A
QUIET MAN

TOM WOOD

SPHERE

SPHERE

First published in Great Britain in 2021 by Sphere
This paperback edition published by Sphere in 2022

1 3 5 7 9 10 8 6 4 2

A CIP catalogue record for this book
is available from the British Library.

ISBN 978-0-7515-7599-6

Typeset in Sabon by M Rules
Printed and bound in Great Britain by
Clays Ltd, Elcograf S.p.A.

Papers used by Sphere are from well-managed forests
and other responsible sources.

Sphere
An imprint of
Little, Brown Book Group
Carmelite House
50 Victoria Embankment
London EC4Y 0DZ

An Hachette UK Company
www.hachette.co.uk

www.littlebrown.co.uk

For Mag

A quiet man is a patient man. He chooses his words with care and speaks only when there is something worth saying. He is a watcher, a listener. He pays attention without seeking it and knows far more about you than you do him. That quiet man is a dangerous man.

ONE

The casket alone cost more than most cars. It had an inner structure of stainless steel covered in a shell of hand-carved ebony. Hand-polished to be impervious to the elements. Fittings of brass and gold. All air, all moisture, removed via expert methods and replaced with inert gas so that the atmosphere inside was pure and would remain so after the casket was hermetically sealed. Resting on soft, white velvet, the embalmed body within this embrace would not decompose, would never diminish. That was most important to them. The ebony, the gold, they were not what mattered. These were trappings, no more. There had to be no doubt that who lay inside would lie there for eternity, until the world, the solar system, ended in some impossibly distant, unimaginable future.

Even that was too soon.

They had no such concerns for themselves. They had no desire for their mortal forms to remain unsullied after death. This gave them much comfort, for it proved they cared more for another than they did for themselves. Despite all other evidence to the contrary, they were in fact good people, selfless people.

Sat in the cavernous cathedral, they thought much about selflessness, about charity.

It was impossible not to do so when surrounded by effigies and murals, crucifixes and candles. So many candles.

They thought much about destiny and legacy too.

Such thoughts were not new, although they were recent when compared with their long lives, and those thoughts had become more frequent of late. With each noticeable week, with each obvious pound of weight lost, with each additional hour needed in bed, they had watched and thought and discussed what should be done.

Not an easy idea even to voice, given that once they had laughed at such a suggestion, had been disgusted by the very thought of it, the implicit insult. They had argued back and forth, and they never argued.

Everything had changed.

Now, what choice did they really have?

Sometimes the only option was the least palatable one.

'I know we have reservations,' he said in a careful tone. 'But I think we should do it. I want to. Only if you agree with me, of course. It must be both our decisions. What do you think?'

She said, 'I've already made the call.'

TWO

A lone guy on a fishing trip would likely have a couple of beers at the local bar in the evening, so that's what Victor had been doing. After returning to the motel from the lake he bathed in the too-small tub, changed, then took the short mile-long walk along the highway to the bar. He could drive his truck, of course, but he didn't want to get stopped on his way back by local law enforcement. Even if two beers were nowhere near enough to affect his ability to drive or do anything else. Because those who didn't drink stood out in all sorts of social situations, a high tolerance for alcohol was a necessity for a man of his profession. Although a drunk could, in theory, do what Victor did. After all, alcohol acted as a catalyst for many killers. Albeit without the same considerable remuneration.

'A beer,' Victor said when the barman asked what he wanted.

This barman was French, Parisian by his accent, and about thirty years old. He had been working each of the

3

previous nights too. On the surface, a civilian. But he had certain features that hummed on Victor's threat radar. The Frenchman was the right age: not too old and not too young; the right structure: strong and trim; he even had the right kind of haircut: no real style yet too short for an assailant to grab hold of. It was also the kind of cut Victor often had after completing a job as a quick and effective way of altering his appearance. The barman's clothes were loose enough so as not to restrict movement yet had a minimum of excess that could catch on protrusions or be grasped in a fist.

Victor had dismissed him as a potential enemy within seconds of first meeting him. It was the way the barman moved. Too slow. He had a stiffness in his back, little mobility in his shoulders. No limberness meant no threat. A professional so impeded would retire or be retired. Which meant the clothes were just clothes. The fit was just comfortable. It meant the similarity in haircut was coincidence. Probably short and forgoing fashion for convenience; simpler to maintain, less time spent in front of the mirror, short enough to be out of the front door straight after towelling post-shower. Nothing to do with the practicalities of either combat or disguise.

Just a barman.

Who looked tired, although the bar wasn't busy. Aside from Victor there were only five other customers. And all drank slowly enough for the Frenchman to spend most of his time doing little actual work. But Victor supposed he could have been on his feet all day after a night when he hadn't slept too much. Black under his fingernails suggested some manual work before his shift at the bar. Maybe fixing up a car. Perhaps digging in a yard.

Draught beer was always better than bottled in Victor's

experience yet a glass's only effectiveness as an improvised weapon was after it had first been broken. A broken glass could kill if thrust at the neck but it was almost useless in any other attack against a target with even a tiny amount of knowhow. A bottle could be broken too and would make an even better stabbing weapon – thicker and more robust – but it could also be used whole as a cosh. A bottle swung at the temple or brainstem could kill, and it could knock someone out if hit on the chin or jaw. It could be used to parry a knife or hit that attacker's wrist or hand so hard they dropped their blade. A bottle could also be thrown as a missile if necessary, although Victor had never yet needed to do so.

No contest.

'I'll take the import,' Victor had said that first night when he was offered the choice.

'Have one yourself,' Victor told him now.

'*Merci*,' the Frenchman said. 'I shall.'

He scooped two bottles from a cooler, using one hand: two fingers wrapped around one bottle neck and two around the other. He used his other hand to twist off the caps and set one of the beers down on the bar surface for Victor.

'Cheers.'

No clink of glass but a raise of bottles.

Unnecessary social interaction was not something Victor often partook in – but he wasn't Victor. He was rarely ever Victor. Only in work, in violence, was he that person. Right now he was a salesman from Las Vegas who loved to fish far away from home. That man was on vacation, albeit a trip that had extended well beyond the original plan. That man bought the occasional beer for another. He didn't make friends but he could be friendly. He was quiet but he was not silent.

Silence was Victor.

The beer was fine in the same way he found most bottled beer to be fine. One golden brew of hops tasted pretty much like any other. Differences were small in Victor's experience. Variations minor. He much preferred a bourbon or a vodka. Still, the Frenchman seemed to enjoy it enough to suggest it was his favoured brand of favoured beverage. Victor had figured him for a wine man given his heritage and didn't like it that his assumption had proved incorrect. He should be more accurate with his judgement. He needed to be more accurate.

His life depended on it.

The Frenchman whispered something between sips, using his native tongue: '*Bien trop bonne pour les lèvres mortelles.*'

Not meant to be heard by Victor, not meant to be understood, but he spoke French. While he had not had cause to speak it in recent times and knew his fluency would have waned, he understood the words.

Too good for mortal lips.

For an instant, he felt like responding in French and flexing his linguistic muscles with a native speaker. He could imagine the Frenchman's surprise, for although French speakers were not uncommon in Canada, they were far more common in Quebec than here at the border. Victor could imagine that after the surprise the barman would smile and respond in kind, equally pleased at the chance to converse in French. Already Victor was rehearsing what he might say when questioned about how he came to learn the language. A reflex, almost, because he had answered many such questions over the years because he spoke many languages.

The salesman from Las Vegas might have lived in Provence for three months one summer long ago. Perhaps he had backpacked across Normandy as a student. Or he had once cohabited with a girlfriend from Marseille for a time and she had spoken little English.

On occasion, if he was feeling mischievous at that moment, Victor would answer such questions by telling people he had to travel a lot for work, which was the truth and hence protocol forbade it. In similar moments he might refer to himself as a salesman who sold something no one wanted, or say that he was in the removals business, a waste management professional or something equally immature. Sometimes the only fun he could have was found in risk and in taking chances. Ironic, of course, because he spent all other waking moments trying to mitigate every conceivable danger.

For a man so careful to stay alive you sometimes act as though you have a death wish, an old associate had said to him.

I don't like to take risks, he had told someone he'd slept with despite knowing she intended to kill him, *but every once in a while I'll roll the dice so I can feel alive.*

The barman was just a barman. Whereas Victor had been wrong to assume his preference for alcoholic beverages, he knew the Frenchman was a civilian. No risk. No danger. It would cost Victor nothing to exchange a few words in French with him, but Victor remained silent.

Perhaps because he was waiting.

Or there could be more to it than that, he thought. Maybe he was tired of lying more than simply speaking, fatigued by the mental exertion of managing a mountain of untruths that was ever growing as every lie was built upon the previous lie.

Could that be it? Could he have finally exceeded his tolerance for deception?

In recent memory he had been injected with a truth serum and he had never known an exhaustion like it. The compulsion to speak honestly had been overwhelming. He had resisted it somehow. Such resistance had only been needed for a short period, although he doubted now whether he could have held out much longer. Did that drug irrecoverably alter his brain chemistry? Did it flip a switch in his consciousness that could not be reset?

He knew what he was doing. He knew he was engaging in self-preservation, perhaps even denial.

He was so tired of lying he was lying to himself about the reason. About why.

He was staying in character, at least. He was a lone man in a bar spending too much time dwelling in self-reflection. Which was a cardinal sin for Victor, against the protocols he had spent years perfecting, the protocols that had kept him alive years longer than he once thought it possible for him to survive. When he had finally understood he had spent too long in the game and had delved too deeply into the life ever to leave his profession, he had reached a peace with it, with himself. All existence was finite. All life temporary. His was no different. Most people died of age-related conditions, some of unfortunate diseases, or accidents, and a few even succumbed to violence. Did it matter how he died? Did it matter that he was certain to be murdered long before he reached an age when heart disease became a risk or when a stroke might occur? The end result was the same.

He wouldn't make it easy for them, however. He was no defeatist and no quitter. When that final shot rang out his killer would have worked hard for it. That murderer would deserve his glory.

'What are you waiting for?' he found himself saying aloud.

The barman didn't hear, of course. Even the mistake of voicing genuine thought was tempered by an unceasing commitment to remaining unnoticed. The barman was watching the wall-mounted television. The news was playing and a reporter was talking to camera, although there was no sound coming through the set. The news item had the Frenchman's attention because there were flashing emergency service lights behind the reporter, who had a grave, serious face. The programme cut to a location shot showing the Chicago skyline and then to B-roll footage of police officers and paramedics.

The Frenchman glanced around the bar, brow furrowed. Frustrated. Looking.

He was searching for the remote. He wanted to crank up the volume so he could hear what the reporter was saying. Chicago was close, only forty miles south.

It took half a minute for the barman to locate the remote, which had been hiding beneath a rag he used to wipe up spills, but it was too late by then. The news item had ended.

'*Merde,*' the Frenchman hissed, disappointed. He turned to Victor. 'Do you know what happened?'

Victor, tired of lying, nodded.

'Yes,' he said. 'There was a murder.'

THREE

Silence comes in many forms. It is not always the absence of sound but sometimes its omission. Silence can be the deliberate withholding of sound and in that way silence is telling: silence speaks in a loud voice.

The silence Victor stepped out of the bar into spoke to him loud and clear. It told him a lot. It told him everything he needed to know.

The night was crisp. Not cold for Victor but he could see his breath in the moonlight. The kind of night people fastened up their jackets. Victor couldn't recall the last time he had restricted his movements in such a way. At least, voluntarily.

Stars offered pinpricks of light in the blackness above and the moon shone with a fierce silver that made steel shine and chrome blaze. There was plenty of both on display in the expanse of uneven asphalt that served as the bar's parking lot. The building was set back from the highway, the lot between the two. No other buildings nearby, just trees. No other reason for so many motorcycles to have parked up.

Except for one reason.

They were no Sunday riders. No boardroom bikers. Their choppers were well maintained yet well used. They were not leisure vehicles but primary modes of transportation. Victor had never owned a motorcycle in the same way he had never owned a car. He had stolen plenty of both, although far more of the latter. Cars were more anonymous. A man sat in a parked car could be almost invisible. Not so easy perched on a motorcycle, although there could be other advantages for a man of his profession in terms of manoeuvrability, acceleration and the ability to go where a car could not.

Still, Victor always preferred to avoid attention rather than to escape it.

There was no escaping it here, however. The nine bikers were all looking his way because they were waiting for him. They were here for him. The choppers formed a rough semicircle that blocked the exit to the highway and stretched the width of the lot.

He had heard them arrive, of course. That was another downside to such vehicles: they were always loud. No chance of stealth. He had taken the time to finish his beer before stepping outside because he hadn't wanted to insult the French barman by wasting his preferred brand.

The leader of the bikers was obvious. In Victor's experience, leaders were always obvious. Not always the biggest, not always the one in the centre, not always the one who stepped forward in front of the others, but they always spoke first. In a strict hierarchy, in a pack, the leader was the first to make his presence known.

Victor's gaze found the one who was gearing up to speak. He was the thinnest, the weakest, the eldest and the most revered. He had a tall, narrow frame and fine, long white hair that hung straight down over his ears and brushed his shoulders, while his pate was bald. The moon gave him a long shadow that stretched towards Victor.

The shadows of the other eight did the same, creating a concave arrangement of jagged black knives all pointed his way.

The bikers wore a lot of denim, a lot of leather. Some had long hair. Some had shaved heads. Others wore bandanas. More than half had beards. They were a range of ages but none were young. All were men, all fully grown. Most were carrying too much weight, but they were strong. Not even one of the nine looked as though they could fight beyond throwing a punch or headbutt, so he didn't have to concern himself with kicks. He didn't expect any advanced grappling techniques. If they were professionals he would have no chance. If they knew he was a professional himself then they would have weapons. They would be armed to the teeth.

Silence is telling.

Their silence told Victor they had no idea he was anything more than a man on a fishing trip. They were standing there and doing nothing but staring because at this point they were still under the impression they were the lions on this asphalt savannah and he was a wildebeest. They didn't understand he was the lion and they were jackals. Dangerous in numbers, in their pack, but every second they stood there in silence gave him a second more to plan and mentally rehearse.

Each second of silence increased his chances of walking away and increased the chances they would be carried.

But nine was an impossible number.

To have even the remotest chance he had to be fast. He had to be faster than they could register. Speed was not purely about reflexes, about fast-twitch muscle fibres. Speed could be manipulated. For a punch to land, the fist had to travel from its starting point to the target, A to B. If that distance could be reduced before the punch was thrown then it would land sooner, there would be less time for the target to react, to attempt to block or dodge or simply flinch. The bikers had their fists at their sides, near their hips. Victor held his hands in front of his abdomen, palm in palm. A relaxed pose, a thoughtful pose. Passive. Unthreatening. Yet his hands were much closer to their final destination. They had less distance to travel. They would be faster.

For the same reason Victor had his right foot a little further back than his left, his torso rotated clockwise to compensate, to give the illusion he was standing square on and disguise the fact he was in a fighting stance. All he had to do was release the tension in the muscles on the left side of his back, and his right shoulder would fall back and he would be acting long before they could react. It would seem inhumanly fast, from zero to a hundred miles an hour, but the engine was already revving. He just needed to release the handbrake.

There would be no pulling punches. Not against so many. Only devastating and debilitating strikes were to be employed. When he hit one, he had to hit him so hard he would not recover. Victor couldn't afford to drop a biker only for him to stand back up a few seconds later and rejoin the fray. Perhaps by then outside of Victor's peripheral vision, unaccounted for and able to attack him from behind when his focus was on another. He couldn't concern himself with accidentally killing someone, with the potential fallout and police involvement.

Kicks only at the beginning, when they were still surprised and before they had a chance to time his movements. Likewise, grappling would wait until the end, when there were fewer enemies. If he took hold of one, he left himself vulnerable to everyone else. He couldn't rely purely on elbows; they were his preferred strike but he needed a punch's range. He couldn't waste precious split-seconds closing that extra step. Damaged knuckles were therefore inevitable. Better than losing, better than ending up with broken ribs and bruised vertebrae, missing teeth and a shattered orbital bone or a subdural haematoma.

Nine was an impossible number, but nine was also too many. Even in a tight circle perfectly coordinated in their timing, it was too many. More than double the number who could realistically attack him simultaneously, and none looked as if they had spent a considerable amount of effort training to coordinate their movements. In the same way one of them spoke first, one of them would make the first move, the first attack.

Then there would be eight.

That would have an effect: a shock factor that might paralyse the others into inaction because events were not transpiring as expected. They would have a mental narrative already in place proved wrong from the outset. Victor's gaze passed over the bikers. He saw no nervousness. He detected no hesitation. These were tough men. Violent men.

Any such paralysis would be fleeting.

Which meant Victor needed to act first. He couldn't wait for that first man. Victor had to be that man instead. He had to ensure the shock of seeing one of their own go down so fast was multiplied by the surprise of witnessing a lone man throwing himself against impossible odds.

Back to eight.

No, seven, Victor saw. The leader had his arms folded across his chest. His eight men had their arms at their sides or slightly raised, hands clenched or fingers flexing in anticipation. The white-haired man's arms were not crossed in a defensive gesture but a relaxed one. He was not a leader in the purest sense. He would not lead his men into battle, he would send them.

Seven was a lot better than nine, yet still too many. However, it would not remain seven for long because Victor had learned never to let an advantage go to waste. He would fully exploit the surprise of that first attack and the shock of the first man going down to launch himself at another. The next closest.

Then, six.

Tough men who were not afraid of violence would be ready by then, they would be reacting, but would still be lacking coordination. They still wouldn't have their timings synced. So it was back to one original opening – one of them attacking first.

Which meant it would then be five.

By that point Victor's back would be exposed. Keeping all threats in his vision was an impossibility with so many opponents. Trying to do so would only slow him down and make him defensive instead of aggressive. That would give them the initiative and it would be over soon after that point.

He had to accept a punch to the kidneys or to the back of

the head or a chokehold snapped around his neck. In return, though, it would then be four.

Four men down, a fifty per cent reduction in numbers, would break the morale of any fighting force and would make any half-competent leader signal a retreat. Yet speed of action was as important as violence of action. If Victor had not reduced the eight threats to four in as many seconds then morale would never become a factor. He would be on the asphalt, kicked to a pulp. That essential speed would mean there would be no time for them to think, no time to doubt, no time for a retreat to be recognised as the right decision.

A good punch to the kidneys would hurt and would stagger him. He might be urinating blood afterwards but it was not going to take him out. He would still be able to fight. None of the remaining four would go down as fast as the previous four by this point. Victor knew he would take some further hits in the following seconds, but it was doable. He could make it work. It would be painful, it would be brutal, and yet after he took the punch to the kidneys the four would join their friends on the ground.

If it was a chokehold instead, it was a problem. He wasn't concerned with the hold itself. They were harder to apply than most people realised and if it was not applied perfectly then Victor had enough tricks to ensure there would be little danger of losing consciousness. The problem was until he escaped the hold, he couldn't deal with the other three bikers. They could hit him while he was immobile or grab his arms so he couldn't actually fight the chokehold. At that point his chances of remaining conscious would be negligible.

A punch to the back of the head, the brainstem, would put him in real trouble. Maybe still on his feet but he would be disorientated, fighting drunk. He would have no speed to drop anyone before they could stop him, no awareness to block and slip the following attacks. They could hit him at will. He might put another one down but he would go down too. Then the kicks to the ribs, the face, would begin.

Before that point, however, he had to deal with the first four. He pictured opening with a stomp kick to fold the first biker in two, driving his heel into the man's abdomen so hard he would likely defecate himself; launching an elbow at the next in line, to the temple given that that guy was a lot shorter than Victor; then, as the biker sank into unconsciousness, a roundhouse kick to the outside of the next closest knee, folding the joint inward with such explosiveness the biker was bound to pass out from the pain alone before he collapsed; pivoting thirty degrees to punch the fourth with a body shot to lower the guard he would be rising by that point before sending a second punch to the face to put him down, crushing the nose instead of aiming for the jaw because Victor needed to spare his knuckles for as long as possible. Maybe one of those first four might require a heel stomp to finish them off before Victor readied himself for the others.

Four seconds. Four down. Four left.

He could predict a lot, he could anticipate most eventualities, but he didn't know what would happen next: the punch to the kidneys, the chokehold or the strike to the brainstem. Two meant defeat, meant pain and injury and potential death. Either through bleeding on the brain or later. Weeks or months or years from now, when the beating Victor took here meant he would not be fast enough or strong enough to survive the next professional who tracked him down for one of the prices on his head.

Which were no kind of odds. Worse than flipping a coin. The best course of action was to retreat back into the bar, to the safety of witnesses and a barman who would no doubt call the police at the first sign of trouble.

The concave arrangement of black knives quivered, restless.

The silence, so loud and telling, was coming to an end.

No further time left to plan, to predict.

The white-haired leader spoke first. 'I've been waiting for this all day long.'

'You have it the wrong way round,' Victor said as he strode forward to throw himself on to the knives. 'It's me who's been waiting for you.'

THREE DAYS
EARLIER

FOUR

He had a name, of course, although Michelle didn't like to use it. Names were, ironically enough, so impersonal. You might be a Hannibal or an Alexander but your parents named you Chad. You should have been Cleopatra or Elizabeth but you're called Tina. Not exactly fair, is it? She understood that injustice because she would have preferred something grander herself. Michelle was an okay name, she accepted, but she longed for something with more syllables, something more classical. When there was nothing to do at the motel she scribbled down ideas and imagined who she should be, who she would have preferred to be. How might things have turned out differently if she hadn't grown up with people calling her Chelle? Could she have made a life for herself and Joshua better than this one? A rhetorical question because any life would be better than this one.

'I was wondering if I could change rooms.'

Not a common request but it happened from time to time. Usually because the dividing walls were so thin they could have had an eating disorder, and people didn't always use motel rooms simply to sleep within. No one ever said that was the reason they wanted to switch rooms, naturally. People were too prudish when it came to such activities. Which had never made a whole lot of sense to Michelle given that everyone did it and the very survival of the species depended on it.

If we were put on this earth to do anything at all, it was that.

She said, 'Let me check the ledger.'

There was no need to check the ledger because Michelle always knew exactly how many rooms were occupied at any one time. It wasn't a skill she was proud of, yet it was one that she'd acquired without trying. The motel was no Four Seasons, after all. There were only three dozen rooms available in total if she included the one currently being fumigated. Plus, it was the off-season. October through to April the motel was never more than half full.

Ah, she was an optimist, she realised, and she never knew it until just now.

'Let me see,' she said as she turned pages. 'I think I can help you out. Is there anything wrong with your current room I should be aware of?'

She asked with a glimmer in her eye and a wry smile because maybe he was different. Perhaps he would surprise her with honesty and say, *The couple next door sound like a pair of rutting elk.*

'It's fine,' he assured her, marking himself as boring as everyone else. 'But I like to keep the window open at night for the air and the mosquitoes are eating me alive.'

'They'll have only just hatched,' she said. 'I don't think I can give you a room that is bug repellent, I'm sorry to tell you. We're not that classy.'

She said this with another half-smile so he knew she was just kidding. Had to have whatever fun you could to battle the boredom of the check-in desk.

He nodded but did not smile in return. 'I'm thinking a room further away from the lake might help.'

'I can put you on the other side of the parking lot but then you'll be next to the road.'

He shrugged. 'I'm happy to take exhausts over bites.'

'You sure? I might be able to dig out some net curtain and string it up across your window.'

He shook his head. 'That's a kind offer but I don't want to put you to any trouble.'

'It's no trouble.'

'I'll take the room next to the road, please.'

She shrugged too. Wouldn't it just be easier to keep his window closed? But, 'Your call.'

'Thank you.'

She fetched him a key and laid it down on the counter. He slid it away with such smoothness, such silence, that she didn't even notice him do so. She only noticed the key was no longer there.

He said, 'I'll move my things and bring the old key back as soon as I'm done.'

'There's no rush,' she said as he left.

He had a peculiar way of leaving the front desk office, she noticed. He backed away from the counter, only turning at the door. It was only a short distance, seven feet at most, but he did this when he arrived too and Michelle, who had become observant of every guest's idiosyncrasies in a prolonged effort to make her job more interesting, had never seen anyone do this before. Had she not become so observant and perceptive it would never have even registered.

There was more than this, she'd also seen. When he walked to his room from the front desk he didn't go straight across the lot like anyone else would do but walked the inner circumference of the U-shaped building. She figured he must be sensitive to sunlight. Maybe that was why his eyes were so dark. Almost black. Almost as if there was no separation between iris and cornea.

He was from across the border like many of the guests that used the motel. Lake Huron was only a few hundred yards away, after all. America was walking distance, yet he was from Nevada. Las Vegas to be precise. That was why he was so tanned, she supposed. Although that didn't fit with her theory about his sensitivity to light. So there must be another reason why he didn't take the shortest distance to his room. Could be he was one of those people who wore those funny wrist watches and were obsessed with how many steps they tallied up in a day. Yes, that made more sense. He had that lean, athletic build. Broad back but narrow waist. A swimmer or a climber. Probably worked out as many times a week as Michelle had a slice of pie. She blamed Joshua for that. She had never been the same since he had come along to brighten up her days. It was like her body refused to accept she no longer needed to eat for two.

Why did you never crave a salad?

She watched him as he walked. In part because she had nothing else to do and in part because he wasn't bad to look at. A little scruffy for her tastes. He could do with a shave and a better haircut. She preferred her men well groomed even though she somehow always ended up with the opposite. She didn't like his faded jeans and frayed plaid shirt. She wondered what he looked like when he wasn't on a fishing trip.

She wondered if he'd ever even worn a suit in his life.

He had been staying at the motel for two days so far. Just him. No partner and no fishing buddy either. He left early every morning, sometimes before the sun had fully risen, and tended not to be back until after dark. She hadn't seen him with a catch but he had a big cooler, so either he kept the fish in there or he tossed them back, and the cooler was for beer. She'd never smelled alcohol on him so it was likely the former.

But what was he then doing with his catch? The motel was just a motel. There were no cooking facilities in the room and even if there had been, the place would stink of fish by now.

She tutted and shook her head, annoyed with herself for not realising the obvious: he cooked the fish before he returned to the motel. What did they say about the simplest explanation being the right one? Perhaps he was not as mysterious as she thought; she wanted to believe he was mysterious in her continued effort to avoid death by boredom. Confirmation bias in action – she'd read about that.

He was just a man on a fishing trip. Nothing more. Nothing less.

She gave monikers to all her guests in an extension of her attempts to liven up her job. Some were used a lot, recycled for multiple guests because folk aren't as unique as they would like to believe. Popular monikers included the Sleazy Guy and the Annoying Woman and the Surly Teen and the Spoilt Brat. From time to time that was a whole family unit right there.

Michelle had struggled to come up with a suitable name for this particular guest. Aside from their brief exchange a moment ago when he'd wanted to change room and an equally brief conversation when he'd arrived he hadn't spoken to her at all. That was unheard of when it came to lone travellers, particularly lone men. They got bored and they got lonely. They found excuses to flirt or just to chat, even if it was only to talk about the weather. This guy didn't do that. She wondered if he would have said another word to her had he not wished to change his room. He was no talker. Not even close.

Therefore, she decided she would call him the Quiet Man.

FIVE

The boy watched Victor every morning. On that first morning the boy had watched from inside the motel's office, two fat little palms and ten fat little fingers pressed against the glass. The second morning he had stood a little closer, out in the parking lot but as far from Victor's truck as was possible. Now, on the third morning, he stood a few feet away as Victor put the fishing rod and tackle box into the truck's load bed. What it was the boy found so fascinating, Victor didn't yet know. The boy watched in silence, with little change in his posture or even expression, yet his eyes held an inquisitive gleam. Maybe the boy found all guests this intriguing. Maybe Victor was no different from anyone else.

The motel was a small establishment, which was one of the several reasons why Victor had chosen it but not the most important. Location was the primary appeal. It provided him with easy access to the lake and the highway.

Pre-summer meant a half-empty motel. Perhaps that was

why the boy watched him. Fewer guests meant fewer distractions for the boy, fewer people to watch. In the absence of more interesting guests, Victor became worthy of the boy's attention.

Except the lone man on a fishing trip Victor played was not at all interesting. He knew this as he did everything possible to seem uninteresting because attention was just about the last thing Victor ever sought. He wore boring jeans and a plaid shirt over a white undershirt. His outdoor shoes were muted and dull. A nylon trucker's hat shadowed his face and he kept that face neither clean-shaven nor with a beard. He spoke little and made no jokes, no insightful comments when he opened his mouth. He did everything possible to avoid attention down to the way he walked because even gait could say a lot about a person. Victor made sure his said he was neither slow nor fast, that he was neither in a hurry nor lackadaisical, that he was neither arrogant nor timid, neither happy nor sad.

In no way was he interesting.

The boy thought otherwise.

He said nothing, so Victor said nothing to him in turn.

The boy stood four feet tall and weighed some eighty pounds, which were just about the only details Victor knew for sure. Victor didn't know the age: maybe he was a big six-year-old or a small eight-year-old or an average boy of seven. Victor was good at reading people, at deciphering strengths and weaknesses, determining when there was a potential threat and when there was none. Children were a mystery to him because there had never been a need to understand them. He had been one, of course, but his had not been a typical childhood and he recalled so little of it – while trying to forget what he could remember – that it offered him no insights nor experience to draw upon.

The boy wore thick-rimmed glasses with thick lenses. Not merely near-sighted or far-sighted but poor eyesight overall. He had a squinting pinch to his expression that Victor presumed came from the magnification of the sun through those dense lenses. For the boy, it would always be bright outside.

Those glasses were skewed, arms stretched at an angle because the boy had a large head. Victor wasn't sure if it was disproportionately so because he figured that children did not always grow in proportion. The boy wore baggy joggers and a T-shirt with horizontal stripes made curves by being pulled tight across a distended belly. A strip of skin was visible between the hem and the joggers. He wore shoes made entirely of some kind of rubbery plastic Victor didn't recognise on sight. Circular holes were cut through the plastic at intervals for ventilation, which meant he could see a superhero motif on the boy's socks. From a comic book or film or both, Victor didn't know.

He knew the boy's name because Michelle mentioned it when Victor had checked in.

'My son Joshua spends a lot of time here,' she told him. 'Just let me know if he gets in your way and I'll tell him not to. He gets . . . bored.'

Joshua seemed uncomfortable whenever Victor looked directly at him so Victor did his best to avoid it. Not always possible because the boy, more confident now than he had been the previous days, kept changing his position to keep track of Victor as he packed his fishing gear.

Which gave Victor the answer that had previously escaped

him: it was not he that was interesting to the boy but what he was doing.

The fishing rod might as well have been a laser sword.

The boy looked at it with the same wonderment Victor had once had as he gazed at trains passing by the orphanage. Commercial trains that went on for ever had been his favourite. So much so that he learned the timetables off by heart – had scribbled the times in a notebook whenever he saw one pass so he didn't miss it – and would race to the window to watch whenever chance allowed. He had always planned to escape by train, jumping on to the siding of a carriage like a cowboy in one of the old black-and-white movies that were sometimes played if the boys had behaved well. The projector made so much noise it was possible to have entire conversations in secret, unheard and unpunished by the stern nuns who tolerated no disobedience.

When Victor had first tried, when he had finally found courage through desperation, he had realised to his dismay he was too small, too weak, too slow to jump up on to the train. He had tried several times, repeatedly failing and falling to the sharp gravel surrounding the sleepers. He shredded his trousers, cut his hands and knees and elbows. He had sat on the track with his nose streaming and his cheeks soaked as he watched the last carriage grew smaller in the distance and quieter as a result. In that quietness he could hear a cruel sound echoing in the night, coming from the open windows of his dormitory as the other boys laughed and jeered at his failure.

The fishing rod felt heavy in Victor's hand. He realised he was squeezing it with such force his knuckles were white and his palm stung from the pressure of his grip.

He swivelled his head to check his flanks, not knowing quite how long he had been lost to memory and weakness, gaze scanning the parking lot, the vehicles, the entrance to the highway, the windows of the rooms, the trees on the far side of the highway. Even a few seconds of idle introspection could mean an enemy sneaking into position unnoticed.

No threats. Only a little boy frightened by Victor's sudden transformation from fisherman to professional.

Victor tried a smile to reassure Joshua there was nothing to worry about, but the attempt failed as Victor had failed to jump on to the train all those years ago.

He opened up his tackle box and took out a bright lure that he tossed the boy's way in a slow underhand throw. Joshua didn't try to catch it and it bounced off his chest and landed before his feet. He waited a moment then leaned over to retrieve it. He examined it with a detective's scrutiny, finding so much to see, so many secrets to unravel in the tiny piece of fibreglass, that he didn't look up at Victor again.

Joshua had gone in the time it took Victor to return to his room for his cool box and backpack. As he placed them into the truck's load bed he realised it wasn't only Joshua that had gone.

The tackle box wasn't quite where Victor had put it. He opened the lid to see there were six hooks in their little compartment instead of seven.

Victor found Joshua at the shoreline nearest the motel. There was no path but the trees and foliage were not dense and made for a short, pleasant walk. The boy did not notice Victor's arrival. Few people were ever aware of Victor's presence unless he allowed them that rare privilege. He didn't want to scare Joshua, however, so he made sure the boy could hear him once there was nowhere for the boy to run to.

Even with Victor no longer lightening his step, Joshua wasn't aware and Victor realised the boy had hearing issues as well as poor eyesight. He didn't know if these were common side effects of his condition or additional ailments.

Joshua was standing on the very edge of the narrow beach, water sloshing around the soles of his rubbery shoes. He faced the lake, so his back was to Victor. Given the hearing problem, Victor opted to walk up alongside him.

Only when he encroached on Joshua's peripheral vision did the boy stop what he was doing.

Which meant he tensed and inhaled air in a sharp moment of surprise, of panic, and dropped his stick.

It was a thin piece of wood no doubt scooped off the forest floor and stripped of any shrivelled leaves and protrusions during his walk. About two feet in length, end to end.

Victor retrieved it from the water.

A piece of twine was tied to the narrowest end of the branch with a crude knot. The twine was thick and old and frayed and might have been from the trash. Certainly, it hadn't been cut for this purpose.

The end of the twine held Victor's seventh hook. It hadn't been tied to the twine: the hole was far too small for the twine to thread through so the hook itself had pierced the twine and pushed all the way through until the wider loop kept it in place.

'I think that's mine,' Victor said.

The boy just stared in response.

'May I take it back?'

32

Joshua was statue still, so unresponsive Victor wasn't sure if he hadn't triggered some kind of paralysing seizure.

Victor shook water from the stick and gathered up the twine into his palm.

Joshua didn't move.

Careful to keep his actions slow and obvious, Victor fed the hook back through the twine until it was free.

The boy didn't protest or try and stop him. He still hadn't moved an inch. If he had blinked, Victor had missed it.

He slipped the hook into an outer pocket of his plaid work shirt. 'May I give you a piece of advice?'

Joshua didn't answer.

Victor continued: 'It's something I learned when I was a little older than you are now. I took things that didn't belong to me, just like you do. I don't think I was greedy for that which wasn't mine so I guess the concept of ownership must have been lost on me back then. Between you and me let's just say it was something of an unconventional upbringing and the rules of polite society did not fully apply. But what I learned is that theft is never tolerated except among fellow thieves. So, if you're going to steal, make sure you steal something that no one knows you want.'

Joshua didn't respond.

'Or even simpler,' Victor added with a wry smile, 'make sure you don't get caught.'

SIX

The lake wasn't far from the motel – a few hundred yards – but it took ten minutes to drive his truck along the highway and then negotiate the back roads until Victor could park it near the shore where his boat was moored.

An inexpensive, practical vessel. Lightweight and durable but too modern, too plastic for Victor's aesthetic tastes. He would have preferred something made of wood, something timeless, but a salesman from Nevada on a fishing trip far from home wouldn't overreach. He was here to fish, to catch northern pike, smallmouth bass and sturgeon in the cold freshwater of the Great Lakes. He wasn't rowing for pleasure, for exercise. The only difference between wood and plastic for that man from Nevada was cost.

Expenses were rarely something that Victor considered. He was wealthy by any standard, made even wealthier courtesy of considerable overcompensation for a recent assignment. Yet he had so few opportunities to exploit that affluence beyond the inevitable and significant overheads of his trade he sometimes wondered what the point was of charging such a high fee. He would never be poor, never go hungry, and maybe that was why. Perhaps it was from all those nights praying for sleep to come and save him from the pain of an empty belly, maybe from the days he could run fingers over his ribs and imagine his ribcage was a xylophone. He had little to spend his money on, but it could be that having it helped him forget a part of his past. Of all his impulses, that was the strongest after the will to survive: he strove to forget who he had been when he was a boy, as a young man, who he had been even yesterday. He longed to live only in the present, with no distractions of unnecessary thought, no memories at all, his mind empty of anything but instinct.

He wondered why he was so self-reflective when he tried to be anything but that, despite the inherent irony of wondering at all.

Change was slow. Evolution took time. Victor was not immune to experience, to nurture. He sought it. He embraced it.

He survived through change. Adaptation was growth. Experiences he had recently lived through unscathed would have killed him ten years ago. Danger he faced back then, that he would not now consider danger, would have killed the twenty-year-younger kid before he'd even understood he was in any danger at all.

His biggest threat was not a younger, faster opponent but an older, slower one who had survived dangers Victor had yet even to face.

Victor loaded in his things and pushed the boat from the beach, which required a little application of strength, then vaulted on board once it was free from the sucking pull of sand and mud. He turned around and sat on the little bench and took an oar in each hand.

Behind him, south, the border cut the lake in half. Boats crossed daily, sailing vessels and fishing boats and the occasional small commercial ship. It would take Victor a couple of hours' rowing to cross and he would be tired and sweating by the time he reached the US. But he would deal with no scrutinising agents and none of his documents would be checked. He could circumvent the security of one of the most fiercely protected borders in the world for the simple price of time and physical exertion.

Then, invisible, he could enter Chicago and do his job.

SEVEN

Victor had once read that all children were close facsimiles to psychopaths because empathy was only developed in the final stages of brain growth, and that didn't occur until a person was well into their twenties. But people also spoke about psychopaths as having personality disorders when in Victor's opinion such a personality was an evolutionary advantage that complemented, rather than competed with, the empathy of others. In the pre-civilised world the psychopath was the warrior first into battle; he protected the tribe from enemies and had no mercy for those that would do harm to his kin. In that context empathy was instead selfish: *Homo sapiens* could not survive the trials of the wild alone. The individual needed the protection of others, so all had to care so as to be cared about in return. Only the psychopath, without empathy, could be truly selfless and that selflessness would have been an invaluable resource.

In the civilised world the psychopath had helped create, however, the psychopath received no thanks.

Which meant Victor would never be out of work.

Client or target, it mattered not to him.

He judged others as he judged himself and he had ceased doing the latter so long ago he might as well have been another person.

His motel room was basic and functional, and the bed offered little comfort. He looked forward to it regardless. The creaky springs, the thin mattress, the lumpy pillows all called to him with the promise of much-needed rest.

Before rest, however, he had to dispose of the rifle. A civilian-grade hunting weapon bought at a gun show for cash and a flash of a fake ID. He had shot it a total of seven times: six at a range to zero the scope and once in Chicago.

At a quiet part of the lake he loaded the stripped-down components into a porous sack weighted with rocks. It sank fast when he dropped it over the side, would reach the bottom by the time Victor had begun rowing away. Scattering the parts across the lake had been another option, but not all components were heavy enough to resist the currents. He didn't want one showing up on the end of a fisherman's line either tomorrow or a year from now.

Victor was exhausted by the time he returned to the motel. He had rowed over forty miles in the course of a single day and completed his job in between.

A simple assignment, but only because he had planned it to perfection and executed it just as perfectly.

Sometimes his job was like that. Sometimes he was paid for what boiled down to mere seconds of actual work. On other occasions things were far more complicated and more taxing. Sometimes the fallout from an assignment could take years to resolve. Some had never been resolved.

Which was why Victor put so much effort into ensuring the potential for such fallout was minimal.

Chicago was close by but also far away, in another country, another world almost. Efforts to find him would be concentrated there. No investigator was going to think the perpetrator had rowed in from Canada and rowed back again. Likewise, no one on this side of the border would have guessed a man on a fishing trip was really a professional assassin preparing for a job in the US. No one would think that when he left the following morning he was, in fact, extracting after the successful completion of a contract worth millions of dollars.

When he returned to the motel, only one person looked at Victor any differently.

Joshua was waiting for him.

The boy's face, so inexpressive previously, now expressed much remorse. He had his hands behind his back, no doubt fingers restless and fidgeting.

Struggling to find his words, Joshua's lips trembled and quivered.

'You're forgiven,' Victor told him.

Those lips formed an O. 'I ... am?'

'And I won't tell your mother.'

'You won't?'

Victor said, 'It would be hypocritical of me to do so given I used to take things that didn't belong to me when I was your age. Do you know what a hypocrite is, Joshua?'

'Maybe. Kind of.'

'I'm many things,' Victor said, 'but I try not to be one of those. In the absence of true virtues I tend to hang on to what's left over.'

Joshua, of course, did not understand the last part. Victor hadn't expected him to do so, which was why he was free to make such an admission. He spoke with honesty so rarely it was almost exhilarating to do so. It felt liberating.

'You really forgive me?'

Victor nodded. 'No harm, no foul.'

The boy thrust out his hand. 'My name is Joshua Joseph Levell and I'm seven and one half years old.'

Victor took the tiny hand in his own. 'It's a pleasure to make your acquaintance, Joshua Joseph Levell.'

'What's your name?'

Victor fished out his driver's licence and held it out low enough so the boy could read.

Joshua said, 'Your name is Wilson Murdoch.'

'That's what it says right there,' Victor told him.

'How old are you?'

'It has my date of birth there too.'

Joshua struggled with the resulting mathematics.

Victor told him Murdoch's age: 'Thirty-five.'

'You're old.'

'I feel even older,' Victor said. 'Why did you want to know my age?'

Joshua hesitated. 'Why do you want to know why I want to know?'

'I'm always interested in people who are interested in me,' Victor said. 'It helps me understand them better.'

Joshua considered this as he watched Victor unload his truck, his gaze finding and focusing on the laser-sword fishing rod.

'Do you like fishing?'

Victor nodded. 'I do indeed.'

'Isn't it boring?'

Victor nodded again. 'That's exactly why I like it. I find it relaxing.'

The boy considered this until-now alien concept: liking something that was boring, that wasn't fun. A contradiction of everything he knew to be true.

'How do you fish?' he asked.

'There are many ways,' Victor began. 'But I use a rod and a lure and a hook. The fish does the rest. In many ways you could say that the fish catches itself.'

Joshua spent a moment thinking on this, trying to imagine how a fish might conspire with the fisherman to be caught. He pulled a face. Not quite a frown because his skin was too young and too plump with subcutaneous fat to crease.

Tentatively, he said, 'Can you . . . show me?'

Victor should have expected this, he realised, even with his limited understanding of children.

'You want me to teach you how to fish?'

With the same tentativeness, Joshua nodded.

'I'm afraid I'm leaving tomorrow morning,' Victor answered, glad to have a genuine reason. 'And even if I were not, I fish out on the lake. The water is very deep and very cold. It's far too dangerous for a young man such as yourself to be out there.'

Joshua was silent.

Victor said, 'You should start off on the shore, where it's safe. I'm sure your father will show you the basics if you ask him.'

He looked at his feet. 'I don't have a father.'

'Your mother then,' Victor suggested, thinking Michelle

seemed like the kind of woman who might enjoy such outdoor activities.

'She hates fish because they stink.'

Joshua's voice was quiet because he was forlorn. As if this was his one chance to learn to fish and Victor was denying him that singular, impossible-to-replicate opportunity. But perhaps by tomorrow Joshua would no longer be interested. A child changed its mind all the time, surely. Today's passion could be tomorrow's boredom, Victor told himself. Still, Victor lived in the present more than anyone and saw Joshua's disappointment, his sadness, in its entirety and its eternity.

'A friend,' Victor said. 'Or a friend's parent might know how to fish and be willing to show you.'

Joshua diverted his eyes. 'No one wants to be my friend because I have too many chrome-somes.'

It took a lot for the boy to make this admission, Victor saw, because to admit it made it real and that made it undeniable. Now, as well as sadness Joshua was lost to despair.

Victor shrugged. 'That's no big deal. I had no friends either when I was your age.'

He said this in an attempt to reassure, to offer Joshua a little hope that things for him might one day be better. Victor, not understanding children, felt optimistic about this reassurance. He realised too late that he had set Joshua up for more disappointment and more despair.

The boy met his gaze and said, 'You got some friends when you grew up?'

There was so much frightened hope in Joshua's eyes that Victor found he couldn't lie. To do so felt like too great a betrayal even for Victor, who was not kind, who had never been decent.

'No,' Victor replied with an honesty that was so easy, so effortless, that he couldn't bear it. 'I've never had a friend. A real one.'

Joshua didn't look away and he didn't say anything in response. Instead, his eyes grew glassy. Then orange light from the sunset glimmered on his cheeks.

Victor admonished himself for making such a clumsy error. Who was he to try and reassure anyone, least of all a child? By his own admission he knew little of children, so it was irrational even to have attempted to comfort the boy. There was nothing else he could do, could say, that would repair the damage he had done. He had failed in his objective. He had underestimated the task at hand.

An amateur mistake.

When victory was impossible, retreat was the only sensible course of action.

A backwards step towards his motel room was easy enough and straight away Joshua seemed smaller and the problem more distant.

Victor took another step away.

One more step and he would turn around and enter his room and pack up the rest of his things and wait up until dawn and in the morning get in his truck and drive away.

His job was over and his extraction would be complete.

Tomorrow he would sleep in another country, on another continent. He would wake up and check his bank balance and feel nothing as he saw the massive deposit of new funds in his numbered account.

Victor thought of trains and laughter in the night.

One more step.

He did not take it.

'Can you swim?' he found himself asking.

Joshua took a few seconds to respond, and when he did so his voice was quiet, unsure. 'Yes.'

'You'll still need a life preserver,' Victor said. 'And you'll have to do everything I tell you. I mean it. Every single thing. If I say it, you do it. No hesitation. No questions.'

Joshua was silent.

'It's too late now,' Victor continued, looking at the fading sun. 'It'll be dark soon. We'll go first thing in the morning instead. Can you get yourself out of bed before dawn?'

'What are you talking about?'

'I'm going to teach you how to fish,' Victor said. 'That is what you want, isn't it?'

Slowly, Joshua nodded.

He had not smiled. Hadn't shown even the slightest bit of enthusiasm. This made no sense to Victor. He did not understand children but he understood that people liked getting what they wanted.

'What's wrong?' he asked.

'Grown-ups don't always tell the truth.'

'Do you think I'm lying to you?'

Slowly, Joshua nodded again.

'Why would I do that?'

Joshua shrugged. He was too young to articulate why adults lied to him and yet it was no new experience. Maybe it happened all the time. Perhaps it happened so often he didn't believe anything he was told. And in this way Victor understood Joshua a little better. No adult had ever told Victor the truth either: not his uncle, not the nuns, not anyone.

'Do you know what a promise is?'

'It means you have to do what you say you will or else.'

'That's exactly why I don't make promises,' Victor explained. 'Circumstances can change even with the best of intentions. You can't fail to keep your word if you never give it, can you?'

Joshua listened.

'So, given this, I've only ever made a handful of promises in my entire life. Because I don't like it if I can't keep my word. I can't really explain why that's important to me but maybe one day you'll know what that feels like too. Perhaps it's similar to not being a hypocrite in the absence of true virtues.' He paused, finding honesty so easy when his entire existence depended on lies. He said, 'Because maybe if I keep my promises, if I don't break my word, I can pretend I'm human like everyone else.'

Joshua was confused.

Victor exhaled. He had felt less vulnerability ambushed and outgunned by entire teams of enemies than he did now with one perplexed little boy.

Victor lowered himself down to his haunches so he was eye-to-eye with Joshua.

'I promise I'll teach you how to fish. First thing tomorrow we're going out on the lake. Do you believe me?'

Joshua gave no answer, but his smile was the biggest Victor had seen in his life.

'Only if your mother says it's okay.'

One additional day, Victor told himself as Joshua rushed off to ask Michelle for permission. Remaining in a staging ground a second longer than necessary was against his strict protocols. Still, the job had gone well and was now complete. He would teach Joshua how to fish and then leave straight away. Maybe in the afternoon, maybe in the evening. Victor would still wake up in a different country, on a different continent, albeit a day later than planned.

A slight delay. That was all.

Any risk had to be minimal.

EIGHT

To be a border guard you had to be more than confident, you had to be more than just smart. You had to be able to see someone and understand them within a matter of seconds. You had to know when you were asking for their identification if you were wasting your time or if there was a chance they would be a problem.

Instinct.

You either have it or you don't.

That's what Derek told people. It wasn't a skill because with a skill you might start off terrible and after lots and lots of practice one day end up pretty good. Maybe even great. Not so with this, not with instinct. Those without it can never learn it, yet those who have it can hone it and train themselves to recognise that instinct when it's talking to them, and after recognition, after hearing it speak, then you can master it. Then you have X-ray vision and can see through people, right to their very soul.

There was no hiding from Derek, no sir.

'How are you doing this evening?' he asked, smiling and polite like any good Canadian.

The woman behind the wheel smiled back at him through the open window, already buzzed down before the car had come to a stop.

Derek appreciated that courtesy. Annoyed him every time he had to gesture, had to make that silly winding motion that didn't even make sense in this electronic day and age. Make him rap his knuckles on your glass and he's going to do everything he can to wreck your day.

So, one mark in their favour from the get-go.

There were another three people in the car. All of those were men. They were all dressed in smart business attire: suits and collared shirts and neck ties, the woman included. Although she wore no tie herself.

Must be the boss if she's driving, Derek decided. He never liked to ride in a car unless he was behind the wheel. Journeys always seemed to take longer that way when he didn't have to concentrate on the road ahead.

She was relaxed and had one of those big white American smiles more dazzling than the surface of the sun.

'I'm just about as good as it gets,' she told him. 'How about yourself?'

People didn't often ask Derek how he was doing so he was starting to like this one.

'I'm only doing average,' he told her, and her smile faded. At least until he added, 'But average for me is better than most can ever hope to do. You might say I tend to look on the bright side even when it's pitch dark.'

'Guess you want to see our IDs,' she said.

'And I don't even charge.'

Was he flirting with her? He wasn't sure because he was so happily married he felt an incredible sense of sympathy for anyone unfortunate enough to be single. Still, he was enjoying this pleasant interaction.

The three guys weren't involved. Weren't doing anything at all. Not even watching. The boss had them well trained was Derek's guess. She didn't look that sort but Derek wasn't sure how that sort should look.

She reached into her jacket to produce a driver's licence.

'Jennifer Welch,' Derek read.

'Like the movie star,' she said. 'Like the bet.'

'I'm sorry?'

'You know, like the bet. Don't welch on a bet.'

Derek said, 'I always thought that was Welsh. Don't Welsh on a bet.'

She shook her head. 'Common misconception. Like card sharp. Most people think it's card shark.'

'Huh, then what does welch have to do with betting?'

She shrugged and smiled again. 'Beats me. But then again what would the Welsh have to do with betting? You ever hear anything about famous Welsh gamblers who failed to pay up?'

'Point taken. So, what's a welch then?'

She raised up both palms. 'You'd think I'd know by now, wouldn't you?'

'Must get pretty tired of getting asked all the time.'

'Takes a lot to tire me. Would you like to see the IDs of my colleagues?'

Still thinking what a welch might be, Derek shook his head. 'That would be unnecessary. I can't imagine you're ferrying undocumented aliens across the border. You're not a coyote, are you?'

She snapped her fingers. 'Darn it, you caught me red-handed.'

He tapped his nose. 'Nothing gets by me.'

'What gave me away?'

'That would be telling,' Derek said with a smile. He might have even winked.

'Just know,' she said with a wink of her own. 'You'll never take me alive.'

Derek laughed and handed back her ID. As much as he was enjoying himself, there was a backlog of vehicles piling up. He knew in his bones there were going to be some assholes to deal with because the later it was the pissier folk got. They could wait another minute, however, because screw 'em.

'What brings you to Canada?' Derek asked.

'Just business,' she answered.

'Isn't it a little past office hours?'

'No rest for the wicked,' she said. 'Time is of the essence because we're already behind.'

'Deal to close?'

'Let's call it putting a bad deal right again.'

'Doesn't sound like fun,' he said. 'But I guess business never is.'

She gave him a look he didn't quite understand. 'Can be if your job just so happens to be your pleasure.'

He would have asked for clarification of what she meant but those assholes kept piling up behind her so instead he said, 'Welcome to Canada, I hope we treat you well,' and motioned for her to drive on.

'Thank you for having us.'

Illinois plates, Derek noticed as the car crossed the border.

City folk, from Chicago. If he'd not been so taken by her smile he would have thought to ask about that breaking news, although what were the chances they would know anything about the shooting? Slim to none, that's what.

Derek took one look at the pair of white trash in the next car with its windows up and knew he was about to take a wrecking ball to their entire week.

Instinct.

You either have it or you don't.

NINE

Victor liked the dawn because it meant he had survived the night. Those first rays of sunlight, of the new day, told him he was still alive, that his unceasing vigilance had been worth the constant effort and the unending tiredness.

He slept a few hours at a time, most often in the morning then later in the day when opportunity allowed. If he slept during the night it was rare and only when he had no other choice, but never all night, never through the early hours. He had slept all through the night once, he was sure, but maybe not since those early days in the orphanage when he had been fooled by the kind words and clean sheets.

He was still angry with himself, with that boy's naivety, his weakness.

He had promised himself never to be weak again.

It had taken most of the night to read his book about the armour of medieval English knights during the fifteenth century, but he had finished it an hour before sunrise. He had then sat through that last hour thinking of nothing but the enemy on the other side of the door and how he would kill them once they were inside his room.

There was no enemy, no assassin readying to make his move, and yet every day was Victor's last until the next sunrise proved otherwise and the cycle started over.

He ferried his fishing gear to the truck in two trips as he had done each day, placing the items in the load bed under the watchful gaze of Joshua.

Only Joshua wasn't watching.

He was not standing in the lot close by as he had done yesterday. Nor near to the office as he had done the day before, nor was he in the office watching through the plate-glass window as he had done that first morning.

Victor hadn't expected this. He had assumed he would find Joshua waiting for him the second he stepped out into the lot.

Victor never liked being wrong.

Michelle's car wasn't parked where it was always parked, he noticed. She drove a little yellow Honda that had faded paint and rust spots. Perhaps she was late for work. Perhaps she hadn't been able to find Joshua's life preserver. It could have been buried among all sorts of junk in a basement or garage or attic.

Something told Victor that she was more organised than this, that she would not have waited until the morning to find it if it had indeed been put away somewhere hard to find.

He recalled her manner when he had asked to change rooms. She'd pretended to look in the ledger to see what rooms were available. She'd looked for his benefit when she already knew. She was an observant type, perceptive. She noticed little things others did not. She noticed because she was so organised, so on top of things, her efficiency gave her too much time in which to grow bored and search for distraction.

She had come to see him, of course. After Joshua had rushed off to ask her for permission, Michelle had knocked on the door of Victor's room.

He didn't invite her inside and she didn't ask.

'Joshua tells me you've offered to teach him how to fish.'

'He asked me to,' Victor corrected. 'I agreed.'

'You don't have to do that, you know?'

'I know.'

'I'm not sure it's such a good idea,' she said.

'Why not?'

'Brutal truth?'

Victor nodded.

'I don't know you from Adam.'

'I understand,' Victor said. 'I'm a stranger.'

'Look, I'm not accusing you of anything,' she said in a careful tone. 'I bet you're the nicest guy in the world. I'm sure there's not a bad bone in your whole body.'

Victor kept as still as he knew how.

'But . . .'

She didn't finish. She looked at him with a sympathetic face, apologetic.

'You can come too,' Victor said. 'We can go in the morning before your shift starts. I can have you both back here for seven o'clock.'

'I don't want to put you to any trouble.'

'You're not,' Victor said. 'You're helping me out. I don't know a lot about children so it would be good to have someone along who does. I can teach you at the same time. Then you'll be able to take Joshua yourself.'

'I don't like fish,' she said, wrinkling her nose. 'But I guess it would be nice to do something outside with him now and again. Fishing isn't so much about the fish but the process, right? I can sit in a boat. No big deal. Anyway, why are you being so kind to us, to Joshua?'

Victor said, 'I wish someone had shown me how to fish when I was his age. My uncle taught me how to shoot but I didn't want to learn. I didn't like guns.'

'Do you feel sorry for Joshua because of his condition? Because you don't need to. He's doing just fine.'

There was a guardedness in her tone, an aggression primed and ready to be unleashed. She was used to defending her son from misplaced sympathy as much as mockery.

Victor said, 'I feel sorry for him because he's lonely. The reason for that loneliness is irrelevant to my offer.'

She didn't smile but her face relaxed. 'Then the answer is yes.'

'I don't recall having asked a question.'

'You can teach him how to fish,' Michelle said. 'It's really sweet of you to want to. But if after you've packed up and left he never shuts up about it I'll make you pay.' She smiled and clenched her fist. 'I'll hunt you down wherever you go.'

Victor raised an eyebrow. 'Get in line.'

TEN

There was no one behind the motel's front desk until Victor used the back of his hand to ring a little brass bell. He hadn't had to do so before.

A guy emerged from a half-open door.

Victor said, 'Where's Michelle?'

The guy was in his fifties, big and round. He wore a white dress shirt made of synthetic fibres so it was a little shiny and a little stiff.

The motel manager, no doubt.

'Michelle isn't here,' he said.

Victor enjoyed sarcasm but he resisted saying 'No kidding' and settled for, 'Do you know when she's coming in?'

'Your guess is as good as mine.'

The guy was annoyed. Let down by Michelle's absence. Frustrated he had to deal directly with guests.

Victor said, 'She didn't call?'

The reply was blunt. 'No.'

'You couldn't get through to her?'

The manager's annoyance was increasing. With every passing second, every word. 'What's it to you, buddy?'

'It was just a simple question,' Victor said. 'You could have answered in fewer words than it took to ask me why I care.'

The guy leaned forward, big hands spreading across the desk. 'Listen to me, okay? Michelle hasn't shown up for work. She hasn't called and I couldn't get hold of her when I called her. Maybe you creeped her out with all your weird questions and she won't be back until you're gone.'

'Funny,' Victor said without inflection.

'But who knows?' the manager continued, scratching at the back of his head to relieve some of his irritation. 'Maybe the no-show is something to do with that retarded son of hers.'

Offence was a concept Victor understood but had no experience of personally. He could not be offended. Words were just words. He didn't like cursing and he didn't like blasphemy for reasons he fought hard not to rationalise, yet there was nothing that could be said to him that would offend him. There was nothing that could be said to him that would make him angry because of the arrangement of syllables used. He was a hard man to anger because he cared so little because so little mattered to him.

He knew, however, that he was not representative of wider humanity. To other people, words could have tremendous power to do harm.

The guy behind the desk was pushing a hundred pounds overweight. His neck was over nineteen inches in circumference but it was thick with fat, not muscle.

It was soft beneath Victor's fingertips.

Squishy.

The windpipe is only a thin tube of cartilage. Even so cushioned by fat, Victor needed only a little of his considerable grip strength to compress the manager's neck until the tube flattened.

Victor's arm had shot out so fast, his aim so accurate, his application of force so sudden, so violent, that the motel manager couldn't even flinch let alone move out of the way.

The whites of his eyes were no longer white by the time his mind caught up with what was happening and he tried to fight back. His fingers snapped around Victor's wrist in an effort to pull the hand free from his throat.

The muscles in Victor's forearm were tight as iron, his grip an immovable vice.

The manager's face was red anyway but it rapidly grew redder and darker.

Now Victor had his full attention.

'I'm told words can hurt,' he said to the manager. 'You wouldn't want to hurt anyone, would you?'

Behind the desk, the guy's face darkened to purple. He couldn't breathe, couldn't wrench away Victor's grip, but he could shake his head. Within a couple of seconds he had shaken his head a dozen urgent times.

'Do you think you can choose your words with more care going forward?' Victor asked in a polite tone. Reasonable.

The guy behind the desk nodded and nodded and nodded and nodded.

Victor released him, and the guy collapsed across the desk, inhaling his first breath of precious oxygen in an eternity before coughing and spluttering for almost as long.

Patience was necessary for a man of Victor's profession, so he had no problem waiting for the manager to regain control of himself. Which took the approximate amount of time Victor expected based on age, weight and general health.

'You shouldn't have done that,' the manager wheezed, backing away from the desk.

Victor remained silent.

The guy's face had returned to its original shade of red but his lips and chin were damp and shiny with saliva. Droplets of it were spattered all over the desk surface.

'You're in deep shit.'

'What did we just agree about choosing your words with more care?'

'I'm calling the cops.'

'No, you're not.'

'You're screwed. You screwed up big time.'

'You're not going to call the police,' Victor said.

With space and the desk between them, the guy felt safe enough and confident. 'You can't stop me.'

'I don't need to stop you. Yet you're going to come to the realisation that it's not the right thing to do in a few moments.'

'I am?'

Victor nodded. 'The red marks on your neck will have faded before they can get here and then it will be your word against mine. The cops are going to talk to us both together, then separately. It might take an hour before we even make statements. Could even insist we accompany them to the precinct to get this sorted if they can't do so here. It'll take all afternoon to achieve nothing more than making the local officers think you're a big timewaster. And who's going to cover here? You're already down one member of staff.'

The guy inclined his chin, gesturing at a CCTV camera overlooking the desk. 'The cops will believe me.'

'It doesn't work,' Victor said. 'That model is pushing twenty years old. Could be even older if it's the previous generation. They used the same shell, so I wouldn't know without taking a look inside. Problem with those early cameras is they run hot. The old electronics require too much juice. You can't be any slouch with maintenance, or dust builds up and the circuits burn out. I guess that happened five or six years ago and you almost choked on your doughnut when the electrician quoted you a repair price. Almost as much as a brand-new system, right? You figured you could just leave it up there as a deterrent. It's not like you ever needed it before. This is Canada, after all.'

The guy was silent.

'Am I close?'

The manager looked from Victor to the camera and back again.

'Now you're thinking "How could he possibly know?" and "he must be bluffing", but the very fact you're standing there in silence thinking that tells me I'm right. So let's skip the part where you try and keep the bluff going because I can see the dust on the lens from here. If the camera worked, you would have cleaned it away once the image on the monitor grew hazy.'

The guy didn't respond.

'Or shall I vault over the desk and check your back office?'

The manager didn't reach for the phone either.

'Take the lesson,' Victor said. 'Learn from it. Don't make another mistake you don't have to.'

The guy said, 'What do you want?'

'You told me Michelle might be absent because of her son. Is this common?'

'That was just a guess.'

'Answer my question, please. The quicker you tell me what I want to know the sooner I'll be gone. That's what you want? It's what I want too.'

'She's never taken a day off before.'

'Not even a sick day? Morning off to see the dentist?'

'No.'

'How long has she worked here?'

The guy said, 'Why does it matter? What's it to you?'

'Don't you find it curious that she didn't show up to work? Didn't call?'

'No,' he said, rubbing at his throat, 'I don't. Sooner or later people let you down. I like Michelle. I like her boy too. Just because I like them doesn't mean she's a good person or a reliable person. I expect she's face down on the sofa after a night drinking and she's going to be calling up to apologise right around noon and begging me to give her a second chance and not fire her.'

'Do you think that's likely?'

'You oversleep on occasion? Ever took a day off?'

'No,' Victor said, 'and no.'

The guy didn't ask for elaboration and Victor didn't volunteer it.

'Are you going to fire her?' he asked.

'If she dropped me in it over a hangover, you betcha I am. If there's a good explanation, then I'll hear her out first. I'm not an unreasonable man. I don't want to see her and Joshua out of their home unless she brought it on herself.'

'Very charitable.'

'Who are you, anyway?'

'I'm just a guy on a fishing trip.'

'You got the hots for Michelle? Is that it? Because I'm pretty sure she has a boyfriend so you might want to set your sights elsewhere.'

Victor said, 'Do you know where she lives?'

'Up on the—' He cut himself off. 'I'm not telling you that.'

'Good,' Victor said as he backed away to the door. 'You did learn, after all.'

ELEVEN

Michelle's house was simple enough to find. He knew it wouldn't be south because south was the border, which left only two highways: north and east. The town proper was north along with the highest concentration of residential properties in the area, so Victor drove north first.

The town was a concise arrangement of buildings, pretty and neat. Overlooking it was a hill bristling with houses.

Up on the— the manager had said before stopping himself saying anything further.

Covering the hill were several neighbourhoods with houses of varying prices all the way up to gated mansions. Victor began at the other end of the scale, taking every street in turn, driving slow enough for his gaze to sweep from the driveways lining one side to the driveways lining the other.

He stopped when he saw a small yellow Honda dotted with rust stains.

It was a one-storey home set back from the street by a strip of overgrown lawn and a narrow driveway of cracked asphalt. The property was separated from its neighbours by a low chain fence that emitted a soft rattle in the wind.

Protocol dictated Victor park at least a street away, but he wasn't working, wasn't even remotely connected right now to his profession. He parked out front, noting that an elderly couple sat on the porch of the house to the right were watching him with more than a passing interest. Perhaps they weren't used to seeing visitors, or they were and knew he had never been here before.

It was a curious experience for Victor to approach the house. Instinct compelled him to put it under surveillance first, to circle it, to check for enemies and ambushes. He knew there was no need here. Michelle was a civilian and no one could have known he would be here. He hadn't planned this course of action so it could not have been predicted either. Yesterday he had made plans to be out on the lake teaching Joshua how to fish. The day before that, he had planned to be on his way to another continent by now.

He passed the Honda on the driveway, running the back of his hand on the hood to check the temperature. No heat. No indication it had been driven this morning.

The sky was grey without a hint of sun.

He stepped up on to the porch and used a knuckle to compress the buzzer.

There could be no ambush here, yet Victor was compelled to step to one side. He didn't want to be standing directly before the door when it opened. He stepped left so his right hand was nearest the door, nearest the likely weapon-holding arm of an enemy who stepped out.

No enemy. No answer at all.

He pushed the buzzer a second time.

He wasn't sure how long to wait. He didn't know how long civilians took to answer their front doors. If the manager was correct and Michelle was prostrate on the sofa with a hangover, she would be in no rush. She might not even hear the buzzer. But if Michelle was indeed unconscious or wishing she wasn't, then Joshua would likely be up.

Was he allowed to answer the door?

Was seven and a half too young to do so?

Victor didn't like dealing with so many unknowns. He would have preferred a full kill team to be hiding inside the house and waiting to ambush him. Then he would know what to do.

He stood still and listened hard.

He heard no voices, no footsteps.

Maybe you creeped her out with all your weird questions and she won't be back until you're gone.

Could that be it? Could Michelle be hiding inside her house with Joshua?

He thought back to his previous conversation with Michelle. She had been happy at the end of it, if not excited, at the prospect of Joshua learning to fish. Victor knew he could never understand how ordinary people behaved, but he was a hard man to fool. He couldn't imagine Michelle having such a dramatic U-turn in opinion as to hide from him.

He was just a guy on a fishing trip.

While they could not see him at such an acute angle, he was aware of the elderly neighbours and how they had looked at him, so he vaulted over the end of the porch and made his way down the far wall of the house where a narrow walkway ran alongside it to the back yard, separated by the low chain fence. He was expecting to pick the lock of the back door but found it unlocked.

He made as little noise as possible opening it and closing it again.

He stepped into the kitchen, seeing the remains of breakfast on the table: two cups for coffee, two glasses for orange juice, and two bowls for cereal. Lowering his head closer to the table told him the milk had not soured.

He heard no one and saw nothing to suggest anyone was home right now. He passed through the ground floor with care nonetheless, finding a neat, comfortable home. Everything was in its place, organised and clean. A plastic crate in the living room held Joshua's many toys. Not a single picture frame was askew.

Upstairs, the beds were made, and a towel was damp in the bathroom. Two toothbrushes stood in a glass on the basin. The mirror was not steamed but the room's air was humid.

Victor had seen enough.

He left the same way he had come in, easing the back door shut behind him. He circled back round to the front, where he vaulted back over the railing surrounding the porch so that when he reached the driveway he did so by descending the short steps and into the view of the neighbours.

They were watching expectantly.

He nodded their way and raised his hand in an informal greeting and they nodded back.

'Good morning,' he said. 'I don't suppose you know where Michelle and Joshua went, do you?'

The woman said, 'Who's asking?'

'Wilson Murdoch,' Victor said. 'I know her from the motel. She didn't show up for work this morning.'

The man said, 'Did she steal something?'

'Not at all. I'm simply concerned about her absence. It's not in her character to let people down. She's as honest as the day is long.'

'Days are still on the short side this time of year,' the woman said back.

'Her car is on the drive,' Victor said. 'And no one's answering when I push the buzzer. I must have tried it a hundred times. I suspect she was driven away by someone.'

'We haven't seen anyone come or go. But that doesn't mean they didn't.' The man leaned forward on his chair. 'She's a good kid. Can't be easy for her looking after her poor boy all by herself.'

'I hear she has a partner,' Victor said.

The woman said, 'They split up. Abe's a real lowlife son of a bitch. Kind of fella with a nice smile so you think he's okay at first and you feel foolish for ever thinking otherwise. Like low-fat ice cream that has twice the sugar instead.'

'He's worse than what you have to scrape off the bottom of your shoe,' the man added. 'I think he used to beat her.'

Victor said, 'And should I wish to speak to this upstanding gentleman, where might he be found?'

TWELVE

Victor didn't know the exact population figure, but the town was on the small side. Maybe five thousand inhabitants at this time of the year, swelling in the summer with tourists arriving to enjoy the lakes. A small population should indicate a small police force. Still, the town was the county capital, and as well as the local law enforcement, regional police were stationed there. The town also boasted the county medical examiner, a criminal court and the District Attorney's office.

The police precinct was located next to the courthouse, which was across the street from the DA's office. A neat, practical arrangement for a neat town. It felt cosmopolitan despite its size, somehow bustling yet laidback, compact yet bursting at the seams.

Victor stopped his truck near to the courthouse but not too near. He wanted to maintain a certain adherence to protocol but didn't feel bound by it in his current circumstances. The radio en route had revealed a few details of the Chicago

job as the police teased out information or that dogged journalists had uncovered for themselves: a known underworld
figure, a suspected kingpin in the organised crime world,
had been killed. The reporter speculated it could be part of a
turf war, although there were no suspects at this time.

Yet there was a doubt in Victor's mind because he
remained too close to the scene of his crime, still within his
staging ground, still using an identity that should have been
erased already.

He approached the precinct from the other side of the
street so he could see it coming, so he could see more of it
and get a feel for it before he arrived. The building looked
about a century old, solid and pale. Pollution had taken
an inevitable toll on the façade, which had darkened and
become stained in grooves and corners. Victor liked such
weathering because it showed fortitude. There was dignity
in such endurance. Victor believed this because it gave him
a hope that if he endured enough, perhaps one day he too
could find dignity when he deserved none.

A tall woman with grey hair stood behind the front desk
and was already looking his way before he was fully through
the revolving door. He didn't like that. He never wanted
to be seen until his presence was obvious, but maybe she
had nothing else to do right now except watch the door
for visitors.

'Why good morning,' she said with a smile, then checked
a clock on the wall above the entrance. 'At least, let's hope so
for the few minutes remaining.'

'Then we should make the most of the morning while we
can, shouldn't we?'

'Are you asking me on a date?'

'Too late for breakfast,' Victor said. 'Too early for lunch.'

'Dammit. Time is the most unwelcome of chaperones.'

Victor glanced at her left hand. 'I'm sure your husband shares the sentiment.'

'I would have declined,' she countered, still smiling. 'Had you asked.'

'Of course you would.'

'I'm guessing you're here to see someone and haven't just strolled in off the street purely to flirt with me?'

'Maybe I'll come back one day to do just that, but right now I'd like to speak with a duty officer, please.'

She gave him a playful look. 'Come to confess a crime?'

'Which one?'

THIRTEEN

The fact that Victor was a career criminal wanted on almost every continent did not escape him as he was led to a desk in an open-plan section of the precinct that swarmed with law enforcement. It was not unreasonable to imagine he was the most prolific, most hunted and most dangerous law-breaker who had ever been inside these walls and yet no one paid him more than a glance's worth of attention.

A name badge on the desk surface proclaimed it belonged to Officer Linette, L. Her chair was empty so Victor sat and waited as he had been instructed. He tried to act like he imagined a regular person would in such an environment for possibly the first time. So he didn't sit still and looked around with a keen curiosity. He gazed at busy men and women in uniforms, listened to murmured conversations on landlines, watched detectives in suits arguing.

In some ways it reminded him what it was like on a military base in a war zone. It had the same atmosphere of boredom and stress that could flip back and forth between the two by the second. Victor had always preferred to be out beyond the wire with bullets zipping over his head and raking the ground than stuck behind sandbags playing cards and chain-smoking while listening out for the telltale screeching wail of incoming mortars.

One of the wily veterans, always restless in inactivity, had told him in such a moment that the best form of defence was to attack.

'If you're hitting them, they're not hitting you.'

Victor had never forgotten that lesson.

Linette said, 'Sorry to keep you waiting.'

'No problem.'

She pulled out the chair a short distance and sat down across from him. He put her in her mid-twenties. She had short, practical hair and a uniform that was a little too big for her frame. The chair was a little too small for that frame, and the arms pinched in her abdomen as she sat back.

'What can I do for you today?'

Victor said, 'I need to report a missing person. Well, missing people. A mother and her son.'

'I'm listening.'

Victor told Linette about Michelle not showing up for work, not being home when he went there, her car on her drive.

'This is today?' Linette said. 'This morning?'

'That's correct.'

Linette had her arms folded and resting on her stomach. 'So we're only talking about a few hours. I'm afraid that's far too early to consider someone missing. How well do you know Michelle?'

'I don't know her at all,' Victor said. 'I'm just staying at the motel where she works.'

'You're a tourist?'

'I'm on a fishing trip. We agreed to meet at dawn to go out on the lake.'

'She stood you up?'

'It wasn't like that. She isn't the kind of woman who would make an arrangement and not keep it.'

'But you don't know her.'

'She's never taken a day off work before.'

Linette said, 'There's a first time for everything.'

'She didn't tell her boss,' Victor said. 'She left her house without tidying up after breakfast.'

'Excuse me, what did she do?'

'She's fastidious. She wouldn't leave a mess.'

'You don't know her,' Linette said again.

'People aren't complicated,' Victor began. 'They have patterns of behaviour. Most of the time they don't even know it but those patterns are set in stone and are only broken when they have no other choice.'

Linette's eyebrows rose. '*They?*'

'Michelle's son Joshua has health problems and development issues. She needs that job. She's never had a day off before yet now she's absent without telling her boss. She keeps a spotless home yet now she's left a mess on the kitchen table. That's not one but two patterns of behaviour broken on the same day. There's a reason why.'

'Like what?'

'I don't know,' Victor said. 'That's why I'm here.'

'That doesn't really answer why you're here. By your own admission you don't know her.'

'Is that important?'

'It makes me wonder,' Linette said. 'Strangers don't tend

to report other strangers missing. It's not something that really ever happens.'

'You don't think she's missing.'

Linette nodded. 'I think something came up and she had to dash out of the house and leave breakfast. That something was more important than calling her boss. So, it's likely because of her kid, Josh.'

'Joshua.'

'You say he has health problems? Maybe something happened in the night and he had to be taken to the hospital.'

'There was breakfast left on the kitchen table.'

Linette was unfazed. 'Could be he had to have some tests done out of town and she forgot until he was crunching cereal.'

'There were two cups of coffee on the table,' Victor said. 'Joshua's a little young to start his day with a couple of hundred milligrams of caffeine.'

'How do you know so much about their breakfast?'

'I peered through the window when Michelle didn't answer the doorbell.'

'And didn't you tell me she kept a fastidious home?'

'Like I said: I peered through the window.'

'What would you like me to do here? I'm confused.'

'Michelle's ex might have been abusive. Hence, he would be a good place to begin.'

'Does this ex have a name?'

'Abe,' Victor answered, using the only name the neighbours had been able to give him. 'He lives at the trailer park.'

Linette rotated her chair, stretched her fingers and set about hitting keys on her computer keyboard. She peered at the screen, which Victor couldn't see, and clicked her mouse several times.

'Abraham Zelnick,' she read, clicking her tongue. 'He has quite the record, including time in the pen for dealing meth, but nothing for violence and no callouts to either Michelle's house or his trailer.'

She rotated back in her chair so she faced him again. She shrugged to say *What now?*

Victor said, 'He still needs speaking to, as do all of her known associates, colleagues and neighbours. Who saw her last and what did they say to her? I would like you to check her bank transactions and see what towers her cell phone has pinged from since she was last seen.' He paused. 'To start with.'

She cleared her throat. 'Would you indeed?'

He nodded. 'I can't do all of that myself, especially when I need to leave town today. I've already stayed longer than I should.'

Linette leaned forward, and that small gesture told Victor the conversation was over before she even opened her mouth.

'It's nice that you're concerned for the wellbeing of Joshua and his mother but at this point there's nothing to indicate they're actually missing. If we investigated every person who missed an appointment, then we'd bankrupt the county while letting real criminals have free rein.' She slid a business card across the desk. 'If there's still no sign of them by tomorrow then call me, let me know.'

'I need to leave town later.'

She held up her palms. 'If no one's seen Michelle or Joshua by tomorrow then I can actually help.'

'And what if they need help today?'

Linette didn't answer.

FOURTEEN

The smartly dressed professionals from Chicago had a list to work through. Just a scrap of paper from the kind of notebook reporters used to use. Welch kept it on her person at all times, but she had memorised the items on the list as a precaution.

'Should be another mile,' she told her associates.

She didn't expect acknowledgement and didn't look for any. She kept her gaze on the road ahead. A narrow strip of winding asphalt flanked by trees. Only a stone's throw across the border and they were already in the wilderness. Civilisation seemed a world away.

They had been working their way through the list all night long. They were tired but no one complained.

The three men in the car spoke only when necessary. They were not friends and not friendly. Not colleagues. Even thinking of them as employees would be a stretch, despite the fact that she was in charge. They would follow her orders without question and without debate.

She said it, they did it.

That was the only way to handle this kind of business. A good system, but it required an uncommon, unshakeable trust. The three men had to, and did, trust that whatever order Welch gave them was the right one. She, in turn, needed to trust that they could handle the task she assigned to them.

She had been let down in the past and would not tolerate disappointment. The three guys knew this well. To say they were happy with this inflexibility would be inaccurate, she knew, but they were paid better by her than they could hope to be elsewhere. She poached good people on a regular basis, usually to replace those who had proved themselves not good enough.

Welch knocked the lever down to indicate and pulled off the highway.

A cute place, she thought. Better than the pictures made out. One of those overpriced bed and breakfasts that attracted couples willing to overspend in an attempt to inject some romance into their anaemic relationships.

The B&B was run by a picture-perfect husband and wife who greeted Welch with warm smiles.

She smiled in return.

'I don't want to take up too much of your time,' she told them, 'but I'm out here looking for a good friend of mine. I think he might be staying here or more likely has already left. He's on his own, on a fishing trip. I really need to find him. It's something of an emergency.'

The husband said, 'Oh, I'm afraid we haven't had anyone stay with us recently who fits that description. In fact, it's rare we have any guests who aren't one half of a pair.'

The wife added, 'But there are a few places nearby that

would be better suited to a fisherman's needs. I could make a note of them if you like.'

'That would be fantastic,' Welch said. 'Thank you so much.'

The wife set about writing on the back of a tourist leaflet while the husband just stood there, smiling at Welch as she smiled at him in return.

Of all Welch's talents her smile was the most used, the most useful. It was her proudest achievement.

No one ever saw through it.

FIFTEEN

On the far side of the hill overlooking the town stood a trailer park of some thirty units. Abe's unit was set away from the others, still falling under the park's boundaries, but to all intents and purposes it was a lone trailer.

Victor found this interesting.

He parked his truck close to the trailer but not so close Abe would be aware of it pulling up outside. Abe had two vehicles already in front of the trailer: a pickup truck and a chopper.

Victor sniffed the air as he approached Abe's front door, noting the acidic, almost metallic aroma coming from inside the trailer.

That made things complicated because Abe wasn't likely to welcome unexpected visitors.

Victor would therefore need to be at his most unthreatening and most polite.

At least, at first.

He rapped his knuckles on the trailer's door.

Music was playing on the other side. Victor didn't recognise the song. He didn't recognise the genre either. Which made him feel a little better about his life choices.

As at Michelle's house, he stepped to the left side of the door in case Abe was even less welcoming of visitors than Victor predicted.

The music stopped.

In its absence, Victor could hear Abe moving about. Just Abe, because he could hear no one else and the trailer's walls were too thin to block much noise. Wherever Michelle and Joshua were, they weren't here.

Abe didn't open the door.

'Who is it?'

His tone was harsh and aggressive but also cautious. As expected, he didn't like visitors. He was wary of them. It wasn't just that he had something to hide. He had something or someone to fear too.

Victor said, 'I need a couple of minutes of your time. My name is Wilson Murdoch and I'm a . . . I know Michelle and Joshua. I'm trying to find them.'

'They're not here,' Abe said through the door.

'I worked that part out for myself. Do you have any idea where they might be?'

'Why would I? I haven't seen that skank since she threw me out.'

The muscles in Victor's jaw flexed but his tone stayed the same. 'When was that?'

'Why do you want to know?'

Victor said, 'Michelle didn't show up for work this morning. That's the first time that has ever happened.'

'You don't work, you don't get paid, so what?'

'That's my point,' Victor said. 'She wouldn't take the day off without warning and without telling her boss.'

'I don't know where she is. I haven't seen her for weeks. I can't help you and I have things to do.'

Victor said, 'She made coffee for someone this morning and given her car is still on the driveway I'm sure she went off with that person too. Does she have any friends you know of, a new boyfriend maybe?'

Abe's voice grew louder. 'Stop bothering me. I told you: I got things more pressing to do with my time than answer some stalker's questions. I don't know where she is and I don't care where she is neither. Beat it.'

'Just a few more questions, please,' Victor said.

Behind the door, a pump-action shotgun racked.

Abe said, 'You hear that, punk? You know what that is?'

'That's a twelve-gauge Benelli,' Victor replied.

'Stalker knows his guns,' Abe said with a measure of mocking respect. 'That's good. That saves us wasting any more time, doesn't it? Get lost. Get off my property before I begin to fear for my life and accidentally discharge this Benelli into your stalker face.'

'Have a good day,' Victor said as he backed away from the trailer.

He had tried being polite.

He had tried being unthreatening.

Next, he would be himself.

SIXTEEN

Abe wasn't going to shoot the stalker. At least, he wasn't going to shoot him right away. He didn't want a bloody corpse on his doorstep even if he could convince the local police he really had feared for his life. He didn't want police anywhere near his trailer. If Castel found out he had done anything to attract the attention of the law or anyone else, there would be all kinds of hell to pay.

Thankfully, stalker boy was a coward and pissed himself the moment Abe racked a shell.

Kind of funny when you thought about it.

Abe peered out of one of the trailer's small windows to watch the stalker back away and to make sure he kept on walking. He couldn't help but wonder what Michelle had done this time. Woman was a whole whirlwind of trouble wrapped up in innocence and artificial sweetener.

Abe was glad to be rid of her. Glad he hadn't fallen for any more of her crap.

Stalker boy might be her latest victim.

Yeah, he looked like that kind of sap.

Abe pulled himself away from the window because he had work to do. Cooking meth was a labour-intensive process and one that a careless person would do well to avoid if they wanted to keep their face attached to their skull.

Abe was nothing to look at, he knew, but he liked his face where it was, thank you very much.

He had pans bubbling on the stove. He had chemicals separating in glass jars. He had residue drying out into hard sheets.

He dropped the shotgun on to one of the vinyl-covered seats flanking the table and set his goggles over his eyes. Like with regular cooking, things spit and splash when cooking meth.

What was that noise?

Within the chorus of bubbling Abe thought he heard something outside. Was the stalker coming back?

Abe flipped up the goggles and reached for the shotgun just in case.

The trailer's door – locked – flung open, kicked in by—

The stalker, charging through the doorway; intercepting Abe as he raised the shotgun, so fast he didn't have the chance to exhale.

Abe could handle himself. Had handled himself on several occasions, yet the shotgun was no longer in his grip because his arms were twisting the wrong way and he thought his elbows might explode with the torque going through them so letting the piece go was his only option to save his joints.

The gun spun through the air, clattering hard against the far wall, knocking over a lamp as it fell, taking them both to the floor.

Abe threw a punch but his fist hit nothing, and he jolted himself off balance as the stalker side-stepped, then pivoted, and a kick to the back of Abe's load-bearing knee dropped him down on to both.

An arm snaked around Abe's neck from behind, and the hard bone of the stalker's wrist compressed against his throat as he was wrenched back into the stalker's savage embrace. The back of Abe's head was against his attacker's torso, trapping him with nowhere to escape the crushing force around his neck.

Pain.

So much pain.

In his neck, of course. But in his head, far worse. All through his head an incredible pressure was building at a ferocious rate, threatening to rupture the blood vessels in his temples, to explode his eyeballs, to force apart the plates of his skull.

Abe couldn't scream because he couldn't open his mouth because his teeth were clamped shut and grinding. He couldn't scream because he had no air to expel.

Fighting back didn't occur to him. It was the last thing on his mind because every other thought was the same: *survive*.

Undergoing such agony, aware that death was so close, created a fear unlike any Abe had ever known. If this was fear, he had never been afraid before.

'Shall we try our conversation again?'

Abe couldn't nod, but he tried.

The stalker released him.

Abe didn't know for how long he coughed. He didn't know how long his eyes streamed tears and his nose rained mucus. He wasn't sure at which point he had urinated, whether before or after he had defecated himself.

'A survival mechanism,' the stalker explained. 'The body shuts down all non-essential functions to provide more energy to where it's needed most. Sphincter control is surplus to requirements when you're about to die.'

The euphoria, the end of pain and fear, became anger, became hatred.

Raging, humiliated, Abe saw from his position face down on the floor that his shotgun was close by – and it was vengeance.

'If you try,' the stalker said behind him, above him, 'we'll just have to go through the same thing all over again.'

The shotgun called to him: not only vengeance but justice. Righteousness.

'You think it hurt the first time,' the stalker said. 'But I was going easy on you.'

Abe could smell himself, his filth.

His humiliation.

'What do you want?'

He said it as a demand and yet it came out as a whimper, a beg.

'I only want to find Michelle and Joshua.'

'I don't know where they are. I haven't seen them.'

'Why would Michelle take an unscheduled day off and not tell her boss?'

'How could I possibly know that?'

'You were in a relationship with her.'

'Doesn't mean I can read her mind, does it? Leave me alone.'

'Soon,' the stalker said. 'The manager of her motel thinks she has a boyfriend. If he didn't mean you, do you know who that boyfriend could be?'

'She dated a guy after me,' Abe said, still prostrate on the floor. 'I don't remember his name but he works at the quarry.'

The stalker said, 'If you've lied to me, if you've withheld anything, I'll come back.'

'Why would I lie to you? I don't ever want to see you again.'

SEVENTEEN

After the stalker had gone, Abe frantically took the pans off the stove to avoid any explosions. He then stripped and threw away his soiled clothes. In the shower, he yelled and cried to release all of the rage and fear and humiliation.

Wrapped in a towel, he stared at the shotgun.

Stared at the vengeance he hadn't taken, at the justice he had denied himself.

Abe didn't like this failure. He didn't like himself for being so afraid, for failing.

He should let it go.

He should be grateful it was over, he knew. He should be happy to have survived.

Let it go, he told himself.

His trailer still stank of faeces. It was going to stink all day long.

He used a cell phone and dialled a number that wasn't stored on the handset but that he knew anyway.

'It's Abe,' he said when the call was answered. 'We have

a problem at the lab. Some guy came by asking questions. I think he's going to be trouble.'

Castel said, 'I don't like trouble.'

'That's why I called.'

'Sit tight. I'll see you soon.'

The call disconnected, and Abe felt a little better.

Abe let nothing go.

EIGHTEEN

The foreman was a skinny young guy named Nieman who walked with a rigid, almost seized posture. Victor could see there was almost no curve to Nieman's lower spine resulting from a posterior pelvic tilt. Maybe overtightness in his hamstrings. Maybe weak hip flexors. Victor didn't expect any trouble from him, but if it ever came to it, Nieman wouldn't run fast and he wouldn't be able to fight with any effectiveness.

Nieman didn't notice Victor's physical evaluation of him because no one ever noticed. Victor was used to making such assessments, his gaze searching for, and finding, weaknesses to be exploited within a mere glance. Nieman was a civilian, not an enemy, but Victor planned to kill everyone he met until he knew for certain there was no need.

The quarry was loud enough that Nieman had to shout just so Victor could hear him.

'Just through here.'

All around them were thousands of tons of machinery

and vehicles, all with huge and powerful engines rippling the atmosphere with thumping, overlapping soundwaves. Victor moved his head more as a result, rotating back and forth to extend his range of vision to compensate for the inability to hear anything but background noise.

A few workers looked his way – he was an outsider – but those looks were only curious, not threatening. Victor was more uncomfortable with such curiosity than he would have been with threats.

Nieman led him to an arrangement of portable office cabins: two side by side, and another two on top of those. Aluminium steps provided access to the top two cabins; Nieman gestured for Victor to go up first.

To maintain his cover he went first even though he didn't like giving his back to anyone, even someone who wasn't a threat. When he reached the top he saw that Nieman was slow to climb the steps, his rigid posture making it awkward for him to do so.

'I know, I know,' Nieman said as he reached Victor, leaning close to be heard without shouting. 'Everyone who comes here for the first time asks why I don't use one of the offices on the ground. But trust me,' he added, gesturing to the steps, '*this* is less hassle than getting them to change.'

Victor said, 'Never pick a fight you can't win.'

'Exactly,' Nieman agreed. 'Let's go inside.'

Victor hadn't expected the cabin to be as effective at blocking noise. Once Nieman had shut the door behind them it proved possible to have a conversation at a normal volume.

Nieman fell into a swivel chair and motioned for Victor to do likewise. 'Take a load off.'

Victor was never quite sure what such phrases meant. Did

other people carry loads? Did they consider just standing or walking to be such a burden that merely sitting down was a relief? Victor preferred to stand. From a seated position it was harder to defend himself or attack another, and it limited visibility.

As the seat had wheels, it was simple enough to reposition it so that Victor could see the door and Nieman at the same time without the action of moving the chair seeming odd or unnatural.

Victor said, 'As I told you at the entrance, I'm looking for someone who works here.'

Nieman said, 'Didn't we talk about something else too?'

Victor reached into a pocket. 'Something about your time being valuable.'

'That's the one,' Nieman said, gaze locked on the cash in Victor's hand.

Because credit cards could be traced with ease, he either carried a lot of cash on his person or had access to currency nearby wherever he was operating. Sometimes that was a stash; other times it might be an expensive watch and other pieces of jewellery that could be exchanged for cash at pawn shops or jewellers. Carrying tens of thousands of dollars through an airport would lead to all sorts of difficult questions but no one batted an eyelid if he put a hundred thousand dollars' worth of Rolex through the X-ray machine.

His funds were almost exhausted because the Chicago job had eaten through them and Victor hadn't expected to require more because he hadn't expected to remain inside his staging ground after the job's completion.

He peeled off a hundred Canadian dollars and handed it

to Nieman, who couldn't snatch the crisp banknote from Victor's fingers fast enough. Nieman shoved it into a pocket with such urgency he almost dropped the hundred on the floor.

'That's my weekend covered,' he said with a grin. 'Who are you looking to find?'

'I don't know.'

'You don't know?'

'I believe we've already covered this,' Victor said. 'I'm hoping you can help me identify him. How many people work here?'

'Including me?'

Victor shrugged. 'Sure.'

'Ninety-one,' Nieman said.

'You work round the clock?'

'Nuh-uh,' Nieman said. 'Six a.m. to six p.m. six days a week.'

'Anyone not show up for work today?'

'Off the top of my head?'

Victor said, 'I'm paying for accuracy.'

'Want me to check?'

Victor nodded.

Nieman sighed because to check meant using a computer, which required him to get up from his chair and shuffle to the other side of the unit to flop down into a different chair and log into a desktop machine. He was a clumsy typist, stabbing at the keyboard with two rigid index fingers, his head bent over so he could look down at what he was doing.

He typed commands and clicked the mouse, and the tip of his tongue poked out of the side of his mouth as he brought up some software Victor didn't recognise, databases with lists of names and corresponding columns holding other information.

'No absences,' Nieman said. 'We run a tight boat here.'

'Ship,' Victor said. 'You run a tight ship.'

'That too.'

'Anyone late for work this morning?'

'Timesheets aren't inputted until later in the day so I couldn't tell you.'

'What about shift patterns?' Victor asked. 'Your employees don't all work seventy-two-hour weeks, do they?'

'I wish,' Nieman said. 'But no.'

'So,' Victor continued, 'who had the day off today?'

'Ah, I see where you're going with this,' Nieman said, happy to have cracked the code. 'But this is crunch week. Got an almighty order shipping next Monday so it's all hands on top.'

'All hands on deck,' Victor said.

'That too.'

'Thank you for your help,' Victor said, standing up. 'I'll see myself out.'

'Oh, we're done already? Sure, whatever you say. Have a good one.'

NINETEEN

After Wilson Murdoch had left the office, Nieman sat in his chair and waited and thought. Should he? Shouldn't he? Nieman didn't like to make decisions and hated to make them on someone else's behalf. That's how you got yourself into trouble.

So Nieman waited a little longer and thought a little harder and tried to weigh up the pros and cons and picture the many potential outcomes.

Still nothing.

Thinking was exhausting, and Nieman didn't like to sweat, physically or mentally.

He hauled himself up out of the chair to peer out of the door to make doubly sure he was alone. He saw Murdoch crossing the quarry towards the exit. Looked like he was taking a longer route than necessary when he could have just cut straight across the open space, but whatever.

Nieman shuffled back inside the office and closed the door, making sure he heard the *click*.

He used the office landline to call a number already pro-grammed into the speed dial.

The line connected.

'This is McAllan.'

'Weird thing just happened,' Nieman said. 'I've just spoken to some guy at the quarry. Gave me money to ask about the employees.'

'What kind of guy?'

'A stranger,' Nieman said. 'From out of town. He was looking for someone but didn't know who.'

'What does that mean?'

'Beats me,' Nieman admitted. 'But I thought you should be aware without delay.'

'You thought right,' McAllan said. 'Strangers are bad news, especially now. Talk me through the conversation. Leave nothing out.'

TWENTY

The elderly couple were not on their porch when Victor stopped his truck. It was a few degrees cooler today than it had been yesterday and a light rain was falling. Victor approached the house with the expectation of finding it to be the same as it had been upon his last visit in the morning. There were no lights on, no windows open that hadn't been before and no curtains repositioned. The little yellow Honda was in the exact same spot.

He didn't ring the bell, instead heading around the house to the back and the unlocked door.

He wasn't sure what a second walkthrough would reveal but his first check had been a cursory one, a scouting mission. Now, he was investigating.

Both beds were made, which told him he had been right to consider the messy kitchen table to be an anomaly. Michelle wouldn't leave dirty crockery out if she had a choice.

So, she'd had no choice.

She had been compelled to leave.

By someone other than Joshua because that someone had taken them away in another vehicle.

Two coffee cups on the table said that she knew that someone well enough to invite them inside her home.

The boyfriend was the most obvious candidate.

Which didn't explain the need to depart with such urgency that it had overridden Michelle's typical behavioural pattern.

What had happened in the morning to make her leave?

Whatever it was, it meant she still hadn't returned, hadn't gone to work, hadn't let anyone know what she was doing.

Victor thought of Abe, his shotgun, his meth lab. Perhaps the new boyfriend was cut from the same cloth. Perhaps Michelle had not left willingly.

The front door had two locks, a deadbolt and a conventional one. Both locks were engaged. Which meant she was careful about security. Maybe someone knew the back door was left unlocked while Michelle and Joshua were home. But then why take the longer route around the house to get to the street instead of using the front door?

Victor knew he was missing something but had no idea what that something might be.

He heard a car stop outside. The street was quiet and there was little through traffic. He moved to a window at the front of the house and peered out between the curtains.

A police cruiser.

Officer Linette was climbing out.

Victor backtracked and left the house through the back door. He circled around to the front in time to see Linette cupping her hands at the window in an attempt to peer inside.

'No one's home,' Victor said.

Linette, startled, took a sudden step back and slapped a palm to her chest.

She glared at him. 'Why did you sneak up on me like that?'

'I didn't,' Victor said.

'What are you doing here?'

'You know what I'm doing. I'm looking for Joshua and his mother.'

Linette said, 'You were supposed to call if they didn't show up.'

'Would you have done anything if I had? You told me to call tomorrow.'

'I know, but I'm doing something now, aren't I?' Linette stepped down from the porch, which took her a little effort, and he met her on the driveway. 'What were you doing?'

'I went around the back,' Victor said.

'You thought they might be in the back yard and couldn't hear the bell?'

'Yes,' he said.

'I checked the hospital just in case,' Linette said and shrugged to say there was nothing else to add on this matter.

'They've been missing all day now.'

Linette said, 'Still not technically missing. Have you tried the neighbours?'

'I spoke to them this morning,' Victor said. 'They hadn't seen them leave nor anyone arrive.'

'I'm thinking back to our conversation earlier and I don't recall why you're so concerned about them.'

'Does there need to be a reason?'

'There's always a reason,' Linette said.

Victor remained silent.

'Wilson Murdoch,' Linette said. 'Thirty-five years old. Resident of Las Vegas, Nevada.'

'You checked me out.'

'I did.'

'Why?'

Linette said, 'Because you don't make sense, Mr Murdoch.'

'I don't?'

'You tell me you're a tourist on a fishing trip. You've been in town all of four days. Yet here you are looking for a single mother you don't really know.'

'And her son,' Victor said.

'You don't know them by your own admission but they don't show up to a scheduled meeting, and this tells you she's not simply impolite but missing.'

'Not alone,' Victor said. 'That combined with the untidied breakfast crockery.'

Linette snapped her fingers. 'Oh yes, we mustn't forget the impossible-to-explain mess on the kitchen table. Such a thing has never happened before in the entirety of human history.'

'People aren't complicated,' Victor said.

'I remember you saying that too,' Linette said.

'And here you are.'

'Here I am, as a cop. Here you are, as . . .'

She looked at him as he looked at her. Linette expected a reaction. She didn't know what, but she needed a sign from him – to believe him or affirm her suspicions about him.

He didn't blink. He didn't look away. He didn't shift his weight. He didn't flex his jaw. He didn't swallow.

She clicked her tongue and opened her mouth to say something but a car slowing took her attention from him, and she frowned.

When the car stopped and four men climbed out, she said, 'Ah, shit.'

TWENTY-ONE

The motel manager was a big, heavy guy with a red face and a white shirt. Welch didn't have to try hard with him because he was the kind of man who wasn't used to anyone smiling in his direction, least of all a woman half his age. It was almost unfair. Almost cruel.

She enjoyed cruelty.

'A very good afternoon,' she said. 'How's today treating you?'

He was rubbing at his neck like it was itchy, like he had the worst kind of razor burn.

'I've been better, but I feel better now,' he said, dazzled by Welch's smile.

'Well isn't that terrific?' she said. 'There was me thinking you were going to be like the other place.'

'Other place?'

'Further west,' she said. 'They were not exactly what I'd call cordial. Not in the least little bit.'

'You'll find we have better manners here,' he told her in a

reassuring, eager-to-help tone. 'How might I assist you this fine p.m.?'

'I have this friend,' Welch began. 'He has ... Let's just say he has emotional issues. Sometimes he likes to get away from it all. And, well, this time he's been gone longer than usual and we're all real worried about him. I don't know where he's staying but I'm pretty sure he's near here. I say "near here" yet he's almost certainly moved on by now. It's a long shot but I think he might have been a guest of yours. I tried the other place and they were most unhelpful.'

'Helpful is my middle name.'

The manager stood a little taller, set his shoulders a little squarer. He was not only going to rush to the distress of a maiden but said maiden had already been let down by his competitors. Welch was sure this was the most alive he had felt, the most of a man he had felt, in a very long time.

'Here's the thing,' she said. 'I don't have his name.'

'You don't know your friend's name?'

'Did I say he had emotional issues? Paranoia is just one of many, so he likes to travel incognito. He doesn't use his real name. But I can describe him to you.'

The manager said, 'I'm sorry to tell you that I don't really deal with our guests all that often so I'm not sure how much help I can really be to you. I'm covering the front desk today because I was let down by an employee.'

Welch hid her disappointment and smiled through her frustration. 'Perhaps I can come back when this employee of yours returns.'

'I have no idea when that will be,' he said. 'I can't get through to her right now.'

'Then would you be willing to pass on my enquiries to her when she returns? I would be ever so grateful. I'm very keen to find my friend before he gets too far.'

'Sure,' he said, sliding a pen and paper closer to him so he could write down details. 'Hit me.'

'My friend is tall, dark-haired. Mid-thirties. He's on a fishing trip. Keeps to himself but can be real intense.' Welch paused. 'You're not going to write this down?'

The manager sighed and shook his head, maybe muttering something under his breath too.

He said, 'I don't need to write down anything because I know exactly who you're talking about.'

Welch fought hard to hide her rising excitement. 'You do? He was here?'

The manager shook his head. 'Not was. Is.'

'*Really?*'

'Really. I mean, not right this moment, but he's still staying at the motel.' He pointed. 'Room 110.'

Welch said, 'You don't know how happy you've just made me.'

'Then perhaps you wouldn't mind giving your friend a little of that happiness because he's one prickly individual.'

'I'm sure once I've talked to him you won't have any more trouble. In fact, I wouldn't be at all surprised if he left immediately afterwards without even saying goodbye.'

'Long as he's paid up he can disappear off the face of the earth for all I care.'

Welch took out a money clip and peeled off bills. 'Why don't I just take care of that? Then you don't have to worry.'

'Suits me.'

'Do you know when he'll be back?'

'Nuh-uh,' the manager answered. 'Far as I know he just fishes on the lake and drinks in the bar.'

Welch couldn't stop smiling. 'Terrific. Let me have a room with a couple of twin beds,' she said. 'We're pretty beat after a night driving around looking for him so could use a rest while we wait for him to show.'

'Happy to have you,' the manager said, grinning.

'But if my friend returns,' Welch said with a frown, 'can you do me a solid and not tell him we're here? Given his issues, I don't want him to freak out and split before I can talk to him.'

The manager nodded. 'I got your back, don't worry.'

Welch smiled at him, then glanced over her shoulder. 'Say, I don't suppose room 109 is free, is it?'

TWENTY-TWO

Victor had no opportunity to ask Linette if she minded not swearing because she seemed to forget he was even there. She headed along the driveway towards the four men. Though Victor had seen none of them before, he had seen their type many times.

Three were large guys, all well over two hundred pounds. Two because they were tall and the third because he was as wide as a phone booth. They had inexpressive faces because they weren't employed to interact any more than they were employed to think. One had scars above both eye sockets, another had an off-centre nose, the third had cauliflower ears.

The fourth man was their boss. He was better groomed and better dressed and a decade older than the eldest henchman. He was almost as big but his heft was almost all around his midriff. It was the weight of leadership and success.

'Fine afternoon,' he said.

Linette glanced up at the grey sky. 'Is it?'

'Who's your friend, Lucy?'

Victor stepped forward and introduced himself. 'Wilson Murdoch.'

A thick hand was extended Victor's way. 'Robert McAllan.'

Victor shook the hand.

Linette said to McAllan, 'What are you doing here, Robert?' Her tone was impatient, almost aggressive.

If he noticed, McAllan ignored it. 'I'm told one of my employees and her son are missing.'

'You own the motel,' Victor said.

He pretended not to notice the three big guys staring at him. He didn't react as they moved through the conversation, slowly surrounding him. There was no pre-determined plan in action, he knew, yet they had a natural synergy. They were dealing with an unknown, a situation that might go any number of ways, and they were instinctively preparing for the worst.

Victor let them because none of the three were going to do anything without McAllan's express permission and he was never going to give that to them with Officer Linette here.

McAllan nodded. 'I own a share, yes. I understand you're a guest there.'

'For the moment.'

'On a fishing trip,' McAllan added.

Victor saw where this was going. 'I had arranged to take Joshua and Michelle out on the lake.'

'And now you're going around looking for them. How come?'

'Because they're missing. That's why you're here too,' Victor said. 'Isn't it?'

McAllan said to Linette, 'If there's anything I can do ...'

'Sure,' she said, sharp. 'I'll let you know.'

McAllan backed away a step. 'A pleasure to meet you, Mr Murdoch. It's uncommonly kind of you to go out of your way like this to help two strangers.'

'It's not out of my way,' Victor said. 'And how nice of you to interrupt your busy day just to swing by an employee's house to check on her wellbeing.'

McAllan hesitated. 'We were passing by. Least I could do.'

Victor remained silent.

McAllan gestured for his men to get back in the car and one held open a door so he could climb on to the backseat.

'How did you know Michelle and Joshua were missing?' Victor asked.

McAllan said, 'How wouldn't I know?'

When all four men were in, McAllan gestured again and the car pulled away.

It was a nice vehicle, an expensive Chevrolet. Showy but not excessive. McAllan didn't feel the need to show off, to advertise his success.

Linette exhaled. She shook her head, thinking of something she didn't share.

'Who was that?' Victor said.

'Local *entrepreneur*,' Linette said, emphasising and drawing out the syllables of the second word. 'He has several businesses in the town and the rest of the county. Mostly construction. The motel being part of his little empire.'

'And the quarry?'

She nodded.

'Why do I get the impression not all of his capitalist endeavours are strictly legal?'

'You're free to hold whatever opinion you like,' Linette said in a careful tone.

'Let me guess,' Victor said back. 'McAllan's name has come up in several investigations yet he's never been charged with breaking any law.'

She said, 'You don't expect me to confirm or deny, do you?'

He shook his head. 'No need. I could see plain enough you're sick of dealing with him.'

Victor had encountered men like McAllan many times. They might be head of the only outfit in a town and as such acted like kings. They kept their crown only because no one had come along to take it from them. That didn't mean McAllan wasn't dangerous. It didn't mean he wouldn't be a problem.

Especially because Victor would be turning his attention McAllan's way.

If the local crime kingpin owned part of the motel then Victor needed to know more about his businesses because maybe Michelle had seen something she wasn't supposed to have seen.

Maybe the little plastic lure wasn't the only thing Joshua had taken that didn't belong to him.

'He won't be involved,' Linette said.

'Excuse me?'

'If something has happened to Michelle and Joshua it won't have anything to do with Robert McAllan.'

There was certainty in her tone. It wasn't just a hunch based on knowing a little of the man and how he operated. She knew a lot more than she had said.

Victor asked, 'How can you be so sure?' because he had an idea.

'You can take my word for it, all right?'

He saw her agitation. Heard her discomfort.

'No, not really,' he said. 'You're going to have to give me more than that.'

She didn't want to give him anything else. That was enough to tell him his idea had been right.

'Who is he?' Victor asked.

'I already told you.'

'That's not what I mean,' he said. 'Who is he to you?'

By now she knew that he knew but she still couldn't say the words. The admission was too great, the embarrassment too acute.

'He's your father, isn't he?'

Linette said, 'He's not a kidnapper. And he wouldn't hurt either of them. Ever.'

'Are you saying that as a cop or as a daughter?'

She glared at him. 'I don't have to justify myself to you. In fact, I don't owe you anything at all.'

'That's right,' Victor said with a nod. 'You don't owe me anything at all.'

'Good. I'm glad we're in agreement on that little fact.'

'But while you wear that badge,' he said, 'you owe Michelle and Joshua plenty.'

She took it on the chin. Didn't try and argue. She gazed into the distance for a long moment, then said, 'How long are you sticking around? You told me earlier you needed to get going.'

'I'm not sure,' Victor answered with honesty.

'You're staying until Michelle and Joshua show up, aren't you?'

He thought about this for a second. 'Maybe I will.'

'How come? I mean, I figure you for a persistent SOB, but still.'

'They're missing,' he said.

'You can head home,' she said. 'I'll let you know if I find them. I'm on this.'

'For how long?'

She stood straighter. 'What does that mean?'

'You said "if" – if you find them.'

'Again: what does that mean?'

'Are you going to keep looking until you find them or until you run out of leads?'

'If I run out of leads,' she said in a measured tone, 'the investigation will remain open until there are new leads.'

'Then I'm staying.'

'You think I'm a quitter?'

He shook his head. 'I think you've just worked a double shift because you don't have enough warm bodies to handle every single case that comes into the precinct. I think you're going to speak to all of Michelle's known associates and check her finances and see if she's withdrawn cash anywhere. When neither of those results in finding them you're going to get some missing posters printed and stick them up around town. And then you'll check out the handful of calls you get as a result, and then when none of those leads you to finding them you're going to move on to a more pressing investigation.'

Linette said nothing.

'Meanwhile Michelle and Joshua stay missing and every day they're not found halves the chances they'll be found alive, and that chance is already hurtling towards fifty per cent.'

'Why are you so convinced something has happened to them?'

'I told you already.'

She rolled her eyes. 'Yeah, I remember. Something about people not being complicated.'

'I'm glad I don't need to repeat myself.'

'So, given that we know people aren't complicated, how do you know so much about how a missing person investigation is conducted?'

'I watch TV.'

She huffed.

'Michelle works at the motel,' Victor said. 'So she works for the local gangster.'

'My dad's not a gangster.'

Victor said, 'She works for a business part-owned by the local gangster and her ex-boyfriend has a history of drug offences.' There was no need to tell her he had seen this was not confined to the past. 'It's no leap of the imagination to see how Michelle might have got mixed up in something she shouldn't have, or Joshua, not knowing any better, might have seen something he wasn't supposed to see.'

'Before you ask: no, my dad has nothing to do with drugs. I mean it. He's in property and construction. Is he up to no good? You bet he is. But he's a white-collar criminal. No drug dealing, nothing like that. He dresses the part and I'm sure he's broken plenty of bones along the way to getting building permits and profitable county contracts, but he wouldn't go anywhere near methamphetamine. He has too much to lose. It's simply not his style.'

'Then whose style is it?'

She fidgeted with her fingers and he saw she was worried about whether she was saying too much. He didn't press her because any pressure would tell her she was right.

'Forget it,' she said. 'You're barking up the wrong tree.'

'If you say so.'

'What's your next move?'

'I'm not sure. Maybe I'll see if I can go buy some meth.'

'That would be illegal.'

He shrugged. 'If you're not going to tell me who runs drugs in this town then I don't see any other way of finding out.'

She rolled her eyes. 'Fine,' she said after a long moment of silence. 'They call themselves the Nameless. They're a biker gang. The real kind, I mean. Old school outlaws.'

'Their leader?'

'Why do you want to know? I've given you plenty already and I really don't want you trying to speak to him. That would be a bad idea. I don't want you getting yourself into trouble.'

'So he's a he,' Victor said. 'And he's trouble.'

'I'm trying to do you a favour here. Let me.'

'What's his name?'

She shook her head. 'No way. Forget it.' She stepped past him, heading for her cruiser. 'I've said far too much and now I'm worried I've given you just enough information so that you can go get yourself in a whole lot of mischief you can't get yourself out of again.'

'You really don't need to worry about me,' Victor said.

'Maybe I'm not worried about you,' she said in return. 'And maybe that's part of the problem.'

TWENTY-THREE

For a few minutes no one spoke. No music played. Only the gentle murmur of the engine and the ambient noise from outside the car interrupted the silence within it. McAllan had his elbow up on the door, arm folded and fingers massaging the side of his skull. There was no pain there, no discomfort, but it helped relax him, it helped focus his mind.

He said, 'Are you all thinking what I'm thinking?'

The man next to him in the back said, 'I don't like him.'

The man in the passenger seat said, 'Me either.'

The driver said, 'He's all wrong.'

McAllan nodded along. 'But the question is: why?'

'Why what?' the man in the back asked.

'Why don't you like him? Why is he all wrong?'

The driver said, 'No guy on a fishing trip interrupts his vacation to go around looking for a missing mother and her kid he's only just met.'

'Why not?' McAllan asked.

The driver didn't answer but the man in the passenger seat did. 'Because he doesn't know them.'

'Why doesn't he know them?' McAllan asked.

The driver said, 'Not enough time. He's only been here four days.'

'More than enough time to fall in love,' McAllan said. 'Do you remember when you last fell in love? Might have taken you months to admit it but you felt it right away, yeah? The double whammy. Just thinking about her makes your heart beat faster and you beat your meat harder.'

The guy in the back smirked and said, 'He didn't seem in love.'

McAllan nodded. 'Now we're getting somewhere. Maybe he's a pure Boy Scout. The last of a dying breed of concerned citizens willing to go out on a limb to help their fellow humans.'

'He didn't seem concerned,' the driver said.

'This is more like it,' McAllan said with a snap of his fingers. 'He's not in love. He's not concerned. Then what is he?'

The driver said, 'That's why he's all wrong.'

The man in the passenger seat turned around. 'I'm lost.'

McAllan explained: 'A guy on a fishing trip looking for Michelle and Joshua is either in love with Michelle or he's concerned about their wellbeing. If he's neither, then he's looking for them for some whole other reason entirely that has nothing to do with common decency.'

'Money?' the driver suggested.

McAllan shrugged. 'Could be money. Could be some other kind of debt. Her ex-boyfriend, Abe, works for Castel.'

'The meth cook, right?'

'What are the odds?' McAllan said.

Silence. Everyone thinking.

The man in the back said, 'This fisherman works for Castel?'

'Does he look like a biker?'

The driver said, 'Could be a partner.'

'Could be,' McAllan said.

The man in the passenger seat said, 'From Las Vegas.'

'Mob?' the driver asked.

'Let's not get ahead of ourselves,' McAllan said. 'We're quite the walk from the Strip. Mafiosos don't need to come all this way to buy their sugar, do they?'

Nods of agreement throughout the car.

'What do we do?' the driver asked.

McAllan's fingertips massaged his skull. 'No one makes any moves until we know who this guy is and what he's really doing here. Get on to our PI in Toronto. Give her this Wilson Murdoch's details and tell her to go ape-shit on the case. I don't care what she bills me so long as she gets me something. Castel or not, mob or not, this guy is no mere fisherman, and he's definitely no do-gooder neither. Whoever he is, whatever he's doing, he's going to be trouble. I can feel it in my perineum.'

The driver said, 'Do we tell Fendy?'

McAllan exhaled. 'Not yet. We only escalate this when we know more. This stays with us until we deem it necessary to share.'

The guy in the passenger seat took out his cell to call the PI in Toronto but paused because:

'Did you see him when we rolled up?' McAllan asked no one in particular. 'Now I may be bordering on presentable but you three certainly miss that mark. With the greatest respect, you look like a trio of hulking Neanderthals who wrestle mammoths just for the fun of it when they're not cannibalising their competition.'

McAllan's men waited for him to continue.

'I don't care who you are, I don't care if you're an untouchable chief enforcer for the entire Nevada Cosa Nostra, the three of you show up without invitation you're going to need a new pair of drawers. This guy? You see him?'

McAllan's men listened.

He said, 'Nothing. Not a tremor. What kind of man gets a surprise visit from three Neolithic savages and doesn't so much as blink?'

No one could answer.

TWENTY-FOUR

Victor reverse-parked his truck in the bar's lot so it faced the exit to the highway. Three other vehicles were spaced out on the rough square of asphalt. None had reverse-parked too so there were no professionals inside waiting for him.

He remembered the manager's words, speculating that Michelle might have been hung-over on the sofa. Perhaps that had been more than a flippant comment. Could be that she was a regular. Victor hadn't seen her there during his visits but he had only been in the area a few days and had only spent a couple of hours at the bar each night.

The French barman had his back to the door as Victor entered. The wall-mounted television had the barman's attention. A soccer game was underway.

Victor's gaze swept over the other occupants in the room to look for threats because he did the same for every room he stepped into. A glance was enough to highlight potentials without alerting them to his analysis. Then, another glance to see if any potential threats were threats.

With only four people besides Victor present, the entire process took a little over a second.

No threats.

Not even close.

That meant he could behave in a natural way. He could slide on to the closest stool at the bar without needing to concern himself with the two patrons behind him. The third was perched at the furthest end of the bar, which might have indicated a professional wanting to sit at the most advantageous position for observing the rest of the space, except the man sitting there was a few decades too old and a few dozen pounds too heavy to represent any kind of danger.

The barman, riveted by the soccer game, only noticed Victor was there once the guy at the far end of the bar gestured to tell him so.

'Pardon, monsieur,' the barman said after he had turned around. He was startled. 'I didn't hear you sneak up behind me.'

'No one ever does.'

'The fish ... they aren't biting today?'

'Not exactly,' Victor said. 'I was going to take someone out on the lake but they didn't show.'

The Frenchman hesitated. 'No? Too bad. For you and for them. Beer?'

Victor nodded. 'Please.'

'Import?'

Victor nodded again.

The Frenchman smiled. 'Un homme de goût.'

'And have one for yourself.'

'Too kind, but I shall indeed.'

Victor put cash on the bar while the barman fetched two bottles of beer from the cooler and twisted off their caps.

When he returned, Victor said, 'Do you know Michelle? She works at the motel.'

The barman set the bottles down. 'She has a kid, right?'

'A son,' Victor replied. 'Joshua. I was supposed to teach them both how to fish this morning, only she didn't show up to work.'

'Oh,' the barman said.

'Does she ever drink here?'

The barman shrugged, thinking. 'A few times, but not often. Excuse me.'

'Sure.'

Victor sipped his beer as the barman went about his duties, checking under the bar for something Victor couldn't see.

The big guy at the end of the bar used the restroom, and when he came back he took the stool next to Victor. The man was maybe seventy, shoulders almost as wide as his midsection. He had a thin sweep of white hair and a haze of stubble.

'You're Wilson?'

A guy on a fishing trip wouldn't keep his name to himself so neither had Victor, but he still didn't like it that someone he had never spoken to before knew his alias.

'Who's asking?' Victor said.

'I'm Big Pete.'

Victor said, 'What can I do for you, Big Pete?'

Big Pete said, 'Nothing at all you can do for me unless you happen to have a cure for sciatica tucked in your back pocket.' He rubbed his lumbar region.

'All out, I'm sorry to say.'

'Well, isn't that just typical? Anyhow, I didn't sidle over here to chew the fat, Wilson, although I'm sure you tell a mean fishing story. I'm wondering if your friends caught up with you okay?'

Victor paused for a second, reading nothing in Big Pete's tone or expression other than simple curiosity. No investment in the answer beyond an involvement in the question itself.

So, Victor nodded. 'If you're asking then I guess someone came here earlier looking for me.'

Big Pete nodded too. 'That Jennifer sure has a pretty smile, doesn't she?'

Jennifer. Pretty smile.

'She most certainly does.'

TWENTY-FIVE

Abe was waiting outside his trailer when Castel arrived. Abe had plenty of notice that Castel was about to pull up because the synchronous roar of several choppers was unlike no other and could be heard a mile away. Almost a pleasant sound at first – faraway surf – before rapidly becoming savage and animalistic, so loud and relentless the tidal waves of sound buffeted Abe's trailer and rattled the dirty crockery festering in his sink.

The noise of Castel's approach gave Abe plenty of warning not to keep Castel waiting, and no one with half a brain kept Castel waiting.

He was a beanpole of a man: thin shoulders, thin waist, with long limbs and a long neck. His skin was the colour of tanned leather except on the top of his head, where it had dark and light patches of sun damage. Unlike many of his crew, Castel never wore a bandana, and helmets were not only a sign of weakness but one of incompetence. Good riders didn't come off their hogs, went the logic.

Abe had a hog but almost never rode it. A truck did everything a chopper did and did it better, and a chopper couldn't do half what a truck could.

He kept such opinions to himself around Castel.

He was the eldest but not old, despite the ring of long white hair that hung from the sides of his skull but no higher. He wore a cracked black leather duster over a denim shirt. His jeans were dark and ripped and clung to his narrow legs as a second skin. Abe had never seen Castel in any footwear other than his snakeskin boots with their shiny spurs.

His crew had never had a name so eventually they began calling themselves the Nameless.

Their insignia became a bone-white skull with a strip of duct tape across the mouth.

Abe coughed a little as the exhaust gases washed across him in a dark cloud. Ignitions were turned off and kickstands lowered. Only Castel climbed from his ride at first. Despite the long limbs, despite the duster, it was a smooth, effortless movement.

As both heels hit the ground he dropped into a fast squat then exploded up out of it on his heels and thrust his arms into the air as if celebrating the small act of arrival. He pumped his fists as if joyous, as if seeing Abe was a rare delight.

Abe knew he was no delight.

He stood still as Castel approached at a slow pace because he was dancing every step, spurs rattling as he clicked his fingers to some song only he could hear, head bobbing and elbows flaring to the beat of those clicks.

Some of his crew smiled at this. Others remained stone-faced.

Abe scratched his stubble. He didn't like the fact Castel appeared to be in such a good mood.

When Castel reached Abe he stopped, but only after spinning on the spot and bringing his hands together in a single, loud clap.

The dance, the song, was over.

Castel wore mirrored sunglasses, so Abe could see himself reflected back at him. He didn't like the nervousness he saw in that reflection.

Castel said, 'You called.'

Abe swallowed. Nodded.

'Talk to me,' Castel said, removing his sunglasses.

He had arctic blue eyes, small and intense.

'This guy came around looking for someone,' Abe began, his throat already hoarse. 'Asking all these questions.'

'What kind of questions?'

'Asking this, asking that. Making excuses to case the lab.'

Castel pursed his lips. 'I see.'

'I told him to get lost or I'd shoot him in the face.'

'You threatened him?'

Abe, thinking of his humiliation, felt better remembering he had scared the stalker away, if only temporarily.

'Why would you threaten him?' Castel asked.

'Because he wouldn't leave.'

'And by threatening him you told him there was a reason worth staying for.'

Abe was quick to say, 'I had no choice.'

'None of us have a choice,' Castel replied. 'Choice is an illusion. We're flesh puppets dancing on a string.'

He mimed this, arms outstretched and flailing wildly. His eyes were wide and almost glowing with craziness.

'Uh-huh,' Abe said.

Castel ceased the act and pointed. 'Why is your front door broken?'

Abe should have let it go.

'Did the stranger break it down?'

Abe had told himself to let it go.

Castel's long fingers squeezed Abe's shoulders, full of tension, and the arctic blue eyes moved closer to Abe's face.

'Did he go inside your trailer?'

Why did Abe let nothing go?

'He saw the lab, didn't he?'

Abe couldn't stop blinking. 'Yeah.'

Castel clicked his tongue and released Abe's shoulders, then turned his gaze away to look at his closest man, sitting on a chopper. 'Go collect all the crystal. Get any supplies worth carrying. We gotta be quick, so hustle.'

The man said, 'Sure thing, chief.'

He swivelled off his hog and entered Abe's trailer along with another of the Nameless.

'He came inside your home,' Castel said. 'Yet you didn't shoot him as you said you would.'

'He ... he took me by surprise. I was cooking your meth. I had my back turned. I can't do everything at once, can I?'

'Is he a cop?'

'I don't think so.'

'From a rival crew?'

Abe said, 'I don't know.'

'Be a pal and tell me something that you do know.'

'He's staying at the motel near the lake.' Abe described the stalker and his truck to the best of his memory.

'Did he give you a name?'

'Wilson Murdoch.'

Castel thrust both fists high into the air. 'Touchdown.'

Abe didn't know what to say so he kept his mouth shut.

The two bikers who had gone into his trailer came out, one with a plastic shopping bag bulging with fresh sheets of unbroken meth. The second carried a nylon sports bag that was heavy with raw ingredients. Both headed back to their choppers.

'Got it all?' Castel asked.

'Everything worth taking,' one answered.

Castel rubbed his palms together while Abe scratched at his stubble. He didn't see a gesture Castel made but he did notice three of the Nameless nearing. One had his hands behind his back. The other carried a jerrycan. The third sucked on a cigarette.

'Lab's gotta go,' Castel said. 'Doesn't matter if the stranger is a cop, a rival or just a neighbour who is sick of the stink. Can't risk it.'

He clicked his fingers and pointed at the trailer. The Nameless with the jerrycan stepped inside and began sloshing gasoline around.

'*Shit*,' Abe said. 'I'm sorry . . . I couldn't—'

'No need to apologise,' Castel said. 'Bad things happen to good people all the time. That's no one's fault. Least of all yours.' He narrowed his eyes to look Abe up and down. 'Unless you're a secret master of the universe and you forgot to mention it?'

'No, I'm not.' Abe managed a half-smile. 'And thank you.'

'Oh, don't thank me,' Castel said.

The biker with the jerrycan stepped outside and threw more of the gasoline over the exterior walls.

'You're good people, Abe,' Castel said, and his arctic blue eyes had never looked so cold.

The two Nameless nearby were on Abe then. He struggled and pleaded as one hit him and wrestled him as the second – the one who had had his hands behind his back – set about binding him with duct tape.

It was over in seconds. Abe was face down on the ground with his wrists bound behind his back and his ankles taped together. He could just about turn his head enough to look at Castel, who said, 'Piece of advice, Abe: never threaten to shoot someone.' He put his sunglasses back on, hiding the arctic blue eyes. 'Just shoot 'em.'

'Listen to me,' Abe said, words fast and desperate. 'I was making it up. The guy wasn't interested in the lab. He didn't care about the meth.'

'Sure he didn't. Why would he?'

'I swear,' Abe said. 'He was looking for my ex, Michelle, and her kid. That's it. He was only a stalker.'

'A stalker?'

'He hurt me,' Abe continued. 'I wanted you to mess him up for me to even the score. Please, I wouldn't lie to you.'

Castel said, 'But you just told me you lied. You wouldn't lie about lying to me, would you? Or are you lying about lying about lying?'

Abe couldn't answer because Castel used the heel of his snakeskin boot to roll him on to his back and the Nameless with the duct tape laid a strip over Abe's mouth.

He yelled and screamed, though only a muffled growl escaped the duct tape.

'Say again?' Castel said.

The two Nameless hoisted Abe up and carried him towards the trailer.

Castel clicked his fingers at the Nameless smoking a

cigarette. 'Once we're done, go to the motel. Get eyes on the fisherman. I want you to know him like you know your own pee-pee.'

The Smoker said, 'Yes, chief.'

Castel clicked his fingers and danced on the spot.

Abe bucked and struggled as much as he could, which had no effect on the two bikers carrying him. They were too big. Too strong.

They dropped him inside his trailer, and he wriggled and thrashed on the floor. The stench of gasoline filled his nose and the fumes made his eyes stream tears. He saw the two Nameless walk away and the Smoker stepped forward to strike a shiny lighter and toss it through the doorway without ceremony.

It landed out of Abe's sight but he heard the *whoosh* of nearby gasoline igniting.

All around Abe the interior set ablaze. Fierce red flames licked the walls and rose up to surround the doorway. It was the only means of escape but, unable to move, Abe could do nothing except watch Castel, framed by fire, dancing on the spot to a song only he could hear.

TWENTY-SIX

As Victor approached the motel he slowed to a crawl. He pulled into the lot with his foot off the accelerator, engine off before the truck had finished reversing into a spot facing the exit.

There was a car in the spot next to him.

That car was the only other vehicle in the lot reverse-parked.

It had Illinois plates.

Victor entered the motel office, surprising the manager who had been playing on his phone. His eyes widened when he saw Victor and he swallowed and took an involuntary step back.

'Michelle's not showed,' the manager was quick to say. 'Hasn't called neither.'

Victor approached the desk.

'I . . . I'm sorry about this morning,' the manager said. 'I really am.'

'Everyone makes mistakes,' Victor replied. 'Everyone deserves forgiveness.'

'Thank you.'

'I have something else to ask you, if you don't mind.'

The manager felt secure enough to step back closer to the desk between them. 'Sure thing.'

'I've been expecting some friends and I can't get hold of them,' Victor said. 'I don't suppose they've stopped by here looking for me?'

The manager squashed his lips together and shook his head. 'No ... no friends. No one's asked about you as far as I'm aware. I mean, someone could have come by when I was in the back, I guess. But I wouldn't have noticed if they had.'

'That's a shame,' Victor said. 'They're pretty keen to catch up with me.'

'Yeah, that's a real shame,' the manager said, feeling the need to look anywhere except at Victor. 'And talking of which, there's a problem.'

'A problem?'

Victor waited for elaboration because the manager took his time to find his words. He took a step back from the counter, recreating the initial distance. Nervous again.

He swallowed, then said, 'Motel's fully booked from tomorrow.'

Victor raised an eyebrow.

'Since you're paying day-to-day,' the manager continued, gaining courage the more he spoke, 'I had to give out your room. I'm sorry but you'll have to be gone in the morning.'

'What's the occasion?'

'Excuse me?'

Victor said, 'The motel has thirty-six rooms, of which only seventeen are currently occupied because it's the off-season.'

He paused. 'One is being fumigated, so including my room you've just taken nineteen bookings. So, what's the occasion? A last-minute no-frills wedding nearby? Or are you telling me you've suddenly had nineteen individual bookings for tomorrow since this morning?'

The manager was silent.

'McAllan called, didn't he? He told you to get rid of me.'

The manager cleared his throat. 'I don't know what you're talking about.'

Victor said, 'You understand that I can make this easy or difficult, don't you?'

The manager stepped even further back from the counter.

Victor shook his head to ease the man's fear. 'You're just doing your job, I get that. But I want you to pass on a message to McAllan for me. Can you do that?'

The manager waited. He didn't nod but he didn't shake his head either.

'He knows why I'm still in town,' Victor began. 'Tell him I'm not going anywhere. Tell him I'm not leaving until I'm done; he needs to understand that it's in his best interests to help me get answers. Are you paying attention?'

The manager nodded.

'It's in his best interests,' Victor continued, 'because I'm going to get those answers whatever it takes. If McAllan tries to hinder that, I'm going to wonder why. I'll wonder what he's hiding and then I'm going to have no choice but to tear apart his entire operation to find out.'

The manager didn't know what to say.

'Will you pass that on to McAllan for me? Every word.'

The manager nodded. 'Uh, yeah. Sure. I'll tell him. He won't like it.'

Victor didn't comment because he didn't care. Instead, he asked, 'Do they have kids?'

The manager frowned. 'Sorry, what? Kids? You mean McAllan?'

'There's a light on in the room next to mine,' Victor explained. 'I'm just wondering if the new guests have children. You know, because of the noise. I want to get a good night's sleep.'

'Ah,' the manager said. 'No. No kids. You don't have anything to worry about like that. They're only staying one night anyway.'

'Have they already paid?'

'Yeah . . .' the manager said. 'How come?'

'No reason,' Victor said as he backed away to the door.

TWENTY-SEVEN

Welch waited because there was nothing else they could do until the man calling himself Wilson Murdoch returned to the motel. Her three associates waited too. One sat on an armchair by the door. The second sat on the bed. The third sat on the second armchair that had been positioned next to the internal wall. The wall that separated their room from Murdoch's.

That third man's role was to listen. He sat and waited and listened for the sound of a door unlocking and opening. No technology was required to assist this process, only silence. No one else spoke. When Welch needed to make calls, she stepped into the bathroom and closed the door behind her and then she whispered.

They were all bored. They were all impatient.

No one liked waiting. No one was good at it.

For this reason, the man sat listening was rotated on a regular basis because it was inevitable that amid such boredom attention would wane. Then, the quiet sound of a door

131

unlocking might be missed. Then, they might miss their opportunity.

Welch didn't listen. She delegated.

She wouldn't do any of the work that came next, either.

It was hard to predict how it might go down, but Welch liked simplicity. She liked doing what she was paid to do, and no more. Why overcomplicate things?

Once Murdoch was in his room they would enter and shoot. Two guys and Welch at the door and one round the back in case Murdoch had a sixth sense and tried to climb out of the bathroom window.

If they could catch him asleep, so much the better. Couldn't count on that, however, and Welch wasn't going to waste this perfect opportunity. Once Murdoch returned to his room, they would enter it soon afterwards. There was no guarantee he wouldn't leave it again and it was nothing short of miraculous they had caught up with him already.

She had expected him to be long gone. Welch had anticipated a lengthy hunt lasting days or even weeks. It almost troubled her that Murdoch was not long gone by now.

Once Welch had completed a job she was in the wind. Once Murdoch was dead Welch and her crew would be in the car minutes later, out of the country within the hour. The motel manager was going to have to go too, but one witness as collateral was no big deal.

That Murdoch was still here, still at the same motel he had stayed in while preparing for the job in Chicago, troubled her. It seemed so dangerous, so unprofessional.

Why had he not left?

She never expected that she would get a chance to ask him that very question.

A QUIET MAN

She never expected that he would knock on their motel room door and when one of her guys answered it expecting a maid or the manager, their target would say:

'May I come in?'

TWENTY-EIGHT

They didn't try and hide their surprise. The guy who answered the door looked back at Victor as if he had spoken in a foreign language, so pinched and confused was his expression.

The door was only opened a quarter of the way, as was sensible when discretion or security was a concern to those inside. Just enough to look out at the person who knocked yet not so little as to seem suspicious and guarded.

There was constrained commotion in the room behind the guy at the door. Victor glimpsed another man rising from a chair near the opposite wall. Another was out of sight, but Victor saw that man's shadow on the carpet. Then, a woman appeared.

Jennifer Welch.

Younger than Victor had anticipated and not smiling as Big Pete had described her. Like the men, she was dressed in smart business attire. The kind of clothes Victor opted for himself most of the time, that he felt most comfortable in because he wore them the most. Reassurance through repetition.

Welch had her right hand behind her back. A redundant action because Victor knew they were armed, but it was a reflex, habitual.

She didn't know what to say.

She didn't know how to act.

So Victor said, 'No reason we can't be civilised about this.'

He had said the same once before, in Minsk.

She hesitated, then said, 'About what?'

'I think we're past the point of being coy.'

The guy at the door was looking at her for guidance, orders. Victor couldn't see the guy's expression with his head turned to look at Welch, but he didn't need to. There was only one question the man would be asking.

Should I shoot him?

Welch took a moment to decide. Victor waited with his heart beating at its resting rate because they had been sitting in the room next to his for a reason – so they were aware when he returned to his room, so they could kill him there without witnesses, without leaving evidence behind.

Welch shook her head.

'What do you want?' she asked.

'I've already said,' Victor answered. 'I want to come inside.'

Welch said, 'Why?'

'So we can talk this through.'

'What's to talk about?'

'Let me inside and find out.'

Her first instinct was that this had to be some kind of trap because she frowned and said nothing. She couldn't know if he was armed, yet they outnumbered him four-to-one and they had guns. He could see none, but no one hunted a professional assassin without them.

She exhaled. Nodded. 'Okay. Let him in.'

The guy at the door didn't move at first. He stayed where he was, blocking the doorway. Only for a second, however, because Welch gave him an intense look of admonishment and the speed at which he took a step back and held open the door told Victor that she was more than simply in charge, more than just intolerant of disobedience.

She was feared.

Victor stepped over the threshold.

The room was the same as his. The only differences were the positioning of the two chairs and the number of occupants. The three men were tense, out of their comfort zone, but controlled. They weren't going to act without Welch's explicit orders. None of the three had guns in hand, but those hands were restless, ready to draw from belt holsters the instant Welch gave the word.

They seemed competent. Neither big nor small. They kept their distance from him as much as the room let them. They knew not to stay close enough for him to attack before they could react.

He stood where he could watch them in his peripheral vision while he looked at Welch.

She was still unsure, still not comfortable, but she was beginning to understand that this was no trick, no trap.

'So,' she said.

'Thank you for making this easy.'

'Don't thank me just yet.'

Victor nodded to say he understood the subtext. 'I know why you're here.'

136

'That's not hard to work out. But that puts me at a disadvantage because I have absolutely no idea why you're here.'

'When I said I know why you're here I wasn't referring to your objective. That goes without saying. I meant I know who sent you. I know why you were sent.'

Welch said, 'I'm listening.'

'I killed your boss,' Victor said. 'Well, the boss of your ... conglomerate. Now, the newly promoted godfather needs to pretend he didn't order the assassination in the first place. He needs to be seen to get revenge. Hence, you.'

'I'm not sure why you're telling me what I already know.'

'Because you need to remember why you're here.'

Welch said, 'I'm not likely to forget.'

'I hope you understand I'm talking purely in facts when I say that your only possible chance was to take me by surprise.'

Welch was silent.

Victor said, 'Obviously, the element of surprise is no longer possible.'

Welch listened. The three guys watched her listen.

'But you're here for revenge,' Victor said. 'Once I've gone, no one but us need know you haven't collected it.'

'What are you saying?'

'I'm saying that the only factor that matters in this is what you say to your boss when you return.' He paused. 'I'm not staying here much longer. Another day, maybe. But when I'm gone, I'll never be back. No one knows who I really am or why I was really here. I'll never return to Chicago either. You could call your boss right now and tell him that I'm dead and there won't ever be a reason for him to think otherwise.'

Welch said, 'Why would I do that?'

'It's easier,' Victor said. 'And safer. You can't take me by surprise any longer.'

'Who says we need to?'

Victor's gaze passed over Welch, over her three men. All standing looking at him, doing nothing while outnumbering him four-to-one.

'You're saying it right now.'

Welch said, 'You go, we go?'

'That's how simple it can be,' Victor said. 'And none of you need die chasing a lost cause.'

'You're here just one more day?'

There was a lot of weight to her question. Victor hesitated because he couldn't be certain, but nodded. 'One more day.'

Welch said nothing. All three of her guys were looking at her. She was considering.

Victor said, 'I appreciate this is a lot to think about so I'm going to leave you now so you can do just that. There's no rush. Take your time.' He paused. 'And if you decide that you can't accept my proposal, I'll be waiting for you next door.'

TWENTY-NINE

The chair in Victor's motel room was one of the best he had ever sat upon. As close to perfect as any he had experienced. As he spent most of a typical night in a chair, he had become something of an expert. Not on chairs in general, but those best suited for him. A connoisseur, maybe. They possessed a rare combination of diametrically opposed features because a chair had to provide an equal degree of comfort and discomfort. If there was the former without the latter, it was too easy to relax and for the alertness needed to keep him alive to lessen. The perfect chair had to keep him upright and support his lower back over long hours of immobility; it had to be so that the soles of his feet rested flat on the floor with his knees above his ankles so he could propel out of it as fast as possible; it had to let his elbows rest on the armrests while his back remained neutral, without elevating his humerus and putting tension in his shoulders; the padding had to be soft enough to cushion his weight without him sinking into it.

This chair was as close to fifty-fifty as he had known.

The only downside to this particular chair was the noise it made. The padding was tight vinyl and was prone to make the telltale friction squeak if he applied too much pressure when adjusting his position. Not loud but noticeable, and the line by which life and death were separated in Victor's world could sometimes balance on such exactitudes.

He had no second book to read – he was not supposed to be here – and rereading the same one had no appeal, so he counted the tiny blobs of raised texture in the wallpaper. There was no uniformity in the pattern because such texture was designed to hide unevenness in the wall behind. Victor was grateful for this as each panel of paper was therefore unique. Each panel's total could not be predicted. Facing the door, he could only count the blobs on two of the room's four walls. When he had finished counting every panel he could see, he started over, checking his previous count against the new one.

With thousands of tiny blobs per panel, no count was the same. He was off by one or two each time. Accuracy above ninety-nine per cent, but not perfect.

The first ray of dawn came before he had completed his fourth round of counting, but he kept counting because he disliked leaving any objective unfinished.

In doing so he realised he had made an additional mistake on the third round. He had settled into a rhythm, a routine.

Victor was not pleased with this lack of focus.

After bathing, after dressing, he stepped outside and noted which cars were still there, which had left, and which were new.

He crossed the lot to check the motel office. The manager

was watching a small TV on the counter. He looked dishevelled. Tired. Maybe he had been up all night too.

The manager shook his head without looking. 'Still nothing from Michelle.'

'Any calls for me?'

'Nada.'

The TV showed a local news broadcast featuring amateur footage of a trailer burning against the backdrop of a night sky. The trailer was positioned by itself, away from the others at the park. Professional camerawork then showed the smouldering aftermath of the inferno, being dealt with by firefighters. A reporter mentioned that one man was thought to have died in the blaze.

Victor watched with interest.

The manager said, 'I've told McAllan that you're still here. I told him what you told me to tell him. Word for word. He's not a happy man.'

'Could be the result of a vitamin D deficiency,' Victor said. 'He was looking a little pale yesterday.'

'You really shouldn't be here.'

Victor said, 'Tell me something I don't know.'

He left the office, thinking about his visit to Abe and the news that Abe was now dead and the meth lab ashes. Victor didn't believe in coincidences. Which meant Abe had told his boss – the boss who was trouble – about Victor's visit and that boss hadn't liked what he had heard. Maybe he thought Victor was a rival or a cop or perhaps he was just a convenient excuse to close the lab down and get rid of an incompetent cook.

But now the Nameless knew about Victor.

Well, Wilson Murdoch.

Then they knew he was staying at the motel, which meant if they were in the least bit concerned about him they knew how to find him.

No choppers were parked in the motel's lot ... but he saw one parked off the highway, on the far side from the motel. There was nothing but vegetation there – overgrown grass with the forest behind: no reason to be there at all, yet the rider was sitting on his vehicle and smoking a cigarette like it was the most natural thing in the world. The gloom of the dawn hid him and the vehicle somewhat, but the rider should have rolled it into the trees behind. He should have at least crouched down in the undergrowth.

The level of incompetence was staggering.

Victor wasn't surprised to see one of the Nameless performing surveillance on the motel given what they had done to their own meth lab, but he hadn't expected them to be so obvious. He reminded himself this was a biker gang, *old school outlaws* as Linette had said, civilians not professionals. Their world and his world were different. Their rules were not his.

He crossed the lot to his truck, acting as if he needed something from the load bed and pretending the biker was inconsequential. He pretended not to notice the Smoker's whole posture change when he realised Victor was the man he was there waiting to see. Abe had told them about the truck, of course.

The Nameless had on a sleeveless leather vest that showed pale arms with lots of tattoos, obvious even in the dim light of an early, grey morning. He wore a black bandana and blue jeans. There were no weapons Victor could see, but the man's knuckles shone with many rings. Even if worn purely for decoration, they would make for effective knuckle dusters.

He had no rucksack, no satchel. No bag attached to the chopper itself. Which meant no supplies, so either he wasn't staying long, or he was ill-prepared for extended surveillance. Maybe his first time ever as a watcher. A rare thrill on paper because he had no idea what watching actually meant. The boredom, the tiredness, the mental fatigue of paying attention for long periods of time, the need to balance watching with unavoidable issues like needing to urinate.

He was no threat in the way no single civilian could be a threat, but he was here because the gang leader considered Victor a threat. But why? Because he had hurt Abe? No, they had killed Abe. So, perhaps they didn't like the fact Victor was asking questions about Michelle and Joshua.

Did they want to know more about the guy asking these questions or did they want him gone? The former, he decided, because if Abe had even hinted at Victor's capabilities, the leader who was trouble would have sent more men to drive him out of town.

Hence, the leader operated with a degree of reserve despite burning down Abe's meth lab with Abe inside. Which seemed contradictory and only increased Victor's eagerness to meet the man.

The Smoker on the chopper didn't yet realise he was the invitation to that introduction.

As Victor left his truck, the smartly dressed crew from Chicago were climbing into their sedan: two men in the back and one in the passenger seat.

Welch had the driver's door open and was standing next to it, waiting for Victor to look their way.

When he did, she held his gaze for a long moment, face expressionless, then nodded a single time at him.

He nodded back.

She climbed behind the wheel and pulled the door shut.

None of the four so much as glanced in his direction as the car drove out of the lot, nor as it joined the highway for the drive south to the border.

He watched them go, thinking that ten years back he would not have knocked on their room door. He would have kicked it in or climbed through the bathroom window to take them by surprise and killed them all without even considering an alternative. He would then have spent the night cutting up their corpses and bagging the pieces. A time-consuming, labour-intensive process because it was demanding work to dismember four people without the right tools, made harder still when it was necessary to avoid leaving an incredible amount of mess behind.

But more interesting than counting blobs in wallpaper, he thought.

The lake would have been the obvious place to get rid of those bagged pieces but given he had already disposed of the rifle that way, he would now be driving off to bury the corpses in the forest. No shallow graves. He would have needed to dig deep holes to avoid animals unearthing them to get at the meat. That might have taken all morning.

Then he would have travelled back to Chicago to kill their boss who had been his client. Almost a repeat of the contract he had just fulfilled only without payment for his time and for his efforts. Far more dangerous too, because his new target would be expecting him to show up given his crew had gone silent. He would be well protected. It would have been certain to end up loud, messy. The chance of injury would have been significant. It would have been no clean kill. There would have been multiple dead. Henchmen. Guards. Maybe civilians or cops caught in the crossfire. Potentially a whole organised crime faction wiped out so he could kill one man and eliminate a single threat. Impossible to do without leaving evidence, without creating a trail for others to follow, whether vengeful associates, dogged detectives, old enemies who had never given up hunting him or other professionals eager to collect the resulting bounty.

All avoided because of a conversation.

Better to side-step a threat than defeat it.

Change was slow but inevitable, Victor told himself as the car disappeared from view.

Of course, he realised, as he returned to his room and heaved open the bathroom window, ten years ago he wouldn't have remained in his staging ground a single second longer than necessary.

He would have avoided the threat altogether.

THIRTY

The Smoker smoked because he had nothing else to do. Castel had told him to get to know the fisherman. But what did that really mean? The Smoker hadn't pressed for clarification and had expected the specifics to become obvious once he was at the motel, but there were so many unanswered questions. How closely was he supposed to get to know him? Take him to lunch? If the fisherman left the motel was the Smoker supposed to follow all the way to Alaska? How long was he supposed to get to know him for? Until they were best buds? With the lack of anything to do but smoke and think, the Smoker spent too long with those questions going round and round his head, and he realised his hand was shaking as he lit up another cigarette.

Of course, he should have asked Castel for more information, but you didn't ask Castel to explain himself. You said 'Sure thing, chief' and got it done.

Or you ended up like Abe.

The Smoker was getting it done. *It* meaning nothing.

Until . . .

The fisherman stepped outside. Which was quite the surprise. The Smoker had assumed he would be in his motel room, sleeping or watching TV or masturbating or whatever else people did before the sun had fully risen.

He first went to the check-in desk, then went to do something with his truck without a care in the world. He didn't notice the Smoker on the opposite side of the road, watching him.

Was this the guy poor dead Abe had talked about? If Castel was worried this guy was a cop or from a rival outfit, he needn't have bothered. Didn't look like much. A regular nobody.

The Smoker relaxed. He could do this. He could watch this nobody all day long if necessary. Idiot didn't know he was a marked man. He was lucky Castel wanted information first because the Smoker could ride right up to him and strike him on the back of the head with a crowbar as he passed.

Wouldn't take much speed and the nobody would be a no one.

The Smoker imagined himself as a knight of old, charging a rival, his chopper a steed and his crowbar a lance. If only there was a fair maiden whose hand could be won, the Smoker's fantasy would be complete.

The fisherman was not exactly out in the open, the Smoker thought, so a little more creativity might be needed. Which was fine with the Smoker. He liked to fight. Had lived for it at one point when he was younger. That was how he had ended up with the Nameless. The Smoker had spent enough nights in lockup after brawling that one of those nights was in the company of one of Castel's crew. With nothing else to do but talk they had bonded, and within a few weeks the Smoker was buying his first chopper with the profits of a drug deal.

He had never looked back.

The fisherman finished with his truck and left the Smoker's line of sight. Back to his room, no doubt. Which was fine. The Smoker would see him when he left again.

Only he wasn't going to leave any time soon. He might not leave for hours.

The boredom grew and grew, and the Smoker did whatever he could to pass the time, to limit the tedium. He cleaned his nails with the tip of his switchblade. He trimmed them with the same knife. He shaved little squares in the hair of his forearm. He held his palm over his lighter for as long as he could stand it. He practised tricks with the lighter. He threw it up into the air and caught it again – underhand, overhand, with the other hand.

The worst part was having to ration his smokes. Once he realised the fisherman wasn't going anywhere and Castel sent no further instructions, the Smoker knew his pack of cigarettes wasn't going to last the day. He had gone through half by the time he worked this out, so he was already up against it.

The flipside to this hell of his own making was that he only lit up when he couldn't put it off any longer, and the resulting rush of relief was incredible. He savoured every inhale, every exhale. He smoked those precious cigarettes all the way down to the filter. He didn't waste a single flake of tobacco.

The cigarettes helped stave off any hunger but they did nothing for his thirst, which grew and grew until he feared death by dehydration more than he did Castel, so the Smoker crossed the highway to go and use the vending machine at the motel.

He had plenty of cash on him and bought himself two bottles of soda and a bag of trail mix.

He downed the first soda before he had left the parking lot and tossed the plastic bottle to the ground before he crossed the highway.

Halfway across he realised something was wrong.

Where was his chopper?

Not where he had left it, that was for damn sure.

He went from a stroll to a jog, crossing the rest of the highway at increasing speed.

He saw the cigarette butts in the grass and the flattened-down areas of undergrowth where the tyres had sat for half the night.

The Smoker slapped the pocket of his jeans and felt the reassuring jab of his keys and the resulting relief that no one could have ridden it away. He would have heard it, wouldn't he?

It was light by now but overcast and dim, and it took a moment's frantic searching until he saw a narrow trail of bent-over and compressed grasses that led from the highway into the treeline.

What the actual . . . ?

Someone was trying to steal his ride by rolling it away. They must have thought he had parked it up for the duration, not realising he was just grabbing a soda.

The Smoker tossed away the second bottle and the trail mix because he was going to need both hands to beat all kinds of hell out of the thief.

You don't mess with the Nameless.

The Smoker hurried into the treeline to catch up with the thief, but beneath the canopy the woods were so shadowed he lost sight of where he was going within seconds. It was impossible to see where the chopper had been led, where the undergrowth had been broken down.

Trees everywhere. Shadows everywhere.

Figuring the thief would have continued the way he was already going, the Smoker did the same, dashed deeper into the trees, angry and urgent.

He loved his chopper more than he did any human being he had ever known.

Every second he hurried forward without sight of it, his fear of losing it for ever increased and his anger towards the thief who had taken it multiplied into a boiling, murderous hatred.

The Smoker was going to kill him. He was going to tear him apart.

The Smoker couldn't find him. The Smoker was lost.

In his desperation, he roared.

In his haste, he stumbled.

In his rage, he fell.

Climbing to his feet, the Smoker yelled '*Where are you?*' at the shadows all around him.

'Behind you,' the shadows answered.

THIRTY-ONE

To his credit, the Smoker didn't panic.

He didn't hesitate. He reacted fast. He was primed, ready. He spun around, pivoting in a rapid one-eighty, left hand rising in a defensive guard as the right dropped to his waist, to the knife holster on his belt.

A click.

A flash of moonlight on metal.

A *swish* of the blade cutting air, rising fast, thrusting for Victor's neck.

The Smoker's eyes glimmered, triumphant.

Victor disarmed him.

A simple action because Victor waited until the last instant, until the Smoker had overextended and left himself vulnerable. Victor struck the back of the Smoker's hand as he hit his inner wrist, both of Victor's hands striking simultaneously.

Sometimes, the shock of the dual impacts meant the knife – or gun, or whatever weapon – flew out of the holding hand, the enemy unable to keep their grip closed. Other times the weapon remained held, but the pain was so great, the nerves so overstimulated, that the grip had no strength. That was the better outcome because then the weapon could be taken.

The Smoker released the knife.

It flashed in a sudden arc before disappearing into the darkness of the trees.

To his credit, the Smoker still didn't panic.

He was already moving forward, so followed through with the momentum, hoping to collide into Victor, to wrestle or headbutt or bite or bulldoze.

Victor wasn't sure of the Smoker's exact intention because Victor was already pivoting on his back foot, slipping out of the Smoker's line of attack.

The Smoker fell.

'Who's your boss and where can I find him?'

The undergrowth cushioned the fall, and the Smoker was up to his hands and knees within a couple of seconds, humiliated more than hurt.

'We can keep this easy.'

The Smoker scrambled up and around, swinging a wild punch in the assumption Victor would be closing. With nothing to absorb the punch's energy, the Smoker swung himself off balance.

'I don't have to hurt you.'

Victor swept his load-bearing leg out from under him.

'But I will.'

The Smoker, down to his hands and knees again, grunted.

'And then you'll tell me everything you know about your boss.'

The Smoker spat out dirt and detritus as he stood.

'You'll be begging to tell me.'

Another attack, even less effective than the previous one because the Smoker was out of breath and letting his rage control him. Victor slipped the clumsy strikes and this time let the Smoker stay on his feet as he stumbled away until his balance recovered.

'Who is he? Where is he?'

The Smoker, chest heaving, grabbed a thick fallen branch from the ground and charged forward, swinging it at Victor's head.

A fast step forward propelled Victor straight at the Smoker, straight into the line of attack, but the branch-club was still mid-swing.

By the time it had finished its arc, it hit only air.

Victor was inside the Smoker's reach, jabbing his right palm into the biker's face; hooking his left elbow over his extended arms, grabbing them and pinning both to his flank; rotating his attacking palm to slip it around the Smoker's head, controlling and pulling the head down into the knee Victor drove upwards at the underside of the Smoker's chin.

Teeth cracked against teeth.

The Smoker became slack.

No exhale, no resistance.

Immediate unconsciousness.

Victor released the Smoker and let him fall face first into the undergrowth.

Faster than choking him out, and Victor needed the Smoker compliant for a moment until he was ready to ensure cooperation.

THIRTY-TWO

The Smoker was unconscious for almost ten minutes. He might have been out for a lot longer had Victor not begun revving the chopper's engine. The sound would carry, of course, but he had rolled it deeper into the woods while the biker was KO'd, draped over it. The trees here were dense, the undergrowth tall. Not a perfect muffler, but good enough for Victor's requirements.

The Smoker spat out blood.

'I'm looking for a woman named Michelle and her son Joshua,' Victor began. 'They're missing. No one's seen them since the day before yesterday. Michelle used to date Abe, your former meth cook, who just so happened to die yesterday. I want to speak with your boss, that's all. I want to know if he knows anything about Michelle's and Joshua's disappearance or if he knows who might.'

The Smoker used the back of one hand to wipe blood from his chin, grimacing and wincing. His eyes shot pure hatred Victor's way.

'I'm glad to see you're back to your regular self already.'

Victor had bound the Smoker's hands together in front of him with his own belt. The resulting bonds were not secure to any professional degree, but they didn't need to be escape-proof. The Smoker wouldn't be left alone to start any kind of attempt.

'Can you talk?'

The Smoker said, 'You're a dead man.'

'Then you have nothing to fear from me.'

'I'm not scared.'

'Good,' Victor said. 'That provides a useful benchmark to work from.'

The Smoker said, 'What?'

Victor explained: 'If you were afraid, if you were desperate, it would be harder for me to know for sure you were telling me the truth.'

The Smoker listened.

'But because you're not scared, because you're defiant, it'll be easier for me to know when you start talking that you're telling me the truth and not what you think I want to hear.'

'I'm not telling you a thing.'

'Even better,' Victor said. 'Keep going with that. It makes this a whole lot easier. For me, I mean. Not for you. In fact, you're making this harder and harder for yourself. Every wall you build up is just one more I need to knock back down.'

The Smoker was not convinced. 'You're nothing. You're not scaring me one little bit.'

'If you think I'm trying to scare you then you're misinterpreting my intent. I assure you that I'm not trying to scare you.' Victor paused. 'But in a few moments you're going to wish I had been.'

The Smoker was silent.

Victor said, 'I'm going to ask you one last time. And I really mean that. I will not ask again. Instead, I'll hurt you. And I'll keep hurting you until you answer. If you don't answer, I'll continue hurting you until you're dead. Then, when your boss sends another to find out what happened to you, I'll ask him. And when he realises what happened to you, he'll talk. He'll be so keen to talk I'll have to tell him to slow down. So, you can't change the end result, but you can change how we get there.'

Victor revved the engine, hard. The exhaust roared. The chopper shook.

'Who is your boss and where can I find him?'

The Smoker spat blood at Victor, who took hold of the Smoker's head and pushed his face against the exhaust manifold.

It was hard to know the exact temperature, but Victor estimated it was between three and four hundred degrees. Nowhere near as hot as it could reach when the vehicle was in motion and the engine was working hard.

Still, it was hot enough so that the Smoker's face sizzled against it. Hot enough that Victor could smell cooking flesh. Hot enough that the moisture in the Smoker's skin boiled and steam hissed and clouded. Hot enough that Victor had to rev the engine even harder, louder, to drown out the high-pitched screams.

The Smoker thrashed in desperate attempts to push himself away from the source of his agony, but with his hands bound and unable to assist he could not match a fraction of Victor's strength.

He kept the Smoker's face against the manifold until the

scent of cooking flesh became the scent of burnt flesh and until the cloud of steam became wisps of pale smoke.

When Victor let go, the Smoker didn't fall. He couldn't because his face was seared to the metal. To escape the burning heat of the manifold the biker had to pull himself free, which meant he had to tear away his face so that a blackened layer of skin remained fused to the metal and where his cheek should have been was a bloody open wound surrounded by a ring of charred crust.

The Smoker collapsed on to the forest floor. He was pale and sweating and whimpering. He was crying.

Victor asked no question.

'His name's ... Castel,' the Smoker answered in a weak voice between frantic gulps of air. 'His house, our den, is on the other side of town ... near the power plant.'

'That wasn't so hard, was it?'

The Smoker lay gasping and trembling.

'I want you to tell Castel what happened here,' Victor said. 'I want him to see your face. I want him to know I'm serious and I'm going nowhere. But I also want him to know I'm not interested in his business, I don't care about his meth. I'm only looking for Joshua and his mother. If Castel knows why they're missing, then he needs to break his back getting that information to me before I come knocking on his door. And if he has them or if he knows who does, then his new number one priority in this world is making sure they're released before I find them. Because if he thinks your face looks bad it's nothing compared to what I'll do to his entire body.'

THIRTY-THREE

Victor left the Smoker in the woods. It would take time for the man to wriggle his hands out of the belt around his wrists, but not too long. Victor didn't want the biker to die out there. Not without first delivering his message. The question remained as to whether the Smoker would do that first or head to a hospital to have his face treated. If he did the latter, then he would no doubt call Castel from there. Not before. He would need a payphone or to borrow a phone because Victor had taken the Smoker's mobile after first getting the man to show him the code to unlock it.

He didn't carry a phone unless there was a pressing need to use one. When he spent so much time and effort to avoid detection it would be counterproductive to have a GPS tracker on his person. Now, however, the benefits might outweigh the risk.

He wanted Castel to call.

Victor had no intention of driving up to the man's house.

That would make him defensive. If he was with his men, which seemed more likely than not considering the Smoker had referred to it as their den, then Castel would feel the need to establish his dominance in front of a threat and Victor didn't want to kill anyone if he could avoid it. The town was small and there had already been one death during his time here. Not that he had killed Abe, but a dramatic rise in the county homicide rate that coincided with Victor's presence was a problem he could do without.

It was the kind of thing that pinged the radar of the kind of people Victor spent his life trying to avoid. A mob boss assassinated in Chicago would have been noticed by those people. A subsequent killing spree in a nearby town would send them into a frenzy with the scent of blood.

Castel's reaction would tell Victor everything that a face-to-face would reveal and bypass the potential for a massacre. Castel would either call him, come after him, or hole up.

If he called, then Victor could ask questions and listen to the answers before deciding his next course of action. If the call never came, there were two options left. If Castel didn't come after Victor, didn't come for revenge or to rid himself of the threat, then it meant Castel was holing up, and Victor would know for sure Joshua and Michelle were either in Castel's possession or had been.

Then there would be no avoiding a massacre.

Beforehand, however, there was time.

But how much time was there left for Michelle and Joshua? The odds of finding them alive were worsening with every day, every hour.

The elderly couple were on their porch when Victor pulled up at Michelle's house in his truck, so there was little need to stop the engine and climb out. Instead, he buzzed down the door window.

'Any sign of them?' he called.

The man shook his head. 'Been out here all morning and I seen no one come or go. No light on neither last night.'

Victor remained silent.

'I'm sure it's nothing,' the woman said.

Victor nodded. 'I appreciate your help.'

'We're just being us,' the man said.

Victor pulled away and headed back to the motel, driving slow. Slow because he had a lot to think about.

He was tired and needed rest, so he slept for three hours on top of the covers of his motel bed. He remained fully dressed because escaping a kill team could be hard enough without doing it naked or burning time to get dressed. He woke up when the alarm in his head, built over years of ceaseless practice, informed him he had rested long enough.

That same ceaseless practice made him reach for his gun – most often tucked into his waistband but sometimes resting on the covers next to him – but he had no gun. He carried one less and less often because he preferred to avoid enemies than shoot them. Still, practice had become instinct at some point and now that reach for a gun was so hardwired into his brain that he knew he would never be rid of it.

No sounds reached his ears that gave any indication a threat was nearby, so he sat up. A visual check followed and, satisfied, he climbed off the bed.

He brought the back of his hand up to his forehead and felt moisture. He realised his pulse was elevated.

Flashes of dreams threatened to form into inescapable memory, so Victor fought to think about anything else.

He checked the room for any signs someone had been inside or tried to gain access but his countermeasures were uninterrupted.

He bathed, changed, and set out.

THIRTY-FOUR

Rowing machines were for suckers, McAllan knew, which is why he was a sucker. He tried to get on it every day and sweat out a few miles, but the boredom was killing him. He expected the physical exertion would be the hard part but no one warned him of the mental toll of exercise. Even the little screen that displayed a digitised route didn't help. He had tried rowing along pixelated rivers, across lakes and down coastlines and none of it made a difference. Maybe it was the incessant, inescapable noise of the chain mechanism with its mocking, rhythmic whirr of irritation.

'Can you turn that up?' McAllan shouted.

One of his men, watching the TV in the nearby kitchen, called back 'Sorry, boss' and turned it down.

'*NO*,' McAllan yelled. 'Up, not down.'

His man appeared in the little annexe that served as McAllan's new gym. He looked confused.

'All those roids have made your neck so thick that not enough blood can get through it and into your brain. Is that it?'

'Boss?'

McAllan rolled his eyes as he rowed. 'The damned television. Crank up the volume for the love of all that is pure in this world.'

'You don't want me to turn it down?'

McAllan, sweating and red-faced and irritated by the whirring and annoyed by his man's stupidity, threw down the rowing machine's cable handholds and climbed out of the seat. He pushed past his man, who had moved closer to seek an answer to his question, entered the kitchen, grabbed the remote off the island and thumbed the volume button until it was maxed and the TV was blaring out some trash show about storage lockers.

Bliss.

He shoved the remote into the hands of his man on his way back through to the gym.

'What do I pay you for exactly?'

His man said, 'My good looks and charm?'

'Well, it's not for your sense of self-awareness, that's for sure,' McAllan said, shoving him out of the way.

Settling back on to the hard little seat of the rower, McAllan took the handholds and started pulling. The blaring sound of the TV in the next room did help to drown out the noise of the whirring, although only for a few seconds before the TV fell silent.

'*Are you kidding me?*' McAllan roared.

He stormed back into the kitchen, finding his man on his phone, nodding and saying, 'Uh-huh.'

McAllan stabbed a finger at the TV but his man shook his head.

He mouthed at McAllan, *Hendon*.

McAllan's rage subsided. He took one of the tall stools at the breakfast bar and waited.

After a few more seconds' interaction, his man took the phone from his ear to tap the screen. He set it down on the breakfast bar and McAllan saw it was set to speaker.

'You're on with Mr McAllan,' his man said.

'How you doin', Hendon?'

She said, 'I'm perfectly fine, Bobby. Working hard at your request.'

'You sound tired,' McAllan said. 'You didn't stay up all night, did you?'

'Don't worry about my hours,' Hendon said.

'You're calling already,' McAllan noted. 'That tells me you've found something I need to know about.'

'It's more what I've not found.'

'Hit me,' McAllan said, eager.

Hendon took a deep breath. McAllan pictured her adjusting her reading glasses and referring to notes. There was a faint rustle of paper emanating through the speaker because Hendon was old school. She wrote everything down by hand. Which McAllan liked, because no one could hack a legal pad.

'I'm going to skip the colour detail,' she said, 'and go straight to the relevant findings.'

'When I pay you by the hour, you'd better.'

'If I charged you for every hour I worked you'd have another stroke.'

McAllan chuckled.

'So,' Hendon began, 'your Wilson Murdoch is an

interesting fellow. He's a native of Nevada and has never left the US until now. Sounds like a homebody or a world-fearing patriot, right?'

'I see.'

'He has his own business that is registered offshore and as such I can't check his finances, I can't see who else works for the company, and I can't even see what that company actually does. It's existed for only ten months so perhaps they're still deciding.'

'I thought you were skipping the colour,' McAllan said. 'On the clock and all that.'

'Murdoch is so clean you could eat your dinner off him.'

'Fat chance. You found out he's not even remotely clean.'

'But only because I went above and beyond on this one, Robert.'

'Stop dragging it out for extra credit. You know I worship you.'

'Anyway,' she said. 'I'm part of a network of private investigators that covers both Canada and the US. I know a guy in Las Vegas. I know him really well, as a matter of fact. I asked him to do me a favour because it annoyed me I had hit a brick wall thanks to Murdoch's offshore company. This friend of mine got in his car and drove out to see Murdoch's parents because Murdoch had an accident a few years ago. He hit his head while skiing in Colorado. No employment records after that until founding his offshore company almost a year back. You know what this friend of mine found when he drove out to see the parents?'

'I can guess,' McAllan said with a frown. 'He found Murdoch in a back room with all sorts of tubes sticking out of him.'

'Bingo,' Hendon said. 'Persistent vegetative state.'

'The parents are religious, then? It's against their faith to turn off the life support.'

She said, 'Sometimes I wonder why you even need me.'

'Because I don't like to work any harder than I have to,' McAllan said. 'Anything else?'

'That's it,' Hendon said. 'Whoever your fisherman is, he isn't Wilson Murdoch.'

'I'll make sure you're paid the same day we get the invoice.'

'I slipped it in the post a minute before I called.'

'Do me a favour, yeah?' McAllan said. 'Never work for the wrong people. I don't want them screwing up and losing you your licence. You're too valuable to me, understand?'

She said, 'Your concern, as always, is appreciated,' and hung up.

McAllan handed the phone back to his man, who said, 'What now?'

'I'd say that's obvious, isn't it?' McAllan said back. 'Now we know who the fisherman is not, we find out who he really is.'

His man nodded.

McAllan said, 'So I'd say we need to go and have a little word with *Mr Murdoch*.'

A loud throat-clearing announced another of McAllan's henchmen entering the kitchen.

This one said, 'A Mr Murdoch is here to see you.'

THIRTY-FIVE

Victor knew little about houses, about real estate, beyond how to break into them and how best to kill those inside. He knew how to jimmy windows, pick locks, avoid motion sensors and disable alarms. He knew what kind of doors would stop a suppressed nine mil and those that would not. He knew where floorboards were likely to creak and where they were firmest. He knew if he snapped someone's neck in the kitchen that other occupants would hear the breaking vertebrae echoing upstairs.

McAllan's house was about three thousand square feet on the ground floor. Maybe another two on the floor above. The grounds were huge. The building was grey stone built in a European style, as if this house was not twenty years old but two hundred, nestled in the English countryside instead of in a millionaire's neighbourhood in Canada.

Victor took mental snapshots as he was led through the downstairs hallways by one of McAllan's bulky henchmen. It was one of the three who had turned up outside Michelle's house. That man had been surprised when Victor showed up here, and had called ahead to someone inside, maybe McAllan or another of his men, and waited for a reply before letting Victor inside. A reasonable system but no obstacle for Victor should it come to it.

Compared to the hardened paramilitaries guarding a people trafficker, the fortress-like casino home of a cartel patron, or the elite bodyguards of an arms dealer, McAllan's security barely qualified as such. He thought it was enough because he had no idea what it really took to be safe. McAllan wouldn't sleep a wink if he knew the truth.

The guy leading Victor through the house kept glancing back over his shoulder as if Victor might not be there, might have slipped away in the intervening seconds. Victor didn't tell him that it should be Victor walking in front, not him, that then he wouldn't need to check.

The lack of effective security suggested Linette was right about her father. Victor couldn't imagine McAllan involved in any business that might have dangerous repercussions if his men didn't even know how to escort a stranger to their boss in their boss's own home.

McAllan was sitting at a breakfast bar, although there was no breakfast before him. He wore a red tracksuit and had a slight sheen to his face, suggesting the clothes weren't just for comfort.

'Wilson Murdoch.'

Victor said, 'Thank you for seeing me.'

'Don't thank me just yet. What can I do for you?'

'Have you made any progress looking for Michelle and Joshua?'

'Any progress?' McAllan asked.

'You told me yesterday that you were concerned for a missing employee.'

'That's right. I did.'

Victor remained silent.

'The answer is no,' McAllan said. 'No progress regarding them. I'm going to take a wild guess and say you haven't found them either.'

Victor ignored McAllan's inquisitive look and the accusatory stares of his henchmen. He ignored the tension in the room because he was the only man not tense.

He said, 'I don't care what you do to make your money. I don't care if you bribe officials or intimidate union bosses or break their bones. I don't even care if you bury your rivals out in the woods. I'm no threat to you. In fact, I can be the best friend you ever had if you help me achieve my objective. All I want is to find Joshua and his mother.'

'I don't know where they are,' McAllan said. 'I have nothing to do with their disappearance. That's not who I am. If that's what you think then you're looking in the wrong direction.'

'Should I be looking in the direction of the Nameless?'

McAllan hesitated, then said, 'Why do you think that?'

'Michelle dated one of their meth cooks, Abraham. I went to see him. Now, he's dead.'

'Dead?'

Victor nodded. 'He's dead, and one of the bikers has been watching me.'

'Has been?'

'I convinced him it wasn't the best use of his time.'

McAllan understood how such a conversation might have gone down. 'And what now?'

'I expect Castel will be in a hurry to speak to me.'

McAllan smirked. 'Rather you than me.'

'Do you and he do any business together?'

McAllan sat back. 'I'm in construction not drugs.'

'That's not answering my question.'

'I don't do business with Castel. I'm insulted at the very suggestion. He's an animal. He's inhuman.'

'But you did once upon a time,' Victor said. 'That's how you know what he's like. Unless you're going to try and convince me you play golf together at the country club.'

McAllan said nothing.

'You're in construction now because you make more money, but that's not how you started out, is it? You and Castel go way back.'

McAllan was silent.

Victor said, 'Why are you trying to run me out of town?'

'Who says I am?'

'You told the motel manager to get rid of me.'

McAllan huffed. 'And a fine job he's done of it. But that was then. That was before. Now, I want to keep you around for a while.'

Victor waited.

'You didn't step into my back yard and expect to go unnoticed, did you? Because I'm like a satellite in orbit with all sorts of lenses fixed on this here fair town, watching, analysing. I see all. I see you before me as Wilson Murdoch, but that must be some kind of magic trick because the real Murdoch is on life support in his mom and dad's back room. He's got tubes stuck in every orifice. Must be hell on the parents, but they're good Catholics. So, you're no magic trick. Just a trick.'

Victor didn't react. He saw McAllan wasn't bluffing. The man had done his homework. Whatever his level of physical security, McAllan made up for it elsewhere. Outside help, Victor assumed, because none of McAllan's guys looked like they knew how to run that kind of background check. But it would take more than checking databases to unravel Victor's legend because it was solid enough to fool Linette. Which made Victor curious as to who McAllan was using because that person was the kind of threat Victor could do without.

McAllan, looking pleased with himself, continued: 'Like I said, I want you to stick around. Because now I know you're not Wilson Murdoch I don't want you going anywhere until I find out who you really are.'

Victor said, 'Do you know what happened to Joshua and Michelle?'

'I already told you.'

'You told me you didn't have anything to do with their disappearance.'

'I didn't, I swear,' McAllan said, leaning forward. He pointed a fat finger at his own face. 'Look me right in my eyes and see for yourself if I'm lying. Well, am I?'

The answer was no, which was why Victor began backing out of the kitchen.

McAllan said, 'But that doesn't mean we're through. Because I can't help but wonder why a man on an innocent fishing vacation needs to travel under a false passport in the name of a guy who pisses in one bag and craps in another. Not the kind of thing that usually happens in a quiet town like this, is it?' He glanced around at his guys as if looking for a correction. When none came, he added, 'Which makes this whole thing a door I'd really like to peek beyond.'

His tone emphasised the implicit threat and his eyes almost shone with a smug gleefulness. McAllan expected Victor to back down because he was used to people backing down.

'Not all doors are meant to keep you out,' Victor said before he headed for the exit. 'Some doors are closed to protect you from what lies on the other side.'

THIRTY-SIX

Castel's house was never quiet. Not in the day, not in the night. Not ever. It was a drum machine set to a continuous steady rhythm of percussion because it had long ceased to be only his house. His home was the home of the Nameless. At least half of them lived here at any one time. As such it buzzed with activity at all hours. He had a small crew but they were always busy. There was always something to do. Business never slept, and neither did the Nameless.

And they partied as hard as they worked. While meth was being bagged in the kitchen, reefers were smoked in the adjoining dining room. While shipments were arranged in one bedroom, dicks were getting sucked in the bedroom next door.

The Nameless were all men, but they had wives or girl-friends – and some had both. Castel encouraged courtships because he never wanted his men to be single. He never wanted them without something to lose.

He welcomed those wives and girlfriends to his house and

173

always took the time to get to know them and to make them feel part of the extended family. He wanted them around even when their men were away for long periods running his business. He wanted them around so those men away on long periods had someone to come back to as well as someone they would have to leave behind should they get greedy.

That had never happened yet, but Castel had been quick to betray every boss he had ever worked for and knew one of his men someday betraying him was inevitable.

He almost felt sorry for whichever wife or girlfriend was left behind as a result because he would have to make them suffer greatly to show his remaining men the price of earning his displeasure.

Because Castel made an effort to get to know those wives and girlfriends he recognised who screamed even though they were downstairs and he was lying on his bed in the last throes of his oxy high.

He dragged himself off the bed and headed downstairs and into the resulting commotion.

'Let me through,' he shouted as he reached the bottom of the stairs.

Most of the Nameless were gathered in the hallway. Wives and girlfriends too. There were many ashen faces, many expressions of disgust and distress and anger.

Everyone was looking at the guy he'd sent to watch the motel for the fisherman. That particular Nameless was slumped on the floor, unable to stand in his exhaustion and pain.

Everyone was looking at the Smoker's face.

'I came ... straight here,' he managed to say.

Castel said, 'Why? You should have gone to the hospital.'

'I came straight here,' he said again.

'The fisherman did this to you?'

The man nodded. 'He's looking for Abe's ex ... her kid. If you know what happened to them ... you need to tell him. Otherwise he's coming.'

Castel lowered himself into a squat. 'He did this to you and then threatened me?'

The Smoker nodded again. Pointed at the huge open wound where one cheek should have been. 'He said ... he'll do worse to you.'

'Will he indeed?' Castel rose and looked at his two men nearby who were waiting in expectation. 'Take him to the hospital. Make sure he's looked after then come back here. Get back here fast. Get back here fast because we're riding out.'

'Yes, chief,' one Nameless said.

'Fast,' the other said.

Castel addressed the rest of his men. Every one of the Nameless was now in close proximity; even those who had been outside or upstairs had been drawn to the screams and commotion.

'An attack on one of us is an attack on all of us,' Castel said, touching his cheek as if the wound was his own.

Nods of agreement.

Murmurs of anticipation.

Castel approached each of his uninjured men in turn, touching their cheeks one after the other. His small ice-blue eyes were fierce and unblinking and glistening with tears.

'I am vengeance.'

One of the Nameless said, 'I am vengeance.'

'I am vengeance,' another said, louder.

Castel screamed, '*WE ARE VENGEANCE.*'

THIRTY-SEVEN

No one watched Victor leave McAllan's property. The guy who had led him through the house followed Victor to the front door, finally getting it right, but only because Victor had begun walking first. The door slammed shut behind him and he approached his truck. It was parked on the gravel driveway, which was circular, set around an elaborate fountain carved in a likeness of the goddess Venus.

The black wrought-iron gates buzzed open.

Not to facilitate Victor's exit but to allow Linette to drive into the property.

She was in her cruiser and dressed for another shift. Surprised to see him.

She parked and climbed out of the car. 'What are you doing here?'

Victor said, 'I could ask you the same thing.'

'I need to speak to my dad.'

'Your dad? He was McAllan yesterday.'

'What's your point?'

Victor didn't answer.

'I'm allowed to have a relationship with my father,' Linette said. 'Whatever he does and whatever I do doesn't change the fact he's my father and I'm his daughter.'

'I never said otherwise.'

'Then why are you trying to make me feel guilty about it?'

'All I'm doing is looking for Joshua and his mother.'

She took a calming breath. Exhaled. 'Still nothing?'

He shook his head. 'I don't think your father is involved in their disappearance.'

'I told you that.'

'But that doesn't mean he's not connected.'

'What?'

Victor said, 'He's done business with Castel in the past.'

'Bullshit.'

'There's no need for that kind of language.'

'When you call my dad a drug dealer then yeah, there is.'

'That's not what I said. He has a past relationship with the Nameless.'

She looked away, then back. 'Even if that was true, what has it got to do with Michelle and Joshua?'

'I'll tell you when I know.'

'Don't say you're going to see Castel next?'

Victor shook his head. He didn't tell Linette that he didn't need to go and see Castel because Castel was going to come to him. He wanted her as far away as possible from what would follow.

Linette said, 'After I've finished here I'll be back at my desk and checking records. If Michelle has used her credit card then I'll know where she's been.'

'She won't have.'

'We'll see,' Linette said. 'I'm not ready to give up on them just yet.'

'I'm not giving up.'

She stared at him for a moment. 'Yeah, I can see that. And I still don't know why.'

'Because if I don't find them no one else will.'

'You know, I'm right here.'

'I'm just being realistic.'

'Yeah, yeah. I remember. You think I'm going to let the case go cold.'

'The case is going to go cold,' Victor said. 'It's not about whether you let it or not.'

'Two things. One: how do you know it will go cold, and two: I'm getting a little tired of your assumptions about my competence. I'm a good cop. I'm going to do everything I can.'

'And it won't be enough,' Victor said.

'There you go again.'

'Do you know where they are?'

'Of course not, otherwise—'

'Do you know why they're missing?'

'No, but—'

'Do you know who they left with that morning?'

'How could I?'

'Do you have a motive?'

'No.'

'Do you have a suspect?'

She said nothing.

'People aren't complicated,' Victor said. 'Something has happened to Joshua and his mother and at this moment in time neither you nor I know what that something is.'

'And I'm going to find out.'

'It'll be too late by then.'

Linette sighed. 'Okay, let's roll with your pessimistic pre-diction. If you have no faith that I can do anything, why the hell should I believe that you can do any better?'

'Please don't blaspheme.'

'Are you kidding me?'

'Not even a little bit.'

She rolled her eyes. 'I'm not even going to waste a second of my mental energy trying to unpack that because I have a missing mother and her son to find. But, you didn't answer my question: why should I think you can actually find them yourself?'

Victor thought about what he knew and what he didn't know. He thought about McAllan and Castel and Michelle and Joshua and the utter lack of answers he had to an expo-nentially growing list of questions.

He said, 'Right now, I don't think I'm going to find them. There's too much I don't understand and not enough time.'

'Have a little faith,' Linette said. 'All we can do is try.'

'I'm going to do more than try,' Victor said. 'I'm going to do whatever it takes.'

With pursed lips she stared at him, and he left her on the driveway. She was still standing in the same place as he drove away.

At Michelle's house the elderly couple on the porch next door were shaking their heads before he'd finished braking. He nodded their way and set off again.

The Smoker's cell phone rang. An unknown number.

Victor answered and said, 'I was wondering when you would call.'

'Where are you?' Castel asked. 'You're not at the motel.'

'I'm close by.'

'Why did you hurt my man?'

Victor said, 'You know why.'

'Nuh-uh,' Castel said. 'I know some lie about Abe's ex and her kid. I don't know the real reason. But whatever the reason, it won't matter. It won't help you.'

'That is the real reason.'

'Nice try,' Castel said. 'I'm not so easy to fool.'

'I'm fooling you and I'm not even trying.'

'What?'

'I'm looking for Joshua and Michelle,' Victor said. 'That's the only reason I went to see Abe. It's the only reason I'm in town at all.'

Silence on the line.

'Do you know where they are?' Victor asked.

Castel said, 'What's it worth?'

'Everything.'

Castel laughed. '*K-ching*.'

'Everything to you,' Victor said. 'To you, telling me where they are is worth everything.'

Castel didn't understand. 'That's a hell of a lot for some skank and her freak of a kid.'

Victor took a breath and held it for a second. 'Did you see what I did to your man's face?'

'You're going to pay for that.'

'I was improvising,' Victor said.

'So?'

'I didn't plan it. I was using what I had to hand.'

'So?' Castel said again.

'So,' Victor echoed, 'if you speak about either Joshua or his mother like that again I won't improvise with you. I'll plan exactly what to do. I'll make sure I bring everything I need.'

Castel laughed. 'Touchy, aren't you?'

'If you know where they are,' Victor said, 'you need to tell me. Right now.'

'Tell me what you're really doing in this town and maybe I will.'

'I can't tell you any clearer than I have already.'

'Are you working for another outfit?'

'I'm alone.'

'Did Fendy send you to keep an eye on me?'

'This is the first time I've heard that name. I work for no one, I was sent by no one. I'm only here to find Michelle and Joshua. Once I find them, I'm in the wind. It can be that simple.'

Castel kissed his teeth. 'We've gone way beyond that point, pal. Whoever you are, whoever you're working for, you messed up laying hands on one of my crew. Because we're not just a crew, we're family. Whatever outfit is backing you up isn't going to save you from the Nameless. We're wild dogs, we are *rabid*, and we are starving. We're going to tear you to pieces. We're going to strip the flesh from your bones with our fangs.'

He howled down the line.

'I'm going to make you the single best offer you've ever had,' Victor said when the howls subsided. 'The best offer you'll ever have in your life, in fact. Are you listening? Tell me where I can find Michelle and Joshua and we never have to meet.'

Castel said, 'You're trying to deal with me after what you did? You're either insane or you're the dumbest fool I ever did come across. You don't negotiate with me, kid, you beg. You *plead* on your belly before my feet and kiss my gnarly toes for all the good it will do. Get it into your skull that we're coming for you and you can't escape our fury and no way do you get to make any kind of deal. Doesn't matter where you hide, the Nameless are riding out. You try and leave town, you try and run, and we'll never stop hunting you.'

'I'm going nowhere,' Victor said. 'Come get me.'

THIRTY-EIGHT

After Linette had gone, McAllan took an airtight food container from the refrigerator and popped open the lid. He took a sniff of the salad inside. Some brown rice thing with all sorts of leaves and beans and crunchy vegetables in a low-calorie dressing. Some protein, some carbohydrates, some fats. Some of everything except taste.

He had shelves full of such containers, each with a healthy meal prepared specifically for him by a nutritionist. McAllan's doctor had called his cholesterol profile a time bomb.

No, an atomic time bomb.

He slid open a drawer to collect a fork and sat back down at the breakfast bar to eat.

He set the fork down after two mouthfuls.

He looked up at his two guys, neither of whom had said a word since the visit of the man going by the name of Murdoch. Both were waiting for McAllan to say something about it. He needed to say something.

McAllan grunted. He thought. He considered. He remembered.

'*Some doors are closed to protect you from what lies on the other side* ...' McAllan mumbled. 'What is that even supposed to mean? Who speaks like that?'

The big guy in the sportswear said, 'He was scared.'

'Oh yeah,' McAllan replied. 'He seemed frightened to death to me when he strolled in here all on his lonesome. Be a pal and mop up the mess he made when he pissed himself.'

The guy with the slicked hair said, 'He wasn't scared. I watched him the entire time. He didn't shift his weight once. He didn't take a step back. He didn't so much as fidget. He's ice.'

'I told you,' McAllan said. 'Didn't I tell you? I knew there was something wrong about him before we even knew about the vegetable with the tubes. This guy is bad news.'

The guy with the slicked hair said, 'The worst.'

McAllan stabbed his fork into the container and speared some leaves. 'He refuses to leave the motel? That's one thing. That's bad enough. Then he comes into my house and disrespects me like that? No, no, no. That's not right.'

The big guy in the sportswear said, 'I would have taught him a lesson had you—'

'Not in my home,' he said. 'Not where I eat. Not where my daughter drinks her orange juice. But there have to be consequences. He's got to go.'

The guy with the slicked hair said, 'Why waste resources? He's no one. Just some guy with too much time on his hands.'

The big guy said, 'Couple more days and he'll be gone, I'm sure.'

McAllan said, 'You're saying we should wait and see?'

'I guess. Yeah. Sure.'

McAllan sat back. 'Since when have I been in the wait-and-see business?'

The big guy in the sportswear knew the tone well enough. He wasn't a man of words, so the definition of a rhetorical question was lost on him. Yet he understood there was no way to answer the boss without getting an earful, so he kept his lips together.

McAllan didn't keep him in suspense long. 'I don't wait and see. You know who does that? Losers. Losers wait and see. Losers hope for the best. Losers don't do, they wait.'

The big guy in the sportswear waited.

'I'm past caring who he is,' McAllan said. 'I want him gone. I don't care if he's a cop, some long-lost associate of Castel, a rival player, a made man from Vegas or even the devil himself. This is my town and he's overstayed his welcome. It's time he hit the bricks or gets hit by them.'

The guy with the slicked hair said, 'You told him you wanted him to stick around.'

'I know what I said. I want him to think that, dummy. You don't tell your enemies what you actually want. You make them think the opposite.'

'We can handle it.' The big guy in the sportswear pushed one fist into the other palm until knuckles cracked. A nonsense gesture, but it made him feel better. Useful. 'Just say the word.'

McAllan sighed and nodded at the same time. 'I know you can handle him. But that's not the important point here. This is no slight to your credentials as professional hard cases. It's not like I pay you for your singing voices, is it? You can work him over. Of that I have no doubt. And then . . . ? We're into aftermath territory. Currently uncharted. So, let's explore this hypothetical. You break his arms, sure, and what then?'

'He learns his lesson or we break his legs too.'

'You break his legs too ... why not? In for a penny ... Sounds so simple, doesn't it? Yet is it? Because in either of those incredibly distinct and unique scenarios he's going to end up in hospital. He ends up in hospital with two or more broken limbs and sooner or later he's going to talk to the police. He talks to the police and we're hauled before a detective. We'll have alibis, naturally, but will that be enough to maintain our careful appearance of law-abiding entrepreneurialism? Is her Royal Highness going to believe we had nothing to do with violating the careful conditions of our continued cooperation?'

'We tell him to stay quiet, he will.'

'Did I say he hobbles to the police himself? No, I did not. I said he talks to the police. Did I say he tells them anything? No, I did not. But do you really think that any cop – and for argument's sake, let's say that dutiful officer happens to be my daughter – isn't going to work out how that fisherman ended up in a double or quadruple cast? I'm guessing she won't be sold when he insists to her that he slipped in the shower while scrubbing at his ball sack.'

His man was silent.

'Whatever you say to the fisherman and whatever he doesn't say to my daughter is irrelevant here. We hurt him, we're looking at scrutiny. Do we like scrutiny now? Because if we do then I'm afraid I missed that particular memo.'

The guy with the slicked hair said, 'Then I'm lost. You want him gone but you don't want us to get him gone.'

McAllan said, 'Do you snake your own drain?'

The guy with the slicked hair said, 'What?'

'When your pipes are all blocked up with tied-off rubbers and great wads of your girl's hair and no matter how much poisonous, carcinogenic, planet-killing chemicals you pour down there it don't do squat … do you roll up your sleeves and bury your arm up to your elbow in all manner of your own filth?'

Silence.

'No,' McAllan said. 'You don't.'

The big guy in the sportswear said, 'We outsource it?'

'Someone's grown a brain in the last ten seconds,' McAllan said with a slow clap. 'It's a Christmas miracle four months too late. Of course we outsource it. Get a crew of wreckers from another town. Somewhere far away. Somewhere I haven't even heard of, okay? I want no one we've done business with before, even at arm's length. And I want a buffer. Use an intermediary to make the arrangement with the wreckers. I don't want them even to know my name, okay? But I want scum. I cannot emphasise that enough. I want wreckers who like what they do. Get me sadists. I'm talking dead behind the eyes, yeah? Because I want them to put the fear of God into Murdoch. Have them hurt him so bad that in a year's time he's still limping. Hurt him so bad that a decade from now the very idea of ever crossing the border again twitches his sphincter.'

The big guy in the sportswear nodded.

The guy with the slicked hair stood. 'I'll start making calls.'

McAllan shoved his salad away. 'And for the love of Zeus will someone go get me a taco?'

THIRTY-NINE

The tail was easy to spot. The driver had no chance of remaining undetected for long because the roads were so free of traffic even an amateur would notice a car following. That car was an unremarkable sedan. A new model. Gunmetal grey paint.

Victor had seen no comparable vehicle near McAllan's property, but it hadn't needed to be close to catch up with him. Victor kept his truck at, or below, the speed limit at all times. Plus, it was a hefty vehicle. A downside Victor could do little about since he needed the truck's off-road capacity.

Past tense, he realised. He had needed that capacity to get to the lake to do his job. The job he had completed two days ago.

He drove on, not watching the car behind him because he didn't need to watch it to know it was there. But he didn't understand why it was following him.

Victor thought he had made himself clear.

He needed to send McAllan a new message.

He applied pressure to the accelerator. The speedometer

turned and the engine revved harder, and the old truck shook under the strain.

The grey car was about a hundred metres behind him. By the time the driver realised Victor was accelerating, it was almost double that.

Smooth empty asphalt lay ahead, flanked by trees. Cool air rushed into the cab through the ventilators. Victor strengthened his grip on the steering wheel to fight the truck's tendency to pull to the right as the speed increased. The road was almost straight on this section but snaked a little now and again. Victor knew that wouldn't last.

Behind him, the grey sedan was accelerating hard to close the distance. A newer, faster car with maybe twice the horsepower-to-weight ratio. Victor couldn't escape it.

He wasn't trying to escape it.

As he drove further out of town the road changed, the snaking becoming sharper turns.

Victor took the first of them and the grey car disappeared from his rear view.

It appeared a few seconds later.

Victor took the second, and the grey car disappeared from his rear view.

It appeared a few seconds later.

Victor took the third turn, and as the grey car disappeared from his rear view he decelerated hard enough to make the truck skid and swerve before it came to a stop.

The grey car appeared a second later.

Going faster than Victor had been driving to catch up, the driver couldn't brake in time, couldn't react quickly enough. He yanked the wheel to avoid crashing straight into the back of Victor's truck.

Tyres smoked and screeched.

The driver fought the wheel and the car fishtailed past Victor's truck, leaving behind a cloud of brake dust, tyre smoke and exhaust fumes.

The car veered right, almost tipping on to two wheels, leaving criss-crossing parallel lines of burnt rubber on the road surface.

For a second it looked as though the driver might keep the car on the road but it was only a brief moment of calm before he lost control and the vehicle entered a spin that took it off the asphalt and tipped it into the flanking vegetation.

It rolled only once, on to the roof, and slid to a stop before it reached any trees.

The driver had managed to force the door open and was crawling out as Victor neared.

'You should be more careful.'

The driver groaned but had no visible signs of injury. He had been wearing his seatbelt.

'I appreciate you're just doing your job, but your boss needs to understand consequence.'

The driver, on his hands and knees, groaned again.

Victor stood over the man and took his right arm and hand, manipulating the limb until the shoulder, elbow and wrist were all locked.

'You can tell people it happened in the crash,' Victor said. 'Dislocated shoulder. Hyperextended wrist. Cervical fractures to both the radius and ulna. Radial fracture to the humerus. Multiple crushed phalanges.'

The man groaned again.

Victor said, 'But you were lucky. It could have been a lot worse. Take a deep breath for me.'

'Wait . . .'

'Tell McAllan this is me being merciful,' Victor said, beginning to twist. 'Tell him—'

'*I don't work for McAllan.*'

Victor paused. There was desperation in the man's voice and fear. Both expected. But something else too. He could tell this wasn't a bluff.

'I can see you don't work for Castel,' Victor said. 'So if you don't work for McAllan either, who do you work for?'

The man said, 'I work for their boss.'

FORTY

The wreckers were hired fast. Three cousins. Two on one side of the family, one from the other. For a moment, a different pair of guys almost got the job, two big-time heavies with prison convictions for violent crimes, but McAllan wanted three guys for the job, not two. He wanted it done right.

McAllan's guy had a former cellmate in Toronto who had a brother in Calgary who knew a bare-knuckle boxer in Regina who worked for a small protection racket in Winnipeg who had used the cousins from time to time. It took four phone calls and less than twenty minutes for the connection to be made.

McAllan had his buffer and then some.

The three cousins ran an illegal gambling ring that doubled as a loan shark business and which also washed some cash now and again. They liked to think of themselves as businessmen on the rise. Capitalists to the core. That their business had been started with money earned the old-fashioned way didn't factor in.

The cousins had robbed liquor stores and convenience stores and armoured cars and even a couple of banks. There had been a fourth cousin once, until a trigger-happy security guard shot him in the back of the skull when they were making a getaway.

That corpse left behind after a robbery meant questions by detectives and the remaining cousins decided to roll back on the robberies before they gave those detectives enough to bury them. The cousins weren't smart, but they weren't stupid.

They had always been in trouble. When they were young they were childhood enemies, fighting each other over the smallest slight. They broke bones. They put each other in hospital. Each one hated the other two. They didn't mind getting hurt so long as they hurt the others more. Until they woke up to the fact they were harder to beat together. They could fight as three and not get hurt at all. Less hurt for each of them meant more hurt that could be caused. None finished high school. Only one of them had not been expelled. All three had spent more of their teenage years in juvenile detention than they had out in the world. They had rap sheets that ran into inches in thickness. Bad to the bone, they liked to think. No one who knew them would argue with that analysis.

But few knew just how bad.

They had robbed for the money and they ran their gambling ring in the spirit of capitalism, but they took pleasure from it too. That pleasure most often came when someone couldn't pay what they owed.

Then, it was open season.

Not on the mark, of course. That wasn't a good way of turning a profit. They went for someone close to the mark and they made the mark watch.

They owned some warehouse space far away from anywhere. Inside was a room. Not quite soundproof but so well insulated it didn't matter. Only someone inside the warehouse could hear what went on in that room. No one but the cousins used the room, and no one but the cousins who entered that room left the same.

In that room they had a dentist's chair.

They had bought it for a fair price from a widower selling off his dead wife's things. They had bought many other things too: scrapers, drills, pliers and more. Not gas, though. Not anaesthetic.

None of them had trained in dentistry but they were enthusiastic amateurs.

No one who watched their loved one in that chair ever missed another payment.

Word got around.

The cousins weren't just bad to the bone, they were beasts. Psychotic. Crazy. Some said they were demons.

Such traits could be useful to others from time to time. The cousins discovered, to their happy surprise, there was much profit to be had in rented cruelty.

The youngest cousin had the best social skills and could even be polite on occasion, so he dealt with people. He could be trusted to answer the phone without starting a turf war.

'Speak to me,' he said.

The voice on the other end of the line belonged to a partner in the protection racket that sometimes employed the bare-knuckle boxer who knew the brother of a former cellmate of McAllan's guy. The partner had recently paid the cousins to torture some of their competitors until they saw sense.

'I have a job for you, but not for us. Good money if you're willing to travel for it. You gotta move fast, though. You need to be on the road before we even finish this conversation. You get me?'

'I'm listening.'

The voice explained the pertinent details in an efficient manner: run some guy out of town and make sure he never comes back. A job for three, so no one sits it out.

'Bring some firepower, just in case.'

'He's one guy. And I don't like driving with a piece. Too risky.'

'I'm only passing on the specifics. They ain't up for negotiation. You want the payday, you do it their way. This guy's a problem. So they want it done right. They don't want any wriggle room for this character.'

'Understood,' the youngest cousin said. 'How bad are we allowed to hurt him?'

'What kind of a question is that? I've already told you. Hurt him real bad. They don't want him ever coming back.'

The youngest cousin fought his irritation and remembered his manners before he replied. There was money on the line, after all.

He said, 'With respect, what you've told me tells me nothing. *Hurt him real bad* can be taken in all sorts of ways. One man's agony might be another's kink.'

'You need me to draw you a picture?'

'I need a number.'

'You need a . . . number?'

'Yeah,' the youngest cousin said. 'Because numbers are inarguable. They don't lie.'

'Okay . . .'

'So, on a scale of one to a hundred, how much are we allowed to hurt him?'

A long exhale came down the line. 'Well, this is not weird at all, but whatever. You want a number? Sure, I'll give you a number. On a scale of one to a hundred I'd say you're good all the way up to ninety-nine.'

'Then consider us on the road.'

FORTY-ONE

Fendy was a very fit seventy-year-old woman. Victor knew she was seventy because it was one of the first things she told him after he entered her office. He knew she was very fit because she told him this too. She seemed proud of both facts and their apparent contradiction.

'The second you're out of here I'll be doing Pilates. Forty-five minutes. Every day. I run every morning too. I row or cycle at the weekends. I bet I can do more pull-ups than you.'

'Uh-huh,' Victor said.

Given the grey sedan was upside down along the side of the highway, Victor had let Sal – the guy he'd run off the road – drive his truck.

Once he had recovered from the crash, of course.

'You weren't really going to break my arm, were you?' Sal had asked as he drove.

Victor nodded. 'Every single bone of it.'

Sal had said little else as he drove Victor to meet his boss and the boss of both McAllan and Castel. He had driven back into town and parked near the police precinct and the courthouse because Fendy was the district attorney.

'My great-grandfather was Indonesian,' she told him to explain her surname.

He hadn't asked.

'Three dollars in his pocket when he stepped off the boat,' she continued. 'Can you imagine?'

Victor remained silent.

She said, 'You're not big on small talk, are you?'

'However did you guess?'

'Okay,' she said, taking a seat behind her desk and gesturing for him to sit in the visitor's chair opposite. 'I like a man who knows when to shut up.'

He sat.

Sal left them and the door clicked shut behind him.

'He's limping,' she said.

'He had a car accident,' Victor said. 'He's lucky it wasn't a lot worse.'

'I'm sure he thinks so.'

'Why are you following me?'

'Why are you stirring up trouble in my town?'

Victor said, 'I'm no trouble at all.'

She said, 'Who are you working for?'

'I'm getting a little tired of answering the same questions over and over again, so I'll make this simple for you. I work for no one. I'm not interested in anyone's criminal activities. I'm only looking for a missing child and his mother.'

'Then why are you making Castel and McAllan nervous?'

'You'll have to ask them.'

'I can't get hold of Castel,' Fendy told him. 'One of his

guys is in the hospital with half a face and Castel's on the warpath. Did you have anything to do with that?'

'He runs a meth-producing operation,' Victor said.

She nodded. 'And you'd like to know how I fit in?'

'The question has crossed my mind.'

'I'm an old Colt .45,' Fendy said, forming a pistol shape with her fingers. 'I'm a peacemaker. *Pow, pow.* I like a quiet county and my job is to keep it that way. I ensure the crime here is as low as possible by putting bad people behind bars, but bad guys are like weeds and two spring up to replace whatever weed you tug out of the ground. That's not in anyone's interest, so I make deals with people like Castel and McAllan. They get a pass if they play by my rules.'

'What rules?'

'The rules of fair play, of course. Namely, don't do anything that would make the front page in the local paper.'

'And make regular donations to the Fendy retirement fund?'

'Hey, I'm never retiring,' she said with faux outrage. 'And also: no. I don't take a cut. I'm a peacemaker not a racketeer.'

'I see.'

'I invited you here because I want to keep things friendly. I don't want you to think we have opposing goals.'

'Reassuring,' he replied. 'But why did you feel the need to reassure me?'

'I can't help it. I'm the last honest lawyer in the northern hemisphere.'

Victor remained silent.

'But, in all seriousness, I don't want you thinking we're enemies when we can be friends.'

'Why would I think you an enemy?'

'Are you going to challenge everything I say?'

'I might.'

Fendy tapped her lip. 'What do the police say?'

'Given there are no signs of foul play and no one has actually reported them missing then there isn't a lot to go on. Officially speaking. Officer Linette is doing what she can.'

'Why do I know that name?'

'She's McAllan's daughter.'

Fendy said, 'Ah, yes. Of course.'

'I guess she uses her mother's name because of the association.'

'She's his stepdaughter.'

'I didn't know that,' Victor said. 'Are they close?'

Fendy chose her words with care. 'I think it would be fair to say that their respective career choices put a certain strain on the relationship.'

'She joined up to rile him?'

'Maybe he became a criminal to rile her.'

She smiled at him and he humoured her with a half-smile of his own.

'I've had McAllan on side for a long time now,' she explained. 'He does what he's told and I'm sure even he would admit he does better for himself playing by my rules. Castel is a more recent addition to the club and a more volatile member, but he's calming down slowly. Now, instead of fighting to keep his turf he calls me. Same as McAllan has always done. Any new players try to muscle in on their respective businesses, or if they know of anyone else setting up shop in my district, they tell me right away and I go after them hard by way of our dedicated boys and girls in blue. Violent crime is almost non-existent in this county, and crime as a whole has fallen year on year for the past three. Like I said: I'm an old Colt .45. *Pow, pow.*'

'I don't care.'

'Excuse me?'

'I don't care how you run this town,' Victor said. 'I don't care about Castel's meth. I don't care about McAllan's corrupt city contracts either. It's none of my business. But if either of them is involved in the disappearance of Michelle and Joshua Levell, or if they know what happened and are holding out on me, I'll burn their clubhouses to the ground before I'm gone. I will rip this entire town wide open if I have to.'

He didn't raise his voice. His tone didn't alter. There was no emotion in his words.

Fendy regarded him with an intense curiosity, almost surprised, as if the man sitting opposite her had become a whole different person right before her eyes.

'You should care how I run my town,' Fendy said after that moment had passed. 'Because if you cause trouble for them you cause trouble for me. I told you we help each other out, didn't I? That means I take care of their problems too.'

'You don't want to come for me.'

She smiled a little. 'I don't? Maybe you should enlighten me as to why not.'

'Right now, as you said, we're not enemies. So you might think that the last thing I want is you causing me trouble. That would be a reasonable assumption given your position in this county and the power it provides. But you really need to trust me when I say the very worst decision you could ever make would be doing something that encourages me to think you are in fact a problem.'

Again, he didn't raise his voice. Again, his tone didn't alter. Again, there was no emotion in his words.

If Victor had transformed in her perception before, he changed again now.

Fendy swallowed, then said, 'You're a salesman from Las Vegas on a fishing trip.'

Victor remained silent.

'All I'm after is maintaining the peace I fought so hard to create,' Fendy said once she had cleared her throat.

'If you want peace then you need to encourage Castel and McAllan to open up. I'm almost out of patience.'

Fendy said, 'You told me you're only here to find Michelle and Joshua.'

'That's correct.'

'Once they're found, you'll move on?'

Victor nodded.

Fendy said, 'Then you and I can help each other.'

'How so?'

'This town is a duck pond. I try very hard to keep the water smooth and glassy, yet you're standing on the edge tossing in pebbles. I want you gone. I want the calm restored. So, I'll do whatever it takes to find them. How does that sound?'

'I'm going nowhere until they're found.'

'I can see that. I didn't mean I would take over the search to get you out of town. I'll help you and then you'll have an easier time of finding them with my assistance. In return, you leave once they're located, and my duck pond can settle back down to glassy smooth again.'

'If McAllan and Castel are involved—'

'Listen, if either of them has anything to do with a missing mother and child then that overrides any prior arrangements

I have with them. I'm not kidding in the least little bit. If they're involved, my professional friendship with them is null and void. My protection vanishes like that' – she made a fleeting gesture – 'and I'll go after them with everything I've got.'

'Then I accept your assistance.'

'Tremendous,' she said. 'I will instruct both esteemed gentlemen to keep their distance for the time being, but you should leave the motel to bring McAllan on side.'

'I can do that but I'm not sure he will back off.'

She exhaled. 'Let me try, okay? And given you burned off half the face of one of Castel's crew he might take longer to convince.'

'I didn't admit to that.'

Her eyebrows pinched closer. 'Nevertheless, you might want to take a road trip until I can talk him down.'

'Don't worry about me,' Victor said. 'Worry that Castel still needs to convince me he has nothing to do with Michelle's and Joshua's disappearance.'

Fendy showed her palms to say she understood.

Victor said, 'Can you get me a list of everyone who works at McAllan's quarry? With their phone numbers, addresses and so on.'

'I can. Why?'

'Michelle might have a boyfriend who works there. So far I haven't been able to find out who he is.'

'You can pick him from a list?'

'This town has a population of about eleven thousand, give or take?'

'Give or take.'

'That's five and a half thousand males,' Victor said.

'Discount half as too young or too old and that leaves two and—'

'I get it,' she said. 'Probably only two hundred men work at the quarry in comparison.'

'Less than a hundred. Maybe sixty guys in the right age range. I'll knock on all sixty front doors if I have to.'

Fendy nodded along as he spoke. 'I'll get right on it. Take my card and call whenever you need something. In fact, call anyway so I have your number in case I find out something and need to get hold of you. Remember: we both want you to succeed here. We both want you gone. And while we're working towards that end, I'd really appreciate it if you can try not to make anyone else in my town nervous. Think you can manage that?'

Victor raised an eyebrow. 'I'll do my best.'

FORTY-TWO

The French barman was not serving when Victor walked inside. Instead, Big Pete was running things. Turned out he owned the bar as well as being one of its regulars. Big Pete gave him a chin-raise greeting and Victor returned it with a nod.

'When I'm not working here, I'm drinking here,' he told Victor as he fetched a couple of bottles from the cooler. 'And when I'm not drinking here, I'm working here.'

'Efficient,' Victor said as he took the beers. 'Saves on gas.'

'I never thought of it like that,' Big Pete said with a nod of approval. 'But that'll be my excuse going forward. I'm going to claim it as my own, just so you know.'

'Then I want my beer on the house,' Victor said.

Big Pete grinned. 'Nice try.'

Linette was waiting for him.

'I want you to know there are no conflicts of interest concerning me and my dad,' she told him as he took his seat at her table.

Victor listened.

'I mean it,' Linette insisted. 'He breaks any law and I'll bust him if there's evidence he did. He's well aware of that. But he's no kidnapper. Why would he even kidnap a mother and her child?'

'He's a criminal. There have to be a dozen reasons why he might need to kidnap someone who works at one of his businesses,' Victor said. 'But if he had kidnapped them then they'd be dead by now.'

'Whoa, hold on a sec—'

'Given I'm looking for them, given you're looking for them, he would be under too much pressure and would either release them – and he hasn't – or he would kill them. Easier to hide corpses than people.'

'You're so full of shit.'

'Don't swear,' Victor said. 'I didn't say that's what's happened. I said if he had kidnapped them then they would be dead. But he didn't kidnap them. They went willingly with Michelle's boyfriend and they never came back again. Either he has them or he took them on someone's behalf.'

'Someone like my dad?'

'He can't be ruled out just because you don't want to believe he's capable of it.'

'But why? How?'

'I don't know why, but the how is simple enough: Michelle's boyfriend works for your father at the quarry so there's a direct connection between McAllan and the boyfriend. Maybe he was coerced. Maybe he was simply paid to do it. Maybe he was never really her boyfriend and the whole relationship was a cover so he could gain their trust.'

'What kind of monster would pretend to be someone he wasn't just to get paid?'

Victor remained silent.

Linette sipped her ginger ale. 'You were right about Michelle, by the way.'

'No credit card has been used since she went missing?'

'She doesn't have a credit card. No bank card either. She gets paid in cash, pays her bills in cash. Her cell is prepaid.'

'Interesting,' Victor said. 'Has that always been the case?'

'For the last two years,' Linette answered. 'That's how long she's been in town.'

'Where did she live?'

'The big city. Vancouver.'

Victor said, 'That's a long way.'

'A whole world away,' Linette said. 'Perhaps Michelle wanted a simpler life. I can't say living in a city sounds particularly appealing to me. All that stress. People are nicer in the country.'

'Did she have a credit card or bank card back then?'

'Not for almost ten years.'

'What happened ten years ago?'

'She got married,' Linette said. 'To some guy named Bellarmien Robidoux. What kind of a name is that?'

'Joshua told me he had no father.'

'They're not divorced,' Linette said. 'They're estranged. Two years is a long time for a kid not to see his dad. Might as well not have one by then. Hell, Michelle and Bellarmien might have been separated before Joshua was even born.'

'Would you mind not blaspheming?'

'Did I blaspheme again?'

Victor nodded.

'Then please accept my most sincere apologies,' Linette said with a glimmer in her eyes. 'Unless you don't like sarcasm either.'

Victor raised an eyebrow.

'How do you even do that? I look like I'm having a seizure if I so much as try.'

'I've had a lot of practice.'

She said nothing for a moment, her attention going to the wall-mounted television that Big Pete was watching with keen interest. Journalists were discussing the shooting in Chicago and the rumours it was related to organised crime.

'Makes me glad to be Canadian,' she said, and swallowed more ginger ale. 'That kind of thing just doesn't happen here.'

'You might want to touch wood for that,' Victor said.

She stood. 'Look, I gotta go, but I'm off duty real soon. If you want to continue this, meet me at the diner near the station in half an hour or so. Best waffles north of the border.'

'Sure.'

Linette turned around, waved goodbye to Big Pete, and headed out of the bar. Victor watched the news while he finished his beer, thinking of Michelle's move out of the big city, having no credit card, a job that paid cash, a pre-pay mobile phone. Linette had joked that perhaps Michelle had wanted a quieter life, yet Victor knew different.

He knew what running looked like.

At the bar, he asked for another beer and bought one for the French barman, who had just taken over for the late shift. After toasting and sipping, the barman, eager to learn more about a breaking development in Chicago, searched in vain for the TV remote. He found it too late.

'Do you know what happened?' he asked.

Victor, tired of lying, said, 'Yes, there was a murder.'

The French barman's eyebrows rose and he grimaced at Victor's short explanation. 'A murder?'

'The head of an organised crime conglomerate, the top guy,' Victor continued. 'The next-in-line was getting sick of waiting for the throne to pass to him so he expedited the succession.'

The barman sipped beer. 'They know all that already?'

Victor shrugged. 'Call it an educated guess.'

The barman shuffled off to serve another customer.

Big Pete was now sat in front of the bar. 'If I'm not working here, I'm drinking here,' he told Victor again. Then he said, 'It saves on gas,' and chuckled.

Victor nodded in return. Regardless of his reasons for still being in town he needed to stick to his cover as much as possible, which was a man on a fishing trip. So, while he waited for Fendy to deliver on her assistance the bar was as good a place as any to think, to plan.

He felt restless because he was stationary. It was rare for him to be in any one place so long, unique for that one place to be a staging ground. He should always be moving, always working, always running.

The Frenchman said, 'You like it here?'

'Excuse me?'

'You're still here,' he said. 'I thought you were staying for only a few days.'

Victor nodded. He had shared his plans with the Frenchman because that's what a lone man on a fishing trip would do.

'There's something I need to take care of first,' Victor explained.

The Frenchman gave him a look and opened his mouth to speak, but Big Pete, close enough to hear, spoke first: 'He's getting friendly with Linette. Wants to get her into a pair of handcuffs.'

He laughed and slapped the bar surface with a meaty palm. The Frenchman smiled apologetically at Victor, who raised his bottle of beer to Big Pete to acknowledge the joke, to show he had not taken offence.

There were a handful of other patrons in the bar who all looked to the entrance. Not all at once, but within a few seconds as the noise grew. Big Pete looked too. So did the French barman.

Only Victor didn't.

Hard to know how many through sound alone, but it was more than one. Half a dozen at least. A cacophony of exhausts rumbling. No mufflers. No revving engines, just the steady loud splutter of powerful machinery outside in the parking lot.

Ignitions turned off and spark plugs no longer sparked. Fuel no longer ignited and engines no longer turned. Exhausts ceased spewing out waste products.

Silence.

The Frenchman glanced at Big Pete, who grunted in response.

'They won't come inside,' Big Pete said to Victor. 'The whole gang is barred. They might be lowlifes but they know better than to try it on with me. They understand Big Pete won't tolerate any kind of thuggery.' He used his chin to gesture at a hockey stick displayed over the bar to emphasise his point. 'Still got my swing.'

'I don't think they're here to drink.'

Big Pete shrugged. 'As long as they stay out there then I don't care what they're doing. They'll be gone before too long. Night's going to be a cold one.'

Victor finished his beer. 'They're not going anywhere.'

The barman said, 'Another?'

Victor rocked his head from side to side to crack his neck. 'I'm done, thanks.'

He stood up from the stool.

Big Pete held up his beer. 'You be good.'

Victor said 'I think it's a little too late for me' as he walked outside to greet the silence.

FORTY-THREE

The meeting took place out of the city and far away from their estate. A long drive, yet a necessary one. They took the limousine because neither liked to drive any more. They used an agency to supply the driver so there was always one available, whatever day, whatever time of day. Once they had a live-in driver, but even servants had to sleep, had to eat, had to have time off from work. Some even had the audacity to complain when politely informed Christmas Day was not a holiday. How else were they supposed to get to mass and back?

This driver was one of their favourites because he never spoke unless spoken to first. He might as well have been invisible, which was perfect. They needed staff to help them through their busy lives but didn't enjoy unnecessary interaction. Staff were only staff, after all.

All of the preparatory work had been done. Each of their personal assistants had been tasked to research, to compile, to narrow down the options. Two separate lists with two distinct yet overlapping goals. Two isolated tasks, each shielded from the other so neither assistant could ascertain the ultimate objective.

But there was only so much that could be achieved with the labours of ignorant parties. Ultimately, they needed to get their hands dirty.

They had come to enjoy getting their hands dirty.

The driver had been given a GPS coordinate and nothing more, and drove them to their destination with no questions, no words. Their favourite.

When the limousine stopped, the patter of rain on the bodywork became louder, almost violent. Raindrops clung to the window glass or snaked down in crooked rivulets. They waited until the driver opened the door for them and they climbed out, one at a time. A slow, awkward process. It had been a tortuously long journey.

The night was chilly, the rain falling in a relentless downpour. They needed to hurry.

The driver shielded them with an umbrella and handed it over before closing the limousine's rear door and returning to the driver's seat to wait until they were finished. They had told him in advance his presence was not required.

Waiting for them in the wash of the limousine's headlights was a lone figure.

'I'll do the talking,' she said.

He nodded. He knew his place. He held the umbrella aloft and they approached the figure.

The man had a tall, boxy frame. He had been waiting for them and was soaked to the skin. This appeared not to bother him in the slightest. They knew he had been a military man. They knew all about him.

His name was Garrett. An African-American gentleman, which neither was pleased to discover, but they could bite their lips for the greater good.

'Thank you for meeting us,' she said.

'No problem.'

'We always prefer to meet our employees, regardless of their reputation.'

'I understand.'

She added, 'Especially when the matter is of a sensitive nature.'

'You're not only paying for my services,' Garrett said, 'but my discretion.'

'You understand what we want done?'

'Yes.'

'I don't like how easily you say that. It worries me. It makes me wonder if you fail to appreciate how important this is to us.'

'If I gave you that impression, I apologise.'

She continued, 'Do you understand loss? Truly understand, I mean?' She didn't wait for an answer. 'Because we do. We know all too well what it's like to have that which you love most wrenched away from you. There is no suffering that comes close. It leaves behind a hole that runs straight through your soul and that emptiness is for ever. It can never be filled. *That* is loss. Nothing can relieve that pain.' She paused to steady herself, lest emotion get the better of her. 'But I want you to try on our behalf.'

Garrett nodded, and she saw that she had made herself clear.

'This cannot be a common request, even for a bounty hunter,' she said. 'There can't be many others in our particular situation.'

'This is the first job of its kind I've been tasked with,' Garrett admitted. 'But far from the first unique challenge.'

'And how successful have you been with these unique challenges?'

Garrett smirked. 'You already know the answer or we wouldn't be here now.'

'We don't want to be connected. We have arrangements in place to protect our interests but we need to know that your end is similarly protected, whatever the outcome.'

'My end is always covered,' Garrett assured her. 'Even in the worst-case scenario, there will be nothing that connects you to me. All of our previous communications were encrypted and have now been destroyed. Once we walk away from here, the last remaining link is broken. You won't know when I make a move. You won't receive progress reports. This is the first and last time you'll ever see me.'

Unable to hold his tongue any longer, a voice came from beneath the umbrella. 'Then how will we know it's over?'

She cast him a sharp, scolding look and he couldn't meet her gaze. She turned her attention back to Garrett.

'Please answer his question. If we have no further communications, how will we know when the task is done?'

'Because it will be done,' Garrett said. 'My guys are waiting outside the town at this very moment. Once we're through here, I'll be joining them. This thing could all be over inside a matter of days.'

'We expect resistance.'

'Resistance is inevitable. And it won't be a problem.'

'Are you sure?' she asked, searching his eyes. 'Are you really sure?'

'I only work with the best. I have a whole team of ex-SF.

I never do things by halves. I never take chances. It's smart business. The fastest route to acquiescence is via overwhelming force. The fiercest of dogs out there cowers before a pack of wolves. But your call. I can take extra bodies if that makes you sleep easier. Just know it will increase the fee and it'll put the brakes on the op.'

'Money is no object,' she was quick to point out. 'And we don't want even the slightest delay. However, that's not what I meant. Are you sure you can really do what needs to be done? Should there be ... resistance.'

Garrett nodded. 'Take comfort in the knowledge there's no line I haven't already crossed.'

'That's exactly what we wanted to hear.'

FORTY-FOUR

The moon was bright and the air as chill as the silence. Many breaths rose into the night.

'I've been waiting for this all day,' Castel said.

Victor approached. 'You have it the wrong way round. It's me who's been waiting for you.'

The concave arrangement of jagged black shadows tightened, sharp knives staying pointed at Victor as he closed the distance. He stopped just out of range.

Castel was surprised to see Victor walk forward across the lot towards the Nameless, surprised he didn't turn and run straight back into the bar. Surprised, but pleased, because he smiled as Victor neared. So pleased he danced a few steps on the spot, hips and shoulders rocking to a soundless melody.

When he stopped, Castel said, 'You need to understand something from the very start, Mr Fisherman. There's nothing you can say that's gonna change anything. Nothing will prevent our righteous retribution. We're way beyond the

217

point of apologies, way past forgiveness. But there is something I can do for you if you do something for me in return. If you tell me who you are and why you're here, then some day you'll walk again. Some day you'll be able to swallow actual whole food again. That'll be nice, won't it? No one likes soup for breakfast, lunch and supper every single day for the rest of their life.'

'Tell me where I can find Joshua and Michelle and you'll still have a crew come morning.'

Castel pivoted his head back so his chin pointed at the night sky and let out a moan of frustration, as if at the universe itself. '*Ugh*, what is it with you and those two no ones?'

'No one is no one.'

'Is he your bastard offspring or something? She your long-lost baby mama?'

Victor remained silent.

'You might have convinced Bobby McGullible with this whole routine, but I sleep with my boots on, you feel me?'

'Not in the slightest.'

'Why were you at my cookhouse yesterday?'

'Abe dated Michelle.'

'The whole town probably dated Michelle. You gonna turn up at everyone's door?'

'If I have to,' Victor said. 'Why did you kill him?'

'I didn't kill Abe. He was always an accident waiting to happen. I'm just glad I got so many batches of crystal out of him before he went and set himself on fire.'

'That's quite a misfortune for such a prolific cook.'

'Or maybe I killed him because I felt like it,' Castel said as he tapped the heels of his snakeskin boots on the asphalt in a fast, rhythmic dance. 'But if I did, I didn't, did I? Because you killed him, not me. You killed him the second you stepped your toes in that trailer. You threatened my meth, my business, my very freedom. That ain't polite. We have manners up here, Yankee.'

'I was no threat to you.'

Castel clicked his tongue, rocked his shoulders from side to side. 'You said "was".'

'That's correct.'

'When we spoke on the phone you did your talking in the present tense. You slipped up, amigo. I see through you like I always saw through you. It's Fendy, ain't it? You're not from a rival crew, you're working for her. She's done sitting on the sidelines. She wants to take my pie all for herself.'

'Fendy only wants to maintain a peaceful county.'

Castel grinned. 'I think that peace has come to an end.'

Victor said, 'When we spoke on the phone, I told you I was no threat to you because it was the truth. I wasn't interested in your crew, your meth, your anything. You could have told me what I wanted to know and it never had to come to this. But here we are. You've brought your whole crew and you tell me there's nothing I can say to prevent your "righteous retribution".'

'Oh yeah, you better believe it.'

Victor nodded to say he did. 'That's why I switched to the past tense. Before now, before this moment, I was no threat to you.'

Castel's small eyes grew smaller, narrowing as he stared at Victor, as he analysed the words and the man before him. Castel disliked what he saw, but what he failed to see displeased him even more. But it was too late to doubt himself and too late to reconsider. He had his entire crew with him for a reason.

'I want him to be able to talk,' Castel said, looking at Victor but addressing his eight Nameless. 'Just make sure he can still talk by the time you're done.'

FORTY-FIVE

The eight Nameless didn't all come forward at once. They couldn't. They weren't communicating and they weren't coordinating. Their semi-circle tightened around him as one stepped forward, then another and another, until they were all approaching. But no formation. No plan.

Victor had a plan.

Four seconds. Four down.

As soon as the closest was within three metres Victor dashed forward one step, then a second, and with his back foot – his left – firm on the ground he shot up his right knee to power out a savage stomp kick with his heel straight into the abdomen of the closest biker.

That man was tall and Victor's heel struck him low at the midpoint between the hip bones, the tremendous amount of energy meeting with little resistance – exploding capillaries in the skin, rupturing the walls of the lower intestines, sending shockwaves of trauma throughout his entire torso. The biker folded and crumpled and staggered backwards all at the same time, his eyes squeezed shut in shock and pain. He dropped to the ground without a scream or grunt, just a powerful rush of air leaving his lungs.

Victor was already moving before the guy had finished the fall, pivoting off his lead foot that recoiled from the kick and springing to close the distance to the next Nameless to the left because that was the shortest turn to make and the fastest.

The elbow hit the biker high on the skull, to the temple.

His head whipped in a sharp rotation until it could go no further and then his shoulders and hips twisted to follow the head and he collapsed mid-pirouette, pupils at maximum dilation, black and empty.

The next closest biker was beginning to react by then, although an instinctual reaction, basic. Primal. That instinct made him back off a few steps, away from the danger.

But his trepidation did not counter Victor's aggression, who covered that extra distance with another dashing step that only increased the force he generated for the round-house kick he delivered to the side of the biker's knee.

Victor struck with the hard edge of his shin at the narrow point where the biker's femur met the fibula, driving those bones inwards and apart, displacing the patella as multiple ligaments stretched until they snapped, one after the other. The leg folded into an L-shape and the biker screeched, hopping on his one good leg for a second before losing balance and falling, clutching in desperation at his ruined knee.

Victor was surrounded at this point. He had expected it but that didn't make it any easier to leave his back exposed. But he didn't hesitate. He kept attacking because he still had the initiative, the Nameless still reactive in their shock at the savage violence.

His next target had brought his hands up and was mobile on his feet, shuffling back and forth in a small area, both preparing for Victor's attack and readying himself for one of his own once the initial shock at what he was witnessing had worn off.

Victor was on him long before that point could be reached, forcing the biker to throw a desperate punch.

The Nameless was a big guy, tall and wide, and he had fast hands, but he didn't know how to use his size or his speed. He closed too much distance and telegraphed the punch by dropping his shoulder back too low, flaring his elbow too far, looping his fist too wide.

Victor had all the time in the world to step inside the biker's reach, to hit him in the ribcage with a hooking punch below the left arm that came down in another defensive reaction, opening up his face to Victor's follow-up palm strike.

Cartilage crushed and bone broke. Blood spattered the biker's cheeks and flowed over mouth and chin. His nose was flattened.

He stayed standing, however, until Victor hit him under the jaw with an uppercut.

A necessary punch but one that cost Victor, who felt the sting of pain signifying damage to the knuckles of his right hand. Those bones were as hard, as dense, as anyone's, but they couldn't compete with the larger, stronger bone of the Nameless's chin.

That biker sank down to a squat as his knees buckled. Then he collapsed backwards to join the other three on the asphalt. The guy with the L-shaped leg had passed out but the first of the Nameless to have gone down was still conscious in a foetal position, clutching his abdomen.

A quick stamp to the face knocked him out and scattered his teeth across the parking lot.

Four seconds. Four down.

The plan was working, but Victor was in uncharted territory. He had four enemies surrounding him on all sides. There was no way he could take any of them by surprise. They had four of their own crew still and silent on the asphalt to tell them everything they needed to know.

He had to pick the right one to attack first so his back was exposed to the least threat. A short man would be ideal because there was less chance of a punch to the brainstem than with a taller opponent. The problem was Victor couldn't waste time rotating on the spot to make sure he went for the best target. Any second of time he burned gave the Nameless more opportunities to overwhelm him with their numbers.

He only had an instant to decide so he went for the greatest danger.

That wasn't the biggest of the four, but the one who had adopted the most threatening fighting stance. That biker was balanced in a half squat, right foot back, torso tilted forward at the waist with his arms out wide. A grappling posture. He was going to bull-rush Victor and try and take him to the ground. Even if that attempt failed, there was a good chance the Nameless would have a handhold and that would be enough to restrict Victor's mobility.

Against four, he couldn't allow any such impairment.

With his arms out in front of him, the grappler came for Victor as Victor came for him, dipping to go for Victor's centre of gravity. It was a hard move to counter because the target's head was low and his chin a difficult target; with the head leading the body the rest of the guy was out of range.

So Victor adopted the same posture, coming forward with his own arms outstretched, his own head forward, denying the grappler the opportunity to get to his waist or his hips to wrap his arms around. But Victor – taller, faster – could reach his target first. Because the grappler was already low and his torso almost horizontal, Victor went lower, going for the biker's closest knee.

He wrenched it out from under him.

The biker flipped backwards, his upper body whipping up and then down to follow the leg that Victor pulled closer.

The back of the guy's head smacked hard on the ground and he went slack with his arms out perpendicular to his body.

Victor released the leg and shot back up to a fighting stance, clearing the guy prostrate on the asphalt because there were still three of the Nameless conscious and dangerous.

Two in front of him.

One behind—

Who punched Victor where the back of his neck met his skull.

The brainstem.

FORTY-SIX

Victor was used to pain. There wasn't a lot that hadn't been done to him. He had been stabbed, shot, burned, electrocuted. He had been strangled and knocked out. He had been tortured. He had suffered pain to the point of paralysing agony but he had learned to accept pain for its purpose: a message. A clear and inarguable communication that whatever was causing the message to be sent needed to stop. An instinctual insurance policy that traded temporary suffering in the hope of avoiding long-term consequences. Imperfect, because pain was not always proportionate to the potential consequences and because sometimes the message could not be heeded – the cause of the pain could not be stopped. Victor's acceptance of pain could not override its unpleasantness but it enabled him to tolerate more of that suffering, to judge it on the consequences separate from the instinctual insurance policy.

The pain he felt in the back of his head was severe but not close to the worst he had endured. It was a dull, pulsing ache reminiscent of a migraine. No great will was required to ignore it, yet Victor knew the consequences were disproportionate to the suffering because those consequences were apparent straight away.

His vision blurred.

Sounds muted.

The ground seesawed beneath his feet.

He found himself stumbling forward with increasingly widening steps as he sought to fight the swaying and tilting parking lot.

He vomited.

One of the Nameless yelled something, although the words were thin and distant. He didn't know if they were directed at him or the other two.

He glimpsed movement in the blur of colours and shapes before his eyes.

He tried to correct his footing, yet he couldn't synchronise his feet. He tried to bring his arms up to protect his head but they were too heavy.

He knew he had been hit again because air rushed out of his mouth. He knew it was a punch to the ribcage because he folded to one side.

Victor swivelled in an attempt to see the attacker, to defend himself from the follow-up, but he lost his footing. He would have fallen had he not stumbled into another of the Nameless.

The one who had punched him in the brainstem, he guessed. He couldn't know for sure, such was his disorientation.

The biker grabbed Victor from behind, wrapping a thick arm around his neck in an amateur chokehold. Amateur because he didn't pull Victor's head against his chest and didn't brace the other arm against the back of Victor's skull to increase the pressure, but effective nonetheless because the Nameless was strong and Victor too slow to counter the choke.

He felt the pressure in his skull from the trapped blood that couldn't escape through pinched veins. He tried to turn into the choke to put the thick muscles of his neck in the way and gain their protection, but it was far too late for that. He should have done so immediately, the instant he felt the arm wrapping around him.

With the pressure in his skull came pain: an intense, pulsating sensation that made his eyes water. He knew his brain was being starved of oxygen, knew unconsciousness was coming in just moments. He was already weak.

'You're done,' he heard the Nameless hiss at him.

For a second, he believed it.

Until he realised he had heard the words, understood them clearly and recognised the tone and the implication.

The effects of the punch to the brainstem were diminishing.

He was weak from oxygen deprivation only.

Fight, he willed himself.

Victor threw elbows at the biker's torso, but he had lost too much strength to make them effective and encourage his attacker to release him. Each strike further diminished his oxygen reserves and further weakened him.

The pain increased as the disorientation from the punch to the brainstem decreased.

But he had mere seconds remaining until he had no capacity to fight or even resist.

His left hand was closest to the biker's torso, so it was that palm Victor pushed flat on his enemy's ribs. Those fingers he used to find the bottom of the Nameless's ribcage. Those fingertips he pushed against the soft flesh there protected by only a T-shirt, hooking them beneath the lowermost, floating rib that attaches only to the spine, not the sternum.

With the last of his strength, Victor wrenched back with his hand and tore that rib free.

The Nameless shrieked.

Victor dropped straight down to his knees as he was released from the chokehold, coughing and gasping, ropes of saliva and vomit hanging from his lips, his chin.

The biker with the detached rib was pale and clutching his side. His eyes were wide and desperate, every breath a hissing agony he couldn't endure. He stumbled a few steps before collapsing to the ground with his back against the wheel of a parked truck. He shook and trembled.

'WHAT ARE YOU DOING?' Castel yelled at the two Nameless who were still capable of acting but were not. 'It's over. *End him.*'

They were hesitant because six of their guys had faced Victor already and five were unconscious and the one who was not sat shock-still, white, shaking, unable to speak, with a look of horror on his face that could not be rationalised.

But their enemy was on his knees and they were as scared of Castel as they were of Victor.

With a glance of encouragement between them, they approached. Neither straight on. One came from Victor's left, the other from his right. They came, but neither rushed.

Victor blinked the moisture from his eyes, grateful for their trepidation, which gave him an extra second to re-saturate his blood with precious oxygen and his senses an extra second to reconfigure after the shock to the brainstem.

The one to his left was in range by the time Victor rose to one knee.

That Nameless swung a punch at Victor's face, the arm angling downwards, aiming for Victor's cheek with a quick hooking shot.

A knock-out blow if it landed.

Victor caught that punch in his right fist – ball in mitt – and squeezed hard enough to shift and creak bones throughout the attacking hand and for the biker to cry out before Victor wrenched the arm closer and used the edge of his left palm at the elbow to lock the limb and twist the Nameless off balance.

Holding the man immobile, Victor stood.

He broke the arm at the elbow, snapping off a chunk of the humerus as he forced the lower arm the wrong way against the joint.

The Nameless wailed.

Then Victor broke the arm at the shoulder too, rotating the limb backwards until the ball ran out of socket and the bone had no choice but to give way.

The Nameless wailed louder.

Victor released him and he fell forward, writhing and crying for a moment until the pain became too much and he went silent.

One biker left.

Who ran.

He rushed back to his chopper, almost knocking it over in his desperation to get on and speed out of the parking lot, leaving only Castel and Victor standing under the moonlight.

Castel didn't back away. He didn't try and run. Misplaced bravery, or pride maybe.

He said, 'That was ... unexpected.'

FORTY-SEVEN

Castel waited. He was frowning, confused and surprised by the events he had witnessed and blinking hard and fast as if he had somehow imagined it.

No doubt he was hoping he had.

Victor approached with slow steps, the dull waves of pain and disorientation emanating from the back of his skull threatening to trip him up every time he lifted one foot from the ground.

The Nameless he had kicked in the abdomen was whimpering and shivering on the cold asphalt as he regained consciousness. Victor had to step around him.

Castel waited.

He had time to flee like the eighth biker had done, yet he remained in place. He did not lead from the front, but he did not retreat either.

A leader.

'I guess you're going to make me suffer,' Castel said as Victor stopped before him. 'That's okay. I can take pain.

I've suffered before. But you can't just replace me. You don't know how to work the routes. You don't have the charm for this. My buyers are loyal to me. They'll wait. You might think you're in charge, but I'll heal. I'll return. Good as new. Better. I'm not even human. I'm an idea. You can't defeat an idea.'

'I'm getting bored of repeating myself.' Victor spat to rid his mouth of the taste of vomit. 'Your business is the last thing I'm interested in.'

Castel, small eyes growing smaller, listened.

'I'm only looking for Joshua and his mother.'

Castel's eyes then widened. 'For real?'

Victor nodded.

'That's not a play?'

Victor shook his head. 'If you tell me where they are, I won't hurt you. But if you don't tell me, if you make me hurt you, then I won't stop until you beg for death. Do you believe me?'

Castel glanced around the parking lot. 'I believe you.'

'Well?'

'I don't know where they are. I never knew. I only ever saw them one time when she was with Abe way back.'

'Then why didn't you tell me that before?'

Castel said, 'Because I needed to know what you were really doing here. I didn't believe you.'

'Then I've maimed almost your entire crew for absolutely no reason.'

Castel's mouth hung open for a moment until he said, 'Sounds kinda dumb when you put it like that.'

'Could McAllan have anything to do with Michelle's and Joshua's disappearance?'

'Bobby's a paper gangster. Even if he had cause to harm

them, he hasn't got the stomach for anything real. But he's connected. He knows a lot of bad people.'

Victor considered this. 'Did Abe ever say why they moved out here from Vancouver?'

Castel thought. 'I don't know. Maybe something about a husband. A real piece of work.'

'Compared to Abe?'

Castel shrugged. He didn't know anything further.

Victor gestured to the seven brutalised Nameless behind him. 'When people ask—'

'I'll think of something,' Castel said.

'That's what I wanted to hear.'

Castel asked, 'Are you going to hurt me now?'

'Do I need to?'

'I'm sorry about what I said before on the phone, about the mom and her boy. I was angry you hurt my guy. It was wrong what I said. I shouldn't have done that. My niece has learning disabilities. I love that little angel to death.'

'Are you still angry with me?'

Castel was quick to shake his head.

'Then I think we can call it quits.'

The bar entrance flew open. Big Pete came rushing out with his hockey stick held high and ready, reacting to the noise and the screams of mere moments beforehand. He looked at Castel and Victor and then at the many prostrate bikers scattered across his parking lot.

'What the . . . ?'

'They fell,' Castel explained.

FORTY-EIGHT

Victor was glad to have an excuse to drive into town. He wanted to create a little separation between himself and the Nameless before ambulances arrived and Linette's colleagues became involved. Big Pete had been quick to call it in.

None of the bikers would say what had really happened. A combination of Castel's promise and their own pride would see to that. Any humiliating story they told was better than the truth.

Big Pete was another matter, but as he had not actually witnessed the fight, there was little he could tell investigators.

Victor found Linette in a booth by the window. It was pretty much the worst seating option in the entire establishment – in full view of the street outside and anyone passing; near to the entrance and facing away from it – but Victor slid into the seat opposite without commenting on her poor choice.

Did anyone else think like this? he wondered.

Linette glanced up from her coffee. 'That's a pensive look if ever I've seen one.'

'I've been doing a lot of thinking.'

'You make it sound like that's an uncommon occurrence.'

'This time is different,' he said. 'This time I'm thinking about myself.'

She frowned, unsure, and didn't press the issue. Instead, she reached for a laminated menu.

'I suppose you don't eat food like this,' she said. 'But that's too bad for you. Luckily, I'm always hungry.' She took a fistful of her midriff. 'If you can call it luck.'

'What kind of food do you think I eat?'

'I don't know. You're all muscle and skin so I'm thinking protein shakes and kale. Maybe a slice of watermelon on special occasions.'

'Hardly,' Victor said, taking a menu himself in his left hand.

The right stung, now the pain in his head had diminished. He could still clench his fist and flex his fingers, so he knew nothing was broken. Swelling and bruises would come later.

She didn't notice he used his left hand to give the right a rest and shot him an approving look. 'You surprise me.'

'I'm beginning to surprise myself too.'

'You make that sound like it's a bad thing.'

'That's because it is,' Victor said. 'I thought I knew myself by now. I should know myself by now.'

'People change. Everyone changes.'

'Someone I used to know said people like me don't change but adapt.'

'People like you?'

Hired murderers, he didn't say.

'It was in a specific context. I don't want to bore you with the details.'

She pursed her lips. 'Then what are you adapting to?'

He wasn't sure how to answer, but then the waitress arrived to take their order and he didn't need to. By the end of the meal he still didn't know what to say.

Linette looked at his bare plate and the empty basket next to it. 'I thought you were bluffing. I thought you'd leave half your burger and I'd eat your fries.'

Victor wiped his mouth with a napkin. 'You can't change the laws of thermodynamics.'

'Say what?'

'Energy in versus energy out.'

'I still don't understand what you're telling me.'

'A calorie is a calorie.'

'So you'd rather eat two thousand of them as burger and fries instead of two thousand calories of salad?'

'Pretty much. But closer to three.'

'Huh,' she said, considering this previously unconsidered idea. 'But aren't you worried about your arteries?'

I'll never survive to an age at which it will matter, he didn't tell her.

Instead, he said, 'I do a lot of exercise.'

She screwed up her face. 'I don't even like walking to my car. But all that talk of thermodynamics makes me think I wish I hadn't passed on the bacon. I didn't want you to judge me.'

'I know what happened.'

'To my bacon?'

Victor said, 'The breakfast left on the table. The

coffee. The car on the driveway. The back door unlocked. Toothbrushes still on the washbasin.'

'Go on.'

'Michelle and Joshua were having breakfast: two bowls, two glasses of orange juice, one coffee. Her boyfriend came round unexpectedly. She made him a coffee but he didn't stay long enough to finish it. He didn't stay long enough because they had to leave. But not for work. He told her something that convinced her to drop everything and go right away. No time to pack their things, no time for Joshua to finish his cereal.'

'What did he say?'

'I don't know, but she was expecting it.'

'If she had expected it then she would have packed. She would have been ready.'

'Would you up and leave your life just because someone told you to?'

'Well, no. But . . .'

'That's my point. You wouldn't. She wouldn't. Unless she was expecting it. Unless they had already discussed it and so when he showed up and told her she was willing to drop everything and leave without bothering to lock the back door.'

'I don't buy it,' Linette said. 'She still would have had something ready for that moment. What do they call it?'

'A go-bag.'

'Exactly.'

'They had discussed it,' Victor said. 'But she was unprepared. Maybe she thought they had more time. Maybe she didn't really believe she would ever need to.'

'Then what was she so scared of?'

'I don't know.'

'But that's why she was out here, wasn't it? No credit card, no bank account. Off the grid. The husband. Has to be.'

'I was told he's a real piece of work.'

'Who told you?'

'I'd prefer not to say at this juncture.'

'That wouldn't have been Abraham Zelnick, would it?'

He shook his head because he knew where she was going with this. 'I haven't had a chance to speak to him yet. But I did hear he cooks meth.'

'The ex cooked meth?' she asked.

Victor, recognising in the choice of tense there was a lot more to that question than the obvious, said, 'That's what I heard.'

'You heard?'

'Yes, that's what I heard. I'm planning on paying him a visit but I haven't got round to it. But I'm working on it.'

'Don't bother,' Linette said. 'Where he lives isn't there any more.'

'I don't understand.'

'A small meth lab burned down yesterday,' she explained. 'With the owner inside.'

'Ah,' Victor said.

'I'm not investigating it so I don't really know what happened beyond an accelerant was used.'

'Sounds suspicious.'

'Abe was burned to a crisp inside so maybe someone killed him – but maybe he was going to torch the place and slipped on the gas and hit his head after lighting a match. People die in dumber and more horrible ways than that all the time. I could tell you stories that would turn your hair white.'

Victor remained silent.

She got a call on her radio and stood to take it, talking out of earshot, but he read her lips well enough to understand the topic of conversation. She returned to the table and took another gulp of coffee, shaking her head.

'What is it?' Victor asked.

She finished her coffee. 'Chaos in the local ER.'

'Define chaos.'

'Aftermath of some kind of battle royale with the Nameless.' She set the cup down, toyed with its position. 'There's seven badly beaten bikers making life miserable for the staff at the hospital and they've only just got there. No one's talking but they got beat up pretty bad. A rival gang, in all likelihood. Must have been a coordinated effort to lay an ambush. Teach them a lesson sort of thing.'

'Do you need to go?'

She rocked her head from side to side in indecision. 'Probably, but not urgently. Call was just a heads-up. The nurses have already rung for assistance to keep the Nameless in check. Doubtful I'll be needed for that, but we'll have to get to the bottom of what happened before they're all fixed up and hunting for revenge.'

'Maybe they've learned their lesson.'

She huffed. 'Wouldn't that be nice?'

FORTY-NINE

Victor's truck didn't start on the first turn of the ignition. Not surprising given it was an old vehicle, so he gave it a moment and tried a second time. Still nothing but the whirr and whine of a starter motor failing to start the engine.

On the third try, Linette knocked on the driver's window and said, 'Do you need any help?'

'Sure,' Victor said.

She had the hood up by the time he had the driver's door open and had climbed out.

'Your lights came on,' she told him without looking at him, 'so it's probably a bad ignition switch.'

'If you say so,' he said.

He had figured as much but would Wilson Murdoch, salesman from Las Vegas, know cars? Victor decided Murdoch didn't spend any time getting his hands dark with motor oil. He paid someone else to get dirty on his behalf. Not a rich man, but one who knew his limits.

Linette said, 'You're going nowhere. You have Triple A?'

'Not for this hunk of junk,' Victor said. 'I figured it would survive a few more weeks, but it seems I was ambitious in that assessment.'

'I'll give you a tow,' she said.

'Don't you have cop duties to do?'

'I did a double shift,' she said. 'Technically, I'm not working right now.'

'Then that's a kind offer and I accept.'

'I'll drop you at the shop. Gino won't rip you off if he sees me bring you in.'

'How reassuring. Isn't it a bit late?'

'Gino's place runs around the clock.'

They fixed up a tow. Linette had all the equipment in the back of her cruiser: straps, rope, even a tow pole. Maybe standard issue.

Linette led him to her cruiser and opened the passenger door. With a flourishing gesture, she motioned for him to climb inside.

She yawned a couple of times on the way to Gino's and even had a nap in her seat while Victor dealt with the man, who had to be no older than twenty yet ran an auto shop of half a dozen mechanics. Victor explained the situation with his truck and handed over his keys.

Relinquishing his keys was not something Victor enjoyed doing, and while he could repair the ignition switch himself, he still needed the parts and the tools and had already decided Wilson Murdoch wasn't good with engines. While there was no pressing reason to stick to that decision, he was already breaking protocol with every minute he remained in the area. He preferred not to add to his list of infractions if it could be avoided.

Gino promised he would have a new ignition switch fitted within an hour as a favour because he knew Linette. Victor acted surprised and touched by this, but knew Gino was just being smart. He wanted to keep the local cops on side. Which meant he was worried some day they would be knocking on his door about stolen vehicles and parts. Victor had known many Ginos in his youth when stealing cars had been the most efficient way to survive.

When he returned to Linette's cruiser, he lightly rapped his knuckles on the window glass to awaken her without a start.

She wiped saliva from the corner of her mouth and sat upright.

'I was just resting my eyes.'

'Thanks for the tow,' he said. 'It's going to take about an hour.'

'Wanna grab a beer while we wait?'

He thought of Big Pete and his hockey stick and said, 'Not for me. And you don't have to wait as well.'

She yawned again.

'Do you want me to drive you home?' he asked. 'I think it's past your bedtime.'

'Against the rules,' she said. 'Even off duty. I'll be fine.'

'Maybe you should head home and get some sleep and leave the beer for another time.'

'I'm fine,' she said again. 'And listen, I'm sorry I snapped at you a couple of times when you were asking about my dad. As I'm sure you can imagine, it's kind of a sore spot for me. You know, being a cop.'

'I understand,' he said. 'And there's no need to apologise. I'm impossible to offend.'

She smiled and said 'Challenge accepted' before sticking a

thumb towards the passenger side. 'Get in. I'll wait with you. I know it's hard to believe, but there isn't exactly a whole lot to do in this town once you take beer off the table.'

'You're sure?'

'I wouldn't have said it if I weren't.'

He said, 'You're too kind,' and climbed into the passenger seat.

'You won't be offended if I take a little nap, will you?'

'Not at all,' he said. 'I'm enjoying the novelty.'

'Novelty?'

'Tonight is my first time inside a police car.'

'What? You're kidding. Never, ever? Not even as a wayward kid?'

'Never, ever,' he repeated.

'Then you're the first non-law breaker I've ever met in my life.'

'Or maybe,' Victor said as he pulled the door shut, 'I've just never been caught.'

'You're saying I should take you to the precinct and book you?'

'That depends.'

'On what?'

'Whether you like paperwork.'

She grunted. 'I hate paperwork. Every cop hates paperwork. Ask ten cops whether they'd prefer to get shot or do paperwork all day and nine will ask you what kind of calibre you are talking about.'

'Then don't take me in,' he said. 'You'll be filling in forms until Christmas.'

FIFTY

True to his word, Gino had the truck back running in under an hour. Linette slept for most of that time and couldn't stop apologising for it once she woke up. Victor thanked her again, thanked and paid Gino, and drove away as Linette took another radio call about the Nameless causing trouble for the ER staff.

Victor needed to keep his hand iced, but he couldn't do that at the motel because he wanted to keep Fendy on side until he knew whether she could help him or not. She wanted him to stay clear of the motel to keep McAllan happy, which meant he had to find somewhere else to stay. Except he wasn't keen on using the Wilson Murdoch legend again now it had been compromised by McAllan's digging. Nowhere in the area would just take cash with no questions asked. People were too law-abiding for that sort of thing in Canada.

Which left him with few options.

He could sleep in his truck or he could buy camping equipment from a sporting goods store to sleep in the woods, but neither provided anything close to even a rudimentary degree of protection. Always better to have walls if they were available.

He had an idea where to go but he needed to clear out of the motel first. Not literally, because he left no belongings in his room, but Wilson Murdoch from Las Vegas, Nevada, would. Even if McAllan knew Victor wasn't really Murdoch, the pretence was still necessary because he had encountered more people than just McAllan. And even though McAllan knew he wasn't Murdoch, he was not aware that Victor left nothing behind in his room when he went out each day.

So, Murdoch would return to the motel.

Victor had stayed there for five nights in total and had seen several other guests in that time and several accompanying vehicles. Mostly trucks and SUVs and the odd sedan. Given the motel was a small, cheap establishment, those vehicles fitted a particular pattern. They weren't new models. They weren't expensive. Often, they were dirty or had rust spots. There were no optional extras.

Which made the big, pristine Escalade a notable presence in the parking lot. It was a brand-new model. Midnight blue. Seventeen feet in length from bumper to bumper, gleaming in the wash of Victor's headlights.

Even more notable was the second Escalade parked next to it. Same brand-new model. Same paint job. Two huge vehicles side by side.

Each could transport eight, including the drivers. A maximum of sixteen, although he expected more like twelve at most. Anyone who could afford two factory-fresh Cadillacs could afford three smaller vehicles instead. No one liked to be cramped shoulder to shoulder, after all. But no fewer than eight people because those who could afford two such vehicles wouldn't want to waste money.

A party of eight to twelve.

Victor didn't believe in coincidences.

He stopped his truck on the opposite side of the lot from them and sat in the dark for a moment. There was limited lighting in the lot so as not to disturb sleeping guests. He angled the rear view to get a better look. There was activity near the SUVs. One of the motel room doors was open next to the Escalades. A man was just inside the doorway, backlit by the lights in the room. That man wore dark jeans and a stonewashed denim jacket.

Victor didn't get a better look at him because he noticed another man exiting the motel office. Again, this one wore jeans. But no jacket. Just a T-shirt. He was tanned and hairy, dense but lean. He also noticed Victor sitting in his truck straight away.

The tanned man had noticed the new truck too. He would have heard Victor arrive when he was in the office and seen the headlights brighten the night. The second he stepped outside he looked in the direction of the new arrival. Perhaps just curious. Perhaps looking for someone in particular.

No reaction.

That was unexpected. Victor was so used to people trying to kill him that it was often hard to accept when potential threats showed no interest.

After the tanned man had glanced in Victor's direction, he looked away again, continued to where the Escalades were parked and opened up the back of one of them. He rummaged around, maybe opening bags, maybe taking something out or putting something inside. Then he closed the boot and headed into the motel room with the open door.

Eight to twelve guys.

They would have three rooms at a minimum. As far as Victor knew, the motel had double rooms, twin rooms and family rooms. The latter sleeping three.

Guys in expensive SUVs wouldn't sleep on the floor.

Victor climbed out of his truck. He took the direct route to the motel office in case any of those guys were watching him without his knowledge. Even if they were no threat to him, he didn't want them learning anything about him he didn't want them to know.

Behind the desk, the manager stiffened.

Victor told him, 'Don't worry, I'm leaving in the morning.'

The manager was surprised. Not in the loop. Fendy would have called McAllan by now but McAllan hadn't called the manager. Not high on his list of priorities.

'Your friend Jennifer paid for you,' the manager said once he had regained his composure. 'So, just drop the key on the desk when you're on your way.'

Victor nodded. He backed away to the door, turned, and went no further. Instead, he opened the door and held it for the man approaching.

Another of the party of eight to twelve.

No denim. This one wore black cargo trousers and an olive polo shirt. About forty. Dark skin. Dark hair touched grey at the temples. He was a little taller than Victor, a little broader.

'Much obliged,' the man said to Victor.

'Nice ride,' Victor said back. 'Rides, even.'

'The planet won't overheat on its own.'

There was a look in the man's eyes as if he knew Victor without recognising him. Victor was pretty sure he had the same look in his own eyes.

'Did he deserve it?'

Victor said, 'Excuse me?'

The man didn't glance down. 'Your knuckles are bruised.'

Victor remained silent.

'Well,' the man said, 'the middle two are bruised. Uppercut, yeah? Guy had a narrow jaw and you clocked him with a perfect shot. Your other knuckles hit nothing but air.'

Victor said, 'It wasn't a perfect shot.'

'Are they ever?' The man smiled. 'But I bet he didn't complain, did he?'

'Not even a little bit.'

'A fast-track ticket to dreamland will do that to a fella,' he said with a smile. 'You didn't answer my question.'

'I just did.'

'No, the other one. Did the guy deserve it?'

'Most assuredly,' Victor said.

'That's what I like to hear.' The man offered his hand. 'Call me Garrett.'

Victor shook it. 'Wilson Murdoch.'

He could feel the strength in Garrett's hand, in the thick fingers and dense bones connected to ropey muscle all the way up his arm. Useful, practical strength. Garrett could have a crushing grip if he so chose. Instead, his handshake was firm but nothing more. He didn't feel the need to prove anything.

Only the weak felt the need to prove their strength.

'Anything I should know?'

'About what?'

Garrett shrugged. 'The town, the motel. Maybe you can offer some insight. You've been here a while.'

Victor resisted saying *How do you know?* because that would mark him as a man who cared why, and he didn't want Garrett to know that particular fact. There were any number of reasons Garrett might know: no keys in Victor's hands meant he hadn't come into the office to check in, so he hadn't just arrived like them; the motel manager might have mentioned Victor in passing, perhaps as a warning. *We have a difficult guest you should stay clear of . . .*

'Just a few days,' Victor said. 'The bar a mile west has good beer on draught.'

'That's my kind of insight.'

Victor added, 'Not much beyond that. It's a quiet place.'

'Except the brawl.'

'Except that.'

Garrett smiled and then glanced at Victor's truck. 'That's a decent model you got there. A workhorse. You'll never get stuck in a ditch.'

'But a bad ignition switch,' Victor said. 'Had to get a new one fitted. If you need an auto shop, ask for Gino. He's young but he knows what he's doing.'

'Thanks, but no need.'

'Escalades are as reliable as sunrise.'

'More so,' Garrett said. 'Not even a chance of cloud cover. But should a sudden hurricane unexpectedly arise we do our own grease monkey work.'

Victor recognised but hadn't heard the term 'grease monkey' for a long time. He thought he hid any sign of recognition because he always did, yet somehow Garrett noticed.

He said, 'Let me guess: Marines.'

Lying would only have drawn more attention so Victor was honest: 'Army.'

There was a pause before Garrett said, 'That's it? No elaboration? Usually a vet can't wait to talk units, ranks. Theatres, tours. Stuff like that. Then they take a guess on me. Maybe swap a war story or two that's usually unsuitable for general sensibilities.'

'I don't need to guess,' Victor said. 'Anchor tat on your forearm. I don't picture you loading torpedoes, so I'll say frogman.'

Garrett rubbed at the skin midway between his left elbow and wrist. 'That little guy is over twenty years old and so faded even I can barely see it.'

'I like carrots.'

'You know where that came from, don't you?'

Victor said, 'World War Two. The RAF claimed their pilots had better vision at night thanks to eating carrots.'

Garrett nodded. 'To hide the development of radar. I'm guessing you're up here to hunt.'

'Up here?'

'You're from south of the border, right? Somewhere east of the Rockies.'

Victor nodded. 'But I'm here to fish, not hunt.'

'Out on the lake?'

Victor nodded again.

'Bet it's beautiful.'

'Peaceful.'

Garrett smiled. 'Even better.'

'You guys are hunters.'

'That wasn't even a question. We that obvious?'

'No one's going to stink up brand-new Cadillacs with bait or fish guts.'

Garrett laughed. 'Ain't that the truth?'

'What are you hunting?'

'Moose. Elk. Maybe a bear.'

'You cast a wide net.'

Garrett nodded. 'A fisherman would know all about that.'

'So would a frogman,' Victor said. 'Good luck out in the woods.'

'I don't believe in luck.'

Victor said, 'Neither do I. But I was being polite.'

'Do you often say things you don't mean, to be polite?'

'Doesn't everyone?'

Garrett pursed his lips. Thought. Shrugged. 'Tell you what, I'll see you later and we can continue the discussion. I can let you know how lucky we got over one of those good beers.'

'I'll have to wonder,' Victor said. 'I'm making a move.'

'What's the hurry?'

'No hurry.'

'You're throwing money away. It's nearer midnight than noon so you must have paid for the night too, thinking you were staying. Something unexpected must have come up and rocked your plans. Hope it's not too serious.'

'It's a long story,' Victor said. 'Needs must.'

'Don't they always?' Garrett said. Glanced at Victor's knuckles. 'Not running from the law, are you?'

Victor stepped to one side, to pass Garrett. 'Happy hunting.'

'I was wondering if you were ever going to continue on your way.'

'Funny, I've been wondering the exact same thing about you.'

'Guess I was testing you while you were testing me right back.'

'Habit,' Victor admitted.

'Likewise,' Garrett said. 'First impressions can tell you everything about a person if you'll let them. I wanted to see how long it took for you to excuse yourself from the conversation, and there you were doing the exact same thing. You're right, it is funny. But what does it mean that you backed down first?'

'That's where you're mistaken,' Victor said. 'I wasn't testing to see if you would leave first. I was testing to see if you wanted me to do so.'

'Huh,' Garrett said. 'Then that leaves me with a question unanswered. Did I pass your test?'

'Did I pass yours?'

Garrett didn't answer.

Neither did Victor.

FIFTY-ONE

The motel manager was neither a brave man nor was he a stupid one. He had his instructions from McAllan and had delivered them as instructed. Only Wilson Murdoch, the fisherman, didn't seem to care. That had put the manager in a difficult position because he neither wanted to tell McAllan that he had failed in his simple task nor did he want to tangle with Murdoch over the issue.

There had been no nineteen new bookings, as he had told him last night, of course. Although those hunters from south of the border had taken up four rooms. The manager had told McAllan at the time that such a claim would not fly but McAllan hadn't cared.

'If we kick him out,' McAllan had told him, 'he has no choice but to go.'

Great in theory, but who was going to kick him out?

Thankfully, it wasn't going to come to that because Murdoch was going of his own accord. The manager could

254

breathe a little easier because he never wanted to see the man ever again. The manager's throat was still a little raw. He was already bored with eating only soft foods.

McAllan hadn't told the manager why he wanted the fisherman gone at all and the manager had asked only enough questions to know he shouldn't be asking any.

What was going on?

Michelle had never been so much as a minute late before; now she hadn't shown up for two days straight and there was a crazed fisherman looking for her, and the motel owner and rumoured criminal was putting pressure on the manager to get rid of the fisherman.

Almost certainly it was best not to know what was going on, but he was starting to worry about Michelle and her boy. He found he missed Michelle's company and missed Joshua getting under his feet. He really was sorry for calling the boy the r-word.

Something occurred to the manager.

He set about looking under the check-in desk for where he had put it. He still wasn't used to Michelle's system and had made a mess of her paperwork organisation.

It took him a few minutes to find the business card.

Still stiff, still pristine. Thick white stock and distinct black lettering. A company name. An Illinois area code. Email address. Cell phone. No logo.

The manager used the desk phone to dial the cell number.

The answering voice said, 'Jennifer Welch.'

The manager introduced himself and said, 'I know it's late, but you said to call any time.'

'I did. It's fine. What can I do for you?'

'You told me to let you know if your friend stuck around,'

the manager said. 'And he has. He's still at the motel. But he's leaving in the morning. So he says this time, anyway.'

'So he says this time?'

'Last night his exact words were: "I'm not going anywhere." Who knows what he will say in the morning. Like you told me: he has issues.'

'He's a complicated individual,' Welch said. 'Those issues run deep. They mean he can act in ways that are definitely not in his best interests. Thank you for letting me know.'

'No problem. I said I would and I'm a man of my word. Will you be coming back? Will you need another room?'

The manager was hopeful but tried not to sound like it.

'We will be coming back,' Welch said. 'But we won't be staying long.'

FIFTY-TWO

Garrett and his guys were all inside their rooms by the time Victor left his own. Both Escalades were still parked in the lot. Big vehicles. Expensive. A team of eight to twelve. Ex-military. A serious operation, but no suggestion they had any interest in him.

Hunters, Garrett had told him.

There was a sliver of truth in the statement, Victor knew. He started his truck and left the parking lot, pulling on to the highway. He headed towards town. Not sure of his next move.

He called Linette. She answered the phone with a sleepy tone.

'I'm sorry for waking you,' he said.

'Don't be. I fell asleep on the sofa. You just saved me a stiff back all day tomorrow.'

'I think I met the husband,' Victor said. 'At the motel. Garrett. He has a crew with him. Claim to be on a hunting trip but they're lying.'

'Wrong guy,' Linette said with a yawn. 'Michelle's married to a guy named Bellarmien Robidoux, remember?'

'He wouldn't use his real name.'

'Why not?'

'Why would he?'

'You say that like it's the most normal thing in the world to go by another name.'

Victor remained silent.

Linette said, 'Tell me about this Garrett. And what do you mean by a crew?'

'Eight to twelve guys including Garrett,' Victor said. 'Two high-end SUVs. They're serious. He wants them back and he's not taking no for an answer.'

'You don't need twelve guys to kidnap a single mother and her kid.'

'He expects resistance.'

'The boyfriend.'

'He's armed. He lives somewhere isolated. Garrett knows this, knows the boyfriend isn't going to give them up without a fight.'

'Shit,' Linette said. 'Shit.'

He frowned.

She couldn't see this, but she remembered. 'In the circumstances, I'm thinking that's warranted. But yeah, sorry. If you're right I have a possible kidnap being planned that includes a possible gunfight and the very realistic possibility of a casualty. This is a sleepy town. Nothing like this happens here.'

'It won't happen here,' Victor said. 'The boyfriend must live deep in the forest. That's why there've been no signs of Joshua or Michelle. They're off the grid.'

'There's a lot of trees out there, a lot of isolated homes. Could be World War Three going on right now in those trees and we wouldn't hear it.'

'Can you get a list of such homes? Cross-reference them with men who work at the quarry?'

'Sure, it will take a couple of days.'

'This thing will be over by then,' Victor said. 'Garrett didn't show up with his crew to sit around twiddling their thumbs. They already have their plan. Now it's time to put it into action.'

Linette exhaled. Victor imagined her staring into space for answers that didn't materialise. 'Unless Garrett has committed a crime, there's nothing I can do. There's not even probable cause to search his vehicles on the off chance there's an unregistered firearm. All I have to go on is your guesswork.'

Victor didn't correct her. He didn't tell her that it wasn't guesswork, that it was deduction based on years and years of experience, of spending almost his entire life observing everything around him for threats, of constantly analysing and evaluating in order to remain breathing one more day, one more second.

By her own admission, Linette could do nothing.

Which meant he needed her further away, not closer.

He said, 'Maybe I'm wrong.'

She yawned and said, 'How do you mean?'

'I'm probably paranoid,' he lied. 'What do I know? I'm thinking the worst. I'm putting two and two together and coming up with five.'

'Dude, don't be putting the fear of God into me and then telling me you're thinking the worst.'

'I'm sorry,' he said, trying to sound it.

'Don't beat yourself up,' she told him. 'You're worried about them. Human nature says we think the worst. Totally understandable. And I'm glad you're paranoid because it means there won't be any kidnapping, any gunfight, and certainly no casualties.'

I wouldn't be so sure of that, Victor didn't say.

Linette said, 'I'm going to bed now,' and hung up.

Victor drove, staring at the road ahead, thinking of plans, options. Going through potential scenarios and their consequences. He thought about Abe and Castel and the Nameless. He thought about McAllan. He thought about Garrett and his team. He thought about Michelle, and most of all he thought about Joshua.

Maybe that was why it took him a little longer than it should have to spot the tail. A black SUV. Not Sal following him on Fendy's behalf again, even in a different vehicle. He wouldn't make the same mistake twice.

Then he watched as red and blue lights flashed from the SUV's grille and inside the vehicle attached to its rear-view mirror.

An unmarked police vehicle.

Victor pulled over and stopped on the side of the highway. He kept the engine running.

The black SUV stopped behind him.

In the dark, Victor could see a man in the driver's seat and one in the passenger seat but no real features. He waited, knowing that waiting was part of the process.

After a minute, the passenger door opened and a man climbed out. Now visible in the truck's tail lights, Victor could see he wore a suit and an overcoat. As he approached,

Victor saw the man was in his mid-thirties and had a shaved head. He made his way to the driver's side of Victor's truck.

'Wilson Murdoch?' the man asked, standing close but not too close.

'That's me.'

He flipped open a leather wallet to flash a badge and its accompanying ID. 'I'm Detective Wall, I'd like to ask you some questions if I may.'

'Sure,' Victor said.

'At the station.'

'What about?'

'I think that's best answered there.'

Victor thought, weighing up his options. He'd already seen a glimpse of a handgun beneath Wall's jacket as he put his ID away.

'Okay,' he said after a moment.

'You need to come with me,' Wall said.

'Excuse me?'

'We'll take you to the station.'

'What about my truck?'

'We'll bring you back afterwards.'

Victor said nothing.

Wall said, 'Don't make this any more difficult than it needs to be.'

FIFTY-THREE

Victor climbed into the back of the black SUV. Wall guided the door shut from outside, rounded the rear of the vehicle, opened up the opposite rear door and climbed into the back.

He heaved the door shut and it slammed.

'All set?' the driver said.

He didn't wait for an answer and pulled away.

Wall sat with his knees spread and his hands in his lap. His gaze was focused out of the window at the grey world beyond the rain.

Victor had his knees directly over his ankles, only his lower spine supported by the backrest, his head over his hips – how he always sat, kinetic chain braced and ready. His hands rested on his thighs.

The driver drove with one hand on the wheel and the other playing with the radio. Talk shows and adverts and music interchanged in a rapid, disjointed melody. Outrage and pop stars and jingles overlapped.

He settled on opera.

Verdi.

Victor approved.

In the back, Wall moved his face closer to the window so he could see better through the downpour. Victor had an idea what he was looking for but wasn't going to help out.

They listened to the aria for a few minutes. No one spoke. Victor did his best not to translate the lyrics in his mind. He spoke Italian, as he did many languages, but preferred to enjoy the melody in as much ignorance as possible. The sound alone moved him in ways that words could not.

In the backseat, Wall rubbed his palms together and then brushed them on his trousers.

When the aria ended and a disc jockey announced what would come up next after a short advertisement break, Victor said: 'What's wrong with the seat?'

Wall frowned, and the driver adjusted the rear view to look Victor in the eye.

'Say again?' the driver asked.

'What's wrong with it?' Victor repeated, gesturing to the empty passenger seat.

The driver said, 'Nothing's wrong with it.'

'Interesting,' Victor said.

Wall sat a little more upright.

'Do you get travel sick?' Victor asked him.

Wall gave a hesitant shrug, then shook his head.

'You're a big man,' Victor said. 'More leg room in the front.'

Wall shrugged again and nodded as if the thought had only just occurred to him.

Victor pretended he didn't notice the driver exchange pointed glances with Wall.

The driver had a beard and dark hair swept back from his

face that reached halfway down his neck. He was tall, like the guy in the back, and so the headrest had been extended.

Victor's left hand shot out and thrust through the gap between the headrest and the seat, taking hold of the driver's long hair in a tight fist and wrenching it down and back.

The driver's head pivoted back, his gaze going skyward, eyes off the road. He cried out in surprise and fear.

Victor wrenched the head back into the rest again and again, which was too soft to inflict much damage but added to the driver's disorientation.

Wall fumbled his draw, his big hands sweaty and clumsy. This wasn't ideal because Victor had to wait to disarm him, holding on to the driver for longer.

Wall kept fumbling the draw. Limited dexterity. Lack of practice. Fear. Pressure.

Victor rolled his eyes.

The gun that eventually emerged from beneath Wall's jacket was a shiny SIG. He drew it with his right hand and had to lift it up past his own left arm and shoulder to aim. He was already reaching out with his left hand to ward off potential attacks.

Victor improvised and went for the exposed hand, snapping a grip across the fingers, compressing them together in a savage squeeze, then withdrawing his arm with just as much speed and power, pulling the bald guy off balance and down to the seat.

Victor struck him on the back of the head with downwards elbows until he heard the gun fall into the footwell as Wall released it to defend himself.

The driver, his gaze still directed at nothing but the car's ceiling, continued to cry out, louder now that his erratic driving was being met with responding horns and screeching tyres.

Without the gun as a threat, Victor was free to loop his right arm around Wall's throat, but before he could fully establish the choke, Wall managed to slither out enough to clear his neck and the vulnerable carotids. That saved him from the choke but not from pain, because now Victor's arm was across the guy's face.

Victor squeezed.

The hard bone of his wrist lay over Wall's cheek. Bone against bone, but there were several hundred more nerve endings in the guy's cheek than Victor's wrist.

He wailed.

Victor kept squeezing, pulling Wall's head against his flank, pinning it there with nowhere to go so all the pressure focused on the sensitive cheekbone.

He wailed and wailed.

The driver lost control of the vehicle and it careered up a kerb at speed, the sudden jolt enough for Victor to lose his grip on Wall, who scrambled away so fast he threw himself against the back door.

Victor released his hold on the driver's hair because Wall, now clear of his reach, went for the gun in the footwell. Victor struck him with an open palm to the side of the head, aiming for the ear where it would inflict more pain, but a hard swerve as the driver sought to regain control of the car threw him off balance and he missed.

The swerve meant Wall failed to retrieve the weapon, almost falling headfirst into the footwell. He struggled to right himself, his left arm reaching out to find purchase but instead finding Victor, who grabbed the hand and snapped the guy's thumb.

Then each of the other four fingers, one at a time.

Snap, snap, snap, snap.

Wall cried out with every break, the volume of his cries increasing each time, pitch heightening.

Victor took the broken fingers into his fist and squeezed.

Broken bone ground on broken bone.

Wall whimpered.

'Stop,' he begged. '*Please ...*'

Victor said, 'Tell the driver to stop the car.'

'Stop the car,' Wall yelled.

'Okay, okay,' the driver agreed, slowing down and pulling over to the side of the highway.

'Keep your hands on the wheel,' Victor told him, compressing Wall's broken fingers to bring forth a cry.

'They're on the wheel,' the driver yelled back. 'Stop hurting him.'

Victor said, 'Take the gun out of the footwell and place it on the seat.'

Contorted and bent over, half in the footwell and one arm outstretched and immobile, Wall had a hard time trying to locate the gun. He breathed in rapid, shallow inhales and exhales, trying to fight the pain from his fingers that Victor kept constant but not debilitating.

'Tell me once you have it.'

Wall said, 'Okay.' Then a moment later: 'Got it.'

'Grip it by the muzzle,' Victor told him, grabbing the driver's hair again.

'Okay.' Wall did as he was told.

'Now hit your friend with it.'

'What?'

'Hit the driver with the gun,' Victor explained.

Wall's eyebrows moved closer together in confusion.

Victor said, 'I want you to pistol whip the driver.'

Wall said, 'Why?'

'You don't need to know why I want you to do it, but why you should do it is because if I have to do it I'll first break the fingers of your other hand.'

Wall looked from the driver to Victor and back again.

The driver said, 'Don't do it.'

Wall said, 'I have to.'

'Please,' the driver said.

'Don't judge him,' Victor said. 'He has no choice.'

Wall shifted in his seat so he could lean through the gap between the seats. He raised the pistol.

Victor kept a tight hold on the driver's hair. 'Hit him on the top of the skull. You hit him on the forehead and all you're going to do is cause him a tremendous amount of pain and then you'll have to hit him again.'

'You're crazy,' the driver whimpered.

'I assure you this is an entirely rational course of action.'

'I'm sorry, dude,' Wall said.

'Don't,' the driver begged.

Wall struck him on the top of the skull with the bottom of the handgun's grip. A good, hard hit.

The driver went slack.

Victor released his hair. 'Where are you taking me?'

Wall hesitated.

Victor said, 'If you don't want to tell me I can shoot you and ask the driver when he wakes up.'

'You can't shoot me,' Wall said in a sheepish tone. 'The gun's not real. It's a replica.'

'You're kidding. Then why did you bother going for it?'

'You know,' Wall said. 'Try and scare you off.'

'Okay,' Victor said. 'If it's just a replica then you can still tell me where you were planning to take me because if you don't I'll beat you to death with it and then ask the driver when he wakes up.'

Wall exhaled. 'Just some place on the edge of town.'

'Let me guess,' Victor said. 'Industrial. No nearby residents.'

'Something like that.'

'Give me the address.'

Wall did.

'How many are waiting there?'

'One.'

'Just one?'

Wall nodded.

'You're not very good at this, are you?'

Wall looked away.

Victor gestured to the driver. 'You'd better check his pulse.'

Wall said, 'Why?'

'Because you're stronger than you look and that was a solid pistol whip. You might have killed him.'

'Wait, what? Seriously? Ah, shit. *Shit.* No, no . . . '

Victor decided there was no point talking to Wall about his use of bad language. Any lesson would fail to be heeded given imminent unconsciousness.

Wall pushed himself through the gap between the seats to take the driver's wrist, which wasn't easy with only one hand. He had to lead through with his good hand and tense and brace to maintain his balance. He also had to give his back to Victor.

Who hit Wall on the back of the head with the replica handgun.

268

FIFTY-FOUR

It was only a short drive to the address Wall had given him. It took almost as long to get the unconscious driver out of the driver's seat and into the passenger seat. A big, uncompliant guy.

The neighbourhood was quiet and dark. Small industrial units for a small town. Some operational throughout the night. Others silent. On the periphery of the larger units was a derelict building. The chain-link fence surrounding it was rusted and warped and absent entirely in places. The gate was open.

Trash had piled up where the wind had pushed it and nature had begun reclaiming the strip of asphalt that had once been a parking lot. No vehicles – all three must have travelled in the black SUV – but faint light glimmered from inside the derelict building, refracting through broken glass that formed teeth in smashed-out window frames.

Victor drove the SUV right up to the front of the building because that's what an incompetent would do.

In similar fashion, the third guy appeared, pushing open a fire exit. He was smiling, pleased the other two had arrived, maybe excited by what would commence now everyone was here.

With the headlights still on, he couldn't see that it was Victor behind the wheel until he was too close.

Victor had already released the catch and slammed the heavy SUV driver's door into the guy, who jolted backwards and fell to the ground.

Victor was out of the vehicle by the time the guy had recovered; he had a passing resemblance to Wall, he saw. Cousins, maybe.

He had no gun, real or replica, because there was nothing in his hands.

He was hurt, unsteady on his feet. He had fallen hard, hitting his head on the cracked and rutted asphalt, splitting the skin of his forehead in a jagged gash above his eyebrows. Blood flooded his eyes.

The guy was far from done.

Trying to blink the blood from his eyes, he came at Victor, staggering more than walking, swiping with his hands more than punching because he was dazed and could hardly see.

Victor stepped back, not needing to parry or dodge the slow, telegraphed attacks. He let the head wound do its job – each second meant more blood leaking from the guy's forehead, further blinding him, further slowing him.

'Fight me,' the guy barked in a slurred voice full of strain and frustration. He beckoned with his fists for Victor to come closer.

'Why?'

The guy growled in response and tried to rush Victor.

A quick side-step put the guy off balance and he stumbled forward, correcting himself before falling only because he bumped into the wall of the building. He pushed himself away from it with a considerable effort, leaving behind a smear of blood, and used that momentum to turn around to face Victor again.

Victor said, 'Give it up. All you're doing is embarrassing yourself.'

'Coward,' the man hissed.

Victor raised an eyebrow. 'Just one of many character flaws I have to live with.'

The guy charged one last time.

He made it three steps before he tripped and fell on the uneven ground.

He was too tired to get back up again.

Victor kicked him in the side of the head to make sure he stayed down.

Inside, the derelict building had one room with lighting via a free-standing halogen work lamp. The kind used in construction. That room had a metal chair in the centre that had been newly bolted to the floor. The chair was too clean to have been here already, so they had brought it with them. Along with several rolls of duct tape. Snacks and drinks were in a bag in a corner because they had planned to be here a long time. A crooked table had been dragged in from somewhere else, judging by the marks in the dust on the floor. Another bag lay on the table, its contents already removed and laid out in a neat line.

A curled length of hose, box cutter, hammer, pliers, bolt croppers, and a cordless drill. The last had several attachments including sanding and grinding heads.

Wall – the guy claiming to be him, at least – came to first. He groaned and shuddered and then his eyes snapped open and he struggled against his restraints. Victor had used their duct tape to secure wrists together, knees together, and ankles together.

The three were next to one another on the floor, backs up against a wall.

Victor waited in the metal chair, facing them.

Wall went to speak but instead grimaced, eyes pinched shut tight. He had been hit on the back of the head, after all.

'Who sent you?'

'I swear I don't know,' Wall said once the moment of pain had passed.

'You need to tell me something.'

'We got a call this afternoon from people we've worked with before. They were passed a job from someone who called someone who called someone. You know how it is.'

'Shy client,' Victor said.

'Yeah,' Wall said. 'You're causing them a problem. They wanted you run out of town.'

'They want me dead?'

'No, no,' Wall replied, fast. 'But hurt real bad so you never even dreamed of coming back.'

'Not a single gun between the three of you suggests I should believe that. Especially given the selection of toys on the table.'

Wall waited. He started to sweat.

'This presents a quandary, doesn't it?' Victor said. 'You're just doing a job, I get that. I don't take these kinds of things personally. Usually, it's to do with work. So this is the same, but different. Any other time I deal with it. I move on. Never think of it again. Yet a permanent solution is going to generate more attention for me, and I already have more than enough of that to deal with.'

Wall, sweating, listened.

'Still, there has to be a consequence. You have to understand the error of your ways.'

'We do.'

'You might,' Victor said, standing up from the metal chair. 'The other two might not.'

'I'll make sure. I swear it.'

'Words are cheap, sadly for you.' Victor perused the selection of tools on the table. 'And time is not on your side. We have to sort this fast. And if we are to avoid a permanent solution then you need a permanent reminder never to repeat your mistake.'

Wall, sweating hard, watched.

Victor settled on the bolt croppers.

FIFTY-FIVE

Derek was looking forward to getting home because Wifey was on the sofa drinking wine and when she drank wine all on her lonesome Derek's head hit the pillow with a smile on his face. She had cooked too, but while she made a mighty fine lasagne with five different kinds of cheese, Derek was only hungry for one thing.

He checked his watch. Three whole minutes had gone by since he'd last checked it. This shift was taking for ever. One of those days when the earth spun in slow motion, when his boots were loaded with lead, when every asshole in North America decided to pass by his booth thinking he was a punchbag for their attitude.

Which was why he didn't return the smile at first.

When you're in a bad mood a smile is the last thing you want to see.

Took him a moment to remember the face behind the wheel.

'You again,' Jennifer Welch said. 'What are the odds?'

Derek's face lit up now. He returned Welch's magnificent smile. 'Of all the border booths in all the world . . .'

'How have you been?'

'Same shit, different day. You?'

'Different day, same shit.'

'Isn't it always the way?'

He leaned down so he could peer into the vehicle and give himself a legitimate excuse for getting a little closer to Welch. He didn't remember the faces of the three guys from last time but he was pretty sure they were the same three. They behaved the same, certainly. They left all the talking to the boss, to Welch.

She reached for the glovebox and Derek waved a hand.

'You sure?' she said.

'Don't tell me you've taken up a false identity since last time I saw you.'

'Who says the one you saw last time was genuine?'

Derek chuckled. 'Where have you been all my day?'

'For a moment I thought you said "Where have you been all my life?"'

'That too,' Derek said.

Damn it, he was flirting. Better get back to business.

'What brings you to Canada . . . again?' he asked. 'Unfinished business?'

Welch said, 'Broken promises.'

Derek said, 'Make 'em pay,' and waved her through, thinking of Wifey's five-cheese lasagne and what would follow.

Welch gave him one final, beautiful smile.

'Oh, they'll pay.'

FIFTY-SIX

McAllan slept like a baby. When his big head hit the down-stuffed pillow it was a fast train to slumber town. The first few years after Janine passed had been rough on him and his sleep. McAllan had taken to sleeping with the bedside lamp on most nights because sometimes he would wake up in the dark and in his drowsiness reach out to her. Then he didn't so much sleep like a baby as sob like one.

That was a long time ago now. He had fixed his sleep over many months of trial and error that he had approached like a big city contract for which he was bidding. He worked hard and took the setbacks on the chin and kept at it until it worked.

He had never felt better.

Once his cholesterol was in check, he would be bullet-proof again. Rebuilt. Or remade? He wasn't sure which was the more accurate description.

The diet and exercise routines were painfully dull and boring, but like his sleep, he would crack them too. He just needed to find what suited him. With sleep, he had learned many tricks that in combination worked a charm: no electronics two hours before bed, a cold bedroom, no lights on at all, not even the standby LED on the wall-mounted television. He went to bed on an empty stomach. He didn't have coffee after dark. He took herbal remedies that promoted relaxation. He meditated. He went to bed at the exact same time every single day without exception. Circadian rhythms had become his bitch.

It also helped to know that two of his crew were always present in the house as security and that the best alarm system money could buy provided additional protection, while a big, ferocious Rottweiler that wasn't fed until the morning stalked the grounds.

Given how well McAllan slept, it came as a surprise to him to wake up in the middle of the night.

He jerked awake from a nightmare, feeling like there was a fat worm or cockroach crawling or slithering over his face, which he brushed off in a frantic, swiping gesture.

He panted. He sweated. He put a palm to his chest. It took a few seconds before he was sure he wasn't having a heart attack.

Not like him to have a nightmare.

Not at all.

It still felt as if something was on his face, and he rubbed at his cheek to scrub away the sensation.

It worked, but what was that smell?

As he brought his fingers down from his cheek he detected an unpleasant, meaty scent.

He held his fingertips to his nose, thinking he must be mistaken.

He was not mistaken.

'What the ... ?'

He fumbled in the dark for the lamp, thumbed it on and saw blood on his fingertips.

'I'm going to ask you four questions,' the man standing over him said.

McAllan gasped. He froze. His pulse spiked. He was naked in bed, pinned in place by a thick duvet and comforter. Standing next to the bed was the man pretending to be Wilson Murdoch. The fisherman.

Only he didn't seem like the fisherman one little bit. Now, he looked ruthless and terrifying, his eyes empty of anything approaching humanity.

The fisherman held a brown paper bag in one hand.

What was inside? A knife? A gun?

McAllan had never been so scared in his life. He thought of his men, his dog, his alarms. None had stopped the fisherman.

'How many men did you hire?'

McAllan, terrified, told the truth: 'Three.'

'Are you going to hire any more?'

McAllan shook his head.

'You need to say it.'

'I ... I ... won't hire any more men.'

The fisherman said, 'Do you know anything, anything at all, about the disappearance of Joshua and his mother?'

'I don't,' McAllan said. 'I swear it. I swear it on my dead wife's name, on my daughter's life.'

'Then get the list of quarry personnel to Fendy. Stop dragging your feet.'

McAllan swallowed. 'Okay. First thing in the morning. I promise.'

'Final question,' the fisherman said. 'Do you ever want to see me again?'

McAllan was shaking by now and his parched mouth made it hard to speak. But he did because he knew his life depended on it.

'No,' he managed. 'I never want to see you again.'

The fisherman nodded as if pleased but his expression showed nothing. McAllan expected death at any moment.

The paper bag rustled as the fisherman lifted it up and emptied the contents over McAllan.

He felt the gentle pattering impacts through the duvet and recoiled in horror while the fisherman backed out of the room.

McAllan was too disgusted, too scared, to count them, but there were twenty-nine in total.

Fingers.

Six thumbs, six index fingers, six middle fingers, six ring fingers, but five little fingers. Some broken first. Hacked off or sawn off, he didn't know. He didn't want to know.

He screamed.

Later, his men would find the thirtieth finger between the mattress and headboard where it had ended up after McAllan had swiped it from his waking face.

FIFTY-SEVEN

The house was quiet. The whole neighbourhood was quiet. The night was cold and windows were dark. No music was playing loud. No one was walking at this hour. Victor parked his truck around the corner, on a perpendicular street. His were the only footsteps on the pavements. His was the only shadow beneath the moon.

The elderly couple were not on their porch, of course. No lights were on in their windows. Victor imagined they had been in bed for hours. They would be waking up at about the same time he would be laying down his head, he expected.

The back door to Michelle's house squeaked a little as he opened it, but the sound would not travel far. If anyone could hear it then they were close enough to see him. He locked the door behind him.

He kept the lights off and stood in the kitchen until his eyes adjusted to the darkness. The air had a faint unpleasant smell from the soured milk in the cereal bowls.

Protocol meant he explored the entire house even though

he knew it was empty of threats. He had been inside twice before, knew the exact layout, and found that nothing had changed, as he had expected.

He returned to the kitchen to drink water and fix some cereal with the last of the fresh milk from the refrigerator. He placed a few dollars down on the countertop to cover the cost. Otherwise, it was stealing.

Michelle and Joshua had been gone for over two days now.

It wasn't time for Victor to sleep just yet – still prime attacking time for any enemies – but he headed upstairs because it decreased the chances of any neighbours or passers-by noticing him inside the supposedly empty house.

The only books he had seen were in Joshua's room. So it was there that Victor sat on the floor to use a sliver of moonlight to read about the many adventures of a team of special needs children who saved the world from evil corporations, mythical monsters and aliens over several short novels. In every chapter a piece of artwork illustrated the dramatic events that had just occurred. The prose was pleasant, and the stories had a relentless pace with a few surprises that even a voracious reader like Victor failed to spot. He imagined Joshua was a big fan. The cracked spines and frayed jackets suggested the books were read either by him or to him with some frequency.

After Victor had finished the series, which took a little under four hours, he lay on the floor with his head resting on his arm to go to sleep. He didn't want to use either Joshua's or Michelle's beds; it seemed impolite.

Within seconds of closing his eyes, they opened again.

A noise.

So quiet and faint he wasn't sure at first if he had imagined it.

But he never imagined such things.

The back door. The little squeak. Joshua's room lay over the kitchen.

Victor pressed his ear to the floor and listened hard. He heard the little squeak a second time.

The back door had opened and now it was closed.

Someone was inside the house.

Victor sat up, then stood. He was already dressed and his shoes were meant for the outdoors, so he kept his movements slow and gentle. By now he knew where all the creaky floorboards were located and could avoid them as he left the room and stepped out on to the landing until he reached the top of the stairs. Victor stopped with his back against the wall, listening.

Now he heard them. They weren't trying to be as quiet as him, so they thought the house was empty. They didn't know he was here.

Dim red light glowed from the floor below. Red because that wavelength of light didn't travel as far as other colours. Which meant red light was only useful for close up, but there was far less chance of the light giving the user away. Red light also wouldn't impede natural night vision.

At first, he thought there was just one, until he heard a whispered voice.

'Essentials only.'

And a second.

'Affirmative.'

Victor waited. There was little else he could do at this point. He wasn't sure what they were doing, so it wasn't smart to act. He kept listening, hearing their footsteps beneath, drawers opening, a zipper being fastened or unfastened.

They were downstairs now, but they would be coming up.

The fact that they hadn't already told Victor they didn't think mother and son were home. They hadn't expected to find them here, but they were here anyway.

They were searching.

For something, not someone.

Within a minute he had identified four separate sets of noise. Four people downstairs. He had heard two male voices but he couldn't be sure about the other two.

'We're through down here,' one said.

Victor backed away from the staircase. There were limited options: the master bedroom, Joshua's room, a box room, a bathroom and an attic. The attic was no good because there was no way to pull down the hatch and the stepladder without making noise, and the bathroom and the box room were both too small to offer any hiding places. Which left the two bedrooms. Joshua's was smaller, yet if the four people were looking for something it made more sense it would be located in Michelle's room, not her son's.

The closet in Joshua's room was full of toys, so Victor slid under the bed on his back. It was a child's bed and not long enough for his height so he had to rotate his legs and bring up his knees. There was enough room to do so but only after he kicked out a large stuffed toy that had been stored beneath the bed.

He lay still, breathing slow, deep breaths. The greatest danger in hiding under a bed was dust and its potential to induce sneezing, but Michelle kept a fastidious home.

The four had spent almost two minutes downstairs and they did the same upstairs. Victor heard them ascend the staircase and then spread out, each checking a different room. Dim red light framed the door to Joshua's room.

The door eased open and the glow from a flashlight bathed the room red. A figure stood in the open doorway for a long moment.

Victor couldn't see the figure from his position under the bed, but he remained calm because he was always calm.

The figure stepped inside the room. Victor saw tactical boots and trousers, coloured red by the flashlight. Those boots approached the bed.

They were so close Victor could see the scuff marks on the toes even in the darkness.

The mattress above his head depressed a little. He heard the tiny squeak of springs inside it.

The figure had placed something on to the bed.

Victor watched as the boots turned around and he heard drawers opening. The mattress trembled above him, responding to more weight being applied to it, and he pictured the figure throwing clothes and perhaps toys on to the bed, into the bag already set down to receive them.

Now Victor understood.

The four were here to collect Joshua's and Michelle's personal effects.

He waited, quiet and calm, while the figure finished up in Joshua's room, zipped up the bag and left, taking the red glow away and easing the door shut.

'All done,' a voice said in the hallway.

Footsteps descended the stairs. Victor rolled his head to one side so his ear was close to the floor. He listened for the back door opening and closing again.

He continued to lie beneath the bed because an efficient

crew like this would have other people outside, for protection and surveillance. Victor wanted to go to a window to gather more intel but it was too great a risk.

He waited a further ten minutes to make sure they had plenty of time to leave the area and to make sure they weren't coming back.

He slid out from under the bed and stood. The drawers had been closed again, he noticed. In Michelle's room too, he found. Clothes had gone, as were toothbrushes, cosmetics and luggage.

The crew had collected up Michelle's and Joshua's belongings to make it appear they had done so themselves. It was to support a narrative: that the mother and son had left of their own free will.

Victor headed down the stairs, unsure what to do next but feeling a growing sense of urgency.

From the darkness, a voice said, 'Strange place to catch a fisherman.'

FIFTY-EIGHT

Victor recognised the voice straight away. It came from the near corner of the room the staircase opened up into, but that corner was set back behind the foot of the stairs. Impossible to see into until further into the room and looking back.

A blind spot.

'You're a patient man,' Victor said, facing him.

'Had you waited any longer I might have begun doubting myself,' Garrett said with a smugness to his tone. 'But I had to even the score from earlier.'

The stuffed toy, Victor realised.

Out of place on the floor of Joshua's room after being kicked out from beneath the bed.

Michelle kept a fastidious home. Garrett had noticed, or already knew. Of course he knew.

He wore similar clothes to those he had been wearing earlier but these were closer-fitting, more tactical. He wore gloves, a rolled-up ski mask, and had a gun in his hand, pointing at Victor. A compact automatic. Suppressor.

Garrett said, 'I thought you were leaving town.'

Victor said, 'I thought you were hunting.'

'It was almost the truth,' Garrett said. 'It says I'm a bounty hunter on my business card.'

Not the husband, but working for him.

'Why do I get the impression that you do a lot more than simply go after those who skip bail?'

Garrett shrugged. 'Maybe you're just of a suspicious mindset. Although, that doesn't mean you're necessarily wrong about me. Am I wrong about you, I wonder? Why do I get the impression you do a lot more than just fish?'

Victor remained silent.

'What are you doing in this house?' Garrett asked. 'You're no more an invited guest than I am.'

'I needed somewhere to sleep.'

Garrett smirked in the darkness. 'Of all the houses in all the world ...'

'I'm looking for Michelle and Joshua,' he explained. 'They're missing.'

'I know they are,' Garrett said. 'I find that quite interesting.'

'Why?'

'They go missing right before I show up. Every other day they're going about their business. Michelle is working at the motel and Josh is doing whatever kids do. Then, out of nowhere, they vanish. Right at the very best moment for them. That's beyond lucky. That's lottery-level divine intervention luck.'

'It was my fault,' Victor said. 'I spooked Michelle. She thought I was you.'

'How does that work? She thought *you* were *me*?'

Victor nodded. 'She thought I was here to take her and

287

Joshua away. That's why they're missing. They've gone into hiding.'

Garrett sighed. 'Well, thank you very much for making my job harder than it needs to be. This was a one-day gig on paper. Perhaps the most profitable single day I ever had. Except it's not because I have to remain in this backwater town longer than I should. I have to play detective.'

'Has Michelle skipped bail?'

'Not that I know of. I'm here on a relocation mission.'

'Kidnapping.'

'That's an ugly word. I'm here to reunite a family. I'm the good guy in this.'

'Michelle came all the way to this town for a new life, not because she wanted to go back to her old one.'

'I'm not here for Michelle,' Garrett said. 'Just the freak.'

It took everything Victor had to remain in place.

Garrett saw this. 'You want to rush me, don't you?'

Victor remained silent.

'Think you can cover ten feet before I can apply six pounds of pressure?'

Victor didn't move.

Garrett said, 'That's what I thought.'

'Michelle will never give him up.'

'I'm pretty sure Mr Smith and Mr Wesson here will be able to convince her that it's in her and the ... the *kid's* best interests to hand him over to me in a calm, peaceful manner. I want to keep this civilised.'

'What happens once you take the boy? You're guilty of kidnapping.'

'I'm sure I can convince the mother it's no such thing. It's all for the best.'

'And if you can't convince her?'

Garrett's silence answered for him. He changed the subject. 'Don't suppose you know where I can find them, do you?'

'No,' Victor said.

'Can't say I'm wholly surprised to hear that. If you knew, you wouldn't be here. Then again, I don't suppose you would tell me if you did know, would you?'

'No,' Victor said again.

Garrett pursed his lips. Nodded. Stared. 'I could make you, you know. If I thought you knew where they were, I could make you tell me.'

'No,' Victor said for the third time. 'I would never tell you.'

This seemed to amuse Garrett, who almost smiled. 'Never? Wow. That's a strong word, Fish. You'd best pray we don't need to test that theory.'

'I don't pray any more.'

'God stopped listening?'

'I stopped deserving His attention.'

'I thought we were all unworthy. All sinners.'

'Some of us more so than others.'

'I'm starting to like you, Fish,' Garrett said. 'But I'm not here to make friends. I'm working. I'm just here to find the kid.'

'Me too.'

'Then the race is on,' Garrett said. 'Although not fair given you've had a head start.'

'You have more resources.'

'Maybe it'll be a photo finish.'

'Maybe,' Victor said.

'But I'm confused,' Garrett said. 'I know why I'm trying to find them, but why have you been trying to find them?'

'Because they were missing,' Victor said. 'Because no one else noticed.'

'That's very kind of you, Wilson. So kind, in fact, that it touches what remains of my decency. I'm not a complete monster, you know, so I'm going to give you some advice. Are you the kind of man who can take advice?'

'I'm aware that there's a limit to my knowledge.'

Garrett said, 'Forget the photo finish. This is a race you don't want any part of. Stop looking for them. Go home. Go back to the States and forget all about Michelle and all about Joshua, and especially all about me.'

'Is this you advising me or Mr Smith and Mr Wesson?'

Garrett said, 'For now, it's me. You've walked into something way beyond your understanding. That's not your fault. And as I said: I'm starting to like you. Hence, I'm giving you a chance to back out and do the right thing. I'm not an unreasonable man and I don't put a bullet in anyone I don't need to.' He stepped back towards the front door. 'I'm going to leave now and then you're free to go – just so long as you go, go. You get in your truck and you don't get out again until your tank is empty. Because this is the first and very last time I'll tolerate you getting in the way of my pay cheque. Am I making myself clear?'

'I understand.'

'Good,' Garrett said, keeping the gun aimed at Victor but backing away to the door until he could open it without taking his gaze from Victor. 'I'm hoping to get this done without shooting anyone at all. Least of all some unlucky sap who picked the wrong mother and kid to befriend and wrong house to crash inside. You've made my life harder but that doesn't mean I need to end yours unless you force my hand.'

'Not harder,' Victor said. 'Better.'

Garrett said, 'What?'

'It's better for you that I spooked them and they've already run.'

'Oh yeah, how did you work that out?'

'Because had I not spooked them, had they still been here, to get to them you would have had to go through me first.'

'I'm not sure how that's better for me,' Garrett said as he backed away through the open door. 'Considering you're only a fisherman.'

'That's just a hobby,' Victor said. 'It's not my job. It's not what I do best.'

FIFTY-NINE

Fendy called the Smoker's cell phone first thing in the morning to say she had the list of quarry workers for him, so Victor drove into town to collect the physical copy. It was four sheaves of white printer paper with a list of around a hundred names, with columns for telephone numbers, addresses, citizenship, ages, hourly wages and other details that were superfluous to his requirements.

He didn't collect the list from Fendy but from Sal, who was waiting outside the building for him, smoking a cigarette.

'How do you feel?' Victor asked him.

'Like I was in a car crash yesterday.' He paused. Almost smiled. 'But it could have been a lot worse.'

Victor nodded.

He took the list the short distance to the police precinct and asked at the front desk for Linette, who came to him after a minute's wait.

He handed it to her when he reached to shake hands in greeting.

'What's the hurry?' she said. 'Beyond the obvious, I mean.'

'I'm just paranoid.'

She gave him a look that said she didn't believe him. 'Really?'

'I have a bad feeling.'

'A bad feeling?'

He said, 'Humour me.'

'I'll work through it as fast as I can,' she said. 'I've been doing everything I can to find them, as fast as I can.'

'I know,' Victor said.

'Has something changed since we last spoke?'

There's eight to twelve bounty hunters scouring the town for Joshua as we speak and if they find him first, they will kill Michelle and her boyfriend because she'll never let them take her son away from her.

'No,' he said.

She tapped him on the chest with the papers. 'Then relax, I'm all over this. I'll have the boyfriend found by nightfall.'

It'll be all over by then, he didn't say.

'You can help if you like.'

'I can't,' Victor said.

She seemed offended. 'Don't want to sully yourself with a menial task like paperwork?'

'It's not that,' he said. 'I have to go fishing.'

She was confused and even more offended. 'Did you say you can't help because you have to go fishing?'

He nodded. 'Right now.'

SIXTY

'Do you have any wet suits?'

She gave him a funny look because it was as obvious as shit on a shoe that she didn't sell wet suits.

'If you can't see one that's because we don't have any,' she said. Plenty of sarcasm but at least she didn't curse.

He nodded. Not annoyed. Not disappointed. Not surprised. He might have asked in case they had a back room with stock not on display. She felt a little bad for her attitude, but she had to deal with a dozen dumb questions a day and sometimes it was simply too much to ask to remain polite through it all. Saints sinned for less.

'We're not that kind of sporting goods establishment,' she added to ease her guilt. 'Might have better luck further east at one of the bigger towns.'

He said, 'I'll bear that in mind,' but she suspected it was now or never for that wet suit.

He had a calm, even exterior. He didn't seem to be in a rush yet he stalked the aisles with such ruthless efficiency, taking items from the shelves with no hesitation, no deliberation, that she could tell he was on the clock. Time was of the essence.

She wondered how a man could be in such a hurry without hurrying.

She ran the items through the register and he packed them into a large sports bag that he had given her first to scan.

He was buying an eclectic collection of goods, no doubt.

Flares.

Four nylon fishing nets.

Thin rope.

Thermal clothing.

Duct tape.

Lead fishing weights.

A box of .338 calibre ammunition.

A beach towel.

A camping stove.

Swimming goggles.

Twelve tubs of petroleum jelly.

With each scan she grew more confused and more curious. It was not her nature to make unsolicited conversation with the customers, but this particular man was testing her resolve.

She cracked when she huffed and struggled to turn the heavy plastic case containing dumbbell bars and an assortment of weights. Had to be thirty or forty pounds. He had four such cases in his cart, lifting each one out with almost no effort.

'Doesn't look like you need them,' she said, taking the second case from him.

He humoured her with a shrug. Not a talker.

'You got another two arms hiding under your shirt?' she joked as the third case was passed to her to scan.

Again, he humoured her. This time with a slight upturning of his lips. Not a smile but something approaching one.

He paid up and wished her a good day.

The cases could not fit in the bag, of course, but he slung it over his shoulder and tucked a case of weights under each arm and carried the other two in his hands. They had handles.

She watched him go, with his eclectic collection of purchases.

She watched him go, all the way to his truck outside in the lot.

A curious man.

A quiet man.

'Excuse me,' snarked a woman with a cart full of diapers, waiting to pay. 'But is this lane actually open?'

SIXTY-ONE

With little wind, the lake was still. The gentle tremor on the surface was only visible up close, at the shore where the water lapped or from up on a boat, looking down. At the centre of the lake floated a two-man rowing boat. A practical, plastic vessel bought for cash by a salesman from Nevada on a fishing trip. The oars were inside, side by side.

His clothes were in a neat pile on one of the seats. A towel was folded next to the clothes, and a camping stove sat next to the towel.

Save for a little lake water sloshing between the seats, the boat was empty. It floated upon the surface, unpiloted and unmoored. From the faraway shores it was not possible to see whether it was piloted or not. From those shores it seemed no different from any other small vessel used by people looking to catch the many cold-water fish in this lake or the others like it.

At this time of year, in April, the lake was around four degrees centigrade at the surface, growing rapidly colder the closer the water was to the bottom, which reached over two hundred metres at the deepest point. Here, below where the boat floated, it was a mere forty metres to the bottom and a little above freezing at that depth.

Typically, a human might be able to stay conscious for around fifteen minutes when exposed to water so cold and would succumb to hypothermia in well under an hour if they didn't first drown after passing out from shock.

It would be several weeks before visitors even paddled at the beaches.

Near the boat, bubbles rose to the surface. Most popped. A few lingered on the surface.

More rose. More popped.

More and more.

The calm, gently rippling surface of the lake ended in a sudden eruption of water as a pale, almost white, hand emerged, followed by a pale arm and then another hand, and another arm, reaching, stretching, coming back down to slash at the already broken surface as Victor's head cleared the water.

He inhaled, gasping, sucking in an urgent, desperate breath, his first for almost two minutes.

He was close to the boat and reached out with one hand to take hold, to make treading water easier, getting back his breath as his bare arms, shoulders and head steamed. His teeth chattered. He shivered. Goose pimples covered his skin. He felt weak. Exhausted.

One minute's rest was all he could afford. One minute's rest meant three minutes' total exposure. Three minutes' exposure meant he had twelve left before he was pushing biological limits. He was far fitter and stronger than the average person, though far leaner. Less body fat meant less insulation. On paper, he had four more attempts. But weaker each time. Slower. Each attempt longer than the previous one.

He was so cold, so fatigued, he knew he had only two remaining, knew he wouldn't have the strength to ascend a fourth time. Maybe not even a third because of the extra weight he had to bring back with him. He might be so slow swimming back up that he never reached the surface, the threat of hypothermia never becoming a risk because he would succumb to hypoxia and drown somewhere below the surface in the icy dark.

With his free hand he slapped himself in the face, hard, replacing the doubt with stinging pain.

Pain brought focus.

He inhaled deep breaths, one after the other, saturating his blood with oxygen.

He took hold of the closest sack of rocks and used the knife to saw through the rope attaching the sack to the side of the boat.

It dragged him back below the surface.

To reduce drag and increase the speed of descent, he kept his ankles together, his thighs pressed together, his shoulders rounded forward and his elbows as close together as his musculature let him. The mass of the rocks pulled him deeper and deeper. He could swim down, perhaps faster, but doing so would burn too much oxygen, create too much carbon dioxide. He needed to conserve every iota of energy for the swim back up.

He was not going deep enough for the bends to be a concern or for decompression to be required, but he felt the ever-increasing pressure in his ears, in his head. He knew it was colder the deeper he descended, but he was already so cold as not to notice that variance.

He had never felt so cold.

As he neared the bottom of the lake, he saw the pale haze of flares colouring the dirty gloom in red. Each one was weighted with taped lead fishing weights. Before the first descent he had thrown and dropped a dozen of them. An imperfect system, but his resources, his options, were limited. His window of time almost non-existent.

Thirty-five seconds to the bottom of the lake and a minute to swim back to the surface left around twenty seconds to search. He needed that light to have any chance.

He released the sack of rocks as soon as the soles of his feet touched silt and sand.

The first descent, he had searched to the east, so this time he searched west. The light from the flares was not as effective as he had hoped because the water was dense with sediment so only small, distant areas of the lake bottom were illuminated with fiery red light. Between them was inky blackness.

Two weighted sacks lay on the bottom of the lake close by, but it was a third one he had twenty short seconds to locate.

If his recollection of where he had disposed of the rifle used for the Chicago job was off even a little, he would never find it. But he remembered the distant spur of land jutting into the lake to the south and the white of the lakeside house to the north.

Twenty, nineteen . . .

The rifle was here, it was close, hiding in one of the areas of blackness outside the pools of red light.

Fourteen, thirteen …

Victor pushed himself through the water, stirring up clouds of silt that only darkened it further. He reached blindly with his hands, his feet.

Eight, seven …

Within just a moment there were only seconds remaining until he had to ascend. Each second increased the burn in his lungs and the compulsion to inhale air that was not available. He exhaled carbon dioxide through his nose, a little at a time.

Four, three …

His fingers touched only sand, his left foot kicked only stones, but his right toes stung against something harder.

One.

No time left to check further.

He should ascend – he had to – but instead he pivoted around, found the familiar texture of hessian.

He grabbed it, pivoted back so he was facing up, and swam.

The rifle weighed ten kilos and another ten kilos of rocks inside the sack made for twenty in total. A manageable weight on land but there were forty metres of water above him trying to force him back down. His ascent was slow, his legs pushing as fast as he could work them but only one arm to pull with as the other hung uselessly and immobile thanks to the weighted sack.

The exertion was extreme.

He had expected it to be as hard as anything he had ever done but the reality was beyond his reckoning.

Gravity pulled him down.

The weight of the lake pushed him down.

He had stayed too long on the bottom, he knew. He had spent precious oxygen he needed for the swim up.

Before, he had ascended in one minute with both arms and no rifle and rocks.

Now, after one minute, he was still surrounded by darkness.

The red light of the flares below had disappeared into the murky depths, and neither could he see the glow of the flare dangling from the boat to guide him back.

There was no more carbon dioxide to release but his lungs burned. The compulsion to breathe was an incredible force that took all his will to fight.

He kept kicking with legs that became more sluggish with each movement, the water becoming thicker and denser as his vision began to fail.

His one usable arm slowed until he could no longer use it.

He told himself to keep swimming, to keep fighting, to never give in.

That voice seemed distant, distorted.

Not his voice but the voice of his uncle.

If I lose another hen you get the strap.

The rifle, disassembled in the sack, was long and unwieldy in his hands. Hard to aim underwater.

He didn't want to shoot the fox.

Wait until it's in range, his uncle told him, but he couldn't. He squeezed, so nervous he wasn't able to wait.

He missed.

But he knew he'd hit. He had seen the flash of red. He had never been able to forget it.

He remembered his uncle's smile, that singular moment of pride that Victor had sought so hard to replicate.

And if he had missed all those years ago? If he had received the strap he had feared so much instead of that unexpected praise?

Would he even be Victor?

Would he be drowning in a lake, alone in the dark, hallucinating as the oxygen deprivation affected his brain's ability to function?

He didn't care.

He didn't care because after hallucination came euphoria. Endorphins flooded his brain and he felt an incredible sense of wellbeing, of contentment.

Maybe his first ever moment of genuine happiness.

His legs, kicking still on instinct, slowed.

His ascent stopped.

Victor had spent every waking moment for as long as he could remember trying to stay alive, yet now he was content to die because he did not want to end this perfect feeling.

Alone in the dark and cold, drowning, Victor smiled.

In the rush of endorphins, he wanted to share that happiness. He needed others to know this feeling. This was life, finally.

Dying was living.

He needed to tell people about it.

He needed to tell Joshua.

Joshua.

Joshua.

Victor kicked his legs with the last of his strength, no longer feeling euphoric but feeling the need to survive another second, another day. He had to survive. He was needed.

He could no longer sense direction. He could no longer sense anything.

He only knew he had reached the rowing boat because he hit the top of his head on the bow.

He ignored the pain because he felt none and manoeuvred clear of the boat, grabbed hold of one of the weighted nets attached to the side with his free hand and pulled.

Nothing happened.

He had no strength left to pull. No energy left to kick. He couldn't force himself out of the water with the weight of the rifle and rocks dragging him down.

Less than an arm's length from air yet he couldn't reach it.

He kicked and pulled with everything he had, with his limbs leaden and his vision almost black and his lungs on fire, and he didn't move.

He kicked and pulled and felt his grip on the net above failing.

Underwater, Victor roared.

No euphoria now.

Only exhaustion and agony and defeat.

He roared and released the sack from his grip.

He kicked and pulled and his head cleared the surface and he sucked in air as the rifle sank back down into the gloom.

SIXTY-TWO

It took a long time before Victor stopped shivering once he was back on the boat. The small exertion of climbing out of the water had almost beaten him. His strength was so depleted and his energy levels so low, what should have taken seconds took nearly a minute of heaving and struggling, hauling and slipping.

Aboard the boat he saw how white his skin had become, so pale it was almost translucent. Veins seemed drawn over him in scribbles of blue ink. Goosebumps covered him. He was sure his lips were even bluer than the visible veins.

Several more nets weighed with rocks hung from the boat, but Victor made no third descent. He was too weak now. He was exhausted. He had been seconds from unconsciousness, seconds from the certain death that would follow, and he had failed.

He had not been strong enough to recover the rifle. He knew he would die for sure the next time he tried.

Victor sat on the narrow bench and dried himself with

the towel he had brought along. A slow, laborious process because his fingers were so stiff he could not fully close his hands to grip the towel with any dexterity.

He was hypothermic, he knew. His core temperature had fallen so far it could not warm itself back up again. He needed an external heat source for that or it would keep falling and his organs would fail.

Expecting this, he had the camp stove, but his unresponsive fingers could not manipulate the dial to turn it on. The dial was too small. He should have anticipated this problem but he had believed himself stronger, his fitness better, his constitution hardier.

Overconfidence.

An amateur error.

The worst of errors.

He pulled on thermal clothing as best he could and collected up the oars. They were thick enough that his hands could grip even with their limited function.

He rowed with a slow, awkward rhythm. His back, wide and thick with muscle despite his lean silhouette, was still strong, but his coordination poor. He was unable to work both oars in synchronisation and unable to keep the boat in a straight line. The weighted sacks of rocks made this more difficult, and yet he could neither untie the knots nor use a knife with his semi-paralysed fingers.

Progress was difficult, although the exertion generated energy and that energy warmed him. Little by little, he shivered less. When he heard the swoosh of oars through the water – because his teeth had ceased chattering – he knew he would make it to the shore.

He knew he would survive.

He was even sweating beneath the thermal jumper by the time he was dragging the boat on to the muddy beach.

He paused, resting against the boat, chest heaving until he got his breath back.

Standing again, Victor paused to look back out at the lake and the rifle lying useless on the bottom.

He gazed out at his failure and the problem it created.

He needed it if he was going up against the bounty hunters. They were no civilians. They weren't a biker gang who let themselves lose a fight against a single man.

Garrett and his crew were different.

Eight to twelve men.

Trained. Competent. Coordinated. Armed.

That wasn't the kind of battle for Victor to throw himself into without a weapon.

But he would because no one else was going to do so in his place.

The sucking mud of the beach was tough to traverse. His feet sank into it with every step, leaving behind deep footprints where the lake water didn't reach to cover them. He saw the path he had taken out of the forest, the footprints becoming more pronounced as the ground became wetter and softer.

He saw a second set of footprints. Bare feet.

Much smaller than his own, and shallow prints, a shorter distance between them.

A woman.

Same height and weight as Jennifer Welch.

Of course.

He had convinced her to back off because he said he would be gone soon. Gone before now.

He broke the arrangement.

He should be gone. There was no sensible reason for him to still be here and every reason not to be here.

Yet he was going nowhere.

The prints didn't reach as far to the water as his own. Victor pictured Welch taking off her shoes before stepping on to the muddy beach and following his own footprints until she stood just shy of the shore, gazing out at the lake and seeing his boat drifting on the water. At that distance, Victor would not have been able to see her in return against the backdrop of the trees.

How long had she stood there?

Not long, he decided, because even when remaining in one spot people rarely stood still for more than a few seconds. Had Welch remained on the shore for any length of time there would be signs of her having shifted her weight, shuffling, or shorter steps back and forth.

She had stood just long enough to see the boat, to picture him on board or in the water, and then she had returned to . . .

Where?

There were no signs of her nearby but there was no reason for Welch or her crew to be close.

They knew where he had been, so they knew how he had come here and where he would be going next.

Had things been the other way around Victor would have waited near the shore to take advantage of the moment of awkwardness of climbing out of a boat and dragging it on to the beach.

An easy kill.

The Chicago crew had not done so because Welch hadn't thought about the footprints in the mud. They were also organised crime enforcers used to operating in an urban environment. The outdoors wasn't their thing. They didn't like the idea of hiding in the undergrowth. Maybe they didn't want to ruin their suits. Maybe they didn't like the idea of being uncomfortable for an indeterminate period.

Each one might be a crack shot, but they didn't have the patience to kill someone like him.

Victor was patient.

He took his time to gather his things, ate an energy bar, and set off into the trees.

SIXTY-THREE

The truck lay fifty metres from the beach, parked off a narrow track that led from the highway. The trees were dense all around it, visibility cut short by trunks and foliage to less than five metres. There was no straight line from beach to truck; it would take Victor only a few minutes to reach it going along a direct route.

He took thirty minutes.

He approached in a wide circle, clockwise to keep his dominant hand and arm closest to any threats. He had no weapon beyond a small knife, but it was protocol nonetheless.

If the Chicago crew didn't have the patience to wait at the beach they might not have the patience to wait in the woods either. Still, Victor had to assume they were there. With four, they could have the truck surrounded, each member of the crew covering a different angle of approach. If he were Welch, that's what he would have done.

Victor circled around to approach the truck from the far side.

He moved from tree to tree, low and slow. He paused every few metres. He peered through the foliage. He listened hard.

By the time he could see the truck, he had seen and heard nothing to suggest anyone was near.

He remembered a time in Russia, on the Black Sea coast near the town of Sochi. In those woods he had believed himself to be alone as he waited to kill a target with a seven-hundred-metre rifle shot. He had been there for days, waiting for the perfect moment. He had not seen enemies hiding in the undergrowth and waiting to kill him. They had been wearing ghillie suits and had blended into the forest as might chameleons.

Welch's crew would have no ghillie suits. They were city people. Competent. Professionals. But not military.

He saw none of them because there were none present.

Which was interesting.

There were no footprints here, yet there were signs of their presence: crushed leaves on the forest floor and bent branches in the undergrowth.

No ambush at the beach.

No ambush here.

They didn't want a direct confrontation. They didn't trust themselves to remain hidden. They figured he might spot them as he had done before. They wanted this done without a firefight. A grievous error on their part, given he had no gun.

So, no ambush, no direct confrontation. Which meant it had to be a trap.

Victor lowered himself into a push-up position alongside the truck. He didn't need to roll on to his back and slide under to see there was something in the undercarriage that didn't belong.

It was nothing sophisticated. No custom-made bomb. Just a Claymore anti-personnel mine rigged with a remote detonator in the form of an old cell phone. They had secured it to the truck with duct tape, right beneath the driver's seat.

A regular Claymore was detonated by a clacker connected to a long wire that had to be unspooled far enough away that the soldier using it wouldn't be caught in the blast radius. Contained within a curved plastic shell was a strip of plastic explosive packed with steel ball bearings. The curvature directed the explosion and the resulting cloud of ball bearings in a sixty-degree arc to cover as wide an area as possible. The killing zone went all the way out to thirty metres with the ball bearings capable of going all the way to two hundred metres.

Detonated directly under the driver's seat, the truck would be ripped in half and Victor turned into a pink haze.

They weren't going for a clean kill but a certain kill. No comeback either, because there wouldn't be enough left of Victor ever to be traced to the Chicago job, the new head of the conglomerate, or Welch and her crew.

The Claymore had been designed way back in the fifties and been used in every US conflict since. There had to have been tens of thousands made, maybe hundreds of thousands. There was little to no chance one could be traced, Victor figured. He couldn't see any markings even to suggest when this one had been constructed.

He disconnected the cell phone from the detonator. Without an incoming call to send a current to the detonator, the plastic explosive inside the mine was quite safe. Years before, in the backstreets of war-torn Kabul, Victor had seen children playing with C4 to sculpt crude figurines while their parents smoked nearby.

He realised those children would be adults now.

Maybe with children of their own.

What were they playing with now, he wondered.

Victor slipped the phone into a pocket and tucked the mine under his arm so he could flex his hands. They were still stiff from the cold.

If Welch and her crew had set a remote-detonated bomb beneath his truck, then they would only set it off when they knew for sure he was behind the wheel and above the Claymore.

Which not only meant they had to see him.

It meant they were waiting for him where they knew for certain they would see him.

Victor was going to make sure they did.

SIXTY-FOUR

Welch wasn't good at waiting. She wasn't patient. Patience as a virtue was overrated. What did it ever really achieve? If you were patient, you just advertised to people that they could take advantage of you. No one took advantage of Welch.

Her guys were bored.

One in the passenger seat of their ride. The other two in the back. She was behind the wheel, of course, which gave her the best view because they were parked off the shoulder of the highway, a way back, but facing the turnoff to the track.

Overhanging branches cast shadows across the windshield and the hood. Those shadows drifted back and forth in a sleepy rhythm as the breeze pushed and pulled at the trees.

The car was no off-road beast. They were from Chicago, after all. Welch had to be careful where she took it up here in the wilds. The track that led to the little muddy beach, for example, was a no-go. Even where she had parked was a risk, with all the slick grass and undergrowth.

Given she hadn't wanted to push their luck, the car was not hidden. When the truck rolled out to the intersection and he looked right he would see them. Maybe not straight away, but a second or two later tops.

It wouldn't make a difference.

It wouldn't make a difference because if he could see them then they could see him.

The guy in the passenger seat had a cell phone in his lap, ready.

Welch wasn't as bored as her colleagues. There was a tinge of excitement teasing her spine, causing her to be restless. She was picturing the moment the red nose of the truck appeared out of the treeline. She was picturing the driver glancing right to check the traffic.

She was picturing his face when she smiled at him.

She was no sadist, but she owed him that much. They had made a deal and he had broken it. He had made Welch look like a fool. Thank goodness her boss didn't know any better and believed the task had been completed because that's what Welch told him. She wasn't just here to right a wrong, but to save her skin.

The guy in the passenger seat knew explosives and had rigged up the bomb. She didn't have a clue how those things worked; that was why she only ever hired good people, the best people.

She just hoped they wouldn't all fall asleep waiting.

It had been for ever since she had stood on the muddy beach in her bare feet and gazed out across the lake. It had been for ever since she had assured her crew they had plenty of time to set the bomb before the fisherman returned.

Turned out she was correct.

Plenty of time had become too much time.

Welch wouldn't share it with her crew, but she was growing concerned he wasn't coming back at all.

That wouldn't just be embarrassing but humiliating. She wouldn't be able to live it down.

Figuratively and literally.

The latter because her boss would have her killed if he so much as suspected that she hadn't done the job she had been sent to do and then lied about it. If the fisherman escaped, Welch would have to kill her entire crew to ensure no one ever told of her mistake, her deception.

It would be quick. She already had it planned out in case she ever needed to do it. It was a simple plan but an effective one. She would have the newest member of the crew killed by the two others. Then, the longest-serving member of the crew would kill the next, leaving only one alive for Welch to handle herself.

Then what would she do?

Hire a new crew.

Back in business with no chance of comeback before the week was out.

'There he is,' one of her guys said.

Deep in thought, she had not been paying attention, but there he was at the intersection.

The nose of the red truck emerged from the trees and the rest of the vehicle came into view, coming to a pause at the stop sign.

'Be ready,' she told the guy in the passenger seat.

'I am,' he said, sitting up, taking the phone in both hands.

Welch watched as the fisherman looked right, checking for traffic.

She watched as he looked her way.
Their eyes met.
She smiled. 'Do it.'
The guy in the passenger seat hit the send button.

SIXTY-FIVE

Did she fall asleep?

Welch wasn't certain, despite the relative ease of answering such a question. Had day become night or had she been dreaming? She couldn't be sure. She couldn't be sure of anything. Her mind was fragmented and disjointed, and it took an enormous effort of will to drag those disparate pieces back together long enough to form coherent thought.

She was drunk and hung-over and awake and asleep all at the same time.

She saw nothing.

She heard ... something. Noises.

A strange crackling sound. Hissing. Roaring?

She moved.

Cried out.

Pain in her legs made tears well in her eyes. She opened them, realising she hadn't been able to see because they had been shut.

She opened them to see asphalt inches away. Dark road surface specked and smeared with blood.

Her blood.

It ran down her face and dripped from her chin. There was a wound on her head, somewhere at the crown. She crept fingers along her skull until she found a sliver of metal buried in her scalp. A single touch of it sent out shockwaves of agony so she left it there.

She was on her front, prostrate in the road.

Her arms worked but not her legs. They were a constant source of unrelenting pain.

She managed to turn her head far enough to look back over her shoulder.

Welch didn't see her legs. Not at first. Instead, she saw the burning wreckage of the car and the eviscerated corpses of her crew still inside. One might have been moving, still alive, but she couldn't see enough to know. There was too much smoke and too much fire.

Her legs were a mess. Shredded trousers, glimpses of bloody skin and bright bone. She wasn't sure her feet were still attached.

Fragments of chassis, bodywork and glass lay scattered across the highway. She saw a door peppered with perfect spherical holes.

Then she understood.

The bomb. The Claymore.

It had detonated as planned but not where it was supposed to have exploded. It had been slipped beneath her car and they hadn't seen. Under the back, which is why she had survived. Sitting in the driver's seat, she had been furthest away from the explosion.

He must have crossed the road far behind them, crept up on them through the trees while all their attention had been set the opposite way.

The target.

Welch saw him approaching through the rippling heat haze as a dark apparition manifesting out of the liquid horizon. He seemed no longer human but pure malice.

Death himself had come.

'I'll do you a deal,' Death said.

Welch struggled to see him. She had blood in her eyes. Smoke and pain made them water.

'I need guns.'

Welch blinked and stared and said nothing.

'If you have one on you or have some nearby, I'll call you an ambulance. The paramedics might be able to save you. At the very least they can make your passing less agonising.'

Welch coughed blood. 'The car ...'

She tried to gesture. She tried to say more but it was too hard.

'All your weapons are in the car?' Death asked.

She nodded. 'Help me.'

Death stood there for a moment longer, peering over Welch to the inferno raging behind her.

'Too bad,' Death said.

He drifted back towards the heat haze, entering the rippling horizon that parted for him and then enveloped him like a shroud, taking him once more from this mortal realm and leaving behind only an empty highway.

'Take me with you,' Welch begged the emptiness.

SIXTY-SIX

Four corpses on the side of the road was far from an ideal situation, but Victor was sanguine. Better to be alive with such a problem than dead without. He felt guilty for Linette, however, who was going to have a lot of work to do in the coming hours and days and weeks and months.

There was no time to clean up the mess and he had no means to do so either. There was a burning car on the side of the road, three corpses inside and a soon-to-be corpse nearby.

He climbed back into his truck and drove away with smoke and flames in his rear-view mirror.

He called Linette.

'How much progress have you made with the list?'

'You mean the list you left with me while you went fishing?'

'That's the one.'

She sighed. 'I'm doing my best.'

'Have you narrowed it down?'

'I'm doing my best,' she said for a second time.

321

'I know you are,' he said. 'I'm not asking if you've identified the boyfriend, but if you're any closer.'

'Halfway there,' she told him. 'I've seen who is married, who cohabits, who lives in the middle of town. I've crossed off those and anyone too old and too young. I've—'

'Tell me where you are. I'll come to you.'

'I'm not done yet.'

'I want to take a look,' he said.

'You do?'

'I want to help.'

'I'm at work,' she said. 'I can't have a civilian sitting at my desk with me, much as I would like the pleasure of your relentlessly witty company. People would talk. They're already talking, I bet.'

The words were light, but he detected a serious undertone. Perhaps her boss had quizzed her already on why she had been seen sharing information with a member of the public, or maybe she had let some other case slip.

He didn't want to push it.

'Besides,' she said. 'We're stretched pretty thin right now with the dead meth cook, the burnt lab and the seven busted-up bikers. I'm still confused how a rival gang rode into the neighbourhood, kicked the crap out of them, and rode out again without anyone noticing.'

Victor remained silent.

'Hey,' Linette continued. 'Since I'm doing you a favour perhaps you can do one for me in return. You seem friendly with Pete, perhaps you can remind him that he's not doing anyone any favours pretending he didn't see what went down outside his bar.'

'Perhaps he didn't see.'

'Funny,' she said without inflection. 'But how is that even possible?'

'I'll talk to him,' Victor said.

'Thank you.'

He drove past the motel. The two brand-new Escalades were not parked in the lot. Garrett and his team were on the move.

'Maybe I can help remotely,' he said. 'Can you see who has a firearm registered?'

'Almost all of them have a licence and own a gun. I can see rifles, shotguns, pistols ... We like our toys here in the Great North.'

'Who has the most guns?'

'Half have two or more.'

'Who of that half has a military background?'

'Let me look ... Seven. Maybe more.'

'Why maybe? Surely they do or they don't?'

'It's not as simple as that. I have two guys on this list who were born overseas so I can't see if they were in the military or not.'

Victor pictured a man with a lean, strong build, yet who was not limber. He now saw that lack of mobility as the result of an injury. An old war wound, he now realised.

Linette continued: 'I have a guy from Mexico and one from France.'

Un homme de goût, Victor thought.

He pictured a bartender starting his shift, tired, with dirt under his fingernails. Tired and dirty not from working on a car as Victor had initially deduced, but at the quarry. A man who questioned why Victor had not left as planned. He had not spooked Michelle, but her boyfriend.

'Look,' Linette said. 'I'm going as fast as I can. It'll be done soon.'

Victor knew that already.

'Let me know if I can do anything,' he said.

'Thanks. I will.'

He hung up and accelerated to the bar, stopping the truck right outside, not taking the time to reverse-park and face the exit.

The door hadn't swung shut behind him before he said to Big Pete, 'Where's the other barman, the French guy?'

Big Pete was standing behind the bar. He tensed when he saw Victor, taking a step backwards in an instinctual, defensive reaction.

'I thought I told you not to come back here. I don't care who started it. I don't care if you threw first or they did, I've had my fill of talking to cops about it. Word gets around. Folk get twitchy about drinking in the same place where people get their limbs broken in multiple places. The register is down by half already.'

Victor approached. 'I need to speak to the French bartender. It's important.'

'Did you not hear what I just said? I need you gone.'

'I'll go and never come back if you help me speak to your bartender.'

'I'm not helping you speak to Naël. I'm not helping you do anything. In fact, I've already helped you. I've covered your ass with the cops, so let's call it quits.'

'A million dollars,' Victor said.

'Excuse me?'

'I appreciate you not calling the police last night and I'm sorry my actions have caused you to lose business. To make up for that, I'll send you a million dollars just as soon as I've left town.'

Big Pete laughed. 'Sure you will. Sure you have a million bucks just sitting around with my name on it.'

'Naël's in trouble,' Victor said.

'He's not working today,' Big Pete said, leaning on the bar surface with his fingers spread out wide. 'I can pass on a message if that helps. He's back in tomorrow night. Leave me your number and I'll get him to give you a call.'

'I have to speak to him in person.'

Big Pete shrugged to say *too bad*.

'Where does he live? I'll go to him.'

'I can't tell you that. I mean, I can. But I'm not going to. I won't. No way in hell, pal.'

Victor frowned at the blasphemy but didn't comment. 'He's in danger.'

Big Pete was sceptical. 'Danger?'

'He's in danger. His girlfriend is in danger. Her child is in danger. They don't know it yet. It's coming for them and it's close and they have absolutely no idea how bad it's going to get.'

Big Pete listened.

'Tell me how to find Naël so I can warn them. If I don't, if you don't help me help them, no one else will.'

Big Pete was frowning. 'What kind of danger are we talking about here?'

'The absolute worst kind. Worse than the Nameless. Worse than me.'

'You're serious, aren't you?'

He nodded.

Big Pete stared at him for a moment.

Victor stared back.

'You'd better be legit, pal. This better be serious like a heart attack. It better be life and death.'

'It is.'

Big Pete exhaled and grabbed a napkin. He started scribbling an address. He glanced up at Victor. 'Just who the hell are you, anyway?'

'I don't even know any more.'

SIXTY-SEVEN

The cabin was set far back from the highway. A single-lane track twisted its way through the dense forest, between thick trees, climbing steadily for almost two miles before it became a driveway of sorts. The building was two storeys of timber beams sealed with pale chinking. The roof of dark tiles rose to a sharp peak. Behind the house the land ascended to form a jagged hill that bordered the lake. Dense trees covered the hill.

A single vehicle was parked outside the cabin. It was a Land Rover, old and reliable. Mud stained the wheel arches and bodywork. Bumper stickers were unreadable.

A diesel generator rumbled at the side of the building. Inside, the cabin was warm and humid. Michelle sat at the dining table. Joshua sat next to her. On the tabletop were specialised learning texts, visual aids, development aids, crayons and colouring books.

'Honey, if the mouse has three pieces of cheese but one has gone bad then how many pieces of cheese can the mouse eat?'

'Four.'

'That's almost right. It would be correct if the mouse had three pieces of cheese and one more.'

'I don't get it.'

'Just try again. If we take one from three, what do we have?'

Joshua stared at the table. He was silent.

Naël, towelling his wet hair, said, 'Maybe he's had enough schooling for one day.'

'He's doing great,' she said without looking. 'Aren't you, baby?'

Joshua said, 'I'm stupid.'

'No, you're not. Don't say that.'

Naël said, 'Maybe he's—'

Michelle cast him a quick look. 'He's stressed. He doesn't understand what's going on. Okay?'

Naël draped the towel over a shoulder and massaged Michelle's neck. 'I don't mean to criticise. I know this is tough for you both.'

'I'm sorry,' she said. 'My nerves are stretched to breaking point. How much longer do you think it will be?'

'I wish I knew. These things take time. Driver's licence is simple, he told me. Passports are a whole other thing.'

She saw Joshua was tense, and stood, guiding Naël away from the table and into the den.

'What if they just take the money and not deliver?'

'They won't do that.'

'How do you know? It's not like we can go to the police if they do. We've handed over all the money to strangers with only their word to go on.'

He held her. 'They're not strangers. My guy vouched for them. Just give it time.'

'How much time do you think we have? The fisherman

is bound to have passed on everything he's found out. They're coming.'

'We have a head start. No one knows you're both here with me.'

'You think no one can find that out? They're coming. I'm telling you they're coming.'

'And we'll be gone when they get here. A little luck and we'll be in another country.'

'I'm the unluckiest person alive,' she said. 'I don't think for one second my luck is going to change now.'

'Have a little faith then.'

'Faith?' She sneered. 'Faith never helped me before. It won't help me now.'

Naël said, 'Then forget luck, forget faith. You can rely on me. I'll never let you down.'

She kissed him. 'I know I can. I know you won't.'

Joshua appeared in the doorway. 'There's someone outside.'

Michelle moved fast, rushing to him and taking him by the hand.

Naël moved just as fast, grabbing a Benelli shotgun from hooks on the wall and opening the drawer of a sideboard to take out spare shells.

'Where did you see him, honey?' Michelle asked, lowering to a squat so she was at eye-level with her son.

'At the front,' he said, pointing. 'I stood on my chair and I saw a man in the trees through the window.'

Michelle looked at Naël, terror in her eyes.

'It's going to be okay,' he told her, stuffing shells into a pocket of his sweatpants and opening another drawer to get his pistol. He took it to her, pushed it into her hands. 'Remember what I—'

She took it. 'I remember.'

Joshua said, 'What's wrong, Mama?'

She wiped her eyes with a sleeve. 'Nothing, baby. We're going to play that game we practised. Like hide and seek.'

'Do I go first?'

'Yes, you first. Don't forget to count to a thousand.'

'Ugh.' He threw his hands to his sides. 'It takes for ever.'

She forced a smile. 'That's why you keep winning.'

Naël, shotgun loaded and a shell racked, nodded.

'Go on now,' Michelle said to Joshua. 'Go hide real good or you'll lose.'

'I never lose,' he said, trudging away.

Once he had gone, she said to Naël, 'If anything happens to him—'

'I won't let it,' he said, peering out of the window at the front.

'Do you see anyone?'

He shook his head. 'Maybe he imagined it.'

'He didn't,' she said. 'This is it. I know it.'

'No vehicle. I can't even hear one.'

'They'd park far away so we didn't know they were coming. We could be surrounded.'

She raised the pistol and aimed it at the door.

He gripped the shotgun in both hands. 'Anyone who comes through that door dies.'

'What about someone who climbed through an upstairs window?' Victor said from behind them.

SIXTY-EIGHT

Frightened civilians with guns weren't known for their self-control, so Victor made sure he was out of the line of fire. He stood on the far side of an interior wall and spoke through the open doorway. It wasn't the best time to announce his presence, but he figured the longer he waited the more anxious they would become, and time was a luxury none of them had.

The French bartender, Naël, shouted at him, 'Show yourself!'

Victor could not see either Naël or Michelle but he knew they were now facing the open doorway and their weapons were pointed his way. The interior wall was comprised of thick timbers like the exterior walls, so there was no danger of them shooting through it.

'I'm afraid I can't do that just yet,' Victor replied. 'But I mean you no harm. I'm here to help.'

'We know exactly why you're here,' Michelle shouted. 'You're here for Joshua.'

'I'm not.'

'I'll kill you,' she said.

'I believe you,' he said. 'But you need to be smart about this. I know you're frightened and I know why, but it's not me you should be scared of. I'm here to warn you they're coming.'

'I know that. I know they are, and I know you brought them here.'

'I assure you that's not the case.'

Naël said, 'You came to the bar. You asked about Michelle, about Joshua. I know you're not just a fisherman.'

'For all intents and purposes I was just a fisherman,' Victor said. 'But now I'm here to help you get out of here.'

'You really think that's going to work?' Michelle said. 'You think we're just going to get into your car voluntarily?'

'That's the plan,' Victor said. 'The sooner we get out of here the better. They didn't know where you were before, but if I found out, so will they.'

'If what you say is true,' Naël said, 'then show yourself.'

'I'm thinking that's not in my best interests right now.'

'Who is "they"?' Michelle said.

'His name is Garrett,' Victor answered. 'He has between seven and eleven men with him in two Escalades. Bounty hunters. They were staying at the motel. They turned up yesterday. They've already been to your house.'

'Why so many?' Naël asked.

'Because they know you're ex-military.'

'Long time ago. When I was young. And I was a medic.'

'But in special forces, right? They've done their homework. They're expecting resistance so they're using overwhelming odds to try to avoid a confrontation. They'll kill you anyway.

They only want Joshua and they don't want to leave behind witnesses to a kidnapping.'

Silence.

Victor pictured Michelle and Naël looking at each other, perhaps mouthing a brief exchange.

What do we do?

I don't know.

We can't trust him.

What if he's right?

He said, 'If I were lying to you, if I wanted to trick you, I would be armed.'

No response.

'If I was sent by your ex-husband I would have a gun. I could have shot you both in the back without saying a word, couldn't I?'

'So?' Michelle said.

'But I don't have a gun,' Victor continued. 'I'm unarmed. I'm going to step out now with hands raised to prove it. I wouldn't do that if I meant you harm, would I?'

Naël said, 'Do it.'

Victor raised his hands and stepped through the doorway.

Naël had a shotgun, a matt-black Benelli pump-action. Michelle had a Beretta 92F. They held them well, Naël's military experience showing in his stance, his aim. Michelle was a pure civilian but she had practised. Both muzzles were pointed Victor's way. Point-blank range.

'See?' he said.

They were closer than necessary. Both within four metres. A slight distraction and he could rush one before they could get off a shot. Michelle first, because the Frenchman wouldn't risk a spread of pellets with his partner in the line of fire.

Garrett's here, he could say, glancing past them at the window.

They would be compelled to look. Their fear would ensure that.

When they glanced back, Victor would have Michelle as a human shield. Then it would be over.

He stood still, hands up near his face.

Naël said, 'It's a trick. He's trying to keep us occupied while the others get here.'

'Then we'll kill him,' Michelle said, her voice strained but her face stern and resolute.

Victor's gaze passed between them. 'I'm here to help.'

'Help?'

'Come with me,' he said. 'We'll take my truck. If the Land Rover is in your name, then they know about it.'

'How?'

'They're bounty hunters. It's what they do. That they didn't already know about this cabin tells me you don't have a lease and you pay cash.'

Naël said nothing.

'Then we're safe,' Michelle said.

'Eight to twelve guys,' Victor said.

'You told us that already.'

'That's eight to twelve guys asking questions. They have your name. They know about your SUV. They know your military experience. The only thing they don't have is your address. But the quarry does. Who else does? Is there anyone in town you've ever brought back here? Is the owner local? Did you ever have a tradesman out to fix something? Ever had someone drop you off? Ever had a delivery?'

Naël's face glimmered with sweat. He didn't answer.

Michelle answered by lowering the Beretta. 'What do we do?'

'Get Joshua,' Victor said. 'Get out of here.'

Naël said, 'He's lying. He's bluffing.'

Michelle approached him. 'He's not. He came to warn us. He's right. If he wanted to take Joshua this isn't how he would do it.'

'How does he know all this? I told you. I told you there was something wrong about him.'

'I'm glad you did,' Victor said. 'You have good instincts. If you hadn't, Michelle and Joshua would have stayed in their home and Garrett and his team would have already taken him back to his father, and I'd have left town before it even happened.'

'They're not trying to take Joshua for his father.'

SIXTY-NINE

Michelle looked down as she spoke. Embarrassed. Ashamed. The Frenchman stepped closer to comfort her, and she shooed him away.

'Joshua's dad wasn't a good husband, but I was young and stupid when I married him and had no self-esteem. It was only when Joshua came along that I understood what a horrible man he truly was. He couldn't handle Joshua's . . . He couldn't love him. When I left, he didn't care. He was glad to see the back of us.'

Victor listened.

'His parents worshipped him,' Michelle continued. 'They're horrible people , yet he was their pride and joy, their only heir. They treated him like a prince. Beyond spoilt. Then he got sick. And he wasn't going to get better. That's when I heard from his parents for the first time in years. They, like their son, had never loved Joshua, but they told me they had had a change of heart. I wanted to believe it. I really did. But I knew, I knew the second we met up with them . . . The

336

way they looked at Joshua. I'll never forget it. The distaste. They didn't even try and hide it. There was no love in them for him. So, no more visits. They got angry. They had all the money in the world, they reminded me. Joshua could have everything he needed if he lived with them. It wasn't about what was best for Joshua. He's simply the last remaining connection they have to their son. They only want Joshua as a replacement. I told them where they could stick their offer. They said it wasn't up for debate. I could either do the right thing or they would do it for me. I knew what they meant. If my husband was awful, they are worse. They always get what they want. When Joshua's dad died, I knew they'd try and take my boy.'

Victor said, 'That won't happen.'

'Why are you here?' Michelle said. 'Why are you doing this?'

Victor didn't answer because Joshua had entered the room. He wore green shorts and a white T-shirt. No super-hero motif on his socks this time.

'Hello, Wilson Murdoch.'

Michelle put her right hand to the small of her back to hide the pistol. Naël set the shotgun down.

Victor turned to face the boy. 'Hello, Joshua Joseph Levell.'

Michelle stepped towards him, lowering herself to his level. 'What are you doing, baby? You were supposed to count to a thousand.'

'I did,' Joshua protested. 'All elephants. Every single one. I promise.'

She wiped her eyes. 'Okay. Good. Well done. You win again.'

He was suspicious. 'Did you even look?'

She hesitated, not wanting to lie.

Victor said, 'It's my fault. They were doing a great job of looking for you, but I turned up and got in the way.'

Joshua blew out a long sigh. 'That's okay. I always win anyway. It's getting boring.' He had an idea. 'Can Wilson Murdoch play? Maybe he can beat me.'

'I don't think we can,' Michelle said. 'We're going to go for a drive first.'

Naël approached. 'I'm not sure that's such a good—'

Michelle kept a smile on her face as she said, 'We don't have a choice, do we?'

Naël looked from her to Victor and back again. Hesitated. Then nodded. 'I'll grab our things.'

'There's no time,' Victor said.

'We have bags already packed and ready. We're prepared for this.'

Victor said, 'Get them.'

'What's going on?' Joshua asked.

His mother stroked his hair. 'Remember I said one day we would go on a road trip?'

'And see the Grand Canyon?'

She nodded, swiping at the corners of her eyes. 'That's right, baby. We're going to see the Grand Canyon and we're going to have ice cream on the beach and we'll do all the fun things we talked about.'

Joshua beamed while his mother tried to hide her tears.

'Is Wilson Murdoch coming too?'

Michelle looked at Victor.

'Sure,' he said. 'If you want me to come along I—'

He didn't finish. He took a few steps towards the front door, towards the window. He'd heard a noise.

Michelle heard it too. 'Oh no.'

Vehicles. Two engines. Two exhausts.

At the window, Victor couldn't see them but knew it was a matter of seconds instead of minutes. They were on the dirt track, a few hundred metres away and hidden by the trees.

Michelle said, 'What do we do?'

'My truck is parked on the other side of the hill, by the waterfall.'

'How?' Naël said, re-entering the room with two pre-packed sports bags.

'I came up the creek in case they had eyes on the track. Go up the hill, not around.'

'Two miles,' Naël said, nodding. 'Up and over. Double that to circumvent.'

'That's right.' He tossed him the keys.

Michelle looked to Victor.

'Go,' he said. 'If no one's here they'll look for tracks. One team will follow you on foot, the other will turn around in their vehicle and head you off.'

She hesitated.

'I'll keep them busy but go as fast as you can.'

Still she hesitated.

'Go,' he said again. 'Every second matters now.'

Joshua frowned. 'Why isn't Wilson Murdoch coming with us?'

Michelle didn't answer. Naël didn't know what to say.

Victor said, 'I'll catch you up.'

Michelle said, 'I don't know how to—'

'You don't need to. Just go.'

Naël took her arm. 'Come on. There's no time.'

She resisted, but only a little, as he pulled her through

the room to the back of the cabin. As they reached the back door, Naël tossed Victor the Benelli.

Victor caught it in his left hand.

'Good luck,' the Frenchman told him.

Victor resisted saying he didn't believe in luck and nodded instead.

Then they were gone.

He had time for one quick recce to familiarise himself with the layout of the cabin before the first Escalade pulled up outside. The second arrived moments later.

Before the first bounty hunter was out of one of the vehicles, Victor had the front door of the cabin open and had fired the shotgun.

SEVENTY

The penetrative power of a pellet of double-ought was negligible, so he didn't aim for the occupants. Not at ten metres away, where the cloud of pellets would spread out to a tennis-ball-size diameter. They would go through window glass, but would deflect as they passed and not hit where he aimed, and if they made it through a door they would have little energy left to cause a severe wound.

Instead, he aimed for the Escalade itself. The closest wheel. The closest tyre.

It exploded.

Rubber stripped away in flayed black snakes. Air rushed out. The nose of the SUV dipped.

He pumped out the empty shell. It smoked and cart-wheeled through the air.

He shot again. This time for the rear wheel. The pellets hit a little too low, some striking the ground and sending up sprays of mud. Enough hit the tyre for the vehicle to visibly drop. That was all he needed. The Escalade was going nowhere now.

It couldn't chase Joshua, Michelle and Naël.

It couldn't head them off either.

The occupants of the disabled SUV were already low in their seats, expecting blasts to come their way. The doors on the far side were opening so they could make their escape.

Victor ignored them for the moment because the second Escalade was shielded by the first and the men inside that vehicle were taking cover behind it, ready to return fire.

Before they could, Victor was back inside the cabin. He'd had the door open only enough for him to see the vehicles. At range, in the shadows, they wouldn't be able to identify him beyond his gender. He slammed the door shut and dropped to the floor as the bounty hunters opened up.

They were well armed, as he had expected.

A deafening unleashing of automatic fire came his way – assault rifles and sub-machine guns.

Dozens of holes appeared through the front door. Splinters and wood dust turned the air thick. Glass shattered. Ornaments exploded.

No rounds made it through the walls, however. Not through timbers thicker than Victor's torso, but he felt the reverberations like a hailstorm on his back. Paintings on the interior wall shook. One fell from its hook.

The shooting was over in a few seconds.

A short, effective show of force from half of the bounty hunters to keep him down while the others hurried into position.

Then, silence.

'It doesn't have to be this way,' a voice shouted from outside.

Garrett.

Victor didn't respond because he didn't want Garrett to know it was him until it was absolutely necessary. He didn't want the bounty hunters to suspect Joshua was already gone.

The longer they thought he was inside, the bigger the lead Victor could give them.

'Hand over the boy and no one has to get hurt.'

To be static in a firefight was to die, so Victor shuffled across the floor on his stomach, reaching the staircase and only standing when he knew there was no line of sight through the window.

He dashed up the stairs.

He entered a small bedroom, made his way to the window, and peered out just enough to see the three Escalades now out front and the bounty hunters taking cover behind them.

Twelve, he counted, disappointed.

The very top end of his estimate.

For an instant, he imagined the hunting rifle in his hands instead of the shotgun. He imagined it dried and greased and assembled. He imagined taking off the scope to use the iron sights for faster target acquisition at close range. He imagined pivoting from his position next to the window, lining up the first shot, squeezing the trigger. He imagined a neat hole in the glass and a thump in his shoulder.

One dead bounty hunter.

A split-second to work the receiver as he adjusted his aim.

Another dead bounty hunter.

Maybe another two dead before they realised where he was and what was happening. The SUVs were armour against shotgun pellets but paper to a .338 calibre rifle round. They couldn't hide from him.

A thirty-three per cent reduction in opposition before they had even returned fire.

But he had no rifle.

Instead, he only had three shells left in the shotgun.

He had to make every single one of those three count, which meant wasting one now at targets too obscured for a shotgun's inaccuracy, but he needed to keep them pinned down as long as possible.

He shot through the window, exploding glass, aiming at the closest bounty hunter behind the closest SUV.

A hit, but not enough pellets to take him down. He cried out, one shoulder bloody, dropping lower behind the vehicle.

Victor was already backing away before bullets destroyed the rest of the window, shredding curtains and plugging holes in the bedroom ceiling and walls. A light bulb shattered. Glass rained over his head.

He made it back downstairs before the shooting ceased. He was at the main window on the ground floor by the time Garrett called again.

'This is the last chance for both of you. Surrender now while you still can.'

Both of you.

They had fallen for Victor's ruse, believing there was a shooter on the ground floor and one upstairs too: Michelle and Naël. That would make them much more hesitant. That would buy Joshua and the others more time.

'You can't win this,' Garrett called. 'One after the other, come out with your hands to the sky and you get to live.'

Victor moved to the front door.

Reached across and turned the handle and pushed it open a little without exposing himself.

344

He pictured half of the bounty hunters now watching the open doorway in expectation while the other half covered the upstairs window.

Which meant no one was watching the ground-floor window.

'Nice and slow and no one has to die,' Garrett continued.

Victor ducked down beneath the window.

'*Do it*,' Garrett called out.

Victor popped up and fired the shotgun.

A snapshot, because he couldn't risk the time it took to aim, but still a good shot.

One of the bounty hunters covering the upstairs window was exposed at the corner of an Escalade, looking up. The double-ought hit him in the flank, between the armpit and the hip. Clothing tore and he fell to the ground, but there was no blood and he scrambled into cover as Victor ducked back down behind the safety of the timbers.

Body armour under the outer jacket.

One shell left in the shotgun.

He would have to go for a limb or a headshot.

This time when Garrett spoke, he didn't call out. Instead, he gave an order to his men.

'Gas them.'

SEVENTY-ONE

Victor didn't have enough time to prepare – they already had a launcher ready – and the best he could do was dash from the window.

He heard the distinctive pop of a compressed-air launcher, a second later the thud of the grenade hitting an interior wall, and then the clatter of it rolling around on the floor.

Then he heard the hiss.

No doubt CS gas because they couldn't risk anything more toxic with a child inside they needed alive. Victor didn't hang around to find out. He raced up the stairs, which would only be a temporary respite until the gas spread upwards, but still a respite.

Yet far shorter than he had hoped because there was another pop and another gas canister entered the cabin through the upstairs window.

They had bought his ruse, of course.

He slammed the door shut to the bedroom to slow down the spread and headed to the bathroom. It was a small space but it did have a shower and that was all he needed from it. He twisted the dial to turn it on and cold water sprayed down. He kept twisting until the pressure was at its maximum. He grabbed a towel, soaked it under the spray, then laid it on the floor outside the bedroom to seal the gap beneath the door.

White fumes were already snaking through it; he coughed, and his eyes watered as the gas entered his system.

He didn't know if they would wait for the gas to do its job and flush the cabin or if they had masks and would use the gas to cover their entry.

Either way, it was bad.

He had slowed the spread from the gas grenade in the bedroom. He couldn't do anything about the one on the ground floor. An opaque white cloud swirled at the bottom of the staircase. The entire ground-floor space had filled with gas. It rose in snaking wisps up the stairs.

Victor knew he had a minute, maybe two.

Then, he would be incapacitated by coughing and blinded by the intense burning in his eyes.

In the bathroom, he stripped off his shirt. Tore a sleeve away at the seam and soaked it under the shower. He then wrapped it around his mouth and nose and tied it into a knot at the back of his skull.

His lungs already felt tight.

His eyes already streamed tears.

Maybe not even a minute.

Whether they had masks and were about to storm the building or were waiting to flush out those inside, the bounty hunters would exploit the distraction of the gas to change positions. Flanking would be the most obvious course of action. They would surround the house to make sure no one could get away.

That they hadn't done so already said that they knew the terrain. There was nowhere to go on foot except near-endless wilderness, so no escape as far as they were concerned. They didn't know about Victor's presence or that his truck was parked at the creek. As far as Garrett and his crew were concerned, there was no escape for Joshua.

He hoped Naël was carrying Joshua and they were running harder than they had ever run before.

He hoped they didn't get lost in the trees. It would be tough-going up the hill. Steep. Difficult terrain. Lots of boulders and outcrops and gorges to avoid.

He moved to a window at the back of the cabin, intending to climb outside, maybe on to the roof or down to the ground if he had time.

He peered out of the window only to immediately throw himself away because a bounty hunter outside was already covering it with an assault rifle and opened fire when he saw a figure at the window.

Sheets of glass fell away from the pane.

A thick splinter of wood the size of his index finger tore away from the frame and stabbed into Victor's chest just below the clavicle.

He used the wall as cover, ignoring the splinter, the pain, the blood.

He told himself to think of something, fast.

Nothing.

No plan. No strategy.

The bounty hunters had the cabin covered. He couldn't leave. He couldn't stay.

He had clipped one and winded another but neither were out of action, so it was still twelve against one and he was down to a single shotgun shell.

He coughed despite the wet rag over his mouth and nose. He blinked away the relentless welling of tears from his eyes that felt on fire.

It was a lost cause.

I never pick a fight I can't win, he had once said to explain the fact he was still breathing despite endless enemies.

He couldn't win this fight.

But he could still buy Joshua more time.

Victor surrendered.

SEVENTY-TWO

He didn't rush, however. He waited. He dragged it out as long as possible. He sat in the bathtub with a wet towel draped over his head and cold water from the shower raining down over him. His eyes still stung and he still coughed, but the CS gas couldn't reach its full effect.

The bounty hunters stormed the house after about two minutes, once it was clear the gas alone wouldn't clear out the cabin.

Five entered.

They wore state-of-the-art masks with charcoal filters that sucked the CS out of the air. They wore body armour – Kevlar vests backed up with ceramic plates over the heart. They had kneepads of toughened polymer, tactical gloves, quality footwear. They wore earpieces and throat mics. They had sidearms holstered at their thighs, ammunition pouches with spare magazines for their pistols and primary weapons. The latter were a range of advanced firearms, suitable for close quarters: Heckler & Koch UMPs, Fabrique Nationale P90s and SCAR carbines, and Mossberg SPXs.

The bounty hunters cleared the ground floor like the pros they were before they came upstairs.

Victor heard their boots on the creaking steps, then on the landing.

He had left the bathroom door open so they would hear the shower and see someone beneath it.

He had his hands up. He had left the Benelli in the doorway so they knew he was unarmed, so they wouldn't come in shooting or throwing grenades.

He couldn't see them when they entered the room, but he heard them, he felt their presence.

A shadow fell across the towel. Then the shower ceased spraying down water.

'What have we here?' a voice asked.

Not Garrett.

The towel was pulled from Victor's head and he only caught a glimpse of the man before the CS gas burned his eyes. He instinctively squeezed his eyelids shut.

'Where's the boy?' the man said.

He didn't wait for an answer. He grabbed hold of Victor and dragged him out of the bathtub.

Victor fought every instinct he had that compelled him to go for joints, pressure points, to grapple and disarm, to choke and strike and kill.

He let the bounty hunter pull him from the tub and shove him to the floor.

He expected a kick and was tensed before the toe of a boot struck his abdomen. He grimaced and grunted.

'The boy?' the man demanded.

Victor acted passive. He didn't resist as the man took a handful of his hair to drag him across the floor. Victor opened his eyes to take a brief look through the burning and the tears to see three other bounty hunters on the landing.

'What is it?' a voice called from downstairs.

This time Victor recognised Garrett's voice.

'White male,' the bounty hunter called back. 'Thirties. Possible match for Naël Lebel. Rest of the upstairs is clear.'

'Bring him to me,' Garrett ordered.

Strong hands hoisted Victor to his feet and marched him down the stairs. He expected to be shoved but they didn't want to hurt him any more than necessary. The Frenchman wasn't the prize and couldn't tell them where to find Joshua with a broken neck.

Victor stumbled on the descent, unable to open his eyes and see where he was planting his feet. Only the hands gripping his arm and shoulder kept him from falling.

On the ground floor, he was pushed through the front door and out of the cabin.

His eyes were still pinched shut by the CS gas.

'You have got to be kidding,' Garrett said.

'He was in the shower,' the bounty hunter who found him in the bathroom said. 'Had a towel over his head.'

'Of course he did.'

Another bounty hunter said, 'Cabin is empty. No sign of the kid or the mother.'

'And no boyfriend either,' Garrett said, tugging down the soaked sleeve covering Victor's nose and mouth.

'Then who's this guy?'

'Claims to be Wilson Murdoch, salesman from Nevada. Here on a fishing trip yet can't seem to keep his nose out of business he has no business sticking his nose in.'

Garrett stood close enough that Victor could smell the coffee on his breath.

'Here,' Garrett said, pushing a water canteen into Victor's hands.

Still blind, he twisted off the cap and poured water into his eyes to wash away the traces of chemicals, trying to open them as much as the pain let him.

'Where are they, Fisherman?'

It took almost the full canteen before Victor could open his eyes fully. They still burned but he could see again.

He glanced around.

Including Garrett, six bounty hunters surrounded him. He imagined the others were either inside the cabin, searching for hidden rooms or compartments, or scouring the perimeter.

Garrett said, 'I won't ask you again.'

Victor remained silent.

Garrett didn't react. At least at first. He didn't speak. He didn't blink. He maintained eye contact with Victor for many long seconds.

Then Garrett nodded, accepting the silence as a definitive answer.

He took a step back, turned, stepped away.

Then he pivoted back around as he drew his sidearm in a swift, smooth motion—

And shot Victor.

SEVENTY-THREE

He dropped to the dirt, clutching his left thigh, experiencing no pain but feeling the warmth of blood pumping out of the wound and welling between his fingers. That blood was bright red, full of oxygen, and he pressed hard over the hole to stop it spraying out in geysers.

'Femoral artery,' Garrett said.

Victor didn't need to be told. He knew the human vascular system as well as a haematologist.

'You're fucked,' Garrett said.

Victor didn't need to be told.

Even with the pressure he was applying, the flow of blood was only slowed, not stopped. All they had to do was pull his hands away and he would be dead within three minutes.

Adrenalin numbed the pain but caused his heart rate to soar. The frequency and pressure of the geyser he was holding back intensified. More blood bubbled out from between his fingers.

'I won't ask you again,' Garrett repeated.

When there was no reply, Garrett gestured to his men.

One bounty hunter grabbed Victor's right arm.

The other took hold of Victor's left arm.

He tried to resist but it was futile. He couldn't match the strength of two strong men. They both pulled simultaneously, wrenching his hands away from the wound.

Arterial blood spurted out of Victor's thigh.

It drenched his jeans and arced through the air at a ferocious rate.

Victor heard it pattering down on the bodywork of the Escalades, several metres away.

Garrett raised his left wrist to make a show of looking at his watch.

'Tick tock,' he said.

For the second time today, Victor knew he was dying. Each geyser of blood arcing from his thigh took him a little closer to death. He weighed about eighty-five kilograms, so there would be about 5.7 litres of blood inside his body. Each pulse sent into the air enough blood to fill a double shot glass.

Garrett waited. He was patient. He was in no hurry.

He didn't need to tell Victor he had no choice.

He didn't need to tell Victor if he wanted to live he had to give Garrett what he wanted to know.

He didn't need to tell Victor how long he had left alive. Victor knew his life expectancy to the very second.

He watched himself weakening. He watched himself dying. Every pulse of blood meant lower blood pressure, meant fewer red blood cells to transport oxygen, meant less energy, less speed, less strength.

Less capacity to save Joshua.

'I'll talk,' Victor said.

'I know you will,' Garrett replied, nonchalant. Then he smiled. Triumphant. 'But do you remember last night when you told me you never would?'

Victor remained silent.

Garrett gestured and the two bounty hunters gripping Victor's arms released him. He pressed his palms back over the bullet hole to stem the flow of blood. There was pain now; when he applied pressure to the wound he grimaced. The adrenalin couldn't hold it back any longer.

The burning in his eyes ceased to bother him.

'We have a case of medical supplies,' Garrett said. 'We have tourniquets and bandages and sutures and disinfectant. We have an extractor. We have plasma. We have bags of every blood type under the sun. We even have Quick Clot. We're battlefield ready here. We're always prepared. You can be right as rain in no time.'

Victor controlled his breathing to stave off the shock his body wanted to go into.

Garrett lowered himself to a squat so he could look Victor in the eye easier.

'I confess I don't understand why you're doing this,' Garrett said. 'And I don't really care beyond a passing curiosity. That curiosity can wait. But what absolutely, fundamentally cannot wait is the completion of my objective. I gave you an out before and you didn't take it. I was fair. I was decent. Now, look at you. You're alone. You're bleeding to death. You're nothing. Whatever you thought you could do, you were wrong. Whatever your goal, you failed. Don't let pride kill you. Pride is just an open wound. All you have to do is let it heal.'

'They're heading south to the border,' Victor said.

'They're going to keep going south all the way to Mexico. That's all I know.'

'Michelle's car is still parked outside her house,' Garrett said back. 'The Frenchie's Rover is right there.'

'I gave them my truck. So you wouldn't be able to follow.'

'What a charitable gesture. When did they leave?'

'An hour ago.'

'An hour ago,' Garrett echoed. 'Then why are you still here?'

'To slow you down.'

'You've slowed us down all of a few minutes, Wilson. Great job. Really excellent work.'

Victor remained silent.

Garrett continued: 'You shouldn't have bothered when they had an hour head start.' He stared at Victor, thoughtful. He stood. He rubbed his stubble. 'Why did you bother?'

Victor didn't answer. He was thinking too. He realised his mistake. He was thinking hard in an attempt to find a way out of it before Garrett worked it out himself.

'Had you not been here to tell me,' he said, 'how else could I have found out what vehicle they were in?'

The other bounty hunters were growing restless, glancing at one another.

'You screwed up,' Garrett said. 'You screwed up big time.' He paused. 'Which doesn't seem like you. Does it?' He paused again. '*Does it?*'

He approached Victor, used the heel of his boot to knock him on to his side.

'Where are your preparations?' Garrett snarled. 'You had an hour to get ready for us, yet you didn't even nail a single door shut?'

His voice was growing louder with every word.

He stamped his heel down hard on Victor's hands, compressing the wound beneath, increasing the pain.

'*What have you been doing all of this time?*'

Blood bubbled out between Victor's fingers.

'They're not driving to Mexico, are they?' Garrett said, pushing down harder and harder. 'They were right here, weren't they?'

Victor roared from the agony.

'Chief,' a bounty hunter called, rounding the side of the cabin, coming from the back.

Garrett didn't ease the pressure. 'What is it?'

'Tracks,' the bounty hunter answered. 'Leading into the trees, going north.'

'How fresh?'

'Fresh,' the bounty hunter said.

SEVENTY-FOUR

Garrett took his foot from Victor's hands, but only to give orders to his men, communicating a lot with only a few words and gestures. The bounty hunters were already split into three teams, one for each Escalade and these three teams were further divided into six two-man units. Garrett sent three of these fire teams to search the woods to the north.

'Track them down,' he told them.

Victor could do nothing but watch the six heavily armed men nod and hurry away. They rounded the cabin and were gone. Into the trees. Hunting.

Another of the bounty hunters took a plastic-covered map of the area from a pocket in his harness. He folded it out and showed it to Garrett.

'There's nothing that way for a hundred klicks,' the bounty hunter told him, pointing. 'Just the hill and a whole lot of forest. No habitation. No roads.'

Garrett examined the map. 'Where does that creek end up?'

'They could follow it to the lake.'

'But why go north first if they need to go east, ultimately?'

The bounty hunter couldn't answer.

Garrett glanced at Victor. 'Where's your truck?'

Victor remained silent.

The bounty hunter said, 'Creek's shallow enough if the truck can handle it.'

'It can,' Garrett said. 'Isn't that so, Fish?'

They studied the map, following the route of the creek, looking for—

'There,' Garrett said. 'That trail.'

The bounty hunter said, 'Creek, trail, road, highway.'

Garrett clicked his tongue. 'That's what you did, didn't you, Wilson? You drove all the way up that creek and came at the cabin through the trees. And that's where they're heading, isn't it? Your truck is parked right there waiting for them on the other side of that hill.'

The bounty hunter folded away the map while Garrett used his radio to relay the information to the three two-man units who had already left in pursuit. Then, along with three of his men, he headed to the Escalade that was still driveable, telling the two remaining guys: 'Plug that wound. I want him conscious in case there's anything else he can tell us. We're getting that kid.'

The two bounty hunters nodded.

Garrett opened the driver's door and called back to Victor, 'Don't go dying on me, Fish.'

Victor said, 'I'm not dead yet.'

Garrett climbed inside the vehicle, his closest men following. The doors slammed shut and mud sprayed as the tyres spun, and the Escalade turned and headed down the track.

In seconds, it was gone.

Even if Joshua, Michelle and Naël made it to his truck before the six men on foot caught up with them, Garrett would head them off. Either on the creek or on the track that led from it to the highway.

They were trapped.

One of the two bounty hunters left with Victor was the guy he had shot in the flank. He still wore the body armour and had a palm over the area embedded with pellets. He carried a camo-painted carbine, a SCAR, in his other hand.

'We should let him bleed to death,' he told the other bounty hunter.

'You heard G.'

He grimaced as he rubbed at his side. 'Maybe we can't stop the bleeding. It happens.' He stood over Victor. 'Sometimes you can't plug the leak. Sometimes no matter what you do, they don't make it.'

The other bounty hunter was resolute. 'Don't do anything stupid, Lex.'

Victor, slowly bleeding to death, just listened.

The bounty hunter named Lex went wide-eyed with faux outrage. 'When have I ever done anything stupid?'

He was lean and strong, wearing a dark brown corduroy shirt over his body armour. Khaki combat trousers covered his legs. His walking boots were worn and well used. He wore a khaki cap with anti-flash goggles perched on the visor. Each arm was attached to the other with a neck cord to ensure they wouldn't be lost.

'Trick question,' the other bounty hunter said. 'So no need to start now. Go get the med kit.'

'Why don't you go get it?'

'Are you serious? That's funny. I leave you alone for two

minutes and I'll come back to find this guy has somehow bled out in the interval.'

Lex grunted, stood for a moment in protest, then approached the disabled Escalade, opening up the back to take out a medical kit the size of a cool box.

While they waited, the other bounty hunter said to Victor, 'What's your story, friend?'

Victor looked up at him.

'I know why I'm here,' he continued. 'But the child's not yours, is he? Then why did you get yourself involved in all this?'

'I had nothing better to do.'

The bounty hunter shook his head in response. Not in disagreement or disbelief but in pity.

Lex returned with the box of medical supplies. He dropped it down on the ground next to Victor.

'You fix him up,' Lex said. 'I'll watch your back in case he tries anything.'

The other bounty hunter sighed and lowered himself to one knee. 'His femoral artery is severed. What's he going to try?'

Lex didn't answer.

Victor watched as the guy on one knee opened up the box and removed a sachet of Quick Clot and a compression tourniquet.

'Keep your hands down on the wound until this is in place,' he said, readying the tourniquet.

Victor nodded, grimacing. 'I'm feeling lightheaded.'

'I'll be quick,' the bounty hunter said.

It was going to be difficult to apply. The bounty hunter had to place one knee between Victor's legs and the other to the outside of the wounded thigh. He had to lean right over Victor, whose grimacing intensified, and thread his arms in and around Victor's own to get the band under the wounded thigh.

Victor ceased grimacing.

He glanced over the bounty hunter's shoulder to where Lex was waiting nearby. He was scratching at the back of his head, bored. Not watching.

Victor pulled both palms away from the wound, and a pressurised geyser of arterial blood jetted from the bullet hole and struck the bounty hunter in the face.

He cried out, blinded, trying to flinch out of the way, but Victor hooked his arms before they could retreat and wrenched the guy closer. He was already turning his head away from the path of the blood.

Which exposed the side of his skull to Victor's face.

The bounty hunter screamed as Victor's teeth found his ear.

Cartilage crushed as Victor's powerful masseter muscles contracted and his incisors pressed together.

Victor bit harder as the bounty hunter screamed louder.

Victor wrenched his head from side to side in savage, violent shakes until the ear tore away from the skull, leaving only frayed strips of skin behind.

Blinded by Victor's blood in his eyes, and screaming in agony, the bounty hunter wasn't fighting back. Too much pain. Too much horror.

Lex, nearby, was yelling for Victor to release him. He couldn't get a shot on Victor with the other bounty hunter over him and acting as a human shield.

Victor released the severed ear, spitting it away, and went for the pistol in the guy's thigh holster.

He pulled it free and started shooting.

SEVENTY-FIVE

With the wounded bounty hunter wailing and thrashing, Victor couldn't take proper aim at Lex, but seeking to intervene, Lex rushed closer. Making himself a bigger, easier target.

Victor squeezed the trigger several times and saw Lex flinch and stagger, although he remained on his feet. Wounded but not incapacitated.

He returned fire with his carbine, loosing off a quick burst, and the bounty hunter on top of Victor shuddered from the impacts. None of the rounds came through to Victor. He had a thick torso protecting him and that had body armour protecting it on both front and back. The reverberations that reached Victor's body felt like finger flicks.

They didn't stop him squeezing the handgun's trigger again and again and again until Lex dropped to one knee, then tipped over on to his back.

The bounty hunter on top of Victor had stopped struggling

by then, and he rolled him clear. One of Lex's shots had penetrated the body armour over his chest. Air hissed and frothy blood bubbled from the wound.

Lex lay on the ground near to the disabled Escalade. He wasn't moving either.

Victor pushed one palm back over his wound, fighting the resulting waves of pain and nausea while he retrieved the compression band. His jeans were now soaked from hip to knee. The dirt all around him had a dark red hue.

With one hand he looped the band around the top of his thigh and worked the lever until it was tight enough to hurt. He locked it in place.

Blood gushed from the wound when he released his palm but only once. He grabbed the sachet of Quick Clot and tore it open using his teeth because his fingers were too slick with bright blood to get a firm grip. He had blood in his mouth also, but far less.

He poured the granules of Quick Clot into the wound.

It stung so much his eyes watered and his jaw clenched hard. A thick, dark crust formed in and around the wound. No fix, but it would slow down the rate of loss of any blood that managed to get through the compression.

He stood. Felt a wave of dizziness in his head. Controlled his breathing to fight the intermittent waves of nausea.

Lex emitted a weak groan.

Victor's shots had hit in several places – arms, legs, lower abdomen – but none of the wounds were fatal in the short term. He was out of action, however, delirious from blood loss and shock.

Victor ignored him.

His instinct was to hurry, and there was every need to

hurry, but he had to take his time. There were still ten heavily armed and armoured bounty hunters and he had a wound that had already weakened him significantly and would kill him if not treated soon, or if it reopened. Despite the danger Joshua, Michelle and Naël were in, Victor was no good to them like this.

In the trunk of the disabled Escalade, Victor found a cool box with blood packs for every blood group, syringes and cannulas and drips. He could rig one up and regain the blood he had lost, but it would take too long. Instead, he rooted through the supplies to find water, electrolytes and glucose tablets. He mixed the electrolytes into the water and drank down the mixture, then chewed on a mouthful of glucose tablets.

Victor took Lex's cap and anti-flash goggles. He took his overshirt too – a brown corduroy garment, baggy and worn. He swapped his own plaid shirt for the corduroy, fixed the cap in place, and would have swapped his jeans for Lex's trousers if not for the compression band preventing him from removing them. He could risk no further blood loss.

He stripped Lex of his body armour because Lex was a closer physical match, took his tactical harness, side carbine, sidearm, ammunition, knife, a single grenade and everything else he had, including a radio and headset. Then he hot-wired Naël's Land Rover. It was an older model and Victor had been stealing cars long before his first whisker had appeared. Within two minutes the engine was revving.

He threw supplies into the back and placed the extra rifle and sidearm from the other bounty hunter in the passenger's footwell and on the seat. He climbed behind the wheel, released the handbrake, put the Land Rover into gear, and ... stopped.

He pictured accelerating away, mud spraying from the tyres as he rushed from the driveway and down the narrow track through the trees. Leaves and branches would brush the side windows, scratching and clattering against the glass. The uneven, rutted surface, narrow breadth and frequent twists were meant to be taken at a slow pace. Victor would accelerate the entire way, fighting a wheel that had no power steering. He would jolt and slide in his seat, every bump and swerve in the track pulsing and throbbing through his leg. The rifles would dance around in the footwell.

On the highway, he would accelerate harder. There would be little to no traffic to overtake. Maybe the odd vehicle passing, going the other way. They would be zipping blurs he barely noticed.

Garrett and the other three in the Escalade had a four-minute lead. Victor had counted every second since they had left. The six bounty hunters, the three two-man teams, had set off on foot three minutes before that. Joshua, Michelle and Naël had a five-minute lead on the six on foot and an eight-minute lead on Garrett, but they would move at a slower pace. They might get lost. Naël might lose the keys to Victor's truck. The newly fitted ignition switch might be faulty, or the fault wasn't the switch in the first place. Or the truck might get stuck going back down the creek. There was no guarantee they would get away and every reason to think they would not.

If anything went wrong the bounty hunters chasing them

would catch up before Garrett and the others traversed the track, the highway, then the creek. If Victor chased in the Land Rover, he was going to arrive too late.

He climbed out of the vehicle.

His leg felt cold already. The lack of circulation caused pins and needles. The pain was there too, but he pushed it to the back of his consciousness, filing it away as a constant, a danger, but one that had to wait.

He had to do this on foot.

Lex's headset crackled.

'How's the fisherman?' Garrett's voice asked. 'Don't let him go dying just yet.'

Victor considered the chances of imitating Lex's voice after hearing so little of it. Even with his considerable skills at imitation, it seemed unlikely he would fool Garrett.

Besides, he didn't want to fool him.

'I'm good,' Victor said, after hitting send. 'Your guys, not so much.'

A long moment of silence.

'Seems we have ourselves an uninvited guest on the air-waves,' Garrett said to the rest of his men in radio contact. His voice was tight with anger, perhaps even grief for the two men he had left behind. 'Kill your comms.'

'First and only chance,' Victor said. 'Withdraw.'

He approached Lex, still groaning weakly.

Garrett said, 'Next time I see you, I won't be aiming at your leg.'

Victor knelt down next to Lex, and said into the mic, 'Remember when I told you fishing was just a hobby? That it's not what I do best?'

Again, a long pause before Garrett's voice came through

the earpiece: 'Yeah, I seem to remember you leaving that particular point hanging in the wind.'

'This is what I do best,' Victor told Garrett as he reached a hand down and Lex's awful gurgling screams were projected through the mic; and as those screams fell into silence, Victor added, 'Ready or not, here I come.'

SEVENTY-SIX

No simple taunt. A distraction. Now Garrett's and his men's focus would shift from Joshua to Victor. Their mission could wait. Staying alive trumped any payday.

Besides, he was just one man.

They didn't want him sneaking up on them from behind, but they could handle a single opponent between them. They had no doubt about that. They had underestimated him once but now they knew what was required.

Kill on sight.

Whatever Garrett had said about cutting comms, the bounty hunters would still be talking to one another. They would have a backup frequency to switch to, denying Victor access to their communications, but it was worth it. He couldn't outrun them, he couldn't head them off. He couldn't even catch them up. He needed them to come for him.

We take care of the fisherman, then get the boy, Victor could almost hear Garrett telling his men.

If they were a tight team, they would be glad of this

change in orders. They wouldn't have changed the frequency until after Victor had ended the transmission. There would be a burning need for vengeance. They had heard Lex dying by his hand. Victor had ensured Lex's screams sent an unignorable message.

He left the spare weapons, and found the tracks left by the pursuing bounty hunters in seconds. They were following tracks already left by the hasty flight of Joshua, Michelle and Naël. Twigs were broken. Leaves crushed. Undergrowth flattened.

He followed, thinking the bounty hunters couldn't be more than a few hundred yards ahead up the hill at the most.

Would they stay put and wait to ambush him or would they be heading this way?

Only one way to find out.

He pushed on, fighting the pain in his leg with every step as the incline increased.

The forest was a kaleidoscope of greens – at least a thousand shades of green within his limited sight. Bright and dark, warm and cool. Some browns and oranges too in the dead vegetation and tree trunks – the former shaded on the forest floor and the latter half covered by mosses and lichen. The canopy put all into shadow except rare spots where unfiltered sunlight could reach and brighten the green into yellows and white.

The rain had only been light so far today – little more than drizzle once it had made it through the maze of canopy shielding the forest floor – but the sky was dark above. The ground was damp but not mud, except where a gap in the canopy had let rain fall unhindered.

Victor found one such place and scooped up mud from the

ground. He smeared it on his clothes and through his hair and painted every inch of exposed skin until he was as dark as the ground itself. He grabbed handfuls of dead and dying leaves and patted them against his clothing, gluing them to the mud's embrace. He did the same with his face, with the backs of his hands and forearms, with his neck, with his eyelids. He pulled free fresh sprigs of bracken to deepen and vary the camouflage.

Finally, he scooped up more wet soil with his fingertips and rubbed it over his lips and gums, and against his teeth until they were more grey than white.

He kept his eyes pinched, almost closed, despite the instinct to open them as wide as possible in the poor visibility. He was willing to trade a little peripheral vision to lessen the amount of bright white cornea on display. Surrounded by the mask of dark mud, that white would stand out even brighter. No point the rest of him blending into the forest if his eyes shone for all to see.

He dirtied up the carbine too. It was painted black, but black did not exist in nature and to a keen eye would be noticeable against the greens and browns of the forest. He was careful not to get mud into any of the working parts.

Against so many, he couldn't use the gun. Not at first. Gunshots would give away his presence. Muzzle flashes would pinpoint his exact location. He might shoot one or two or even three, but at some point they would surround him and it would be over.

So, stealth.

He had to kill as many as he could as silently as he could before it went loud, so that when it did go loud they didn't have the numbers to envelop him.

He slung the carbine on his back, its strap over his shoulder and across his chest in a diagonal line. He tightened it to keep the weapon as still and stable as possible. He didn't want it rattling around or catching on foliage. It would be slower to take off, but he deemed it an unavoidable compromise. If he needed the gun in hand quicker, then the situation had already become untenable.

The knife taken from Lex had a razor edge along seven inches of high-carbon steel. The gladiator point was just as sharp. No tool.

This was a formidable killing weapon.

It felt good in his hand, like it belonged there.

Victor used mud to dirty the blade but kept the edge clean in a single line of shining steel destined to become red.

SEVENTY-SEVEN

Victor had no home. Had never had a home in the truest sense. But there were places he felt at home. He felt it in nature, in the woods, waist-deep in bracken and undergrowth; all around him endless wilderness untroubled by the neighbouring civilisation it would outlast. Here, back against a moss-covered boulder while he surveyed his surroundings, was his primordial home. Here, there were no guests, only trespassers. Here, Victor belonged.

He moved on, walking on the balls of his feet. A slow, careful gait. He felt for secure ground, for dry twigs waiting to send a *snap* echoing through the trees. He kept low, moving with legs bent and his shoulders down. The loss of height meant a restricted view, yet sight was a secondary sense in the wilds. Even the tallest man, the most acute eyes, could not see far in this primordial home. To rely on sight here meant to be surprised.

Victor listened.

He was close now, he knew.

If the bounty hunters were coming for him he would have encountered them by now. Instead, they were waiting for him to come to them.

He heard the gentle rustle he made as he pushed through the bracken. He heard the swish of wind through foliage. He heard the creak and scratch of branches.

He heard no wildlife. Every mammal and bird had wisely left the area upon the intrusion of nature's most dangerous creation.

The rustles and swishes and creaks and scratches became a series of notes, forming a melody in Victor's consciousness. He listened for a note out of place, a harmony where there should be none, the introduction of a new instrument altogether.

He was both conductor and audience to this primordial orchestra and would tolerate no interruption.

But the bounty hunters were no strangers to such a performance. They were musicians in their own right; only their music went unheard by him.

Against ten, he had to be invisible to twenty eyes and silent to twenty ears.

Impossible.

Against civilians, yes.

Against bounty hunters, no.

Victor, conductor of the primordial orchestra, changed the symphony.

He found a thick, dry twig with the toe of his shoe and stepped down on it.

Snap.

A sudden, sharp sound. Loud to Victor and noticeable to any hunters close by, but noiseless to others outside the immediate area.

Victor dropped down on to his stomach, palms on the damp earth of the forest floor. The scent of wet soil and detritus was strong and comforting.

It was home.

He listened.

He waited.

Quiet at first, but distinct and clear to Victor's ears, undergrowth rustled. With the confusing echoing effect of the trees it took a moment to place the source.

Left.

West.

Victor, invisible on the forest floor, remained in position. He didn't need to see the bounty hunter to know he was there and to know he was approaching. The man wouldn't be able to identify the exact location of the snapping twig but he had been close enough to be sure of the general area.

In the absence of other indicators, such an invitation could not be ignored.

With an enemy announcing his approach, it had to be investigated.

The rustling grew louder.

Victor heard footfalls. The careful placement of one boot followed by the next. Slow, tactical.

Smeared with mud and vegetation, Victor was indistinguishable from the undergrowth.

Then the bounty hunter was so close Victor could hear the man's breathing. Deep and regular.

In many ways you could say that the fish catches itself, Victor had told Joshua.

When the bounty hunter turned around and headed away, Victor let him.

He waited.

He rose into a squat, a tree trunk behind him, his eye level at that of the tallest bracken leaves. He watched the bounty hunter go. The man moved well, tactically, sweeping back and forth.

Alone, but he wouldn't be alone.

Victor watched.

The pins and needles in his left leg had gone. A double-edged relief because he knew that meant the lack of circulation was so bad he was losing all feeling. Cramps would follow soon afterwards. Then the leg would become unresponsive.

He almost did not notice another bounty hunter passing by so close he could smell him.

Victor stayed motionless.

The bounty hunter walked with slow, careful steps, gun up and sweeping back and forth with his gaze. He looked left. He looked right. He looked near and he looked far. But he did not look down.

The second of the two-man fire team.

Five metres behind the first. Close enough to cover the first man but not too close.

A classic, universal tactic. The buddy system, as some referred to it. Each man looked after the other. Safer and more effective than operating solo.

But it had a single downside.

Relying on another meant an inevitable reduction in individual awareness. When another was tasked with watching your back, you didn't watch your own.

Victor, who relied only on himself, never lowered his guard. He watched his own back.

He crept up behind the second man until less than a metre remained between them. He matched his gait, step for step.

When he had timed the man's movements to perfection, Victor used that noise to close the two steps he needed to wrap his left palm over the man's nose and mouth, simultaneously muffling any cry while yanking the head back to expose the neck.

Victor drove the point of the knife into the flesh to the left of the bounty hunter's Adam's apple until he felt the hard resistance of the spine, then dragged the blade in a fast arc through to the right, severing the windpipe, carotids and jugulars, and withdrawing the blade in one swift, efficient motion.

He released the man and stepped back as a torrent of blood spattered the bracken in a sudden bright-red rainstorm, and the bounty hunter collapsed to his knees.

With so many severed muscle fibres at the front of the neck, the man's head lolled all the way back, gaze straight up and skyward. With no link between lungs and mouth, his screams were silent.

Victor was back down prone in the undergrowth before the man tipped forward in front of him and went into convulsions for the few seconds it took to lose consciousness.

Steam rose from the bracken in many places.

Victor waited for a reaction, for the lead bounty hunter to respond to the quiet but unavoidable noise, but the only sound Victor heard was the gentle patter of blood dripping from sodden leaves.

It made for a pleasant melody with which to finish his symphony.

By the time the first man realised his buddy wasn't following, Victor had circled around to his flank.

Blade against his throat, the bounty hunter froze.

'Don't worry,' Victor told the man as he dragged him down into the undergrowth. 'It's not me who's going to kill you.'

SEVENTY-EIGHT

Moisture saturated the cold air. No wind blew through the forest but the canopy above swayed and rippled. Mist filled the gaps between the trees, darkening the afternoon to a thick gloom of grey.

They found their man within a few minutes because of the screams echoing through the trees, drawing them irresistibly to the area where they saw the erratic sway of bracken and undergrowth. Until they were close, they could not see what was causing the plants to move.

'Shit,' Garrett said when they were close enough.

The man was alive and writhing in obvious agony on the forest floor. He lay on his back, hands pressed over his abdomen. Blood soaked his shirt and covered his hands. It was smeared all over his face and neck too, leaking out of his mouth.

'That's grim,' one of the three bounty hunters with him said.

Garrett frowned. 'Show some respect. He's one of us.'

The wounded man on the ground saw them and moaned louder. He had already been moaning, but upon seeing his comrades the pitch of the moan changed from one of suffering to one of communication.

'What's he trying to say?'

The moans were incomprehensible. No words. Not even a syllable.

But the man was raising his head up to gesture down at his body.

Garrett said, 'Do what you can.'

The bounty hunter alongside him whispered, 'When someone's lost that much blood . . .'

'I know,' Garrett interrupted. 'But do what you can.' To the other two, he said, 'Guard the perimeter.'

They did, spreading out, angry faces displaying their need to even the score.

The bounty hunter with Garrett knelt down next to the wounded man and reached out to the man's abdomen and the two hands pressed over some kind of wound. It was hard to tell exactly what had happened to him with all the blood.

'I think he's been gutted.'

When the bounty hunter went to take a look, the wounded man moaned louder and shook his head. Blood bubbled from his mouth.

'Easy,' Garrett said. 'We're just going to take a look.'

The man continued to shake his head.

He resisted when the bounty hunter tried to prise his hands away from the wound.

'We're trying to help you, okay? Just let us take a look. Maybe we can staple you back together.'

The wounded man did not cease shaking his head. He resisted when the bounty hunter again tried to move his hands away.

He turned to Garrett, exasperated.

Garrett squatted down low.

He looked his wounded man in the eye.

'Listen,' he told him, 'you have to let us look. Let us help you.'

More moaning. More head shaking.

Garrett wiped some of the blood from the man's face, finding no wound.

'You're cut inside your mouth?' Garrett asked him.

The man nodded. Moaned.

'Let me see.'

The man hesitated, then parted his lips, opening a dam that released a flood of blood that spilled over his face, neck, shoulders.

'Jesus,' Garrett hissed.

'What is it?' the bounty hunter asked him.

Garrett winced. 'His tongue's missing.'

'What—'

'It's been sawn off.'

'What the . . . ?'

Garrett opened up a pouch on his harness, removed a pressurised injector, flipped off the cap and stabbed the needle hard into the wounded man's shoulder.

He shook his head in desperation, moaning and moaning until the morphine was carried by his blood into his brain, and he became sluggish and sedate.

He still shook his head, although it was in slow, heavy movements.

'See?' Garrett said. 'We can help.'

The bounty hunter said, 'Why did the fisherman hack off his tongue?'

'Because he's crazy,' Garrett said, then pointed to the wounded man's abdomen. 'What's the deal there?'

The bounty hunter could now prise away the wounded man's hands. He still tried to resist but had no strength thanks to the morphine's influence.

With the hands out of the way, it was still hard to see through the blood-sodden clothes what was going on, but the bounty hunter moved the clothes out of the way until the bare abdomen was visible.

He hadn't been gutted. At least, not in the way they expected.

The hands had covered a grievous wound: a cut that split the flesh of the abdomen across the belly button. Grievous, but not fatal because the wound was not deep and had severed no arteries.

A deliberate, strange wound.

Made stranger because it was wide, the skin distended and stretched from within.

Despite the width of the wound, no innards were visible. Instead, there was something smooth and dark. Thin. Curved.

'What the hell?'

The bounty hunter didn't understand. Not at first.

Garrett did. His mouth opened and his eyes widened. The wounded man's missing tongue made perfect sense now.

No tongue. No warning.

Garrett stumbled backwards a step, then spun around and sprinted away as fast as he could while the bounty hunter on one knee took another second to understand that the thin, curved object was a lever.

And another second to realise there was a grenade beneath it, yet without the pressure of the wounded man's hands on the lever, it was now detached.

After that, there was no time left to come to any further revelations.

'Oh ... shit.'

SEVENTY-NINE

The sound of the explosion was muffled by flesh and organs, skin and bone into a dull thudding pop. An Mk67 fragmentation grenade threw out shrapnel in every direction up to over two hundred metres, given clear terrain. Few pieces reached a fraction of that distance after they had shredded the bounty hunter. Some were dragged to the earth by blood and chunks of skin and muscle. Others hit trees. A few didn't make it through the ribcage. Others still embedded in the skull.

The overpressure wave took viscera in a blooming sphere that painted foliage and undergrowth and left a cloud of atomised blood mixing with smoke and dust to colour the air.

Garrett didn't need to look to know his man was dead.

He could smell him.

Hell, he could taste him.

Garrett lay on his stomach, having thrown himself down after a short sprint. The overpressure wave caught him just before he hit the ground. Hot shrapnel hissed in his body armour. A piece had caught in his fatigues. Another had sliced his shoulder. He'd been in the kill radius – fifteen metres – when he hit the deck, but far enough away and low enough for the blast wave and shrapnel – which rose as it expanded – to go over him for the most part.

He lay winded for a moment, his ears ringing, but there were no injuries he could detect. Tomorrow he would be covered in bruises, he was sure.

Tomorrow could wait.

Tomorrow was far from certain.

Tomorrow had to be earned.

Garrett fought through the pain and willed himself to move. Murdoch was nearby. He had to be close and moving closer.

He had set the trap. He had picked the location for a reason. Here, the hillside was jagged and jutted with outcrops and narrow gorges and all sorts of places to hide and launch ambushes.

On the ground, buried by undergrowth, Garrett was invisible. A temporary cloak, however. A decent tracker would see the trail easy enough and Garrett had a feeling Murdoch was far more than a decent tracker. He had proved far more in every other regard.

Garrett, not prone to intense emotion, hated this particular adversary.

He told himself to control that hatred because there was no benefit to it. Emotion in combat never helped. Only in the removal of all humanity could the perfect soldier be realised.

Garrett waited.

Murdoch did not appear.

But the forest came alive in a ripple of movement and

violence. A form blurred through the undergrowth, coloured as the forest but separate from it, almost a wind of death disturbing vegetation. Malevolence made whole.

The first of the two bounty hunters Garrett had set to guard the perimeter didn't see the forest take form, nor hear that malevolence behind him.

Garrett could only watch as the blur swept over his man and then was gone again, and there his man still stood, only now he trembled and raised hands to a gaping neck that spilled blood as a ferocious, red waterfall.

The second bounty hunter heard the gurgling rush of spilling blood and spun to face the threat, yet instead faced only the mist-shrouded forest.

Garrett groaned. He tried to move.

He tried to call a warning to his man when the forest manifested itself once more, darkness melting out of the mist behind the bounty hunter.

This time his man heard, or felt, the danger and turned to kill it.

But the forest could not be killed.

It sprang at Garrett's man, dark limbs wrapping around in a sudden, deathly embrace, and dragging him down beneath the undergrowth amid a chorus of screams and gunfire.

Garrett rolled on to his stomach and crawled.

Away.

Crawled anywhere.

Anywhere but here.

The gunfire ceased behind him. The cries of suffering continued a little longer.

The forest could not be killed and its bloodlust was far from sated.

Garrett could feel that bloodlust, that unquenchable thirst, and knew he could not escape it. He tried anyway. He dragged himself through the undergrowth, fingers digging into the soft earth and carving trenches of dread. He saw bugs and worms in those trenches, waiting to feast on what the forest left behind. He pictured many mandibles stripping away his skin in countless tiny bites. He imagined fat, satiated worms wriggling inside his hollow eyeballs.

Such horror energised him to crawl faster and reminded him he was still alive.

Dazed, disorientated, but alive.

Each second of life was one more second of recovery. Each second made his vision a little clearer, his hearing a little sharper, his chance of remaining alive a little better.

'Ten seconds,' a voice said through Garrett's headset.

Reinforcements were coming.

The forest had not yet won.

EIGHTY

Rain fell. At first, a fine patter, light and cold. Then, within seconds the fine drops fattened, falling harder and faster. They pelted Victor's head and shoulders, plastering his hair to his skull and sluicing away the mud that covered him into a feral pattern of streaks and blotches.

Visibility worsened in the downpour. His own footsteps became undetectable. The rustling his movements made through the undergrowth fell silent.

He had killed two in the aftermath of the explosion yet in doing so had lost sight of the third – Garrett. Nearby but hidden in the forest and the mist. He could be mere metres away, yet he would not be heard through the rain.

Maybe Garrett was dead too.

Or maybe not.

Victor slipped the knife away and unslung the carbine from his back.

The remaining bounty hunters were all here or close – or

would be in mere moments. The explosion, the gunfire, had drawn them in. No more chances for stealth.

No more clean kills.

But Victor had picked the terrain of his choosing. To the east, the hill fell away to the lake, and to the north narrow gorges cut into the hillside. The bounty hunters would come from the west or south.

Victor pulled back the receiver to check the chamber contained a round. It did. It always did. He had checked the chamber maybe a thousand times and without fail saw the brass case of a bullet. But he would keep checking because only in the acknowledgement of his own capacity for imperfection could he hope to overcome it.

He had killed many killers who had believed themselves to be perfect.

He waited.

He rocked his head to the right, then left, to crack his neck.

Silence.

Calm.

There was always this moment.

Violence rarely commenced without an introduction. Even a sudden, surprise attack had cues.

Thunder only clapped after lightning struck. That lightning was always there but not always seen. Thunder was always heard.

He used that moment to take a deep breath into the bottom of his lungs and held it there to override the body's instinctual responses to danger. He didn't want excess adrenalin and cortisol in his system, meant to help primitive man run or fight, to interfere with the small motor units needed to aim with accuracy and to swap a magazine at speed.

The breathing slowed his heart rate and forced his body to relax when countless physiological processes wanted the opposite.

Before he fought, he fought himself.

Practice makes perfect, as they said. Victor understood why. He knew that through repetition the brain insulated neural pathways with fatty acids to increase the speed of the electrical pulses required to perform a given task. In this way he knew that his brain was quite literally wired to kill.

Some people were master musicians.

Others were incomparable artists.

To each his own, he thought.

Victor took in one last deep breath and felt his heart rate slow almost to resting, adjusted the way the stock sat against his upper chest, and swivelled out of cover.

He shot as he moved, stalking forward with the carbine's stock firm against him and his head positioned so his gaze was a straight line through the iron sights.

At the limits of his vision through the rain and mist and foliage, a shape rippled to the west.

The bounty hunter was already moving too – maybe having seen Victor take cover behind the tree in the first place – and was dashing into cover as the rounds came his way.

They shredded leaves and exploded bark from the tree trunk he got behind, if only for a moment.

They exchanged fire. Close range, but each a fast-moving target obscured by the rain, shielded by trees.

Victor moved laterally to a new position an instant before the bounty hunter returned fire, shooting blind from behind the tree and spraying rounds into the area where Victor had been.

He saw no others but they had to be close. He had to make every second count before he was outgunned.

Thumbing the selector to single shot, Victor aimed for the exposed rifle, missing by millimetres, and the bounty hunter withdrew the weapon before Victor could adjust his aim.

He changed positions again, seeking to get an angle on the far side of the tree where the bounty hunter was hiding and knowing that any kind of competent gunman wouldn't stay in that same spot for long. Either he would move directly back or he would rotate around the tree, away from the line of fire.

If he was good, he would back off, creating distance and opening up his field of view so whichever way Victor circled around, to his left or to his right, the bounty hunter would see him.

So Victor didn't circle.

He approached the tree in a straight line.

On one knee, he waited for a long moment. He wanted the bounty hunter fixated on the forest in his peripheries. He wanted him to begin to doubt. He wanted him to grow concerned that Victor was flanking him from so far out that he couldn't see him.

Then, when Victor peered out around the tree trunk he had an extra few seconds to locate the bounty hunter where he was crouched low in the undergrowth, head rotating back and forth, focused on his flanks and not on what was right in front of him.

Selector still on single shot, Victor triple-tapped him in the upper chest above the body armour's protection.

It was too far to see individual wounds, but Victor knew at least one of the rounds had severed the spinal column because the guy flopped straight down with almost no reaction.

Not an instant kill, but the bounty hunter was paralysed from the neck down, and the three holes in his chest would make breathing increasingly difficult as essential pressure leaked out from the thoracic cavity and his lungs filled with blood.

The only question was whether he suffocated first or drowned.

A slow, messy death either way.

Victor left him to it.

EIGHTY-ONE

Victor retreated as automatic fire came his way from the right. Bark tore from tree trunks. Leaves shredded. The forest was a thunderstorm of gunfire.

Multiple shooters.

Two. Maybe three.

He took cover behind a corner of jutting rockface. Watched as rounds blew away shrapnel of stone and plumed out a grey cloud of dust.

He changed positions during a lull in the shooting. He wasn't counting the enemy's bullets – there were too many coming his way from multiple shooters for him to keep track – but he guessed they were reloading.

At nine hundred rounds per minute, the SCARs would empty their mags in less than three seconds of continuous fire.

Victor dropped the first guy with a headshot when he rounded the corner of the rockface in a hasty pursuit and took a snapshot at the second as the corpse fell, but that bounty hunter was already moving out of the line of fire.

Shooting again to make sure he stayed put, Victor changed positions, not flinching as the bounty hunter popped out of cover to put rounds his way. They blasted holes in the rock. Debris peppered his arm.

A round thumped into the carbine and it jolted from his hands.

No time to retrieve it – and a good chance it was disabled – so he shuffled fast into a narrow gorge, knowing the third guy had to be flanking because it would be the easiest thing in the world to circle the outcrop while the other two had pushed forward. If Victor hadn't made it through to the other side before the third guy had manoeuvred around the rocks, then he never would.

He drew the pistol on the move.

A compact SIG.

In close confines with many blind spots, he kept the gun in a double-handed grip near to his chest. Leading with a weapon further from the body increased the risk of someone taking it. At point-blank range he didn't need to use the iron sights to hit a target.

Point. Shoot.

Kill.

He approached a junction in the ravine.

Corners were always dangerous – a gunman could be waiting unseen, ready to fire – but reaction was always slower than action.

Victor darted out fast but low, in a bent-over half-crouch, right arm across his chest, gun beneath his left armpit.

The guy waiting to ambush him saw Victor at the same time Victor saw him, but the bounty hunter was reactive, not active.

A double-tap hit him in the throat.

A third bullet tore a hole through his jaw.

He went down shooting, muscle spasms compressing his finger on the trigger. Rounds plugged holes in the side of the gorge until the magazine was dry and rock dust and fragments thickened the air, covering him in a pale burial shroud.

The gunfire drew attention, as Victor knew it would.

He was ready for the next guy, who took the same approach Victor had done, coming out at speed while low and relying on action being faster than reaction.

But he didn't see Victor at the same time Victor saw him because Victor was prone on his stomach, hugging the rock-face in the bounty hunter's blind spot.

The guy rushed right past him.

Victor's first trigger squeeze put a bullet in the back of the man's closest knee before exploding the kneecap on its way out.

He screamed and fell straight down, providing Victor with a clear and easy shot to the back of his head.

Blood and brains painted the rocks.

Victor jumped back up to his feet.

Another three down meant only one remaining.

Garrett.

EIGHTY-TWO

Garrett approached with more caution than the others, moving away from the rockface to improve the angle. He had his right arm outstretched with his left bent at the elbow, left hand cupping the end of the grip to support his hold on the pistol.

A stable, effective stance, yet the pale sun was behind him and his shadow inched forward ahead, rounding the corner before he did and giving a split-second warning.

Victor never let an advantage go to waste. He dashed out of cover, deflecting Garrett's pistol with his left hand as he went out shooting, gun near to his chest, aiming at centre mass. The muzzle barked three times in rapid succession, brightening the dark forest in a trio of yellow flashes.

The bullets struck Garrett in his body armour, none penetrating but hitting him with thousands of joules of energy.

He grunted and recoiled, releasing his double-handed grip on his own pistol to grab at Victor's weapon before he could adjust his aim for a headshot.

Both guns went off as they wrestled for control of the weapons. One bullet struck the rockface and blasted debris into Victor's face.

He felt warm blood on his cheek, but worse were the tears that flooded his eyes in response to the rock dust that entered them.

Blinded, he fought with touch, with instincts.

He twisted and wrenched the pistol from Garrett's grip, who then batted it out from Victor's hold and threw a downward elbow strike at the back of his other wrist to jolt the SIG from his hand.

Blinking in an attempt to clear his vision, Victor threw short punches to the body and palm heels to Garrett's head to keep him from attacking with strikes he could not see to defend against.

Garrett backed away from them, then went low beneath Victor's reach to tackle him around the waist and drive him back to the rockface.

The impact stunned him for an instant, and Garrett punched and elbowed him with blows that made his ears ring and his blurred vision darken.

Victor raised a high guard that caught and deflected the next strikes to give himself a second to recover.

His eyes streamed water, yet his sight cleared enough for him to glimpse Garrett loading up for a powerful right cross. Victor dodged, but not fast enough, and the punch caught him on the side of the head.

He staggered away, dazed, although his eyes were now free of dust, and he turned to catch the following punch thrown in the exact same way as Garrett sought to repeat the previous success.

Even dazed, Victor controlled the arm and threw elbows into his enemy's face, splitting his lip, opening up his cheek.

Garrett turned his face away, shrugging his shoulder to help defend it, and grabbed hold of Victor's shirt to pull him closer and twist him off balance.

They pivoted on the spot, Victor on the back foot and Garrett exploiting that to put knee strikes into Victor's abdomen.

He slipped and went down to the ground, using that sudden shift in weight to drag the bounty hunter down with him and throw him over his head.

Victor scrambled from his back to his front, rising slower than he was used to because of the weakness in his left leg. Garrett was faster to his feet, attacking Victor before he had risen fully upright, but the ground was uneven, the gradient made worse with the earth churned to mud.

They both staggered, both unbalanced, pushing and pulling until they fell.

They tumbled down the sloping gorge, Garrett's arms around Victor, pinning Victor's arms to his torso until they hit a tree and came apart, Victor winded and Garrett dazed. They slid in the mud, Victor on his back and the bounty hunter on his front.

Garrett recovered first but was unsteady as he climbed to his feet. There was no hill behind him, just empty air. The lake far below.

Diaphragm paralysed and gasping for air, Victor could only watch as Garrett rose and then turned on the spot to collect his bearings. He reached out with his arms, as if seeking handholds in the empty air, and shook his head in an effort to regain his senses quicker.

When he did, his gaze locked on Victor.

He grunted as he approached, kicking for Victor's head, which he jerked to the side, before rolling away from the heel that propelled downwards at his face.

'Why won't you just die?' Garrett growled.

His chest heaved for air and he didn't go after Victor. Garrett was happy to take a rest and shake off some of his disorientation.

With space between them, metal glinted as Garrett drew a combat knife with a serrated back edge and a hooked point.

Victor's knife was dirtied with mud and blood. He took it into his hand as he rose.

Garrett attacked with fast slashes and faster thrusts. Short movements, precise and considered, as he used his left hand to ward off counter-attacks or attempts to disarm.

Victor kept his blade moving in fluid diagonal arcs, a relentless rhythm – high low, low high – seeking to slip past Garrett's parries.

The bounty hunter had too much speed and experience to leave himself open. He fought with restraint. He preferred to move his own knife along the horizontal and vertical planes in short, quick slashes. A thrust was faster, the point travelling in a straight line, but that line offered almost no defence of its own – unlike a cut, which blocked lines of incoming attack as it attacked.

Their blades clashed several times with dull clangs.

Victor blocked a slash to his face with the back of his wrist.

Garrett accepted a cut to the shoulder to spare his neck.

Victor matched him move for move. Garrett fought in a Kali-inspired style. Short, fast moves perfected in the Philippines over generations. Fluid, effective. Victor fought with no style. He subscribed to no methodology. Violence was violence. He used what worked, what beat and maimed and killed in the most efficient manner. Fluidity was nothing without efficacy. Style was synonymous with martial arts, yet art had no place in combat. Sometimes the ugliest move worked best. Often, a martial art was only effective because both parties adhered to the rules.

Victor had only one rule.

Garrett was not prepared for that savagery.

'It's like that, is it?' Garrett said, dabbing the back of his hand against the frayed skin of his cheek that Victor had ripped with his teeth when they had been close.

It was impossible to dodge or parry every attack. Victor's wounded leg halved his speed and dulled his reactions. For every cut he landed on Garrett, Garrett sliced him three times.

There was only one outcome for that kind of exchange.

He could not exploit the terrain because there was none. They fought on an outcrop overlooking the lake. There were no trees. No escape except back up the steep gorge down which they had tumbled.

When Garrett next moved in, Victor dropped his knife to go for Garrett's arm. It took the bounty hunter, expecting a counter-attack with a weapon, by surprise.

Victor caught the incoming arm by the wrist, moving to take control of the knife, but Garrett slammed him before he could apply the lock, driving Victor back into the rockface.

Water erosion had smoothed away any sharp protrusions, so no new wounds opened, but air rushed from his lungs and his ribs burned from the impact.

He maintained his grip on Garrett's wrist, keeping the

knife immobile, and hit him in the side of the head with his left hand, an open palm strike, followed by an uppercut to the guts as Garrett's free arm rose to ward off an expected second blow to the head.

Victor threw more body shots, lefts and rights, hitting Garrett's ribs, his sternum, his abdomen in a relentless barrage.

He wanted to hurt him, but more than that Victor wanted to attack with the body shots to leave his own head exposed long enough that his enemy couldn't resist throwing a punch that—

Victor slipped.

Garrett's left fist collided with the rockface.

He cried out, multiple bones in his hand fractured. Maybe his wrist too.

In that moment of weakness, Victor batted the knife from Garrett's other hand, and the bounty hunter retreated, face pinched and contorted in agony.

Victor, exhausted, only remained on his feet because of the rockface behind him supporting some of his weight. He couldn't feel his left leg any longer.

He realised he had taken a knife slash above his knee and not even noticed.

Garrett had his left arm bent at the elbow so the broken hand was cradled near his shoulder. He was exhausted too.

'What's it going to be, Fish?' he asked. 'Are we going to keep doing this until we're both dead?'

Victor said, 'What do you suggest?'

'If we carry on like this, neither of us walks away. Last man standing will never make it out of the forest. Victory doesn't taste so sweet when you bleed to death a few minutes later.'

'I'm listening.'

'I can cut you in,' Garrett said. 'We can split the payday. Walk away rich men. That kid is worth a truck of money. I don't know why those two old creeps want that grandson for themselves so much and I don't care neither. But they're richer than sin. I'm talking retirement money. I'm talking never having to work another day for the rest of our lives.'

Victor said, 'I don't need the money.'

'What is that boy to you? He's not yours. You don't know him.'

'I said I'd teach him to fish.'

Garrett waited for more, and when none came, he said, 'You have got to be kidding me. You said you'd teach him to fish? This is a joke. It has to be. You're going to die here in the rain for nothing.'

'I made him a promise,' Victor said.

EIGHTY-THREE

'I try not to make promises,' Victor continued, 'because I don't like it when I can't keep my word. I told Joshua the same thing. I told him that in the absence of true virtues I tend to hang on to what's left.'

'I get it,' Garrett said. 'I could have killed you before at the house. But I didn't. I acted with honour. I showed you mercy.'

'You did.'

'You remember what it was like to have honour?' Garrett asked. 'You wore a uniform once, just like me. I bet you miss it too, don't you? I know I do. Not the rules, not the bullshit. I miss the camaraderie. Nothing comes close to it on the outside. Not friendship. Not love. When you fight shoulder-to-shoulder with your teammates it changes you. You're never the same again. I was never the same again.'

'Me either,' Victor said.

'Then you and I are as good as brothers because we understand one another. You'd never kill a man you fought alongside, would you?'

'Never.'

Garrett said, 'You kill me, you kill one of your brothers.'

'They're all dead.'

'Who are all dead?'

'My teammates,' Victor answered. 'My squad. I was the only one who made it.'

Garrett listened.

'Ambush,' Victor explained. 'We walked straight into it. They had the flanks. Higher ground. We were trapped with nothing but dirt and dry grass for cover. We called for air support. Jets were already in the sky. Six minutes out.' He paused.

'Felt like a lifetime, did it?'

'Those six might as well have been sixty. Heavy machine guns. Mortars. Sniper fire would have ended it in seconds had the mortar shells and machine-gun rounds not turned the air into a giant dust storm. They couldn't see us, but we couldn't see them either. We were shooting blind at the hills, counting the seconds, praying those jets could break the laws of aerodynamics and get to us sooner. I don't know who died first, but I know it was a mortar. There was an explosion so close to me the shockwave popped the buttons on my fatigues. I heard a scream. Saw a pair of legs with no torso attached. I had seventeen pieces of shrapnel in my back and I didn't feel even one of them. We'd been fighting for maybe thirty seconds at that point. Five and a half minutes still to go until air support arrived.'

'What did you do?'

'Fought. Put so many rounds into those hills I ran out of ammo and had to scoop up another rifle. I didn't know who was dead and who was alive in that dust storm, but it didn't matter. The mortar was picking us off. I couldn't see it but I knew how fast a good team could launch a shell and they were raining down on us like clockwork every nine seconds. Seven-second flight time meant three hundred metres away. Two hundred metres of ground to cover and I could get a bead on them. I could buy a reprieve.'

'Did you?'

'Yes,' Victor said. 'I killed the mortar team.'

'But?'

'Enemy rushed my team's position. Overwhelmed them.'

'Then you're lucky to be alive.'

'Unless I had stayed in position,' Victor said. 'Maybe with another friendly we could have driven them back until the jets reached us. Some could have made it. Instead of just me.'

'You don't know that for sure.'

'You said I was lucky to be alive,' Victor said. 'Do you believe in luck?'

'No.'

'Neither do I, but sometimes I wonder.'

'Why?'

'Because there are more than seven billion people on this planet and of those seven-plus billion people to which to show mercy you picked the absolute worst one.'

Garrett said nothing.

'Even for the two of us, neither of whom believes in luck, that seems pretty unlucky, doesn't it?'

'You don't have to kill me.'

Victor said, 'You might be right.'

And tried anyway.

He charged Garrett, and together they toppled over the edge of the outcrop.

They twisted as they fell, Garrett's greater strength forcing Victor around, and he sucked in a hurried breath an instant before he hit the lake first.

A sudden thump of resistance jolted him before the water parted in a huge splash and the lake swallowed both men.

The water, freezing cold, was a second jolt of pain, but Victor already knew it well and had survived it once already. Now, the cold was more intense, the pain more profound. Deprived of blood, his body had less ability to fight the temperature.

With their combined mass they sank fast, a tumble of limbs and violence. Bubbles all around. Water coloured with blood. Muted sounds. Pain and anger.

Garrett went for Victor's thigh, for the wound he had created. He punched it, grabbed at it with desperate fingers until he found the compression tourniquet and unhooked the fastening.

The pressure released and blood raced through Victor's leg, and the dark lake water around them became a shroud of swirling red.

Victor kept fighting, working on his position, his grip, the movement of his legs. He let Garrett attack the wound because it kept the bounty hunter focused, busy on his own actions and not on Victor's.

They twisted around in a savage embrace, tumbling deeper, sinking faster.

Light faded with every second until they were almost blind, struggling in darkness.

Victor, losing more blood after already losing so much, knew he would run out of oxygen long before Garrett. All Garrett had to do was wait, not fight, but he fought hard with aggression and rage. He spent more oxygen than he needed to. The price of hatred.

Garrett's fingertips found the bullet hole in Victor's thigh and clawed at it, trying to rip it open, to widen it.

The pain made Victor lightheaded. He cracked teeth keeping his mouth closed against the instinct to open it and scream. He couldn't afford to waste a single molecule of oxygen.

Victor wanted to be behind Garrett but it wasn't going to work. He was weak from blood loss, dizzy with pain. Disorientated in darkness. He couldn't wait until his position was perfect because he would die before he worked himself into it. He settled on getting chest-to-chest with him, releasing Garrett's arm so he could wrap both arms around the man's back.

Victor grabbed his own forearms as close to his elbows as he could, grappling Garrett as tight as possible.

He braced and retracted his scapulas in a single, powerful instant, withdrawing his shoulder blades as fast and hard as he could with the strength he had remaining, driving his hands, his arms, against Garrett's back and compressing Garrett's ribs against him in a sudden, forceful squeeze.

A cloud of bubbles expelled from Garrett's mouth as his lungs were pinched shut and forcibly emptied of air.

Garrett panicked.

He ignored the wound, ignored the fight entirely, and tried to free himself from Victor's embrace.

Garrett pushed and kicked and screamed beneath the water.

Victor closed his eyes and steadied his mind and held on, accepting the elbows and punches Garrett threw at him, ignoring the fingers that went for his eyes.

Garrett, airless, weakened fast.

The attacks became sluggish.

Then they stopped.

Victor opened his eyes to see Garrett's own, wide and red, staring back through the gloom without blinking.

Releasing him into the lake's embrace, Victor began his ascent towards the surface. He was so weak he could barely swim – his left leg couldn't move at all – but the distance was not far. Even wrapped together, they had not sunk deep.

He headed towards the daylight above, but instead of the water growing clearer as he swam, it darkened further, and he heard the faraway voice of his uncle calling to him.

EIGHTY-FOUR

They hadn't made it to the truck. Not even close. Naël couldn't move with speed with his old back wound and neither could Joshua with his little legs. It had taken too much time to navigate the forest. As the truck had come into view, they had heard an approaching vehicle. The same deep rumble that had come to the cabin, only louder, faster, more urgent.

Backtracking, they had gone to the rocks, the caves. There, they had hidden for a long time, shuddering at the boom of an explosion and the roar of nearby gunfire and then waiting in terror after it had ceased. Naël had held Michelle tight as she held Joshua.

It's just fireworks, baby.

When the gunshots had ceased, they had waited and waited and waited.

Between Michelle and Naël they had whispered about whether they should stay or go. An impossible choice. In staying, they might lose their chance to escape. In going, they might lose their chance to remain hidden.

They figured the bounty hunters would find them if they stayed, sooner or later.

Naël went first, to Michelle's protestations, but there was Joshua to consider. Naël had to leave first and scout ahead to see if it was safe. It had to be that way.

He found much blood and many bodies.

He picked up a rifle.

He found no signs of life at all.

It was over.

He fetched Michelle and Joshua and led them a different way back to the cabin, one that avoided the corpses. He told Michelle to get their things and pack them into his Land Rover. They were leaving.

Joshua asked about Wilson Murdoch.

Was he still coming with them to see the Grand Canyon?

They exchanged questioning looks over Joshua's head that he could not see and told him that Wilson Murdoch would come and visit them some day in the future. But they would send him a postcard.

Michelle told Joshua to go fetch his vacation bag, and she and Naël talked back and forth. They had to go. They couldn't stay a single second longer than necessary. But maybe he was still out there. Maybe he needed them.

Could they really leave him behind?

No, was the answer.

They went back. They searched.

Naël knew the forest and he knew how to track.

They found Murdoch on the shore, face down in the mud where he had exited the water but then fallen, the last of his strength spent, or perhaps where the lake had washed up his listless form. The water lapped over his unmoving legs and small waves broke over his torso and head, covering him for a brief moment before withdrawing again. He had been washed clean. Blood loss and the icy coldness of the lake had paled his face to brilliant white.

Naël dragged the body out of the water, stumbling and fighting the sucking mud with every backwards step. He shooed Michelle away when she tried to help because without his mother's hand to steady him, Joshua approached, compelled by curiosity, and Naël did not want the boy to see a corpse up close.

There were many wounds – cuts and contusions and even a bullet hole in his thigh. Despite Naël's medical knowledge it was hard to know if the wounds had killed him or if he had drowned or died of hypothermia, or a combination of all.

Adieu, ami.

Michelle called from where she stood some metres away, holding back an increasingly anxious Joshua, who was not convinced by her assurances.

Naël shook his head in answer and Michelle used a hand to stifle a cry. She turned Joshua away as he asked his many questions, and she tried to distract him by any means.

Look at the forest. Look at the leaves. The colours. Look anywhere else. How old do you think that tree is? I bet it's a thousand years old, don't you?

Joshua looked where his mother told him to look. He gave no answers, and Michelle wiped her eyes.

Then Naël called to her, for her. Loud. Urgent.

Desperate.

Confused, she hesitated. Naël pleaded, and she told Joshua to stay facing the forest. To try and count the trees.

She rushed to Naël and saw the pale, horrid form lying in the mud with him. She gasped in disgust and sympathy.

There. Naël pointed to a trickle of bright blood on the washed-clean, corpse-white skin. Fresh blood from a heart that still pumped.

Together they dragged and heaved until they were free of the cold mud and were on firmer ground.

Naël pulled off his jacket and his shirt and tore his shirt into strips for makeshift dressings and tourniquets. They stripped away sodden clothes and Naël used the jacket as a blanket.

Because of his old wound, Naël needed Michelle's help to get Murdoch on to his shoulders. Every spare moment she reassured a teary Joshua that it was fine, that it was all a game that adults played from time to time.

Naël could not move fast but he hurried every step through the trees, fighting back the burning in his lungs, in his muscles, in his joints, and the agony in his back. It was the very least he could do.

He was so exhausted by the time they reached the truck he could not climb inside once they had laid Murdoch inside first. Michelle had to help Naël get behind the wheel and she and Joshua rode in the load bed, where she hugged him and sang his favourite songs.

Accroche-toi, Naël willed.

Hang in there.

EIGHTY-FIVE

Linette had never known anything quite like it. By the time she arrived on scene, the car had stopped burning. All that remained of the fire was a plume of black smoke rising from the charred shell of metal. At first, no one could get close enough to see how many corpses were in the car. Was it two or was it three?

The one on the road was a mess. Stumps where legs should have been.

Days would go by before they understood what had transpired. No one in Linette's department knew anything about explosives. Experts had to be called in. A computer simulation was built to recreate the incident.

Stainless-steel ball bearings would turn up for weeks afterwards. They never found them all.

Jennifer Welch was simple enough to identify given the ID in her wallet. The three sets of remains in the car took a little more work. Dental records to the rescue.

Welch and the three guys all had links to organised crime

in Chicago. A crime boss had recently been assassinated, and there were rippling waves of secondary violence in the wake of the killing. A detective had been looking into Welch and her crew for years. He was not surprised the dangerous lifestyle she'd led had resulted in her ultimate demise. Though no direct link to the assassination in Chicago could be established, Welch was known to be an asset of the wider crime network. Was she killed for revenge or business or was it an accident? It was a question that would go unanswered.

Linette had to take that one on the chin. She never liked leaving something unresolved, but there was no more she could do.

At least the missing mother and child turned up. Michelle and Joshua came right to the station. She'd heard people were looking for her and her boy and didn't know why. Joshua played with toys while Michelle explained she had spent a few days with her boyfriend at his cabin. She seemed a little twitchy to Linette, who asked several times if she was okay. She insisted she was and everything was fine.

Did a man named Wilson Murdoch contact her?

He had, Michelle answered, and added that she didn't like him. He was strange. A bit obsessed, even. Michelle's boyfriend had seen him off and they hadn't heard from him since.

Neither had Linette.

She was annoyed at herself for getting swept up in a stranger's fantasy. He had seemed so convincing and sure of himself. But she agreed with Michelle, he was peculiar.

Linette thanked Michelle for letting her know she was okay, and saw her and Joshua to the exit. Michelle's boyfriend, the French bartender, was waiting in his truck to take them home.

Linette's phone rang, and she half expected it to be Murdoch. It wasn't. It was her dad calling again. He didn't appreciate how busy she was dealing with the corpses from Chicago. He was driving her nuts with questions. He had become suddenly and intently interested in upgrading his home security system. She didn't understand it. He already had one that cost more than she earned in a year.

What could he possibly be so afraid of?

EIGHTY-SIX

Business had never been great. It would be charitable even to pretend it had ever been good in the first place. At best, it survived. Ticked over. No one ever got rich running a bar and plenty of folk lost everything trying to keep their simple dreams alive. Big Pete had seen it happen. He had seen it happen far too many times. Margins were tight to begin with and even the slightest downturn in the economy meant things went south fast.

Big Pete was fortunate in that he had been running his bar so long the mortgage that had once seemed high had become almost manageable. That gave him breathing room. He could survive a slow month. He could survive two or even three.

But when was surviving ever enough?

Last few weeks the bar had ceased to be considered surviving and was now officially terminal.

A slow, painful death.

Big Pete might find a way to turn it around, sure. If he

scraped by for a while longer, the tides might change. The summer would bring in an inevitable boost in business, but July was for ever away.

Besides, he was too old to scrape by and had long ago decided that when life wasn't worth living, no longer would he be sticking around just for the hell of it.

Big Pete had no patience for that.

Since the Nameless had ended up in broken pieces in his lot, the bar's already sparse selection of regulars had thinned to a skeleton. Despite Big Pete's efforts to convince folk it was safe, Officer Linette and co turning up every other day told them otherwise. And even those with a little more back-bone were spending less. No one was going to risk an extra sip before driving home with the law hanging around.

Naël quitting like that had been a blessing. He'd called. Assured Big Pete everything was fine and there was no danger and never had been, but he wouldn't be coming back to work. Saved Big Pete from letting him go further down the line. That would have stung. Big Pete didn't quite think of him as a son – because Big Pete's real son was a lowlife of the highest order, so that would be an insult – but they were close. Real close. As good as family. Naël had packed up with almost no warning and moved on with that lady of his and her sweet little boy. They'd all stopped by the bar to say farewell and Big Pete had fought hard to keep his misty eyes from becom-ing full-blown waterfalls. He was going to miss them all, but they had the rest of their lives ahead of them, and he was glad they were throwing caution to the wind and starting over.

They told him they didn't know where they were going.

Maybe they hadn't wanted anyone to know.

Best of luck to them.

The young always left behind the old. It had to happen. Life had to move on. But with his bar's doom an inevitability and his lack of appetite for a drawn-out demise, why did it have to move on so damn fast?

When the phone rang, Big Pete could hardly be bothered to get off his stool and answer it.

He only did so because he could feel the irritation of the skeletons around him.

Since when did the undead get so tetchy?

'Yello?' he answered.

A polite city voice introduced himself with a respect and formality Big Pete was neither used to nor appreciated. He liked folk to get to the point, yet this guy was talking in all sorts of terms and phrases Big Pete had no time for even when he wasn't feeling so morose.

'Whoa, whoa, fella,' he interrupted. 'I'm taking in only about one quarter of what you're telling me and I'm only understanding a quarter of that.'

'My apologies,' the voice said. 'This is purely a courtesy call to introduce myself and explain a little of what I can do to help.'

'When have you banks ever helped anyone aside from yourselves?'

'Well,' the voice said, a little tight, 'there's a lot I can do for a man in your situation, and I assure you as your newly assigned WMA that's precisely what I'm best placed to do.'

'Let me revise my earlier statement on only understanding a quarter. Now, it's making sense. You can smell blood in the water, can't you? I'm bleeding cash, but that doesn't mean I'm a sucker going to fall victim to one of your vampire loans. And I don't want to remortgage to some incomprehensible new interest rate so you can steal my home even quicker. So, you're wasting your time. But, sleazy banker as you are, I know you're just doing your job. You got bills to pay, same as everyone else. Which means I'll do you the singular courtesy of saying goodbye before I hang up ... Goodbye.'

'*Wait*,' the voice pleaded, and Big Pete hesitated. 'I assure you I'm not looking to sell you anything. Given your newly acquired liquidity you now qualify for our wealth management scheme and I'm your new adviser. That position means I work for you and will make sure your money grows in the fastest possible way.'

'Did you just say my *newly acquired liquidity*?'

'Yes,' the voice said. 'Your checking account now sits very healthily at a little over one million dollars thanks to the recent offshore transfer, so the first thing I suggest is moving that money to a more appropriate account with some urgency. If for no other reason than to safeguard it from things like identity fraud. I can help set that up right now over the phone. After that, we can discuss how to use your new wealth to its fullest potential and ensure the taxman takes as little of it as possible.'

A little over one million dollars ...

'Uh-huh,' Big Pete managed to say after a long moment, mouth hanging open so wide even the skeletons were wondering what was happening.

His new wealth management adviser carried on talking about account options and interest rates and fees and savings and shares and investments and pensions, but Big Pete was only half listening.

Instead, he was thinking about a man he barely knew. A fisherman. A quiet man.

Big Pete smiled.

You crazy son of a bitch.

'Do me a favour?' Big Pete asked the polite city voice. 'Call me back tomorrow. I have a lot to process.'

'Certainly, sir,' the voice said. 'I'll do just that. I look forward to continuing our conversation.'

'Me too.' Big Pete set the receiver back on the cradle, used the tips of a couple of fingers to check the thundering pulse in his neck, and then called out in a loud voice, 'You skeletons thirsty this evening?'

Eyes turned his way, but no one said anything. The undead were such a distrustful breed.

'Because,' Big Pete said as he began popping caps from beer bottles and setting them in a line on the bar, 'from now until close, all drinks are on the house.'

EIGHTY-SEVEN

Was a politician at the very bottom of society's decency ladder or was it a lawyer? They weren't sure, because where would that leave them? They were surrounded by plenty of both. It seemed where one gathered the others couldn't keep away. All about money, of course. Both the politician and the lawyer would sell their mothers – if only they could find someone to buy them.

Over the years they had been to many such functions. They were neither profession, had never been, but they had more money than anyone could spend in ten lifetimes, so both the politician and the lawyer tripped over themselves to chit-chat.

No one had actually tried to sell their mothers to them.

There was still plenty of evening left, however.

They were not going to stay long. They had been in no mood to come at all. However, they were sticklers for good manners and had accepted the invitation to the event long before they could have known they would be in bereavement.

Some knew. The wily politicians seeking campaign contributions made sure to pass on their condolences and tutted from afar at those who had not done their homework and flattered shamelessly.

They were known to respond well to flattery. Not that they were vain, but they enjoyed watching those with power reduced to begging courtiers.

Such cruelty could generate no fun tonight.

She said, 'I want to leave.'

He nodded.

Exiting took its own time because there were still many beggars who had been waiting for their chance all night long and now saw it slipping away. It took a whole twenty minutes to cross the hotel lobby alone.

Outside, they ignored the driver who held open the limousine door for them as they climbed inside. It was a slow process because they were both beset by many ailments of old age and further burdened by the exhausting pain of grief.

Neither spoke for a while as they were driven out of the city, until he said, 'I'm becoming concerned.'

She was too, of course, although she was also made of sterner stuff. To voice worry was to show weakness. He had always been weaker than her.

'He said we would never hear from him again. We would know only when it was done.'

'How long does such a thing take?'

'If I knew that, why would we need to employ him in the first place?'

Silence for a moment.

She said, 'We will give him a few more days.'

He said, 'A few more days.'

'It's not as if we're in a hurry to wipe up any more drool than we need to, is it?'

She rested a hand over his because for all his weakness, all his faults, he had always been loyal, and in their son he had given her the only joy she had ever known.

A grandson could never replace that joy, least not such a problematic creature, but even if a sliver of her unbearable sadness could be taken away then it would be worth the otherwise unpleasantness.

Anger rising, she stabbed a finger at the button for the intercom.

'You missed the turning,' she snapped at the agency driver. 'Are you blind as well as a cripple?'

He had a problem with his left leg, she had noticed. An awkward gait.

No response.

Another turn. Another wrong turn.

She didn't like him. He was too quiet. She never liked such men. A quiet man is a patient man. He chooses his words with care and speaks only when there is something worth saying. He is a watcher, a listener. He pays attention without seeking it and knows far more about you than you do him. That quiet man is a dangerous man.

'Answer me,' she demanded, buzzing down the privacy panel so she could meet his eyes in the mirror. 'You're going in completely the opposite direction. What is this? Where are you taking us?'

Those eyes that met her own were dark, almost black.

They held her gaze in a way she had never before been looked at in all the days of her long life.

Those eyes sent a terrible chill right through her.

'Try and relax,' the driver said. 'It'll all be over soon enough.'

EIGHTY-EIGHT

It wasn't Lake Huron. That would have been foolish. Foolish even for a man who had already acted as such more times in the space of a few days than perhaps in his entire life before that. So, another lake. Far, far away. With bright blue water beneath a cloudless sky. Busy with pleasure craft but calm at the point he had chosen. Where he deemed it would be safest.

The vessel was a beautiful rowing boat fifteen feet in length. Wood, not fibreglass or plastic. Handcrafted by a master boatwright. A work of art.

Because it was made of wood it was heavier, and therefore harder work to operate. The rower had been very strong and very fit yet had weakened through long weeks of convalescing. Each pull of the oars was tiring and caused him pain in many places, yet he kept the suffering from his face for the benefit of his passenger.

Who was so excited he could not keep still.

His eyes were wide and his head was in constant motion,

gazing out at the other boats, the jet skis and paragliders, the yachts and the dinghies. Even the lake itself held almost irresistible wonder, but he knew – had been told by his mother many, *many* times – not to lean over the side for a closer look at the water.

The passenger wore a life preserver so big and bulbous his arms could not hang at his sides and instead protruded out at forty-five degrees. He kind of liked it. He felt huge. Powerful. Like a superhero.

The rower stopped where he deemed it best and withdrew the oars into the vessel, and the passenger's excitement shot up to even greater heights. The rower wiped sweat from his brow and spent a moment catching his breath and managing his pain before he set about preparing the equipment.

They had discussed what would follow and had practised the intricacies on land. But now this was it.

Finally.

The overjoyed passenger took the rod into his little hands.

'The most important thing is keeping quiet,' Victor whispered to Joshua as he helped the boy cast out his first line.

ACKNOWLEDGEMENTS

This book would not exist without the kindness and encouragement of Liz Barnsley, Bodo Pfündl, Lidia Teasca, and Graham Wall. Thank you all.

His name is a cover
He has no home
And he kills for a living

Victor is an assassin, a man with no past and no
surname. His world is one of paranoia and obsessive
attention to detail; his morality lies either dead
or dying. No one knows what truly motivates
the hunter. No one gets close enough to ask.

When a Paris job goes spectacularly wrong, Victor finds
himself running for his life across four continents, pursued
by a kill squad and investigated by secret services from
more than one country. With meticulous style, Victor plans
his escape ... and takes the fight to his would-be killers.

In this first novel in the explosive Victor
the Assassin series, it's not about right and
wrong – only about who lives and who dies.

AN ASSASSIN HAS ONE RULE:
KILL OR BE KILLED

THE ENEMY

TOM WOOD

A VICTOR NOVEL

An impossible mission, for a man who barely exists

The mysterious assassin known only as Victor is
locked in an uneasy alliance with the CIA. And he
has a list: three names, three victims. Worst of all,
Victor is given just two days to take down his targets,
forcing him to compromise his usual extreme care.

With each name Victor crosses off his list, the game
grows far more complex – and far more lethal. A
conspiracy begins to unwind and suddenly this
perfect assassin becomes the perfect target.

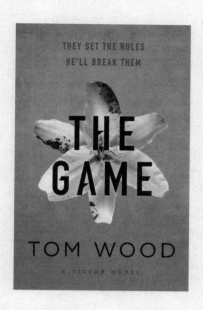

THEY SET THE RULES
HE'LL BREAK THEM

THE GAME

TOM WOOD

A VICTOR NOVEL

Victor is the perfect killer.
He has no past.
He will stop at nothing.
And he can find you anywhere.

In sweltering Algiers, ultra-efficient hitman Victor
executes a fellow assassin. But when the CIA comes
calling, Victor must pose as his victim to identify
the dead man's next mark, a mission that takes him
across Europe to the bloody streets of Rome.

Working alongside a group of vicious mercenaries,
Victor faces an impossible choice: to do what's right, or
to sacrifice the only thing he cares about ... his life.

HE'S PAID TO KILL
NOW HE'LL PROTECT

BETTER OFF DEAD

TOM WOOD

A VICTOR NOVEL

A hitman must be anonymous, amoral ... and alone

Victor is the face in the crowd you don't see, a
perfect assassin with nothing to live for.

But when an old friend turns to him for
help, he finds he can't refuse. For once his
objective isn't to kill, but to protect.

Hunted through the streets of London by ruthless
enemies, Victor needs to be more than just a
bodyguard ... but his every move leads danger
closer to the very person he's vowed to defend.

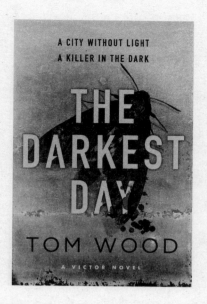

A CITY WITHOUT LIGHT
A KILLER IN THE DARK

THE DARKEST DAY

TOM WOOD

A VICTOR NOVEL

He is darkness. She wants him dead.
In a city starved of light, she might just succeed.

She moves like a shadow; she kills silently: Raven.
This elegant assassin has been on the run for years.
This time though, she has picked the wrong target.

The hitman known only as 'Victor' is as paranoid as
he is merciless, and is no stranger to being hunted.
He tracks his would-be killer across the globe, aiming
not only to neutralise the threat, but to discover who
wants him dead. The trail leads to New York ...

And then the lights go out.

Over twelve hours of unremitting darkness, Manhattan
dissolves into chaos. Amid looting, conspiracy and
blackout, Victor and Raven play a vicious game of
cat and mouse that the city will never forget.

A HITMAN WITHOUT CONSCIENCE
A TARGET WITHOUT REMORSE

A TIME TO DIE

TOM WOOD

A VICTOR NOVEL

Even a killer can be a hero

If the assassin known only as Victor once had a moral
compass, it is long since buried, along with his many
victims. Yet some men are so evil even Victor accepts
they must die for reasons other than just money.

One such is Milan Rados, a former commander in
the Serbian army who has escaped trial at The Hague
to become a formidable criminal power. Tracking
down and killing this brutal man will win Victor a
reprieve for his own recent crimes on British soil.

But Victor isn't the only one who wants Rados dead.
A woman, whose family was butchered on the tyrant's
orders, will do anything to see Rados' blood spilled on
the snow of Eastern Europe. Now Victor has an unlikely
ally – but an army stands between them and justice.

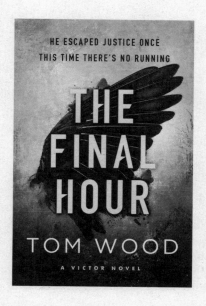

HE ESCAPED JUSTICE ONCE
THIS TIME THERE'S NO RUNNING

THE FINAL HOUR

TOM WOOD

A VICTOR NOVEL

Former CIA agent Antonio Alvarez has been tracking a vicious murderer for years, a nameless hitman responsible for numerous homicides.

Once, the Agency deflected him away from his search, but now promotion has given him a second chance to right the past.

Only problem is, the killer has vanished.

Thousands of miles away, the professional known as Victor has stopped working – recently he began to care; he made mistakes. But there's another assassin, Raven, who needs his help – and she is hard to refuse ...

A FAMILY AT WAR
A KILLER FOR HIRE

KILL
FOR
ME

TOM WOOD

A VICTOR NOVEL

For years, two sisters have vied for the turf of
their dead crime boss father. Across the streets
of Guatemala City, bodies have piled up; the US
Drug Enforcement Agency, operating far from its
own borders, is powerless to stop the fighting.

But now one sister has a weapon that could finally win the
war – a cold, amoral hitman known, fittingly, as 'Victor'.

Freed from previous employers the CIA and MI6, Victor
is a killer for-hire whose sense of self-preservation trumps
all else. Yet as betrayal and counter-betrayal unspool
in the vicious family feud, Victor finds himself at the
centre of a storm even he could be powerless to stop.